FRENEMY MATRIARCHS

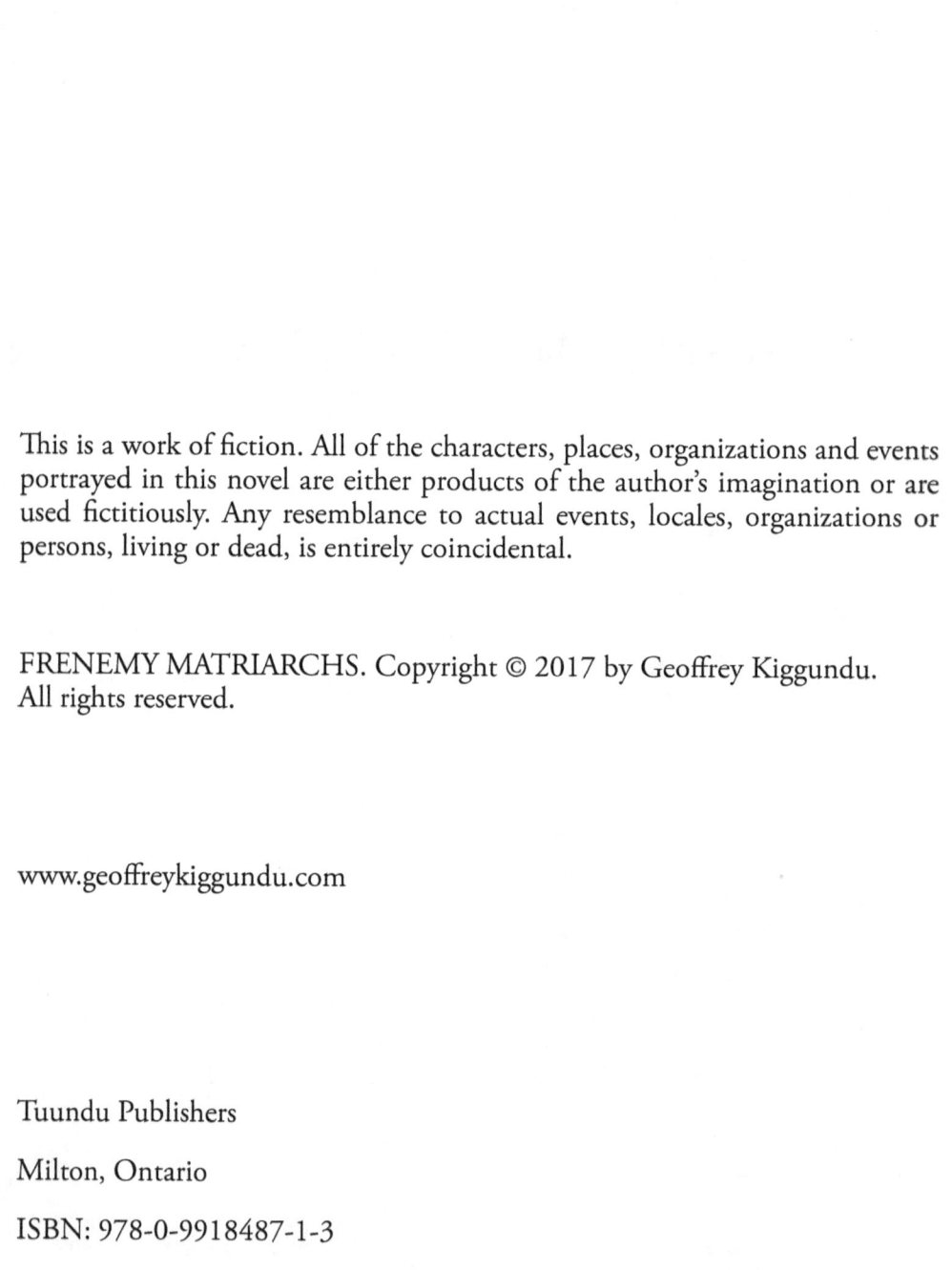

This is a work of fiction. All of the characters, places, organizations and events portrayed in this novel are either products of the author's imagination or are used fictitiously. Any resemblance to actual events, locales, organizations or persons, living or dead, is entirely coincidental.

www.geoffreykiggundu.com

Tuundu Publishers

Milton, Ontario

ISBN: 978-0-9918487-1-3

IN MEMORY OF MY GRANDPARENTS

YAKOBO AND MALITA MATOVU

Many thanks to the following people for their help with this novel:

My father, Edward, for being an invaluable resource for
historical information; my editor, Barbara Feldman, for her thoroughness
and attention to lexical and structural detail; and my wife, Sarah,
for her encouragement.

1

JUNE 1945

FIFTEEN-YEAR-OLD Merab Nantamu knew that this was the day when, upon returning home from school, she saw her aunt Abigail chatting with her father Levi under the mango tree in the front yard of the house. Merab suspected that the conversation was very important because the talkative Abigail rarely sat to speak to a person for long.

Not this time.

Levi was sitting on a wooden folding chair and Abigail was sitting on a mat facing Levi, her big brother. Merab knelt about three metres from where her father and aunt were seated to greet them.

"Come closer, dear. I don't bite. I am very glad to see you, Merab," Abigail said as she stretched her hands out to hug her niece. Her unusually enthusiastic greeting made Merab even more suspicious of her aunt's intentions.

Merab went inside to greet her mother, Dolosi, but soon found that her mother was not in the house, but in the outdoor kitchen, preparing dinner. The aroma of smoked beef was a sign to Merab that it was going to be a special dinner; the family never ate beef on weekdays. She stayed in the house, hiding behind the front door so she could eavesdrop on the conversation still going on under the mango tree.

"...don't think he is a Christian. When I asked what his Christian name was I got no answer," Merab heard Abigail say.

"I knew his father," she heard Levi reply. "He was not a Christian. We can therefore conclude that since the father was not a Christian, his son is not a Christian."

When Merab saw her aunt rise up from the mat, she quickly went to her bedroom, put her books on the floor and changed from her school uniform. Before Merab could leave the room, Abigail came in and closed the door behind her. She had done the same thing the year before, Merab remembered, when she had turned fourteen and her aunt had talked to her about sexuality.

"Merab, I am an unannounced visitor this evening," Abigail said, "and..."

Of course, I know that, Merab thought.

"I have come specifically to see you," Abigail continued. "I have got great news for you. Sit down."

Merab took a mat that was in a corner and spread it on the floor so that she and her aunt could sit. She now had no doubt what the news would be.

"We have found a man to marry you," Abigail said.

I didn't know that you have been on a quest all along.

"He is from a well-known family in Kalasa..."

Oh no! Merab had been looking forward to completing her primary education, going for further studies to become a teacher, and marrying an important man in Kampala, not someone from a rural area like her own. She did not want to live in the country all her life. Her cousin Philemon, one of Abigail's sons, worked in the city, and judging from the stories he told, it was a great place to live. She'd aspired to marry there.

"Not only is he from a well-known family, he is a successful farmer, from a family that both your father and your aunt Namagembe know well," Abigail continued. "Actually, your aunt Namagembe is the one who recommended your future husband to us."

So my father and Aunt Namagembe know the man well—but I don't.

"Your future husband will be coming to pay us a visit in two weeks' time."

That's too close. It leaves me no time to prepare myself, and I am not interested in marriage! I am still very young—why should I get married now when I am still in school?

"...and there will no longer be a place for you in this home," Merab's aunt's words broke into her thoughts. "You are marrying for life. As I am sure you know, no woman in our family has ever divorced her husband."

I guess staying in the marriage or not depends on what kind of man one is married to, Merab thought, looking at her finger nails.

"Last time I talked to you about cleanliness, but I must emphasize it again..."

Can't you talk about something else? I'm known for my cleanliness.

"Before you serve a meal, make sure you are clean. Never serve meals while wearing soiled clothes or when you are sweaty after working in the garden. And when you serve food, serve your husband first. Give him enough food, preferably on a large plate. He should never ask for a second serving. When you cook beef, goat meat, chicken or game meat—I don't know if your future husband enjoys hunting—his piece or pieces of meat should be special and bigger than the other pieces."

How well did her aunt Abigail and her father know the man they wanted her to marry? Merab wondered but she couldn't dare to ask; her parents had trained her to listen, not to talk back. But she'd wished to marry an educated man, maybe even the headmaster of a school, so that her life could be different, more exciting.

"...a string if you have one," her aunt's instructions continued. "That way it will be easy for you to identify his piece of meat. Do you understand?"

Abigail had noticed that Merab was only half-listening. "You've got to listen to me attentively, young woman! What I am telling you will be important in your marriage. Remember, we are marrying you off for good. You will still be welcome here in your father's home but only as a visitor. There will no longer be a place for you here."

Of course there will always be a place for me here. This is my father's home.

"Listen attentively. I don't want to repeat myself," Abigail said, raising her voice a little. "In some homes when they cook meat, the whole saucepan of meat is given to the man of the house, the head of the family, to serve himself first and to choose the pieces he wants before the other people in the household are served. However, this is not what I am suggesting you should do. Do whatever you can for your husband to know that he is special. When you choose his piece of meat before you cook it and tie it with a string, you can easily identify it when you serve him."

Merab almost burst out laughing but restrained herself. In their home Levi, her father, was not treated in the way that her aunt was describing. Although he sat alone at a small table in the living room to eat while everybody else in the family sat on mats on the floor, his meals were served just like for the other family members. He was neither served special pieces of meat nor given any overly special treatment. But Merab was also aware that because Levi was a catechist—a teacher of the Christian religion—he was mild-mannered compared to the rest of the men of the village.

"You've got to cheerfully welcome all visitors to your home, whether they are invited or not, whether you like them or not," Abigail added, her voice loud and authoritative. "You should never be a sulking wife. Sometimes, it may be hard to deal with members of your husband's family but for the good of your marriage, don't quarrel with them. Treat every one of them respectfully."

I guess I, too, deserve to be respected.

"It also goes without saying that you've got to be hospitable. Every person who sets foot in your home must be fed. Don't be a miser. You've got to cook enough food for everyone in your home and when you cook, it is better to prepare more than you would for the members of your household, assuming that you will receive visitors, than to receive visitors and not have enough food to offer them..."

That's assuming there will be someone to help me with the cooking. I can't cook for the entire village day in and day out.

"...cleanliness. Your bedroom must always be neat and tidy. Your husband would not want to spend a night in your bedroom if it was not clean."

Here we go again—another lecture on bedroom matters, sexuality, whatever! Merab recalled the last time Abigail had visited, embarrassing her with explicit sexual talk.

"Your future husband has three children. I know it is not easy to deal with stepchildren but you should love and care for them as if they were your own children."

What? I'm going to marry a man who already has children?

"Your future husband and some members of his family will be visiting soon to be formally introduced to our family. I am going to finalize the details with your father," Abigail said as she rose to go to the living room for dinner.

Merab stayed in her room, crying. She wanted to stay in school. She did not want to get married.

When her older brother Absalom came in for dinner and noticed that his sister was not seated in her usual place, he went to her bedroom and asked her to come out for dinner, and she came. He saw that she was upset but didn't want to ask her why, not at least in the presence of the entire family.

❋   ❋   ❋

Two weeks later, Merab, her mother Dolosi and her aunties Abigail and Namagembe thoroughly cleaned the house. Absalom and his father swept the bare ground in the front yard and trimmed the shrubs near the house. When the cleaning was done, Abigail and Namagembe sat with Merab in her bedroom, giving her more tips about marriage while two women friends of the family, who'd arrived in the home early that morning, helped to prepare a sumptuous lunch, cooking plenty of chicken stew, beef stew, groundnut sauce, *matooke* plantain and sweet potatoes.

When the visitors arrived towards noon, Merab's uncle Mulinda met them at the front door. Merab's future husband thirty-two-year-old Lutalo, was accompanied by his elder brother Lumu, their sisters Nakirijja and Nalwanga, and Lutalo's friend Kabali. Mulinda greeted them formally, and then asked in the customary way, the reason for their visit.

"We are here to request you to let us become children in this wonderful family," Lumu, who was the visiting party's spokesman, answered. Other than the greetings, Lutalo was not expected to utter a single word.

"You want to become children in this family?" Mulinda asked, pretending to laugh. "In our family, children don't ask to become children here. They are just born into the family."

"Somebody told us that we can be born into this family and since we very much love to be a part of this family, we didn't hesitate to come," Lumu replied.

"And the person who told you that is a member of our family?"

"Yes, she is a member of your family."

"Then I will allow you inside our house. Please come in," Mulinda said, stepping aside to let the visitors enter, as was customary after the initial greetings.

There were three extra wooden chairs for the men and two mats for the women, who sat down while the men shook hands with Mulinda, Levi and his brothers-in-law Reverend Mukuye, who was Abigail's husband and Kyazze, the husband of Levi's sister Namagembe.

After the greetings, Mulinda addressed the men of his family. "These people," he said as he turned to face the visitors, "are here to request our permission to become a part of our family. Do you think it would be a good idea for us to welcome them?"

"Yes indeed," Reverend Mukuye answered.

"Where are you from?" Mulinda asked Lumu, as if he did not already know.

"We are from Kalasa, about thirty kilometres from here."

"Oh, that's quite far from here. You came all this way just because you wanted to become a part of our family?"

"That is the major reason," Lumu said and paused. "But there is another reason. We know how great your family is. The man of this house has an excellent reputation as a great teacher. We couldn't wait to meet him."

Levi beamed, happy to hear that he was known beyond his village.

After Lumu had answered more questions satisfactorily, Abigail was called into the room in the company of Namagembe, her younger sister, to confirm that these were indeed the visitors that she'd been expecting. The women seated themselves on a mat before greeting the visitors. Then Mulinda asked Abigail, as was the custom, "My sister, look closely at these people and tell me if you know them."

"Yes, I know them."

"Were you expecting them?"

"Yes, I have been expecting them."

"What do they want?"

"Sir, my niece Merab is ready for marriage and before us is the gentleman who would like to marry her," Abigail said, then paused.

"Please go ahead," Mulinda said after a few moments. "This is going to be very interesting."

"Before I go ahead let me bring Merab out," Abigail said as she and Namagembe rose.

While they waited for Abigail to return Levi sat silently while Mulinda chatted with Lumu. When the women returned, Lutalo gazed at Merab, whose eyes quickly scanned the visitors as she wondered who of them was her suitor.

She is a beauty, Lutalo thought. *I wish they could let me take her home today.*

"My brother," Abigail said as she shifted on her mat to face Mulinda, "I would like to introduce to you and to all who are gathered here today the gentleman who would like to marry my niece Merab."

She then turned to face Lumu who touched Lutalo's shoulder, saying, "He is the one."

Merab glanced up to see who it was she was about to marry. *He is so old! I wish they would realize how old he is and send him away.*

"Sir, I would like to thank you for welcoming us to your home," Lumu said to Levi, "and it will be a great honour to us if you accepted my brother's proposal to marry your daughter."

"Please introduce yourselves before we respond to your request," Mulinda replied. "We wouldn't like to marry our daughter off to a long-lost relative."

Lumu stood up. "Gentlemen and ladies, I would like to introduce my brother to you," he said, touching Lutalo's shoulder once again. "His name is Lutalo. He is a son of the late Chief Lumu of Kalasa…" Levi nodded in approval. He knew the late Chief Lumu. "…a grandson of Lutalo, a great-grandson of Kulumba. He is of the Sheep clan. He is a successful farmer and businessman. He lives in Kalasa."

"Good," Mulinda said. "You are not our relatives. We don't have any relatives in the Sheep clan. You are in the home of Levi Bukulu, son of the late Geresomu Bukulu, grandson of the late Lwere and great-grandson of Sentamu. We are of the Buffalo clan."

"We are very glad to meet you," Lumu said, "and happy to be here today."

Namagembe escorted Merab back to her bedroom.

Mulinda then motioned for Levi to follow him outside for a consultation. While her brothers were still outside, Abigail brought in her sister-in-law Dolosi, Merab's mother, and Merab's older sisters Eseza and Nawume to greet the visitors.

After this last greeting, Lumu and Kabali went outside to where they'd left their bicycles leaning against the outdoor kitchen's wall, loaded with goodies they'd brought with them. They'd also brought a calabash full of banana beer, which they now untied from one of the bicycles along with some empty gourds, bringing them back into the house just as Mulinda and Levi were also coming back in. "Sir," Lumu said to Mulinda, handing him a filled gourd, "please drink our excellent beer."

"My sister, should I drink this beer?" Mulinda asked Abigail as he raised the gourd to his lips.

"Yes, sir, drink the beer," Abigail answered.

Mulinda sipped the beer twice, then said, "Men of the Sheep clan, you've travelled this far in search of our beautiful daughter. And I'm glad to say that you have our permission to marry our daughter Merab."

"We thank you for accepting my brother's proposal," Lumu said, beaming. He and Kabali then went back outside to their bicycles and untied the presents they had brought for Merab's family. Lumu gave them out on behalf of Lutalo: for Levi a *kanzu*—a robe—and for Dolosi, Merab and each of Merab's aunties enough cloth for making *gomesis*—ankle-length dresses. There was even a live rooster for Absalom, Lutalo's future brother-in-law. After thanking Lutalo for the presents, Mulinda served a gourd of banana beer to each person in the room. The two women who had helped Dolosi with cooking helped to serve lunch then they and a few friends ate outside, under the mango tree, leaving Levi, Dolosi and their visitors to have lunch in the house. The sumptuous meal was accompanied by cheerful conversation.

Lumu thanked the hosts for what he called "the best meal they had ever had the pleasure to enjoy." Then to symbolize the sharing of both friendship and new kinship, Mulinda opened his woven bag and took out some packets of dried banana fibre containing roasted coffee beans, carefully opening each of the packets and passing the beans around to share. Levi ate the roasted coffee beans to show how happy he was with his younger brother's gesture, but inside, he was fuming. Why had his brother not sought Levi's permission to perform this custom in his home? Mulinda was not a Christian, but as a staunch Christian and a catechist, Levi was not sure whether the age-old custom was in line with Christianity and he would have liked to think about it first.

After the coffee beans had been eaten, Mulinda asked Lumu when the wedding would take place. When Lumu hesitated it was clear that this matter had not been discussed, and he asked for permission to go out to consult Lutalo.

"Yes, and feel free to walk around and see our property," Mulinda said proudly.

Once the three men were outside, Lutalo told Lumu that he wanted Merab but did not intend to marry her.

"But since they are Christians, they are likely to insist on a church wedding," Lumu said.

"I don't want a church wedding," Lutalo said, shaking his head. "I am not ready to commit myself to that extent."

"I know what you mean—you want to have more than one wife, like some of us," Kabali said. "I understand Christians are not allowed to do that."

But Lutalo didn't respond to Kabali's comment.

"So?" Mulinda asked when the three men returned to the living room.

"My brother is ready to take your daughter but there will be no wedding," Lumu said.

"What do you mean? Do you think you can take the catechist's daughter away just like that?" Mulinda said. "Don't insult us! That cannot happen. You can only marry her in a church wedding."

Lutalo and Lumu went outside again to confer. "You see? I told you that they would insist on a church wedding," Lumu said. "What are you going to do?"

"I don't know," Lutalo answered.

"The young woman is beautiful," Lumu said. "Are you going to let this opportunity pass because you can't make up your mind?" When Lutalo did not respond, Lumu continued. "Accept whatever conditions they impose on you, and then later you can decide what to do."

"Okay, tell them that I will marry her in church," Lutalo said.

✳   ✳   ✳

After the visitors had left, it was obvious to Dolosi that Merab was anxious; she was so quiet and preoccupied. "What's wrong with you?" Dolosi asked.

"Mother, the man is too old and I wouldn't know what to do as a wife. I am too young," Merab said.

"You are not so young. I married your father at exactly the same age as you are and although I was unsure about what to do, my aunt encouraged me and everything went well afterwards. There were no difficulties too big to bear."

"Aunt Abigail told me that the man already has children. I love children but how am I supposed to raise children who are not mine?"

"It is not something that I would wish for you. It is true that I did not have to raise stepchildren, but many women do. Don't worry, the children are still young. Besides, you love people and you love children. You will raise your husband's children as you see fit. Love them and care for them."

"But I don't want to get married now," Merab said quietly.

"Don't say you don't want to get married! It is our duty as women to get married and to raise families. It is also our duty to look after every member of our families. You *will* get married and I hope you will have children and raise them like I have raised you, your sisters and your brother."

"It seems Eseza is not happy in her marriage—" Merab, who had seen a look of sadness in her sister's eyes, began.

"Sometimes there are problems in marriage. However, telling me that you don't want to get married simply because there are problems in marriage is like saying you don't want to have children because there is pain in labour."

"I don't want to get married now," Merab said again, her eyes glistening with tears.

"You have no choice; you have to go with the man we have chosen for you. And, remember to treat your husband's children well, they are your children too," her mother told her. "And please don't meddle into your husband's private matters. For example, don't ever ask about his former wife or entertain rumours about her. If she ever visits—most probably she will never visit—you must be courteous to her."

His first marriage failed. Why should I be married to an old divorcé?

"Merab, it's also important to be careful not to talk back to your husband. Some men don't like it when their wives talk back to them. Your uncle Mulinda is one such man. In fact, many men will beat their wives for talking back to them. Your father is rare among our men—he lets me and you four children reason with him and even talk back. Don't take that same attitude into your marriage. If you do, it will get you into trouble."

Mulinda's daughter Scovia was the same age as Merab and knew that it would soon be her turn to get married off, too, but she, like her cousin, didn't want to get married. That evening, when the two girls were alone, she told Merab that she would run away if her family chose a man for her to marry.

✴   ✴   ✴

A month later, a crowd of about a hundred people were sitting on the grass under a large jacaranda tree at the village's fortnightly market, listening to the news that a man with a high-pitched voice was reading aloud. His audience clapped vigorously when he reported that the war that had been raging in Europe had ended. Levi beamed when the newsreader came to local news and announced that his daughter Merab would be marrying Lutalo, a son of the late county chief, Lumu of Kalasa.

Reverend Mukuye, Abigail's husband, had had to delay the wedding for a month until Lutalo had completed his catechism classes, been baptized and given the Christian name Jonah. *I have been christened but it will not stop me from enjoying my life*. Lutalo thought.

2

JANUARY 1945

IT WAS A hot sunny afternoon and fourteen-year-old Ruth Wamala was sweeping the front yard of her parents' large beautiful home located on a hill in Rubaga, a few kilometres from Kampala. Ruth's chore was almost complete when her father Collin drove into the front yard.

"Good afternoon, Ruth. This is for you," Collin said, handing her a letter as he stepped out of the car. When Ruth saw that the envelope bore the logo of Buweela High School she dropped her broom and rushed to the veranda to open it. She only read the first few lines, then ran into the house and into her parents' bedroom where her mother Eunia was ironing laundry.

"Mummy, I have some exciting news for you!" Ruth said, handing the letter to her mother. "I have been admitted to Buweela High School."

"That's very exciting, Ruth. I am very happy for you, my dear," Eunia said as she took the letter from her daughter. "Even though you had good marks, I didn't think they were good enough for you to get admitted there."

"I can't wait to begin classes in Buweela!"

"You should write a list of the things you'll need in school," Eunia said.

"Yes I will. I will work hard in high school for excellent results," Ruth said, in an attempt to pre-empt her mother. Ruth's mother could be very demanding—she was the deputy headmistress in Rubaga Primary School, where Ruth had been a student.

"Good," Eunia replied, smiling. "I am glad to hear that and I expect nothing less from you."

❋   ❋   ❋

The following morning, Ruth waited until her mother had left for work before going into her parents' bedroom to talk to her father. "Daddy, I would like to go pay a visit to my friend Sanyu later today," she said.

"Sanyu? Is that Mr. Bulega's daughter?"

"Yes."

"You know that your mother doesn't want you to go places alone."

"She wouldn't mind if I went to see Sanyu so long as I have done my chores."

"You can go, then," Collin said. "Just make sure you've done your chores before you go."

When Ruth arrived at her friend's house, Sanyu's older brother Cornelius greeted her from the veranda, where he'd been reading a book. "Hello, Ruth. You're looking happy. Have you been admitted to Buweela?"

"Yes," Ruth replied, smiling. "How about Sanyu?"

"She will tell you herself," Cornelius said, rising to go call his sister.

"Hey, Sanyu, how are you?" Ruth said as soon as Sanyu stepped out of the front door.

"I am very well. I've got news. I've been admitted to Buweela."

"Me too," Ruth said. "Daisy must have been admitted there, too!"

"I don't know yet."

The girls sat under a nearby tree to chat. "I can't wait to go away to Buweela to get some freedom," Ruth said.

"Me too," Sanyu said. "I think the holidays have been too long for my liking."

"But your mother is not as demanding as mine. I need a break from her," Ruth said.

"Ruth, you exaggerate things sometimes. Mrs. Wamala was my favourite teacher. I don't think she is too demanding."

"You were just her student, not her firstborn daughter. She seems to want to control every aspect of my life."

"But she does that out of love."

"Yes, of course, but it's too much. As soon as I start schooling in Buweela, I'll work for some independence from her."

"What?"

"What I mean is I'll gradually start thinking for myself and doing what I want."

"Really? I think we are too young to do whatever we want."

"You would understand what I feel if you were in my shoes."

After chatting with Sanyu for about an hour Ruth was in a hurry to get home—she wanted to get there before her mother returned.

❄   ❄   ❄

Eunia seemed to be happier than Ruth was that her daughter would be joining Buweela High School. That her firstborn daughter was going to study in the "great" high school would be further proof to her relatives and all those who had doubted her chances for success that she, Eunia, the daughter of poor peasants, had secured her place among the rich.

The day before Ruth left, Eunia checked all the items Ruth was going to take to school while Ruth packed them into her suitcase, one by one. "Ruth, you are going to school and for the first time in your life, you are going to be on your own—away from the family," she said as they packed. "I don't want any mischief. I want excellent results. You are going to school not for tourism and not for fun. You are going to school to study. Is that clear?" Ruth nodded. "You are going to school to study," Eunia repeated. "Is that clear?"

"Yes, it is clear, Mummy," Ruth answered. She knew her mother disliked non-verbal responses.

"I will accompany you to the school. We will be taking an early morning bus."

※　　※　　※

"Is the school far from here?" Ruth asked nervously as soon as they had boarded the bus the following day. She had never visited the school. Several passengers were still waiting outside in the queue.

"No, it's not far. We should be there in about one hour and a half."

"It's quite far, then."

"Not really. It's less than thirty kilometres away but the bus stops frequently for people to embark and disembark."

Ruth looked out of the window and imagined the next few years of her life as a boarding student. She knew that there would be other students at Buweela from her junior school, but other than Sanyu, she had not met with any of them since the results had been released, so she did not know which. In her previous school her friend Daisy had been even brighter than Ruth, so Ruth was certain that she too would be admitted.

"Buweela High School is a big school," Eunia said. "Things will be different there than they were in Rubaga Primary School, where everybody knew you as the deputy headmistress's daughter. You'll need to work harder to cope both academically and socially."

"Yes, Mummy, I will work hard for good results."

"Not just good results; I want excellent results," Eunia said firmly. "Do you know what career you would like to pursue in the future?"

"No, not yet. I will think about it later."

"Now is the time to think about it. I don't want you to study aimlessly."

"Shouldn't I get used to the school first before I think about hard things like my career?"

"Do what you've got to do. All I want is for you to focus on your studies for excellent results. And I want you to be involved in various activities in school because you are a natural-born leader."

"Yes, Mummy. I'll join the netball team," Ruth said, hoping that her mother would change the subject, and when a woman that Eunia knew came into the bus with her daughter who was also going to Buweela High School, and found seats behind them, her mother's attention was diverted.

As Eunia and her acquaintance talked, Ruth thought about how hard her mother had worked to raise her two sons, Mark and Thomas, and her two daughters, Hannah and Ruth. Ruth smiled when she recalled the school day mornings. Eunia would be discussing family matters in Luganda as she walked to school with her daughters, but as soon as they arrived at the school gate, she would switch to English, just as quickly switching from being their mother to taking on her role of teacher.

When the bus stopped at the dirt road that led up to the school, Eunia's mind was flooded with her own memories. As she and Ruth walked up the kilometre-long hill, she noticed that although there were now more houses in the area, the village looked almost the same as it had twenty years earlier, when she herself had come to board at Buweela High School for girls.

Born to poor rural parents, Eunia had been a very determined young woman. Before the beginning of every school term, she and three other girls would walk for four days from their home town of Masaka 130 kilometres away to come to the school, making stops on the way to rest at strangers' homes, where they would be given free food, lodging and a lot of encouragement. Throughout Eunia's four years at Buweela this had worked very well except on one occasion. During her last year, a man in whose house the girls had spent the night said he wanted to take the oldest girl, Belinda, to be his third wife. They had thought he was joking, but when they thanked him for his hospitality and were preparing to embark on the next leg of their journey, the man was fuming. Did they think they would get away with free meals? So to pay for the food and accommodation he forced the girls to stay an extra day to pick cotton on his plantation. It was during Eunia's course at the teachers' college that one of her teachers had introduced her to Collin Wamala, an introduction that had changed Eunia's life. Collin, a builder and son of the prosperous owner of Wamala & Sons Construction, Lutti Wamala, would become her husband, soon after she finished her studies.

When they arrived at the school, Ruth was impressed by how beautiful everything looked. The grounds were planted with flowering trees and the school seemed vast, comprising so many buildings. The largest, the administration building, stood in the middle of a large compound, in front of a row of classroom buildings. Farther up a hill stood some of the student dormitories. The teachers' houses were on the other side of this hill, as were the largest student dormitories. These had huge water tanks beside them, for collecting the rainwater from their corrugated iron roofs. Ruth also noticed a door marked "Students' Infirmary," and was very happy to see a netball field; she loved netball and played it very well.

While Ruth was waiting in line to register at the administration building, she observed several returning students in their well-ironed uniforms, navy-blue dresses whose length was a few centimetres above the ankle. The girls looked good.

"Hey, Ruth!" Ruth turned to see who was calling out her name, and waved when she saw Daisy and Sanyu at the back of the line. The three friends were able to hug each other and talk once they'd completed their registration.

Eunia had been standing near one of the classroom blocks as she waited, talking to one of the teachers, Mrs. Sekatawa, who had been at school here with her twenty years earlier. After she said hello to Daisy and Sanyu and they'd left to go to their dormitory, Eunia introduced Ruth to her old classmate.

"Mrs. Sekatawa, meet Ruth. She is my first-born daughter."

Mrs. Sekatawa shook Ruth's hand. "Hello, Ruth. I'm glad to meet you."

"Good morning Mrs. Sekatawa," Ruth said.

The women chatted for a few more minutes before parting. "Please keep an eye on my daughter," Eunia said.

"Yes, I will," Mrs. Sekatawa answered.

Eunia then accompanied Ruth to her dormitory to help her make her bed and see where she'd be living. She was happy when she realized that Ruth would reside in Speke Dormitory where she had also lived during her years here. "I have wonderful memories of this place," Eunia said as they entered the building. "I lived three years in that corner before I got my own cubicle as the deputy head prefect. I hope you'll like it as much as I did."

"I hope so too," Ruth said.

Once Eunia had bade her daughter farewell and gone back home, Ruth was very conscious of her unfamiliar surroundings. The first night inside her dormitory she watched the matron for some time. The woman was so strict and stern and her actions as she went back and forth seemed so automated that she reminded Ruth of a machine.

❋   ❋   ❋

The following morning, the headmistress, Miss Cook, an Englishwoman, addressed the first assembly of the year in the presence of most of the teachers. During Ruth's first class the teacher spent the whole lesson time helping students get to know each other and explaining the gist of the subjects they would take. The next lesson, Ruth studied English before she returned to her dormitory.

The students were talking excitedly about their new school when an older student with an air of authority entered the room. "Hello everyone, welcome to Buweela High School. My name is Clotilda ..."

Not again! Ruth thought. It was Clotilda Kayiza, who had been two classes ahead of her in Rubaga Primary School.

"I am the prefect in charge of students' welfare..."

Ruth could not believe her ears. *What? Who puts Clotilda in charge of students' welfare?*

"I am also a resident here in the great Speke Dormitory."

"No, not again," Ruth murmured.

"Speke is a fun place; we welcome everyone regardless of their background, academic or other," Clotilda said as her eyes swept through the room.

Liar! Clotilda had been a notorious bully in Rubaga Primary School.

"We encourage all the students to participate in the various organized social activities, which include sports, the bi-monthly tea party and the debating club."

Another student entered the dormitory and stood next to Clotilda. She, like Clotilda was older than the new students, but although it was obvious that she was also an official, Clotilda did not acknowledge her.

"Most importantly though, I want to inform all newcomers," Clotilda said, while emphasizing 'newcomers,' "that cleanliness is of paramount..."

Now that's the Clotilda I know, Ruth thought—"*newcomers.*" Ruth had heard Clotilda's condescending tone by which she'd meant to express her superiority.

"...importance. Beds have to be made every morning, clean clothes must be neatly arranged in your suitcases, and dirty laundry must not litter the floor. Is that clear?" Clotilda said. No one responded. "Am I speaking to someone?" Still, there was no response. Clotilda stopped talking.

"Hello, ladies," the other older student said. "You are welcome to the great Buweela High School. I am Jane Nabirye. I am the school's timekeeper."

Clotilda walked away as soon as Jane began speaking. Ruth felt it was awkward.

"Ladies, I can't emphasize enough the importance of timekeeping," Jane said. "Here, we follow our schedules strictly and we are expected to be on time in everything we do. The first bell of the day rings at 5:45 every morning. So before you get out of bed at exactly six o'clock you have fifteen minutes to do whatever you want. You'll find more details on your dormitory's notice board."

Walking back from her cubicle, Clotilda glanced at Jane before leaving the dormitory and Ruth could sense the tension between them.

❋   ❋   ❋

Shortly after all the students had sat down for lunch, a young teacher entered the dining room who immediately captivated Ruth with her beauty and demeanour. "Hello, ladies. I am Miss Catherine Nannono, one of the two Home Economics teachers. I also oversee students' nutrition," the young woman said. "I don't intend to keep you waiting because I know you are hungry. However, there are a few things I would like to point out to the new students. By the way, you are all welcome to the great Buweela High School."

"Those who already know how to use cutlery should bear with me, but as you know, not all of us have had the chance to use it in our homes," Miss Nannono said as she and Clotilda demonstrated table etiquette. Ruth wondered whether there was anyone who did not know how to use these things, but many of the new students were watching attentively. "I would also like to inform the new students that each month, one class prepares a special meal for the entire school to enjoy. This is an opportunity for you to show off your culinary skills and it is very exciting. One other thing, you are free to have conversations in the dining room but please remember to keep your voices low. Be courteous to the kitchen staff and place your plates onto the racks after your meal. Any questions, don't hesitate to ask me," Miss Nannono concluded before leaving the dining room.

❈　❈　❈

Ruth enjoyed the Home Economics lessons very much. Not only did she love the beautiful and friendly Miss Nannono, she also enjoyed the subject, learning how to weigh food and cook while following recipes. She also learned how to economize by preparing just enough food. "There are millions of people in this world who don't have enough food," Miss Nannono said in one class. "Because we get free food from the school farm, some of us don't realize that food is actually a big expense for people elsewhere. Most families in this country rely on the rain and grow their own food but the headmistress says that people who live in cities in England buy all their food from supermarkets. This will be the case here as our country continues to urbanize and people abandon their farmlands to move to the city. And just imagine how hard it is right now for people in Europe to get food due to the war."

❈　❈　❈

Ruth soon realized why people said that Buweela High School produced "well-trained hard-working women." Academic excellence was pursued but social development was also a top priority. The students woke as soon as the first bell rang at 5:45. During the fifteen minutes when each student was free to do what she wanted, some prayed, some daydreamed, some squeezed in a few extra minutes of sleep, but after fifteen minutes sharp, the matrons would tour the dormitories, ensuring that nobody was still in bed. At 6:30 AM all students were required to be in the dining room for breakfast, and classes started immediately afterwards. Every minute was accounted for.

Every Saturday after breakfast, the students would gather in the backyards of their respective dormitories to handwash their clothes. Ruth wondered whether boys' high schools followed the same routines and wondered how her brothers Mark and Thomas, who relied on their mother or sisters to wash their clothes, would cope.

❋   ❋   ❋

One afternoon, several months after they had arrived, Ruth and Sanyu were standing near the main entrance to their dormitory, arguing about the recently-ended war, and Ruth was talking at the top of her voice. When Clotilda walked into the dormitory and asked the two girls to keep quiet, Sanyu stopped talking but Ruth talked even louder.

"Wamala, keep quiet. Other people have better things to do than listen to you ranting," Clotilda said, intentionally addressing Ruth by her last name to annoy her. Ruth had always defied Clotilda because she was a cruel prefect in Rubaga Primary School, stubbornly challenging her authority. She did the same now, and kept talking.

Clotilda walked quickly towards her. "Shut up or else…"

"Or else what?"

"You have to obey my orders. Shut up," Clotilda said as she pushed Ruth, who fell on the floor.

Ruth was crying as she walked out of the dormitory. Several students asked her if she was okay but she did not answer. She walked past the nearest classroom block and continued towards the administration building, her hand covering her face. Clotilda, who was following her from a distance, was shocked to see Ruth go to the headmistress's office, because disputes between students here were always reported to the teachers, not to the headmistress as in Rubaga Primary School. Clotilda continued watching from a distance. Miss Cook was so respected she was almost out of the reach of the students—surely Miss Cook or her secretary would send Ruth away.

Miss Cook was surprised to see the sad-looking young student walking straight into her office. Moments later, the headmistress motioned Clotilda into her office. "Honey, these are girls," Miss Cook told her. "You've got to handle them with care. Please treat them well and don't let this kind of treatment happen again."

"Yes, Madam," Clotilda said and walked out of the office. *I'll try to treat the other girls well—but not stubborn Wamala.*

3

JULY 1945

LEVI AND MULINDA sat under the mango tree at Levi's home to plan for Merab's pre-wedding party.

"I will donate a bull to be slaughtered," Mulinda said. "It is a great honour for us to be marrying off our daughter."

"Thank you very much," Levi said. "I will be forever grateful."

"Half of the meat will be served here and the other half will be sent to Kalasa as our contribution to the wedding reception," Mulinda said.

"Sending half of the meat to Kalasa would be a good idea but do you think the remaining half will be enough to feed our people here?" Levi asked. "We don't know how many people will turn up."

"Half of the bull will be enough because we will also serve goat meat and chicken."

Levi and Dolosi's relatives and friends also brought food to donate for the feast. "We and our daughter Merab are indeed honoured by your gesture," Dolosi said politely, knowing that it was customary for people to donate food on such occasions.

Abigail came at the beginning of the week, bringing a new pair of shoes that Lutalo had bought for Merab for the wedding. Merab was very happy to receive the shoes but that did not change her feelings toward Lutalo—she neither knew him nor loved him. Dolosi did not want anybody else to see the shoes before the wedding but she encouraged Merab to wear them inside the house to practise walking in them before the big day. It was Merab's first pair of shoes ever.

Now Abigail was at Merab's side at all times. She continued to talk to her about what was expected of her as a wife and as a mother. Merab listened without interrupting or asking any questions. Several other women also gave her their own advice.

Merab's older sister Eseza had been married in the nearby village of Bulimu. On the eve of the wedding she sat down to talk to Merab. "I thought that they would let you complete your primary education," Eseza said. "After all, you have been doing well in school."

"I thought so, too. I only found out that they were planning my marriage when I returned from school one day and heard Aunt Abigail talking with Father," Merab said.

"It would have been better for you to stay in school," said Eseza, frowning. "And Mother told me that you are going to get married in Kalasa."

"Yes."

"That's another rural area. I wish we could run away to escape from these marriages that we did not choose for ourselves!"

"I thought about that. Can't I run away?"

"Run away? To where?" Eseza said. "I thought about running away myself but I am still stuck in my marriage, in a village where there's absolutely no progress."

"What is wrong with your marriage?" Merab asked.

"Poverty, mostly. Look," Eseza said, pointing to her husband, who was splitting firewood in the yard in front of the kitchen. "Is that the best thing for a son-in-law to be doing now?"

"Don't blame him. He is giving what he has," Merab said. "Free labour."

"That's exactly what I'm talking about! Because he is poor, he can't contribute money to your wedding or even give something as little as a few chickens. And that makes me sad."

While they were chatting, Levi called Merab over to talk. She took a seat on a mat in front of her father, who sat above her on his folding chair. "Merab, it is never easy to embark on a new leg in our journey through life," he said. "I know that your upcoming marriage must be stressful for you but you should not be afraid."

Of course I have to be afraid! Merab thought. *You chose a man for me who I know nothing about and I did not want to get married now.*

"I know your aunt has prepared you, so everything should go well. I don't have much to say to you now but I encourage you to keep up the good work. You are very hardworking and I know you will be a blessing to your husband and to your future family."

"Father, where shall I begin, in a home that is not familiar to me?" Merab asked.

"One important thing that you should remember is to never neglect your values—our values—honesty, love, kindness. You will be in the home not as a visitor but as the wife, and you'll be able to do many things your way. Above all, you should always pray. Lead your family in the daily evening prayer like we do here and all will be well with you." His words were interrupted by a group of musicians who'd started drumming as soon as they arrived in the front yard. "We will continue this conversation when we get a chance later," Levi said. "Now you should get ready for the party."

❆　　❆　　❆

"I want us to organize a wedding reception that our people in Kalasa and beyond will remember and talk about for a long time," Lumu had said to his younger brother. Lutalo had agreed.

"At first I didn't want a wedding but I'm now excited about it," he'd said.

Not only did they want to make their people happy but they wanted to keep their father's legacy alive—the late county chief Lumu was known for his generosity; a party at his home had usually meant that he'd be treating the whole village to both lunch and dinner.

But now, as Lutalo, Lumu and their friend Kabali planned the menu, Kabali asked, "Why don't we organize a tea party instead?" Kabali had just recently moved into the village and had no idea of the magnitude of the late chief Lumu's house parties. "Wouldn't it be too much to prepare such huge amounts of—"

"No," Lumu answered even before Kabali had completed his sentence. "Our people will enjoy the wedding more when they eat real food. We men of the Sheep clan are known for our generosity. Besides, we have plenty of food."

A large shed made with newly cut poles and roofed with a large tarpaulin was erected in Lutalo's front yard. The shed was nicely decorated with wild flowers and banana trees. Two fattened bulls, several goats and many chickens were slaughtered on the eve of the wedding and the more than twenty men and women who'd volunteered to cook started in the middle of the night. Banana beer seemed to be in unlimited supply and more than two hundred people spent the eve of the wedding drinking, singing, dancing to drums and having fun at Lutalo's home.

The wedding itself took place in Levi's church in Senge, thirty kilometres away. The service started when Levi walked Merab down the aisle. Many jubilant friends and relatives of the family attended, and were impressed by the photographer Merab's cousin Philemon had brought from Kampala and his tripod-mounted camera. Only one person, the bride, seemed not to want to be there. Merab had her eyes fixed on the floor as she walked with her father, and Dolosi worried that her daughter was about to cry.

A few minutes into the service, Reverend Mukuye called out, "Who is giving away Merab to be married to Jonah?"

Absalom had performed the same ceremony twice before when he had given away his younger sisters Eseza and Nawume but he was not ready to give Merab, his youngest sister, away. He thought she was too clever to be married at such a young age, and to such a rural man. As he walked to the altar he hesitated for an instant. And after he returned to his seat next to his father, his duty done, he tried to concentrate on the wedding ceremony. But his thoughts drifted and he could not overcome his disappointment. Absalom was his parents' oldest child, now twenty-four years old, and he felt like a failure even though he had already built a small mud house on land his father had given him. He lived alone. He had hoped that his beautiful, clever and hardworking youngest sister Merab would have a different life than his two other sisters. He thought about the acre of maize that Merab had planted. It was about to yield a plentiful harvest, but all her energy had been wasted, he thought, because she would not be there to harvest her crop.

As the wedding ceremony progressed, Merab's thoughts drifted, too. *This is not at all what I wanted. I think I will stay in the marriage for only a few weeks. Then I will run away.*

"Merab, do you take Jonah as your husband, for better, for worse, for richer, for poorer, in sickness and in health, till death do you part?" Reverend Mukuye asked.

"I do," Merab answered.

Her reverend uncle then turned to Lutalo. "Jonah, do you—"

Lutalo, who had memorised his vows and was eager to take his bride, interrupted. "I Jonah Lutalo, take thee, Merab, to be my wedded wife, to have and to hold, from this day forward, for better, for worse, for richer, for poorer, in sickness and in health, to love and to cherish, till death do us apart, according to God's holy ordinance and therefore I pledge myself to you," he said, not stopping for breath.

The congregation clapped and cheered.

✳ ✳ ✳

After the wedding, the photographer took several photographs outside the church. The first bicycle then set off carrying the groom, followed by the one that carried the bride and a procession of several others over the long journey back to Kalasa. In the villages through which the wedding party passed, well-wishers gathered along the road to cheer and congratulate the new couple. Merab enjoyed the attention as so many young people admired and cheered for her. And where it was hilly and she had to get off the bicycle to walk, she had no trouble walking in her shoes because she had practised for several days.

The bridegroom and bride were received first and refreshed themselves at Kabali's home, where they rested for about half an hour before being taken to their own home. The dirt road had been decorated with banana trees and wild flowers, and on both sides people stood to cheer the new couple. Merab felt overwhelmed by all the attention, which was mostly on her. "The bride is too young," she overheard someone say.

The couple were welcomed into the overcrowded front yard with cheers and drumming. The drummers who had performed at Levi's home on the eve of the wedding and a local group were both there and some friendly competition ensued.

After the bridal couple had been seated at a high table, the feast began with banana beer served in gourds and mugs. Lutalo beamed with joy and waved to several friends and acquaintances but Merab just looked preoccupied and worried. Lumu, the Master of Ceremonies, called out the names of the various villages that were represented at the wedding party. The people from these villages would follow the usher who showed them their allocated spot, sitting before they were served a copious meal of *matooke* plantain, sweet potatoes, rice, beef, goat meat and chicken.

Merab's family members were served their meal in the living room together with the bridal couple. Lutalo enjoyed his meal while he conversed with Philemon but Merab hardly touched her food. Her aunt Abigail, who was next to her on a mat, tried to get her to eat but Merab was not in the mood for food.

After they had eaten, Merab's family bade her farewell to return home before dark except her aunties Abigail and Namagembe. The bridal couple retired to their bedroom towards midnight, after a weepy Merab had received a brief but stern last-minute lecture from Abigail. The drumming and drinking continued till the wee hours.

In the morning, Abigail asked to see the couple's bedsheets and Lutalo presented a live goat to Abigail as a gift, proof that Merab had been a virgin.

4

April 1946

BY THE FOLLOWING YEAR, both Clotilda and Ruth had grown into tall beautiful young women who could not go unnoticed wherever they went. Clotilda was a couple of years older than Ruth but that did not stop Ruth from standing up to her, even in situations when other students would simply walk away. The two seemed to be opposites and therefore natural enemies, Clotilda doing everything to bring others down, Ruth fighting injustice at every opportunity. On several occasions, the two girls clashed—especially during netball practice. For two years before Ruth joined the school netball team, Clotilda had enjoyed the limelight as the team's top scorer. Both girls were tall and very fast runners, but their coach, Mrs. Sekatawa, soon realized that whenever they were on the same side during practices, each would try to monopolize possession of the ball in order to score. And so to alleviate the situation and to balance the strength of the practice teams, she would put Ruth and Clotilda on opposite sides. More spectators than ever showed up.

One Saturday evening Clotilda could be heard through the wide-open door in the dormitory, loudly telling two girls that as a prefect, she worked very hard but that people like Ruth did not seem to appreciate her work.

"What kind of work do you do for us?" Ruth asked as she rose from her bed and walked towards Clotilda.

"I plan the menu, I make weekly reports about your likes and dislikes, and that is a lot of work because everybody does not like the same food. I—"

"I don't care!" Ruth said. "In any case, your role is useless because the food is terrible."

"The food is terrible!" said a girl who Ruth had not realized was in the room.

"The food is terrible, the food is terrible!" A large group of girls who happened to be rushing into the dormitory took up the cry.

The matron stood in the doorway. "Report to Mrs. Kyeyune's office first thing tomorrow morning," she said to Ruth before turning and walking away. Mrs. Kyeyune was the head of the Disciplinary Committee. How long had the matron been there? How much of the conversation had she heard? Ruth didn't know, but had no doubt that the woman would testify that she had heard Ruth say, "The food is terrible."

In the morning, Ruth knocked on Mrs. Kyeyune's office door. The teacher told her to enter. "What is your name?" Mrs. Kyeyune asked.

"My name is Ruth Wamala," Ruth answered, shaking.

"I see. You were involved in a commotion in Speke Dormitory last evening that caused a lot of disturbance for the rest of the residents. Is that correct?"

"Yes, but I was trying to defend myself against—"

"You were trying to defend yourself by making statements that can lead to riots in the school? Did you say that the food you are served here at school is terrible?"

"Yes," Ruth answered, knowing that if she denied having said so, another case would be opened against her, "but only because I was provoked and I lost my temper."

"Learn to control your temper," Mrs. Kyeyune said. "Since this is your first time to be involved in such misconduct, you've been suspended for three days. Take this warning letter and have your parents sign it before you return to school. Now, get out of my office. I'll see you back here on Thursday morning."

Ruth went out of the office with the letter in her hand. She was still crying when she went to the dormitory to pick up a few of her belongings and off the campus to wait for the bus. Clotilda and a few other students saw her walking past the school gate, and Clotilda laughed.

Mrs. Kyeyune soon investigated the matter, talking to some students who told her that Clotilda had set Ruth up, that she'd planned to get Ruth in trouble with the school authorities. The following day she summoned Clotilda to her office. The girl was trembling as she waited to learn her fate.

"Clotilda, you should know that you are lucky that the Disciplinary Committee has given you only a light punishment," Mrs. Kyeyune said. "You have been suspended for one week. Collect your belongings and walk off the school property immediately." As Clotilda stepped out the door and was about to close it behind her, Mrs. Kyeyune added, "Let me remind you that if this happens again, you will be expelled from the school forthwith."

When Ruth arrived home, she just told her mother she wasn't feeling well, afraid to admit that she'd been suspended from school. At dinner that evening her father noticed she looked troubled and worried, and when he inquired further after dinner, Ruth confessed what had happened. Eunia was furious. She yelled at Ruth, threatening to send her away from home if she was expelled from the school. Ruth cried.

"So, Ruth," Collin said after Eunia had calmed down. "Tell me what exactly happened."

"Daddy, I am sorry I made a stupid mistake—"

"No, no—go on. Don't we all make mistakes?" Collin said.

"Clotilda attacked me in the dormitory—"

"Who is Clotilda?" Collin asked.

"Clotilda is Kayiza's niece," Eunia answered.

"I was in the dormitory when out of the blue Clotilda accused me of not appreciating her work," Ruth said.

"Is she in a position of authority?" Collin asked.

"Yes she is. She is a prefect. We argued for a short while and when she said that she plans the menu, I said that the food is terrible—"

"What?" Eunia asked.

Ruth continued. "A matron heard what I said and reported me. I was suspended for three days."

"You are setting a bad example for your sister. Do you remember what I told you on the first day of school?" Eunia asked.

Collin didn't wait for Ruth to respond to her mother's words. "Be more careful when you go back and try to obey the school rules," he said gently. "Go to bed now."

Ruth was relieved. As she went to her bedroom, her parents continued to quarrel. "Clotilda is a troublemaker and Ruth knows that well," she heard her mother say. "She mustn't provoke her."

5

July 1945

WHEN CHIEF LUMU'S will had been read a few months after his death six years earlier, his friends and relatives had been surprised to learn, contrary to what they had expected, that his youngest son, Lutalo, had been chosen as his heir, to inherit his home and most of his property. Lutalo's home was very large, with five bedrooms, a large living room and dining room and a spare room that was used for storage, now full of newly harvested cotton. Several smaller houses stood in the large compound as well, some vacant.

After the wedding, Merab was kept in the bedroom for five days and nights. She was served all her meals there and those who wanted to talk to her would go to her room, especially members of her husband's family, many of whom also lived in Kalasa. This was considered her honeymoon, since she did not do any work, but Lutalo resumed his work on the farm two days after the wedding.

Each day he would return at around noon, bathe, eat his lunch, and then take a nap while Merab sat beside him in the bedroom weaving a mat of dried palm leaves. On the third day, as Lutalo slept, Merab quietly lifted the cloth that was covering his feet, noting that his feet were clean and not cracked. *Thank goodness! That's impressive—it's good that he grooms himself well. All the same, it's a terrible thing to be married to such an old stranger.*

On the last day of Merab's honeymoon, Abigail joined her niece's new family for lunch. Afterwards, while they were alone in the living room and Abigail was preparing to leave, Merab told her that she missed home and wished Abigail could take her away with her.

"I know marriage is sometimes difficult especially in the later years but you'll get used to it. Stay focused, work hard and take care of your husband and the family," her aunt said firmly. "I expect no mischief from you. Your aunt Namagembe will be coming frequently to check on you." Abigail's sister lived in the neighbouring village of Lukwate, half an hour's walk away.

Merab said goodbye to her aunt in tears.

The first thing she worried about was the chore of cooking meals for the many people who lived in the big house. In addition to Lutalo's three children—the girls, five-year-old Nabbosa and four-year-old Nakiyingi, and the boy, two-year-old Kulumba—there were more than ten other relatives living there as well as servants who lived in the smaller houses in the same compound. The men worked on Lutalo's vast coffee, banana and cotton plantations. All had to be fed.

During Merab's first week as a newlywed all the meals had been prepared and served without her involvement, so she decided to keep it that way. All she needed to do was to plan them. The servants harvested the food from the garden and brought it home and the task of cooking could be left to Lutalo's cousin Nabukalu, who, although she was several years older than Merab, didn't seem to have any trouble taking orders from her. And Cousin Nalunkuma, also living in the house, seemed to be indifferent toward her cousin's new wife.

But even though the responsibility of feeding so many people was shared, Merab was still overwhelmed by the large homestead when her real life in her new home began. It took a few weeks for her to gain confidence as the wife in the large home until Lutalo said, "This is your home; you are in charge. Organise it as you please." The head servant, Yafesi, was cheerful, talkative and welcoming, and Merab soon noticed that she talked more with him than with Lutalo, her introverted husband. The four other servants were more reserved, though very respectful of their master's new wife.

The only time that Merab cooked was when the menu included meat, especially chicken, Lutalo's favourite. Many chickens scratched around the coffee and banana plantations near the house, and whenever Lutalo wanted to eat some, Yafesi or any of the other servants would slaughter three or four and chop the birds in pieces. Then Merab would take over, tying a string to each of the pieces meant for her husband for easy identification at the time of serving, as her aunt had advised her to do.

As a woman, Merab was not supposed to eat chicken at all—it was a delicacy reserved for men, and although her father Levi did not see any sense in the practice because he was a Christian, Merab knew her own mother Dolosi had never eaten it. Usually, even in Levi's house, women would prepare chicken and serve it to the men but eat another type of meat themselves, like beef or fish. Now, however, the fact that she was not supposed to eat chicken did not stop Merab from sneaking some. Having her own home and cooking in the outdoor kitchen by herself provided her an opportunity to taste it. So unless Yafesi counted the pieces after he had slaughtered the chickens and told Lutalo how many there were, Lutalo would not know that Merab secretly enjoyed the delicious meat. Nobody knew.

❋ ❋ ❋

"Will you please follow me?" Lutalo said to Merab one morning, picking up a machete. "I would like to give you a tour of the property."

Merab followed him in silence. She was never sure when to talk to Lutalo without appearing to interrupt his thoughts. He talked so little. The only time he seemed to talk freely was when he was drunk.

"This banana plantation covers about seven acres," Lutalo said. "It was my father's favourite area, and the only area where he worked himself. The rest of the land was under Yafesi's care. My father hired Yafesi many years ago."

Merab did not respond but Lutalo did not seem to care.

"Beyond the banana plantation is the coffee plantation," Lutalo said, indicating its direction with the machete. "My father cared a lot for his coffee. It was his number one source of income. He had many children, some of whom you'll get to know with time. He took good care of us. We didn't lack anything."

❋   ❋   ❋

In the following weeks, Lutalo was pleased to see Merab getting involved in the activities on the farm. She woke up early every morning, and he was pleased to note that after he had given her the tour of the land, she knew what needed to be done and led the rest of the family to do the work.

She thought of ways to make money, and before long, she'd realized that she could sell firewood like her father did back home. She asked Yafesi and the other servants to help her cut down some trees.

"Yes Mother," Yafesi had answered. "My men would be glad to do that job. After all, they don't have much to do in the afternoons."

"How do you get paid for your labour?" Merab asked Yafesi, a little embarrassed that a man who was older than her was calling her 'Mother.' "Are you paid per month or for each job you complete?"

"We are paid per month but don't worry about the money, Mother. We will do the job for you. We are members of the family."

Once the trees had been cut down, chopped and laid out in the backyard to dry, it was ready to be sold as firewood. Merab would carefully count the money the men who came to buy the wood gave her, handing it over to Lutalo—how it was spent was neither her concern nor within her power. She had enough wood to sell for a few months, but she could see that at the rate it was selling, there would soon be no trees left to cut. Merab also asked Yafesi and his team to clear a large swampy area where they later planted sugarcane. The farm prospered under Merab's care and Lutalo thanked her.

❊   ❊   ❊

Every evening, Merab would spare a half hour to prepare the following day's activities for the whole family. She allocated chores and planned meals. Lutalo noticed that there were fewer quarrels in the family with his young wife in charge. He nicknamed her *Mufuzi* (the Administrator).

Lutalo usually finished his farmwork at 11:00 AM. He'd return home, take a bath and sit in the living room to wait for his lunch, which Merab would serve him exactly at noon. He ate the meal in silence, even when she sat down on a mat to wait on him, and as soon as he was finished, he would then hop onto his bicycle and go to his shop in the centre of Kalasa. Merab would rarely see him again until nightfall.

The house she lived in now was the largest Merab had ever seen. On some days she felt lost in it and lonely, wishing she could run away, back to her father's home. But she knew there was no longer a place for her there—Abigail had made that very clear. And she and her siblings had been brought up to be very obedient, so how could she disobey her parents by running away from the man they had chosen for her? She cared for and loved Lutalo's three children, especially two-year old Kulumba, but deep down, she wanted to have children of her own.

Sometimes during the first few months, she felt strange in the company of people who were older than her, especially the men who came unannounced to talk to Lutalo about their farming businesses. Sometimes, especially when she saw young people of her own age giggling while on their way to and from the stream to collect water, she felt as if she was still the child she had been in her father's home. *My life here is very boring*, she'd think. *Sooner or later I will have to run away*. Merab missed her mother so much that sometimes when Lutalo was not home, she would sit in her bedroom and cry. She felt trapped in the large house with the husband she did not love. And because he was older she feared him.

The situation was worsened by the fact that Lutalo rarely talked to her. The few times he spoke at home it was to bark orders at the children. During her

47

bedside prayers, Merab wondered what to pray for. *Should I pray to get used to life in this home or should I pray for something like a beating, so that I will have an excuse to run away?*

However, realizing that she had no alternative, Merab soon adjusted to her new life and began following her aunt's instructions faithfully. Every evening, she would warm water in a clay pot and pour it into a metal basin to have Lutalo's bath ready for him as soon as he returned, then wait for him to change. Then she'd lead the family in evening prayers before Nabukalu and Nalunkuma served dinner. As Merab and Lutalo waited for dinner to be set up on the living room floor, her sitting on a mat and Lutalo on his chair facing her, she would ask about his day. In most cases he'd respond in monosyllables.

However, she soon realized that her husband was generous. Every Saturday evening he would bring something from his shop just for her, whether a set of handkerchiefs, or underwear, or a blouse.

A few buildings at the intersection of two roads comprised the village of Kalasa's small town centre, and Lutalo's shop was one of four to be found there. Among the many items he sold the best-sellers were paraffin, bar soap, tea, dried beans and sugar. His customers liked him because of his willingness to sell to them on credit. Borrowers could buy whatever they needed and pay up what they owed, without interest, whenever they had sold their coffee or cotton. Because of that, many people, including those from the villages neighbouring Kalasa, bought from Lutalo's shop. He used an exercise book to keep track of all the accounts.

During the few times that Merab went to fetch water, out of boredom rather than necessity, she met other married women there at the stream, but the other women were all older than she. When she went to the stream alone, young men would sometimes talk to her, trying to persuade her to run away from the "old man."

A few months after she had moved to Kalasa, Yafesi accompanied Merab on her first visit to the village's bi-monthly market. When a young man she didn't know said to her, "There you are with your bodyguard—why don't you leave the old man for me? I will give you a better life," it was the word "bodyguard" that caught her attention. Yafesi usually came with her while they worked on the farm. Was he actually monitoring her movements for Lutalo? She quickly dismissed the thought—Yafesi was simply a polite man who cared for and respected her.

That week Lutalo bought Merab a beautiful dress; he seemed to be proud of her and she was gradually beginning to fall in love with him. But Merab still spent a lot of time encouraging herself to persevere and still thinking. *I will stay in this marriage only for a short while...maybe I will produce a couple of children but I will leave this man eventually. I don't want to live here all my life; I want to live in the city. I've got to do whatever it takes to go live in the city.*

Merab was very skilled at hand-weaving palm leaf mats, a skill that her mother had begun to teach her when she was seven years old. Now every afternoon, after lunch, she would sit for hours weaving mats in the shade of a tree beside the house. A friendly older woman named Nakatudde soon joined her, and they'd spend most afternoons weaving mats together while chatting.

6

June 1947

IT WAS THE turn of Ruth's class to cook the monthly special meal for the school. Some of the students peeled *matooke* plantain in the backyard of the kitchen while Ruth led a group of ten students to cook beef and beans.

When these special meals were being prepared, students who were not members of the class were not allowed into the kitchen. Although Clotilda knew this, she came into the kitchen anyway, to check on the progress of the dinner. She was the prefect in charge of students' welfare, after all.

"We need to cook the meat in several pans; that will enable us to cook faster," Ruth was saying as Clotilda came into the kitchen. "Remember we have hundreds of students to serve."

"Shut up, Wamala," Clotilda said. "Don't you think the others know what to do?"

The other students laughed but Ruth did not respond as Clotilda made a quick tour of the kitchen and walked out.

Ruth was quiet for a few minutes. "I think three of us could go set up the dining room while the rest of you continue with the cooking," she finally said to her classmates in the kitchen.

"You are a know-it-all, Wamala," she heard Clotilda say from where she stood just beyond the door. Ruth had not realized that Clotilda was still there. "Let the others think for themselves."

"Clotilda, can you please leave me alone? You are not supposed to be here anyway," Ruth said.

"For your information I'm the prefect in charge of the kitchen. Who are you to tell me where to be or not to be?" Clotilda said as she walked towards Ruth. When she pushed Ruth against the wall, students started talking at the top of their voices, telling Clotilda to get out of the kitchen.

"Get out or else—" Ruth herself began.

"Or else what?" Clotilda said, pinning Ruth to the wall. The noise behind her stopped suddenly. Clotilda turned, and saw a matron who had walked in quietly through the back door.

"Clotilda, are you part of the class that is preparing this evening's dinner?" the matron asked.

"No, madam," Clotilda answered, trembling.

"Then what are you doing in the kitchen?"

"I am the prefect in charge—"

"I know that, but even though you are the prefect in charge, should you be harassing the people that you are supposed to be leading?"

Clotilda did not have an answer to that question.

"Get out of the kitchen," the matron said. "I'm going to report you to Mrs. Kyeyune."

"No, please don't report me. I will not cause trouble again," Clotilda said. But the matron was already walking out of the kitchen.

When Clotilda knocked on the door of Mrs. Kyeyune's office the following day, there was no response, so she sat on the veranda as she waited for the teacher to come. Several students passed by and the smirks and even joy on their faces annoyed Clotilda. She knew how unpopular she was among the students, and it was obvious that they already knew that the matron had caught her mistreating Ruth.

When Mrs. Kyeyune arrived, she opened the door and went into her office without talking to Clotilda, leaving the door wide open. After about two minutes, she returned, saying, "Come in." Clotilda went into the office, trembling.

"Close the door," Mrs. Kyeyune said coldly, her facial expression a sign that the punishment would be severe. Clotilda was terrified.

"You can remain standing," Mrs. Kyeyune said sternly. This was another bad sign—as a prefect, whenever Clotilda had gone to Mrs. Kyeyune's office before, she'd sat on a chair.

"What is your name?" Mrs. Kyeyune asked.

"Madam, you know me. You know who I am," Clotilda answered.

"It is an administrative procedure," Mrs. Kyeyune answered while perusing a document in front of her.

"My name is Clotilda Kayiza."

"You were caught misbehaving in the kitchen, yet you were not supposed—"

"I was trying to maintain order in the kitchen," Clotilda said. "And Ruth Wamala—"

"Were you supposed to be in the kitchen at that time?"

"No, but as the prefect—"

"You've answered the question I asked and that suffices for me. You admit that you were not supposed to be in the kitchen. Clotilda, when you were appointed prefect you swore an oath to lead by example—"

"I've done my best—"

"Don't interrupt me. You have failed to lead by example and you have received a warning in the past. Your behaviour has forced the Disciplinary Committee to expel you from the school," Mrs. Kyeyune said as she stamped the expulsion letter and handed it to Clotilda.

As Clotilda stood there, incredulous, there was a knock on the door.

"I've got other matters to attend to," Mrs. Kyeyune said. "Get out of my office and leave the school property immediately."

Clotilda left Mrs. Kyeyune's office in tears with the letter in her hand. Nobody she passed approached to talk to her but several students cheered. When she went to the dormitory to take out her belongings, the same matron who had caught her was there, waiting for her to hand over the key to her cubicle and to ensure that she did not take anything that did not belong to her.

A few minutes later, as Clotilda walked out with her belongings, Nabirye, a fellow prefect met her at the door. "Clotilda, what's going on?" she asked.

"I have been expelled, yet it was Ruth Wamala who caused the trouble."

"What?"

"I have been expelled," Clotilda repeated as she walked away. "But I will pay Ruth back in the future."

Several people walked by as Clotilda waited at the roadside bus stop with looks of pity on their faces, but no one said a word to her. They knew that the sight of a student standing outside the school with all her belongings during the school term meant that she had been expelled. After a while, a man stopped to talk to Clotilda. He was drunk.

"Hey, so you've been expelled from the school, haven't you? Were you causing trouble?" he asked.

Clotilda, who said nothing, gave the man an angry look.

"You don't have to go back home; you can stay in my house," he said.

"Leave me alone, you stupid man!" Clotilda yelled.

A woman who was working in her garden nearby heard the commotion. "Kamese, don't be a nuisance!" she yelled. "Leave the girl alone. Go find yourself a job."

In the two hours before the bus finally came, a crowd of people had gathered, and Clotilda felt uneasy as she heard several people discussing her and her expulsion from the school in hushed voices.

Clotilda did not know how she would tell her uncle Walter that she had been expelled from a school in which many girls wanted to study but did not have the chance to do so. How would she tell him that she had been expelled after another unprovoked attack on Wamala's daughter? When she'd been five years old, her father—Walter's brother—had died suddenly, and her uncle had taken on the responsibility of raising her and her older brother Claver. When she'd completed junior school, her uncle had wanted to find a man for her to marry but since she was doing well in her studies, his wife had persuaded him to enrol her in high school. Now, she had been expelled during her final year of high school.

It was the middle of the day by the time Clotilda arrived home with her belongings. She thought that Uncle Walter would not be home, so she was surprised to find him seated in the living room as if he'd been waiting for her. She put her luggage on the floor by the front door and knelt to greet him. Before she could say anything, he asked, "Is it the end of the school term?"

"No," Clotilda answered.

"Then why are you home? Are you sick?"

"No, I'm not sick. Ruth Wamala got me into trouble again and—"

"You've been suspended from school?"

"She got me into trouble and it was not my fault," she said. "I've been expelled from the school."

"You know very well that we have done everything we could to help you," her uncle said angrily. "Now, listen to me. I will not let you live in this home any longer if you don't have anything useful to do. But I will let you use the remainder of this month to find something to do."

"I am sorry—"

"Get away from my sight now," Walter said.

Later that day, Clotilda walked the three kilometres to the home of Jude Kiyaga, the man who she'd always planned to marry someday. Jude was a few years older than she was and preparing for post-secondary education. However, he'd never showed much commitment to her, which worried her. Jude's father, Dawson, was a wealthy businessman and Clotilda had hoped that going to Buweela High School would elevate her social status enough for Jude to begin a serious relationship with her. She wondered whether she should tell him that she was no longer in school now and was ready to marry him.

Clotilda walked slowly once she arrived at the dirt road by the front yard of Jude's parents' large family compound, hoping that Jude would see her. She then sat down under a tree about two hundred metres away from the Kiyagas' home. But what would people think if they saw her seated idly by the roadside at that time of the day? After about ten minutes, she decided to walk back. The fact that Jude had not come out to meet her meant he was not home.

As soon as she rose, she saw him riding his bicycle towards her. He was smiling and seemed to be in a jovial mood. She sat back down under the tree.

"Hello, Clotilda. How are you?" Jude said, getting off his bicycle and sitting down to face her.

"I am well but I missed you," she began, smiling. "That's why I decided to come over to see you." At this, Jude's face was expressionless, showing his usual lack of interest. "Do you have time to talk?" she asked. "There are important things I would like to tell you."

"Hey, before you do," Jude said, "I have some exciting news. I have been admitted to Cardiff University in Wales. I am going to study there for four years. I will be leaving next month. I can't wait!"

"Oh, I am glad for you," Clotilda said, trying to hide her disappointment.

"So what's going on with you? You look worried," Jude said. "Aren't you supposed to be in school?"

"It is a long story. I really need time to explain everything to you, but you seem to be in a hurry now. Can we talk?"

"Listen, both my father and mother are home now and they wouldn't be pleased to see me with you," Jude said. "I will come to see you this evening."

"Can I count on you?"

"Yes, I will see you this evening," Jude said, hopping onto his bicycle and riding away.

But that evening he did not show up. As Clotilda waited, she remembered that he had not told her where they would meet.

*　*　*

"Clotilda, it's been a week since you were expelled from school," her uncle said. "What are you planning to do next?" She looked at him but she did not say anything. "I'm going to talk to Mrs. Wamala," he continued. "I think she is the only person who can help you to find a job—maybe a teaching position in a school. I hope she is not aware that you have been harassing her daughter."

"Ruth caused all the trouble," Clotilda said.

"I don't believe you," Walter answered. "The school authorities wouldn't expel you without first investigating the matter. I know how big-headed you are."

That evening, Walter went to Eunia Wamala's home to talk to her about Clotilda. He was relieved to note that even though she was sorry to learn about Clotilda's expulsion from the school, Eunia did not seem to know the reason. Two weeks later, with Eunia's recommendation, Clotilda got a job as a teacher in a small private school, Lungujja Primary School.

The school's owner, Tito Mbogo, was happy to have a former student of the great Buweela High School as a teacher in his school and he began to use that as a selling point to recruit new students. Soon after Clotilda started teaching there, she assigned herself the job of spokeswoman for the school, going door to door in Lungujja and the surrounding villages to tell the parents how great the school was. A number of parents agreed to register their children.

A few months later, Clotilda told Mr. Mbogo that if he gave her a bit of money for every student she recruited, she'd increase the student population even more. In less than two years, she had managed to triple the school's student population through her door-to-door visits, and was more visible at the school than both its owner and Mr. Kiboneka, the headmaster. "Since Clotilda is so active let's make her your deputy," Tito said to the headmaster. "Let's put her in charge of students' affairs so you can concentrate on general administration."

"I think that's a brilliant idea," Kiboneka said.

But when Clotilda took over students' affairs, Kiboneka spent a lot of time away from school to take care of his other businesses, and Tito noticed.

✳   ✳   ✳

There were no more upsets for Ruth at Buweela High School during the next two years, and her younger sister Hannah now attended the school as well. One Sunday Eunia came to visit her daughters, bringing a home-cooked lunch for them.

"Ruth, I visited the National Teachers' College last week," Eunia said as they were eating. "I thought it would be great for you to study there."

"Yes, I would like to study there," Ruth answered. *But my first choice of career would not be to become a teacher.*

"And I got a chance to talk to one of the tutors there—"

"You want to become a teacher, Ruth?" Hannah asked.

"There isn't a better profession," Eunia said before Ruth had a chance to answer. "I enjoy teaching. You get a chance to change the lives of many young people. I am always glad when I meet my former students, some of whom I may have forgotten, who tell me how well they are doing in life."

Ruth pretended to agree, but inwardly she was rebelling. *Don't decide for me*, she was thinking. *I will disappoint you when I choose a different career.*

❇   ❇   ❇

As Ruth met Miss Cook several times in her office over matters she referred to as "cases of injustice," she became acquainted with the headmistress. The other students were not surprised when Ruth was appointed Head Prefect in her final year, because she was a great role model. She was organised, punctual, her books were in good condition and her bed was very neat. As Head Prefect, Ruth even got the rare opportunity to visit Miss Cook's home when the headmistress invited her to tea.

They had a conversation on her veranda, and Miss Cook told Ruth about her life in England. Ruth listened attentively without asking any questions. "I gladly took up the opportunity to come to teach in Uganda," Miss Cook said. "Obviously I was more adventurous then than I am now. I was young, wasn't I?" She laughed. "Never pass up a good opportunity while you are still young."

Ruth listened even more attentively.

"When I arrived at this school obviously I didn't know anybody," Miss Cook continued. "But people gladly welcomed me even though they limited their interactions with me. At first I thought they had not accepted me but later I found out that as headmistress, I was given more privacy than I wanted. Of course I had a lot of questions to ask, especially about the Baganda culture. I was fascinated by your clan system, and how you use animals as symbols for your clans."

"Actually, Miss Cook, more than mere symbols," Ruth said. "For example, a person is not allowed to marry someone from his or her own clan, even if there is no known blood relationship. You can tell to which clan a person belongs depending on his or her last name. I for example, belong to the Bushbuck clan."

"Fascinating, isn't it? Oh, what a bad teacher I am! Shouldn't I be talking to you about new things instead of things you already know?"

"It is an interesting conversation," Ruth reassured the older woman.

"Have you thought about what career you would like to pursue now that you are about to complete your secondary education?"

"I've thought about it, but not seriously. My mother would like me to become a teacher."

"And is that what you want?" Miss Cook asked.

"No, but she seems to think there's no other option for me. I might disappoint her, though. I would like to pursue my own dreams."

"Do what you love. Obviously you need her advice, but you should choose for yourself."

❊   ❊   ❊

The next time Ruth visited Miss Cook's home was on a Sunday afternoon and after tea and biscuits, she and the headmistress took a walk around the school grounds.

"Women like you will play a major role in the development of this country," Miss Cook said as they strolled. "I am assuming that you are planning to pursue your education—"

"Yes, I will pursue my education."

"Great! I know that many girls in Uganda are not enrolled in school. How does one hope to develop a country when a large section of the population is not educated?"

*　*　*

To be seen to be a friend of the headmistress was a great honour and the other girls watched Ruth with jealousy. But it was not just Ruth's fellow students who noticed her closeness to the headmistress—the teachers noticed, too.

"What does the head prefect want from the headmistress?" Mrs. Musana asked.

"Whatever it is, it must be important," Mrs. Sendege answered. "Otherwise, how did she get Miss Cook's attention?"

One afternoon while Ruth was walking back to her dormitory, she met Mrs. Musana, who looked a little nervous. "Ruth, can I talk to you for a minute or two in the staff room?" It became obvious to Ruth that it was a planned encounter.

"Sure. What is it about?"

Ruth's question caught the teacher off guard—students never answered her with questions.

"Nothing to worry about."

When they sat down in the staff room, Ruth watched Mrs. Musana in silence as the teacher fidgeted with a drawer, pulling out an exercise book and putting it back in. Mrs. Musana had never encountered a student with such a level of confidence. Usually in such circumstances, the other students would be nervous and would avoid direct eye contact. Ruth was different, she thought. The girl had such beautiful eyes, so big and fierce-looking, that her stare was unnerving.

"Ruth, I have noticed lately that you are close to the headmistress," Mrs. Musana managed to say. "What do you talk about when you meet her?"

"We talk about studies, my future plans and things like that," Ruth answered, surprised.

Mrs. Musana hesitated before she spoke again. "Do you also discuss other matters—"

Ruth looked impatient, as though the teacher was wasting her time. "Like what?"

"Like teachers, teachers' performance and things like that."

"Why would we? Why would the headmistress discuss such matters with a student?"

"No no, I was just thinking aloud. Not that I thought you would discuss that."

Ruth continued to stare.

"Anyway, that's all I wanted to ask you," Mrs. Musana said, surprised that she did not have the courage to ask further questions. "But please don't ever tell the headmistress that I asked—"

"No, I won't," Ruth said as she rose from the chair and walked out of the staff room.

As soon as Ruth had left the room, in came Mrs. Sendege through the back door. "So, did you talk to Ruth?"

"Yes I did," Mrs. Musana said. "I asked her what she talks about with the headmistress."

"What did she say?"

"Her answers were not straightforward. And she was rude."

❋   ❋   ❋

Ruth admired the headmistress and was very eager to learn from her. Miss Cook, too, found Ruth very intelligent. When she invited Ruth to her home for the last time, she advised her to set goals and to check them off whenever she accomplished them.

"We women work like donkeys. I guess you understand what I am talking about, but you've got to remember that you can't do everything at one go. Tackle your tasks, even big ones, one small step at a time. My mother used to ask me whenever she thought that I was overwhelmed: 'How do you eat an elephant? One small piece at a time!'" Miss Cook smiled. "Get an exercise book, a notebook or anything else to write down your list of things to do and your goals. Have a plan for everything you do. Keep a diary where you can note your feelings, your thoughts, your fears and what you are grateful for. And remember, live in the moment. To do that you have to pay close attention to what you are doing. For instance, take time to enjoy your life, your food and everything else that life offers."

The very day that Ruth completed her end-of-high school examinations, Eunia went to the National Teachers' College to pick up admission forms for her.

❋   ❋   ❋

When she visited homes to recruit students, whenever a parent said that a child, usually a teenage boy, had refused to go to school, Clotilda would confront the child. "If you don't study, what alternative do you have? Do you know how hard your life will be if you drop out of school at this age?" In most cases, she would end up persuading the child to join her school. Clotilda became so influential that people in the area began to refer to the school as "Clotilda's school."

This became more a reality when the ailing Tito entrusted all the school's affairs to her and fired Kiboneka. Then Tito died, and during the funeral service, it was announced that the school would continue operating under Clotilda and that she would also take care of the education of Tito's own children who were still in school.

Clotilda's true colours manifested themselves just months after Tito's death. "You've got to work hard to ensure that your students pass their examinations—otherwise, there's no guarantee that you'll keep your jobs," she told the teachers. "Those who want to try to find jobs in other schools are free to do so."

7

TOWARDS HER FIRST wedding anniversary, Merab was overjoyed one evening when Lutalo told her that he was sending her to visit her parents. He handed her a letter addressed to her father.   "Here," Lutalo said. "Give this letter to the old man as soon as you arrive home. You will be visiting for ten days." He also gave her a woven bag full of groceries—sugar, tea, two bars of soap, salt and four kilograms of beef—to take to her parents.

Lutalo lent his new bicycle to Yafesi to take Merab to her parents' home. Dolosi shouted for joy when she saw her daughter when they arrived there around noon.

They greeted each other joyously.

Levi too came out of the house. "I am very glad to see you Merab."

"I am very glad to see you too Father," Merab answered. "Mother, Father, meet Yafesi. He's been very kind to me. He assists me with a lot of the work on the farm."

"Hello Yafesi," Levi said as he shook hands with Yafesi. "I'm glad to meet you."

"I am glad to meet you Father," Yafesi said.

After the greetings, Levi asked for the letter he knew his son-in-law had written. Merab took the letter out of her bag and handed it to him, and he read in silence.

> *Dear Sir,*
>
> *I hope you and everyone at home are doing well. I have given permission for this one to pay you a visit for ten days, starting today the 26ᵗʰ of July, 1946. She has been working very hard on the farm during the past year and since she joined me, my harvest has been more abundant. I am very happy about her blessed hands. Now that it is the dry season, there is not much work to do at the farm. Therefore I think the ten days will not be too many. She also needs some rest.*
>
> *Your humble son-in-law,*
>
> *Lutalo*

Levi took the letter inside the house and tucked it away in a book.

After lunch Yafesi rode back home, and Merab and Dolosi settled in for a chat in the front yard under the mango tree. After Dolosi complimented Merab on her good behaviour—Abigail had not reported any complaints from Lutalo—she told Merab that her cousin Scovia had run away from Mulinda's home after he had tried to marry her off.

"Did Scovia tell anyone why she did not want to get married?" Merab asked.

"To whom do you think she would tell her reasons?" Dolosi asked. "Your uncle is not someone to negotiate with. The very day your aunt Abigail informed Scovia that they had found her a man to marry, she ran away."

I should have run away too, Merab thought.

"Your cousin Philemon saw her in Kampala and still in school, although we don't know who pays her school fees. The worst thing in all this is that her father disowned her."

"What?"

"Yes, he said that since she had disobeyed him, he would no longer consider her his child and that he did not want to see her again."

Levi joined them, and from the look on his face, it was clear to Dolosi that he did not want Merab to hear more about Scovia's adventure. He asked Merab about the children in her home. At the end of the ten-day visit, Levi handed a letter to Merab, addressed to her husband.

> *Dear Sir,*
>
> *Yes we are doing well. Thank you for letting your wife come to pay us a visit. I am glad that she is making a difference at the farm. She has always been a hard worker. Thank you also for the groceries that you sent to us. Let Merab continue the good work and you will be blessed even more. We were very happy to see her and ask her to convey our warm greetings to you. Her visit has ended today, the 5th of August 1946. Your father-in-law,*
>
> *Levi Bukulu.*

Dolosi loaded Merab's woven bag with dried beans and dried nuts for Merab to take to her husband. "Mother, you didn't have to give us these foodstuffs," Merab said. "We already have plenty of them back in Kalasa."

"I must heed the wisdom of our culture, must I not?" Dolosi answered her daughter. "When you came to visit, you brought a bag full of goodies; when you go back to your home, you have to take back a bag full of goodies!"

When Yafesi returned to take Merab home, he reported that all was not well at home. Three-year-old Kulumba had been sick for the past three days—by the time Yafesi had left that morning he'd had such a high fever he had been convulsing. Merab was so worried about the child that she refused to eat her lunch. She regretted having left the little boy behind.

"Father, I think it was a mistake to marry off Merab before she completed school," Absalom said to his father once Merab and Yafesi had left. "She was doing well—she should have been given a chance to study. She could have married later on."

"What do you mean? Why are you saying this to me now?"

"Merab was a very happy young woman when she lived here but she has changed. She is no longer happy, and I don't think that marriage will enable her to become the person she was meant to be."

"Maybe you are right," Levi said, thoughtful. "I noticed that she was more pensive, but I thought that was just because she is now older and has more responsibilities."

"No, I don't think it has anything to do with her age," Absalom said, his voice rising. "She is only sixteen years old—still a child."

"She is still a child?" Levi asked, laughing. "What is wrong with you young people these days? You think a married sixteen-year-old woman is still a child?"

"Yes, she *is* still a child, but one with a lot of responsibilities, like raising children who are not her own."

"Your thinking is wrong, Absalom. I hope you did not share your opinions with Merab. Such thinking would make marriage hard for her."

"No, I didn't discuss anything with her. I am simply sharing my observations with you."

"But what makes Merab special? You have two sisters who married at the same age but you did not express any concerns for them."

"I love and care for Eseza and Nawume as much as I love and care for Merab," Absalom said. "But they were not as promising as Merab, neither as far as their schoolwork was concerned nor their work outside of school."

"You are right," Levi nodded in agreement. "But even if Merab could have studied and gotten further with her education, she would still have ended up married and raising children."

"But she wouldn't have to be just a wife and a mother. She could have had a career as a teacher or as a nurse. I know that she aspired to be a teacher. Philly says that more and more women are now working in those professions in the city."

"But she is already married now. What do you suggest we do? Annul the marriage?"

"That's not what I am suggesting, but—"

"I am actually surprised that you are more concerned about your sister than you are about yourself. You are twenty-five years old and don't have a job."

"Philly promised to help find a job for me," Absalom said, avoiding his father's gaze.

"That's all good, but while you wait for Philemon to find you a job," Levi said, trying not to smile, "why don't you find something to do here in the meantime?"

Absalom now realized that the conversation was going to be about him, and he quickly walked away.

❋　　❋　　❋

As soon as Merab arrived home, she spoke to Kulumba's aunt Nabukalu, who told her that she had bathed the boy in water mixed with herbs and had given him another bitter herb to drink. The boy had vomited most of it up again.

Those herbs don't work; it's a waste of time! Merab thought. "Thank you for your help but let's take him to the health centre right away," she said instead, rushing into the house to dress the shivering child.

"I am ready when you are, Mother," Yafesi said. He knew it would be an anxious ride. The health centre was twelve kilometres away.

Nabukalu turned to Yafesi. "There is no need to take him to the health centre," she told him, indignant. "Now that I have given him some herbs and some hot tea, he should be fine."

Merab emerged with the child a few minutes later and they set off.

When he returned home that evening, Lutalo knelt on the mat where Kulumba was sleeping. "How is he doing now?" he asked, his hand on the child's forehead to feel his temperature.

"The medical assistant diagnosed malaria and said he would be well after an injection of quinine," Merab told her husband. "He sweated a lot after the injection but he is doing better now. I cried all the way to the health centre because he was convulsing. I didn't know if he would still be alive by the time we got there."

"Thanks for caring for him," Lutalo replied. "You treat him better than his stupid mother."

That was the first time that Merab had heard Lutalo mentioning the children's mother. She did not comment. How could she discuss a woman she had never met? "I will have to take Kulumba with me the next time I travel," was all she said.

"You don't have to," Lutalo said. Then he went to the living room to wait for her to present him with the letter from his father-in-law.

※　※　※

A week later, Philemon rode his brand new Raleigh bicycle to Senge to visit his cousin and show it off. "What a beautiful bicycle, Philly! It must have made it quicker for you to get here from Kampala," Absalom said.

"Oh, yes! It took me just a little more than three hours to get here—before, it would have taken me five hours," Philemon said, jumping off the bicycle. "Any news about Merab?" he asked.

"Merab came home about two weeks ago. She's fine but I don't think she's settled there," Absalom said.

"I think I should pay her a visit one of these days," Philemon said.

"Merab is clever and hardworking—I didn't think she'd end up married so young to an older farmer."

"You are right. But I think she is stuck in that marriage," Philemon said.

"There must be a way to help her get out of that village," Absalom said, and neither cousin spoke for a few moments.

"I actually have some good news for you," Philemon finally broke their silence. "My boss, Mr. Mitego, is a member of the Central Cooperative Society. Last month, his friend Patel was elected as the new chairman of the Society. Now the Society is looking for someone to buy dried coffee beans in this region. I talked to Mr. Mitego about you and I told him that you are hardworking, honest and you love talking to people—just the kind of person they are looking for," he said. "Mr. Patel is offering you a job!"

"That's excellent news," Absalom said, excitedly hugging Philemon. "Where will I be working?"

"I don't know yet but I will find out—and since a lot of coffee is grown in the same area where Merab is living maybe I can convince them to post you there so you will get the opportunity to fulfil your mission of helping her move away," Philemon answered, smiling. "Mr. Patel will send someone to train you."

"Thank you very much," Absalom said. "I can't wait to start a real job. Please tell them that I am ready to begin work anytime."

"So, if you move to Kalasa, what will you focus on? Your job or helping

Merab to escape from Lutalo's home?"

"Both," Absalom said, laughing.

Absalom moved to Kalasa to start his job as a coffee buyer and was housed in a single room at the back of a newly constructed building that had a store in the front where he'd be buying the coffee from the farmers. Merab was glad that Absalom was now living just two kilometres from her home in the same village. She sent Yafesi every day to deliver lunch to her brother and expected him to come to her home every evening for supper. But Absalom did not want to. He didn't like Lutalo, and he wasn't happy that his sister was married to "an old man" whose children and household she had to take care of, even though she did not yet have children of her own.

Absalom noticed that people in Kalasa seemed to have a lot of free time and he soon made friends. People came to the coffee store even when they did not have any reason to, just to talk to him. Some would sit around for hours there, watching him as he weighed and paid for the coffee. And Philemon started making monthly visits to Kalasa, too, to see his cousins Merab and Absalom and to tell them about his progress in the city.

By the following year, once Absalom had noticed that he did not have to open the store so early in the morning because the coffee sellers were usually still at work in their plantations and that he'd have idle seasons when there was no coffee to buy, he asked Lutalo to lend him a piece of land to cultivate. Lutalo agreed right away, and Absalom started growing cotton, cassava, bananas and beans.

One evening when Absalom met with a group of men in the town centre to drink, he found himself the topic of their conversation.

"You are a grown, responsible man, Absalom," Lumu said. "Why don't you look for a woman to marry?"

Absalom did not respond.

"Single men like you are misers," Kabali said, smiling. "You don't want to share your food or your wealth with anybody!"

"Everyone, can I have your attention, please?" Lutalo said, rising from his seat, waiting for the group's attention. "I have an announcement to make," he said, turning to face Absalom. "My brother-in-law, you gave me a beautiful wife. Now it is time for me to pay you back. The land on which you are growing your crops belongs to you from now onwards."

Absalom was very surprised and, for a while, speechless.

"I confirm what my brother has just said. It is a family decision," Lumu said. "Our brother-in-law Absalom should never be called a miser again. Our next mission is to find him a wife!"

It was only then that Absalom realized that the conversation had been planned, and for a moment he thought Lutalo was trying to bribe him to gain his approval. "There are moments when you feel that 'thank you' is not enough," Absalom said as he rose to hug Lutalo. "This is one such moment, but what should I say? Thank you, my brother-in-law, for the very generous gift. May you get many more rewards in return."

8

RUTH AND HER friend Daisy began their studies at the National Teachers' College. Their friend Sanyu went to Makerere University to study Chemistry, Biology and Maths. In the second and final year, Ruth did her teaching internship in Kampala in City Central School while Daisy did hers at Mukono High School in Mukono, about twenty kilometres east of Kampala.

At the end of the internship, while the two friends prepared to look for employment, Daisy told Ruth that the school where she'd done her internship could employ them. "I think the school is great; the students are well behaved and the teachers are all friendly," Daisy told her.

"Don't you know that I'm a city girl?" Ruth said.

"I know that, but they will provide us accommodation, too," Daisy answered. The school would be providing a small two-bedroom house for Ruth and Daisy to share. "You can visit Kampala on weekends," she added.

A few weeks after Ruth and Daisy started their new jobs, Cornelius Bulega, Sanyu's older brother, reported to work in the same school as its new deputy headmaster.

❊   ❊   ❊

To celebrate the return of his son Jude, Dawson Kiyaga organized a party in his new home in Kampala's posh neighbourhood of Kololo, and invited, among others, his friends Collin and Eunia Wamala. Many people, including some who hadn't been invited, turned up for the party to see the man who had been overseas. Jude had moved to London to work from Cardiff University after completing his course in engineering there, but now his father convinced him to return home.

Then one Sunday, a month later, Dawson paid a visit to the Wamalas, joining them for lunch. A friend did not need a luncheon invitation—he simply showed up. When they were chatting in the living room after eating and Dawson cleared his throat and paused, Collin realized that his friend had something important to say.

"Collin, you and I have been friends for twenty-five years," he began. "I want us to cement our friendship by asking you to let my son Jude marry your daughter Ruth."

"Good, I like the idea," Collin said right away. "There is nothing that would prevent our children from getting married. What does Jude think about it?"

"He would be very glad if you let him marry your daughter. I will ask him to pay you a visit to discuss it further."

"Yes, let him come next Saturday," Collin answered.

When Dawson left, Collin called Eunia to the living room to break the news to her.

"*Kabiite*," he began—"Darling, Dawson has a proposal that I think you will like. He would like his son Jude to marry Ruth."

Eunia hesitated before she responded. "Yes, that would be good," she finally said.

"I'm glad you think so," Collin said, his tone revealing that he'd heard the glimmer of doubt in his wife's voice.

"There would be one problem though—not with Jude but with his mother," Eunia said. "I wouldn't want my daughter to have Belinda as her mother-in-law."

"I know your relationship with Belinda is not good, but Ruth would be marrying Jude, not his mother. I don't see why you would be concerned about her."

"Belinda is a very difficult woman," Eunia replied. "She wouldn't let them live in peace. She would always meddle into their affairs."

"How do you know? You know her as a friend, not as your daughter's mother-in-law. Sometimes—"

"Believe me. I've known Belinda since we were both young girls, and she's always been a know-it-all who wants to impose her opinions on others. Ruth would have a hard time dealing with her."

"How about Jude? Do you like him?"

"I like Jude."

"Then let's give it a chance. We will talk to Ruth to see what she thinks."

❋   ❋   ❋

"Jude, you know Ruth Wamala, don't you?" Dawson asked as soon as Jude walked into the living room.

"You mean Mrs. Wamala's daughter? Yes, I know her but I haven't seen her in years."

"Ruth completed her studies this year. She is now a teacher and she has become a very beautiful young woman. Your mother and I thought it would be a good idea if you two got married," Dawson said.

"Great, that would be good, yes. I'm single and have been searching. But isn't she too young? And—"

"You should see her. She is a beauty, and I know she would make an excellent wife," Belinda said. "We have made an appointment for you to pay a visit to her parents on Saturday."

But although he was excited to meet Ruth, Jude did not like the fact that his parents had already made an appointment for him to visit her. He would have preferred to first break up with Clotilda, with whom he was not really in love.

"And, remember Jude, when you visit the Wamalas," Dawson said, interrupting his son's thoughts, "I want you to be respectful."

"I am usually respectful, Daddy," Jude replied.

"Not just 'usually'—you should always be respectful."

"Listen, Jude," Belinda said, "because what your father is telling you is very important. Be respectful because the Wamalas might be your future in-laws. For instance, don't sit like you are sitting now, with your legs crossed like that. Don't interrupt when they talk to you and please, listen more, talk less."

"I know Jude understands what we are telling him," Dawson told his wife, smiling. "He doesn't need a lecture from us."

❋　❋　❋

On Tuesday, Eunia went to see Ruth at Mukono High School and asked her to come home that weekend in time to receive "a visitor" on Saturday. But she wouldn't tell her who would be coming.

When Ruth arrived home on Friday, she was surprised to see her mother more excited than usual to see her. "So, what do you think of Jude Kiyaga?" Eunia asked her with a smile on her face.

"How do you mean?" Ruth asked. She knew that Jude was an engineer now and that he had just returned from Europe.

"He will be visiting tomorrow."

"Tomorrow? Is there anything special about his visit?" Ruth asked.

"Yes, but I will let your father tell you the details." It was unusual for her mother to beat about the bush, and Ruth sensed immediately what Eunia was not comfortable telling her, so she went to the living room to talk to her father.

"Mr. Kiyaga paid us a visit last weekend and told us that Jude would like to marry you," Collin said. "Would you be interested?"

Here we go again, Ruth thought. *My parents chose a career for me and now they want to choose a husband for me.* "I don't know Jude well," she said to her father. "The last time I saw him I was still a young girl. Why doesn't he talk to me first?"

"Mr. Kiyaga and I have been friends for over twenty years. He is a loyal friend and a good man. I assume that his son is a good person, too, and you are a good person. I think you would make a wonderful couple."

"Thanks Daddy. I will think about it and decide after I have talked to Jude," Ruth said, and left the room.

❊   ❊   ❊

Jude arrived at the Wamalas' home at 3 o'clock the following day.

"You returned recently after completing your course. What university was it again?" Collin asked the young man before Eunia came in to greet him.

"Cardiff University," Jude replied. "I'm working now at the hydroelectricity dam that's under construction in Jinja. It's going to generate enough electricity for a large part of the country."

"That's great news," Collin said.

"Yes, Uganda will soon have electricity in every home that can pay for it."

Eunia came into the living room, sitting on a mat to formally greet Jude, who responded both politely and attentively to her greeting. She liked him immediately.

When Ruth came into the room to greet Jude, he could not hide his joy at seeing her again. He had last seen her when she was in her last year at Rubaga Primary School and was amazed to see the beautiful woman she had become.

Ruth too had a good first impression of Jude. "Hello Jude," she said, stretching out her hand to shake his.

"Not so fast!" her mother said. "Get a mat and please sit down for a proper greeting."

I have to sit on a mat to greet a potential suitor while he is seated on the sofa? Is it not such practices that make our men feel superior to us? But Ruth did as her mother insisted, getting a mat and sitting down. It felt so odd to greet Jude in such a formal way and she wished her parents would go away so she could have a one-on-one conversation with him. But they both stayed put.

Eunia was the first to leave a few minutes later, but she went to a bedroom next to the kitchen so she could continue to hear the conversation. Collin chatted with Jude and Ruth for a few more minutes. Then he too left the living room and joined Eunia in the other room. Left alone in the living room, Ruth and Jude switched to English and Ruth got up to sit on the sofa.

"I wonder why they choose to speak English, like they don't know Luganda!" Eunia said, annoyed. "It sounds strange."

"Oh, now you are not happy to reap the fruits of your labour?" Collin asked. "You and your fellow teachers spanked those children in school whenever you caught them speaking Luganda. Did you tell them that they should speak English only while at school and not when they are in the real world, as adults?"

After Jude left, Eunia and her daughter spoke in the young woman's bedroom. "Ruth, we arranged for you to meet Jude, but I do want you to make your own independent decision about whether to marry him or not."

"I think I like him," Ruth answered with a smile.

"Don't rush to decide," Eunia said, sitting beside Ruth on the bed. "Take time to think about it."

"Yes, I will think about it," Ruth answered firmly. It was plain she thought the discussion should end there.

"I've already told your father that I have no problem with you marrying Jude. But I've got serious reservations about his mother. She is a difficult person."

"Okay. I'll think about it, then," Ruth said as she walked out of her room.

✳　✳　✳

When Ruth returned to Mukono High School the following day, she was very happy. "Daisy, I've got news! I met a wonderful man, and it seems he'd like to marry me! His name is Jude, and I can't wait to introduce him to you."

"I'm very happy for you! Where is he from?"

"His father and my father are great friends, actually—he is Dawson Kiyaga's son. You know Mr. Kiyaga, don't you?"

"I've heard about him," Daisy said. "Isn't he the one who manufactures Sunshine Coffee?"

"And several other products, as well," Ruth nodded. "And from the conversation his son and I had, I think Jude is also an amazing man. I have another date with him next weekend."

The following Saturday, Jude and Ruth met for dinner in a small restaurant in the city. Jude seemed to be enjoying the conversation during the meal but then Ruth noticed that he'd become a little nervous.

"Are you all right?" she asked.

"Yes, I'm all right, but I must confess that I've never felt what I'm feeling now," Jude said, his heart racing. "I love you very much. I would like to marry you, Ruth. What do you think?"

"I think you are a wonderful man. Yes, I would like to marry you," Ruth answered.

"Thank you. I'm very happy to hear that," Jude said, kissing Ruth's hands.

She felt a little embarrassed—the waiter was just a few paces away, coming to collect the bill.

"What do you think about my lady?" Jude asked the bemused waiter.

Jude promised to visit Ruth at her school the following weekend so he could see where she worked and meet her friend Daisy. When he drove into the front yard at exactly 11 o'clock that morning, just as he'd said he would, Ruth said to Daisy, "That's the kind of man I want to marry. Among other things, he's good at being on time."

As Ruth hugged him at the door and led him into the living room, Daisy was waiting inside her bedroom. Through her open door, she could see the look on Jude's face as he scanned the sparsely furnished living room. She didn't like what she saw. Jude had both hands in his pockets as he walked behind his fiancée and his face was full of disdain.

While Ruth went to Daisy's bedroom, Jude sat down in the armchair, leaning back and continuing to inspect the room, his leg over one arm of the chair.

"Jude, meet Daisy," Ruth said when she and Daisy returned to the living room.

"Hello Daisy. I am Jude," Jude said as he rose to shake Daisy's hand.

"I am glad to meet you Jude," Daisy said.

Would you like a cup of tea?" Ruth asked.

"Yes please," Jude replied.

"Where are you from Daisy?" Jude asked when Ruth left for the kitchen.

"My parents live in Kampala but we are originally from Lugazi."

"Lugazi? Oh, where's that? How did you get here?"

"Um, what do you mean?"

"Lugazi. That sounds far. It's far, isn't it?"

"Actually, it's not far from here."

After a short conversation over a cup of tea, Daisy went out for a walk to let Ruth have some time alone with her fiancé.

"How do you like it here?" Jude asked Ruth as soon as Daisy had closed the front door.

"I like it. I enjoy being a teacher although I don't think that's what I'd like to do all my life. But for now, I am following in Mummy's footsteps," Ruth said. "Actually, it was she who encouraged me to become a teacher. I don't earn much but I love what I do."

"That's all right," Jude said. "I make enough money myself. Besides, we wouldn't want you to make more money than I do, would we, darling?"

Ruth did not respond.

Half an hour later, the deputy headmaster Cornelius Bulega looked out his window and saw Ruth walking out of the house with Jude. Cornelius had never found the courage to speak to Ruth about his strong feelings for her and now he was jealous. He looked on helplessly as the two lovers drove off the school property.

"Jude is a wonderful man, Daisy," Ruth told Daisy later that evening. "I am so excited I can't wait for the big day!"

"Are you sure you want—" Daisy began, but realized the question she wanted to ask would upset her friend. "Oh yes, I think he is wonderful."

❃   ❃   ❃

"Miriam, Ruth is about to get married," Collin had come to speak to his younger sister at her home in Rubaga, where she lived along with their sister Eva. "Please talk to her to prepare her for marriage."

Miriam thanked her brother for entrusting the responsibility to her.

She was impressed by Ruth's makeup and her dress when her niece came to see her, but also felt a little intimidated by the educated young woman and wondered whether Ruth would listen to her advice.

"Ruth, I am glad that you have found a man to marry..." Miriam began.

Found? I didn't find him, Ruth thought. *He was chosen for me.*

"It is a good thing that you have waited to be a little older before marrying. Marriage will be easier for you..."

Oh yes, I think it will be sweet and easy.

"Some of us married too young and marriage was a nightmare."

Tell me about it, Ruth thought, turning uneasily on the mat, uncomfortable because she was not used to sitting on the ground.

"Marriage is very important and you should take it seriously. Although you are educated and have a job, your work should not take precedence over your husband," Miriam said. Ruth's direct gaze was making her uneasy.

Ruth had noticed her aunt's uneasiness. She looked down at her handbag.

"This is very important, my dear," Miriam said. "I repeat. Although you are educated and have a job, your work should not take precedence over your husband. But since he is also educated, I think he will understand that you have other things to do..."

I hope so.

"There are some small things you can do to maintain your husband's love for you. Show him that he is more important than anything else by giving up whatever you are doing when he returns home. Serve him a cup of tea and listen to him. Ask him about his day and be attentive while he is talking to you..."

Attention should be reciprocated for the relationship to work, Ruth wanted to respond but she didn't want to offend her aunt.

✳   ✳   ✳

After Ruth had left, Eva asked her sister how the conversation with their niece had gone.

"It was difficult to talk to her. I really doubt whether what I told her will be of any use to her," Miriam said. "She is too educated. Although she was calm and polite, she seemed to question everything I told her. It seemed like I was an old woman, just wasting her time."

"I blame her mother for her behaviour," Eva said. "Eunia gave that girl too much freedom to do whatever she wanted, and Collin could do nothing about it. Some people think that he is in charge, but it's Eunia who runs the home and who's in control."

"I don't like it when Eunia talks to me like she would talk to her students either," Miriam added. "She thinks that being a deputy headmistress of a school is such a great thing."

"She instilled the same attitude in her know-it-all daughter," Eva said. "But I don't think her marriage to Kiyaga's son will last—that boy is equally arrogant. At that party his family had when he returned from overseas, he made his speech in English, as if after being away for a few years he had forgotten Luganda! They are all stupid."

✳   ✳   ✳

Walking home from her aunts' home, Ruth tried to replay Miriam's monologue in her mind, feeling a bit guilty that she had not retained much of it. Her attention had dwindled at "Show him that he is more important than anything else…" *No wonder men feel so entitled!* She thought, indignant again. *And with the kind of information our aunties pass on to us, it won't be easy for us women to break free of the yoke that is our men, either.* She felt angry that her aunt had not said anything that would add value to her as a woman, but recognized that such thoughts were unfair to her aunt, who, although she was now divorced, was only relaying the same message she'd gotten from her own aunt. *It will be up to us modern educated women to choose the good things in our culture to pass on to our own girls*, she thought. *And to reject the things that subjugate us as women.*

9

JUNE 1948 – AUGUST 1951

ONE EVENING AFTER Lutalo closed the shop, he went to his brother's home and found Lumu and their friend Kabali outside, chatting and drinking banana beer. "Yozefu, bring a chair and a gourd for your uncle," Lumu called out to one of his sons.

Lutalo sat down, joining Lumu and Kabali in conversation.

"My wife Nakasi is expecting a third child," Kabali told them. "So now I will have seven," he added, glancing at Lutalo. His friends knew that Kabali also had four children with his wife Nakuya.

"Congratulations," Lumu said, but Lutalo did not comment. He knew what Kabali was driving at with the conversation, and it did not take long for Kabali to say what it was.

"My friend, how long have you been married to your new wife?"

"A little more than two years," Lutalo answered.

"She has not conceived yet. Isn't that a sign that she can't have children?"

"I have three children already."

"Three? How many children did your father have? I don't think he would be pleased to know that his heir has only three children."

"Having children with just one woman is risky," said Lumu, who had three wives. "Chances are all of the children will have similar problems, like poor performance in school. One needs to diminish these chances by—"

Just then a young woman that Lutalo had never seen before came to the yard where the three men were seated and knelt to greet the two visitors.

"That young woman is my wife Nagitta's cousin Zabali," Lumu told the men after she had left. "And she is single."

* * *

From that evening on, Lutalo frequented Lumu's home to talk to the young woman, and one evening he even invited her to visit his shop. When she came, she stayed for hours, sitting on a mat on the veranda and chatting with Lutalo.

In the following weeks Lutalo did not go straight home after he had closed his shop. He'd go to Lumu's home to talk to Zabali.

"The young woman seems to like you," Lumu told his brother. "Why don't you take her?"

Lutalo did not respond but his mind was made up.

When Lutalo returned home late those evenings, Merab, assuming he was busier at the shop, would serve dinner to the family and then patiently waited for him to return so they could eat together. When her friend Nakatudde finally told her that "people" saw a certain "youngish" woman speaking for hours with Lutalo at his shop almost every day, Merab ignored her. *You gossip too much, Nakatudde*, she thought.

But three months later, Lutalo asked his cousin Nabukalu to move out of her room to one of the smaller houses in the compound. And, one evening, Merab and the rest of the family were surprised when Lutalo returned home with a woman that none of them knew. She was carrying a load on her head, and he walked alongside her with more items on his bicycle.

"This is my new wife," Lutalo said after the family had greeted who they'd assumed was only a visitor. "She will occupy the first room to the right of the corridor from now on," he said, the room that had been Nabukalu's. He did not say anything else, and Merab, too, was silent as she walked away and went to her bedroom.

Was Lutalo joking? She had never heard him tell any jokes before... and she could have no doubt about Lutalo's seriousness when he spent the night in the new wife's bedroom.

Merab slept very little that night, feeling that Lutalo had betrayed her. *Isn't he satisfied with the work I do in this home? Is it because I don't have children?* She decided to leave because Lutalo had breached his vows.

Lutalo woke up earlier than usual the following morning and went straight to his shop while Zabali woke up late. She had to put on a brave face because it was obvious the family did not welcome her presence. When Merab said "good morning" to her and the new wife answered in a respectful tone, Merab could see that she was embarrassed. "You are welcome to our family," Merab said to her and kindly asked the woman her name.

Merab still went ahead with her plan to leave but, noticing that Kulumba had not woken up yet, went to check on him in the children's bedroom. She found that the little boy had a stuffy nose and a very high fever. She'd learned that convulsions would follow and so asked Yafesi to go with her to the health centre with the child.

When they'd returned Merab, seated on a mat, held Kulumba on her lap until he fell asleep. Zabali approached them, timidly asked how the child was, before returning to her bedroom. Merab noticed that she was nervous. *Men! I wonder what Lutalo found attractive about her*, she thought. *She is ugly! Her nose is too big and she walks with a funny gait.*

Two days later after Kulumba was better, Merab went to see Absalom and tell him the news. When she arrived at the coffee store, Absalom was still serving a customer, so she sat on the veranda to wait. Absalom saw that his sister was not happy. As soon as his customer had left, he asked her to come into his office.

"Can you believe it, Absalom? Lutalo got himself a concubine," Merab said, beginning to cry.

"How did that happen? Did he talk to you about it before—"

"No, he returned in the evening two days ago and just said, 'This is my wife,'" Merab answered, crying even more.

"To be honest with you, I've never liked that man," Absalom said. "Leave him. Just walk away."

"I actually thought of leaving the other day but Kulumba fell sick, so I stayed to nurse—"

"That's his responsibility. Let the new wife take care of the children," Absalom said. "You've got nothing to gain from that marriage. You should simply walk away. If you want, I can let him repossess his land and then we will return home together."

Merab worried about what she would tell her parents as she went back home to get ready to return to Senge. She thought that the fact that Lutalo had brought another woman into the home was enough for her to leave him but doubted that her parents would let her return to their home. While she was thinking about her predicament, she heard her aunt Namagembe's voice in the front yard and guessed right away that Namagembe had heard about Lutalo's new wife. Lutalo often sent Yafesi to her home to deliver presents like sugar or beef.

Merab went outside to welcome her aunt, then came with her into the living room, placing a new mat on the floor for her aunt to sit on, choosing an older mat for herself. Several members of the family came to greet the visitor, but not Zabali.

Once Merab was left alone again with her aunt, she started crying.

"Don't cry, my dear," her aunt told her. "Calm down and talk to me."

"My husband breached his vows. He brought another woman—"

"Many men do that and it's all right. You can't stop him from doing whatever he thinks he has the right to do."

"But that's not the kind of marriage I wanted! I'm going to leave him."

"You can't do that, Merab. You can't leave. Unfortunately, these are the kinds of problems that make us women grow. Live your life as if there was no other woman in the home. Do your best…"

What more can I do for him? Merab thought, angry. *He has betrayed me.*

"I, too, went through a similar situation, as you know. My husband got two other women—for twelve years there were three of us in the home, but he sent them away one by one. They called me a witch then but my marriage remained intact to this day."

"Yes, I know your story, but I still don't think I can stand this."

"Be strong, don't give up. You'll have children of your own and you'll forget about the other woman. And don't let the fact that your husband has another woman affect your loyalty to him. You should remain loyal to him—in fact, if you love him even more than before, you'll remain his favourite wife."

Namagembe left later in the evening. After their long discussion, she had convinced Merab to stay.

❊   ❊   ❊

Absalom was so annoyed by the fact that Lutalo had breached his vows by bringing another woman into his sister's home that he went home to Senge to talk to his father about it.

"Father, Lutalo is not the right man for my sister," Absalom said as soon as he had greeted Levi, and sat down with him under the mango tree in the front yard. "He brought another woman into the home. Merab now has a sister wife."

Levi looked at his son in disbelief. "How did it happen?"

"Merab told me that her husband just returned home one evening with a woman and he said that she was his new wife."

At that moment Dolosi was returning from the garden. She had a basket of sweet potatoes on her head, which she placed on the ground, sitting on a mat to greet her son. Levi's face was buried into his hands as he waited silently for Absalom and Dolosi to end their greetings.

"I've just informed Father that Merab now has a sister wife," Absalom told his mother.

"What? Was there a wedding?" Dolosi asked.

"No, Lutalo just returned home one evening with a strange woman. Merab couldn't believe her ears when he told her that the woman was his new wife."

"Is that how he's decided to treat my daughter simply because she has not yet borne a child for him?" Dolosi asked.

"I don't think that is the reason," Levi said. "He already has children."

"That's not what I wanted for my daughter," Dolosi said.

"I advised Merab to walk away but she won't budge," Absalom said. "Is she stupid or what?"

"You can't do that, Absalom. You should learn to control your temper. That's not your home—" Dolosi began.

"He breached his vows; that's what he did. I don't have anything else to say. I'm very disappointed," Levi said, getting up to go inside the house.

"How is your work going, Absalom?" Dolosi asked.

"My work is going well but now we have that new challenge."

"The new challenge is not yours, Absalom," Dolosi said. "It's not what I wanted for Merab but she should stay in her marriage. Don't encourage her to walk away—Merab will handle it herself."

Absalom asked his mother about his other sisters, then said, "Even though their husbands are poor, I think Eseza and Nawume are better off than Merab. Her husband is very stupid."

"Absalom, my son, that's not the right thing to say about your brother-in-law. You know that we don't tolerate such language here," Dolosi said.

"I'm sorry, Mother, but I've never trusted Lutalo and this proves I was right."

When Absalom was preparing to return to Kalasa after lunch, Levi said to him, "Please tell Merab that we are not happy about that new development in her home but encourage her to persevere."

As Absalom hopped on to his bicycle, he told his parents he'd be back in a month, hoping that they would ask him to bring Merab back home with him then. They disappointed him when they did not.

※　※　※

By the third week, Zabali was used to life in her new home. Merab had decided to be courteous to her but Zabali was not as polite. She was short-tempered and did not hesitate to spank the children when they misbehaved, and had spanked Nabbosa twice already in the first month. Merab protested each time—she did not want anyone to spank her children—but Zabali disagreed. "If you don't discipline them now, they'll become big-headed and not listen to you when they get older," she said.

Lutalo liked the way Zabali disciplined the children, calling her *Mukuza*—"the one who raises children."

Mukuza gave birth to a son by her first anniversary in the house, and the baby was named Jonah, the same name that had been given to Lutalo before he married Merab. The fact that the new wife had borne a son while she was still childless worried Merab. She started doubting whether she would ever bear children and her worries kept her awake most nights.

Then Abigail came to pay Merab a visit and told her niece how displeased she was that Lutalo had breached his vows by getting a second wife. But, like her sister Namagembe, Abigail encouraged Merab to stay in her marriage. "I must have forgotten to tell you that it is things like your husband getting another wife that will make you grow as a woman," Abigail said. "Unfortunately, you're not the first and certainly not the last, to go through such trials. Persevere."

It's easy for you to say that; you *don't have a sister wife*, Merab thought.

Merab prayed for and hoped to have children. Namagembe, too, desperately wanted Merab to have children, especially a boy—a heir for Lutalo—and whenever she came to visit, she'd bring herbs that she'd mix with water, that she'd ask Merab to drink. But Merab refused—as a staunch Christian, she believed that it was wrong for her to drink such an herbal mixture.

"Then I will bring other herbs for you to bathe in," Namagembe said.

Merab didn't want to do that either, but she did it anyway in order not to displease her aunt.

❈   ❈   ❈

A year and a half later, Zabali gave birth to her second child, another son, named Dunstan. She continued to spend most of her time looking after all the children, including the older ones, resolving their disputes and disciplining them. Merab became even more desperate. She continued to pray for at least one child.

One Saturday when she went to the bimonthly market, she saw the famous medicine man Nsigo-Emeluka selling his medicine—these were bars that he made out of a mixture of clay and herbs, thoroughly dried. He had a bar in his raised hand and was reciting a list of illnesses that he said it cured, including whooping cough, diarrhoea, pneumonia, body aches, headaches, stomach aches, high blood pressure, ulcers, mumps, measles, sore throat and infertility. Many people bought the clay bars but Merab watched them with scepticism. *Aren't these people just throwing away their hard-earned money? Do these things work?*

So when Namagembe returned two days later, Merab was surprised when her aunt brought one of Nsigo-Emeluka's bars for her, and a piece of a broken clay pot in which to scrub a bit of the herbal bar to dissolve it in water for Merab to drink. Namagembe prepared the mixture and after Merab had drunk some, told her niece to keep the bar and clay pot piece for use every morning. She told her that the medicine would help her to conceive.

After Namagembe had left, Merab threw them both away. *I don't want to contaminate myself with these things.*

✳   ✳   ✳

"*Mwami*—my husband, Yafesi and his colleagues have been living here for years and I don't think they will be going away," Merab said to Lutalo one evening. "I think it would be good if you gave them some land so they build their own houses and get some independence."

"That's a good idea, Mufuzi and I have been thinking about it for a while now," Lutalo said. "Let me tour the land this week; I'll see where to allocate them land by the end of the week."

So Lutalo gave two acres of land to each of the men. They worked together to build mud houses thatched with grass for each of them and moved out of Lutalo's home a few months later, but they continued to work for him.

About a month after the servants had moved out of the houses in the compound, Lutalo asked Yafesi to thoroughly clean the house he used to live in. The two wives, Mufuzi (Merab) and Mukuza (Zabali) wanted to know why the house was being cleaned but they didn't dare to ask Lutalo, and Merab knew that he would disclose the reason when he felt like it. When he did, both women were shocked when he told them it was for a third wife.

The woman joined the family two weeks later. When she moved in, Merab welcomed her as soon as she arrived and did not complain. *What's the point of complaining about it? Mwami has made his decision and no amount of complaining will make him change his mind.*

Mukuza did not welcome Lutalo's third wife, however. On the day he announced that the third wife would be moving in, she didn't leave her bedroom but stayed there, crying, and no one dared to go to her because they knew she would react in a rage. Lutalo did not seem to notice, though.

He did not go to work on his farm that day—he left on his bicycle and returned home two hours later with the new wife. Lutalo carried her few belongings on the bicycle while she walked along behind him, carrying a few more belongings on her head that were neatly wrapped in a cotton cloth. Along with them was a boy of about six years, whom she later introduced as her nephew.

When the trio walked into the large front yard and Kulumba ran to meet them, his arms outstretched to hug the boy, Merab saw him and did not like it. Was Kulumba going to bond with the new wife because of the boy who had come with her?

Merab placed a mat in the shade of the small tree that stood a few feet from the new wife's house and asked her to sit down. All the members of the household but Mukuza came out to greet the new wife. Lutalo noticed Mukuza's absence but it did not bother him—he figured that she'd eventually get used to the fact that she wasn't the boss in his home. He put the new wife's belongings in her house's doorway, hopped on to his bicycle and went to open his shop for the day.

Merab found it strange that Lutalo had not waited for lunch but didn't comment about it. Maybe he was nervous because of Mukuza's reaction to the new wife's arrival.

She asked Nabukalu to serve lunch in the shade of the tree where the new wife was seated. Merab felt pity for her—the young woman wasn't saying anything and seemed to be uncomfortable. *Poor woman, I don't think any of us is happy to see her. If I were her I would return to wherever I came from.* "What is your name?" Merab asked the woman.

"My name is Erina."

"Where are you from?"

"I'm from Sentema."

"Sentema? Where's that?"

"You wouldn't know; it's quite far from here."

Merab wanted to ask Erina how she had met Lutalo but she decided not to. It was none of her business.

10

CLOTILDA WAS VISITING her uncle Walter, and he mentioned Jude's upcoming wedding. "Jude is getting married to Wamala's daughter Ruth," he told her. "The wedding will take place in three weeks' time."

"Oh, good for them," Clotilda said, knowing that neither her uncle nor his wife knew about her relationship with Jude. But her heart sank and she felt both sad and angry. She had tried to see Jude since his return from Europe but he'd seemed to be avoiding her.

It is because of Ruth that my life turned out differently than what I had planned, Clotilda thought. *She got me expelled from school, and now she is taking my man! We will share him.*

Two weeks before her wedding, Ruth went to Buweela High School to deliver an invitation card to her former headmistress, Miss Cook.

"Who is the lucky man?" Miss Cook asked.

"His name is Jude. His father is a family friend."

"Good. So you knew him before you decided to marry him."

"Yes, I knew him."

"I was not as lucky," Miss Cook said. "Although not many people here know it, I am divorced and have a daughter. You probably saw her at least once when she visited. When I met my future husband, I thought I had met the most wonderful, charming man in the world. Little did I know that I was about to marry a moron!"

Ruth laughed, surprised.

"Oh, it's not about me. Let's celebrate your upcoming wedding with tea and biscuits, shall we?" Miss Cook said, getting up. "I will be glad to attend your wedding."

That same afternoon, Ruth brought wedding invitations to the headmaster and her fellow teachers at Mukono High School. But although Deputy Headmaster Cornelius thanked her for the card, he did not seem to be happy for her. Ruth wondered why not but decided not to think about it.

Two days before Ruth's wedding, her fellow teachers were in the staff room talking excitedly about the wedding when Cornelius said to Daisy, "Can I tell you something? I don't think I'll have the courage to attend Ruth's wedding." He hesitated before speaking again. "I have a confession to make, Daisy. I not only care about Ruth, I love her a lot."

"You love her?" Daisy said, surprised. "This is the first time I've heard about it."

"It's because I've never had the courage to tell her."

"Poor man, your lack of confidence has made you miss out on a wonderful girl."

❄   ❄   ❄

Collin spoke on behalf of his family at the wedding reception. "Ladies and gentlemen, my name is Collin Wamala. I am Ruth's father. Let me also introduce my dear wife, Eunia."

Eunia stood up and waved to the guests. They clapped and cheered for her.

"I am very happy to note that my daughter has today married Jude, a son of my long-time friend Dawson Kiyaga. It is a great honour to the family for our daughter to marry the son of the industrious Dawson Kiyaga."

Later in his speech, Collin said, "Ruth, trust and love your husband. I know that once in a while there will be challenges in your marriage. However, you should follow our age-old wisdom: *eby'omunju tebittottolwa*—what happens in the home, stays in the home. If you have a problem that's too big for the two of you to solve, don't tell it to your next door neighbour. If you must talk to somebody, you have lots of support—your aunties, your uncles and others in both families. We wish you a long happy marriage. Be blessed, have children, educate them and help build the nation."

When he spoke, Dawson mainly highlighted Jude's achievements. "Jude studied in the great Musasa High School, but he did not stop there. He is an alumnus of Cardiff University. It is the contribution of young educated people like him and Ruth that our nation needs to develop."

Cornelius Bulega had decided at the last moment to attend the reception, but he walked out of the hall while the bride and the groom were cutting the cake, no longer able to stand the sight of Ruth and Jude exchanging loving smiles and glances as they enjoyed their big day.

Among the presents that Miss Cook gave Ruth was a pocket diary, and the headmistress told her that at the end of the school term she'd be retiring and going back to England.

Just as the newlyweds were leaving the reception hall, Jude's parents took them aside to talk to them privately. "Jude, there is something important you don't seem to have thought about," Dawson said. "Where will you and your wife live?"

Jude smiled and looked mischievously at his father. "Oh, are you kicking me out of my bedroom?"

"Really, Jude, you should have prepared that before you asked Ruth to marry you!" Belinda said, smiling, as she handed a pair of keys to Jude.

"What are these for?" Jude asked.

"They are the keys to the new house we built down the hill for you and your wife to live in," Dawson said. "It's yours from now on. It is our wedding present to you"

"Thank you very much," Jude said, shaking hands with his parents.

Ruth knelt before them. "Thank you very much for the wonderful wedding gift," she said.

Ruth knew that her father's company, Wamala & Sons, had recently built a house for the Kiyagas. Her brother Mark had told her that the new house was located near the Kiyagas' home. *I don't want to live near my parents-in-law's home*, Ruth thought. *More so because my mother says Belinda is a difficult woman.* But the house itself was large and beautiful and the newlyweds were very pleased with it.

Two weeks later, as Ruth prepared to return to work, Jude asked her to quit her job. He didn't want her going away to Mukono.

"Why should I resign from the school I love?"

"It's far. How long would it take you to travel to and from that school every day?"

"Sorry we didn't discuss this before the wedding but I had hoped to continue teaching there. I could continue living in my school's house and return home every weekend."

"What? Would I then consider myself a married man when my wife was not home most of the week?"

"I have established good relationships in the school, with my fellow teachers and with my students. I wouldn't like to abandon them."

"If you were to choose between them and me, who would you choose?"

"You, of course," Ruth answered, surprised by the question.

"See? We can find a school for you to teach nearby. After all, there is a need for teachers all around the city."

"I wasn't expecting an argument so soon in our marriage," Ruth said. She thought, *I hope I didn't rush into this marriage.*

"Don't be silly. It's not an argument. We can't live apart when we are married. It doesn't work that way," Jude replied.

"But you are not home on some days. Sometimes you are away working at the dam."

"I can live away from home some days because I'm the husband. Remember?"

"Yes, you are the husband. You win, sir."

Ruth got a teaching position in the prestigious Kololo Secondary School and two weeks later, she resigned from her previous job.

❋　❋　❋

A month after the wedding, Jude went to pay a visit to his parents and invited them for lunch at his home that weekend. His parents looked forward to the first meal in their son's home.

But when Belinda and Dawson arrived at the house they surprised Ruth, who hadn't been expecting them, and Jude wasn't even there. But Ruth didn't tell her in-laws that Jude hadn't let her know they'd be visiting. She welcomed them to the living room and after they had sat down, she knelt to greet them. It was clear to Ruth that Dawson was happy to see her but Belinda seemed distant. She scanned the room with a look that seemed to be critical and her responses to the greetings were barely audible. *What kind of mother-in-law is she going to be?*

"Can I serve you a drink?" Ruth asked after she had greeted her parents-in-law.

Belinda looked at her blankly. *You should never ask visitors such a question; simply serve what you have.*

"Yes please, I'll have a Tusker beer if you have some," Dawson answered.

Half an hour later, when Ruth put two small plates of salad on the dining table, Dawson looked at them in surprise. *Collin is a generous man. I wonder why his daughter is a miser?*

"I made this salad with fresh vegetables I bought from the market this morning and I hope you will enjoy it. I will also serve tilapia curry with potatoes," Ruth said cheerfully.

Belinda looked at her and smiled. *She sounds like a waitress in a restaurant.*

Ruth was finding her parents-in-law too reserved for her liking. *Either they don't like me or they are judging me. It's going to be difficult to deal with them*, she thought, returning to the kitchen.

"Hello, Mummy. Hello, Daddy," Jude said, entering the dining room. "I am sorry I'm late. I had forgotten that you two would be joining us for lunch."

"Jude, you didn't tell me that Mummy and Daddy were coming!" Ruth said. "I would have prepared a more presentable meal."

"Uh, don't worry. It's just Daddy and Mummy. They can eat whatever is available."

Belinda scrutinized Jude. *No wonder my son has lost weight. She doesn't feed him correctly.*

✳   ✳   ✳

Two years into the marriage, after Ruth became pregnant, a live-in maid was hired to help her with the housework. Ruth respected her and treated her well but Jude yelled at the woman and called her uneducated whenever she did something that displeased him, and he refused to eat the food she cooked. Ruth had to wake up earlier than necessary to prepare his breakfast despite her morning sickness.

"Darling, I will put your tea in a thermos flask so that all you will have to do in the morning is to pour a cup for yourself," Ruth said one morning.

"No—why would I prepare my breakfast and eat alone when I am married?" Jude answered. "It wouldn't make sense, would it?"

The maid quit abruptly just two months before Ruth was due to deliver her baby. That weekend, when she met her mother at the wedding of her friend Daisy to Nathan, a manager in the Grindlays Bank, she told her mother that the maid had left, letting her know without going into details that Jude was the problem. A week later, Eunia brought her cousin's daughter Nampa to help, asking Ruth to tell Jude that Nampa was her relative so that Jude would show her some respect.

But when Ruth and Jude's son Herbert was born three weeks after Nampa moved into their home, Ruth soon realized that Jude was not ready to change.

"Ruth, will I be late for work this morning simply because you delayed breakfast?" Jude asked as he straightened his tie in the mirror one morning.

"Are you joking?" Ruth asked.

"Why would I be joking, woman?" Jude answered, a stern look on his face.

"You do realize, darling, that the baby had a restless night? He was immunized yesterday and his thigh is still sore, and he has a fever," she said. "I was up most of the night."

"Get your priorities right. Did your aunt tell you who comes first in this family? Is it your husband or your child?"

"I'm stunned that a man of your calibre, a loving father, can say that when—"

"Come on, I will be late."

That afternoon, Belinda came to visit. Nampa welcomed her into the living room and greeted her but Belinda did not answer. "Please have a seat," Nampa told her. "Ruth has taken the baby to nap. I'll let her know that you are here."

"Thank you," Belinda said, but she did not sit down. She rearranged the sofas and dusted the small table in the centre of the room using the cloth that had been placed on it to decorate it. She went to the kitchen and fetched a broom then started sweeping the living room.

"I've already swept the house and mopped it," Nampa said.

Belinda did not answer.

When Ruth came out of her bedroom, Belinda was sweeping the living room. Ruth knelt to greet her. Belinda responded without looking at her.

"Your house is not clean enough although it should be even cleaner since you are home these days and especially since you have a baby. Babies should be raised in a clean environment," Belinda said.

"The house is clean; we've already cleaned it. I don't know why you felt it necessary for you to sweep it again," Ruth said.

"How is Herbert doing?" Belinda asked, not responding to what Ruth had just said.

"He cried a lot last night after he had been immunized but he is better now."

"I understand, but while the baby is napping, you've got to take a look around the house to see what you can do to make it a clean, welcoming home. Don't leave the responsibility to your maid."

Ruth was losing her temper but instead of responding, she went back to her bedroom. From there she could hear Belinda giving instructions to Nampa. Belinda was still there by the time Jude returned and Ruth knew that she would complain to Jude about her. *Let them talk. I don't care.*

* * *

Herbert was three years old when his sister Kate was born, joined two years later by another sister, Victoria. Belinda, saying that she adored her grandchildren, was visiting Ruth's home at least once a week.

11

SOON, THE THIRD wife got a nickname. Merab had noticed that even three weeks after her arrival, the woman was still keeping to herself and saying very little. "Like the two of us, you need a name which will be used to address you. What should we call you?" Merab asked the new wife.

"Let's call her 'Musirise'—the quiet one," Mukuza suggested.

"Great, your name is Musirise. I think it suits you well. Do you mind being called Musirise?" Merab asked the woman.

"No, I don't mind."

"Musirise is your name from now on," Merab said.

Like Mukuza, Musirise produced a baby within a year, a boy named Roger. Roger's birth made Merab to feel even worse about not having children. Whenever visitors came to the home, cheering and laughing with the children, Merab felt she was invisible, the childless woman who no one remembered.

Meanwhile, Absalom continued to pressure her to leave Lutalo. "He now has three wives. What are you waiting for? Leave him! I don't think he's done collecting women—if you stay you might end up sharing your bedroom with a fourth!"

Merab's aunt Namagembe was also troubled by the fact that even newcomer Musirise had borne a child before Merab. She consulted healer after healer and gave Merab many herbs to drink and to wash herself with, but her frustration increased month after month when Merab still did not conceive.

As a husband to three wives, Lutalo would sleep in turns in each wife's bedroom, one week at a time. It was the duty of the wife in whose bedroom he slept, to cook for the family, to serve his meals, to wash his clothes and to warm the water for his baths when he returned in the evening. Each wife's turn with him was called a *kisanja*.

"I find it quite unfair to the wife doing the *kisanja* to have to do all the work. Why don't we share the work since we are all still married to him whether we are doing the *kisanja* or not," Mukuza said one day.

"Can you imagine that I did all this work by myself before the two of you came on board?" Merab asked her sister wives, almost stopping in the middle of the sentence when she realized her statement could be interpreted to mean that she was grateful for having them.

"You were the only wife; you had no choice. But now that there are three of us, why don't we work together?" Mukuza said.

Merab frowned, knowing that Mukuza was only suggesting it because it was not her *kisanja* that week. She did almost no chores during her "off" weeks, unlike Merab and Musirise, but she was complaining because whenever it was Merab's *kisanja*, the rest of the members of the family worked together to ensure that everything was done on time, especially hardworking Nabukalu. The house was cleaned and the meals were served on time, and the credit went to Merab.

Merab found Musirise friendlier than Mukuza and during the weeks when it was Musirise's *kisanja*, Merab would give her tips, happy to be helpful. "Musirise, I see you are preparing cassava and sweet potatoes for lunch," she said one day to the young woman. "Didn't we have the same food for lunch yesterday? It's good to vary your meals. We have yams, we have maize. You could serve those with some fresh beans. Then you can cook the sweet potatoes or cassava tomorrow."

Mukuza, overhearing Merab's words, came to talk to Musirise as soon as Merab had left. "Isn't it annoying for someone to think that it is okay to tell you what to do, like you were her child?"

"It is very annoying," Musirise agreed. "I wonder whether she realizes that we too are grown women with our own sense of judgment."

"I don't think she does, but one of these days I will give her a piece of my mind," Mukuza said.

"This is already the third time this month that you are saying that. Why don't you talk to her about it?" Musirise asked.

"I will. But I think it is *Mwami* to blame for that—he knows this woman mistreats us but he doesn't say or do anything to stop her behaviour."

"I don't like it when she gives me instructions but I wouldn't say that she mistreats us," Musirise answered.

"Don't you dare defend her!" Mukuza shot back. "I'll talk to her because complaining to *Mwami* will not help. He only cares about himself. I don't think he cares about what goes on in this home beyond his meals and clean clothes."

❋   ❋   ❋

Mukuza remained angry. It was her *kisanja* the following week. Nakatudde's husband Ezra came for lunch shortly before noon that Sunday, as he had most Sundays for years. Mukuza was in the kitchen finalizing preparations for lunch when she saw him getting off his bicycle in the front yard.

She walked straight up to him, pointing her finger at him. "Sir, I think you are getting too familiar with us. Don't think you'll be having lunch here every Sunday—you have your own home and you have a wife. Let *her* prepare you the Sunday lunches that you crave. Go home now."

Lutalo had watched the exchange from the living room but couldn't hear what Mukuza was saying. By the time he decided to go out to see what was going on, Ezra had cycled away.

❈　　❈　　❈

Like her aunt Namagembe had advised her, Merab did everything she could to retain Lutalo's favour. Whenever it was her *kisanja*, she prepared a special side dish for him with every meal, usually his favourite vegetables or a portion of fried meat, like beef liver, just for him. Whenever she sold some crops or firewood, she would set aside some of the money to buy him a shirt, underwear or a pair of trousers on market days. She kept the clothes she bought in her bedroom and while her sister wives procrastinated on washing laundry, Lutalo always found clean ironed clothes in Merab's bedroom to wear. He noticed. Her gestures ensured a steady supply of her usual Saturday-evening presents from her husband.

Mukuza finally gathered courage and complained to Merab that Lutalo favoured her to the detriment of the other wives. Merab said nothing to her. She just went to her room grumbling under her breath. Nalunkuma, who'd never liked Merab and had been in a corner of the dining room weaving a mat, heard what she said, and saw her opportunity to worsen the situation.

"Do you know what Mufuzi has just said?" she asked Mukuza. "She said that it is obvious that she is Lutalo's favourite wife and that you've got to get used to the fact that she is the legally wedded wife. You two are just concubines."

Nalunkuma's statement caused such a quarrel that Merab asked Lutalo for permission to go to pay a visit to her aunt Namagembe for a few days.

Abigail happened to be visiting Namagembe at the same time, and the day after Merab arrived, an argument ensued between her aunts. Namagembe accused Merab's sister wives of bewitching Merab so she could not bear children.

"That's nonsense," Abigail said, "Merab is still young; she will bear children when the right time comes. I don't like it when people get into problems and they claim that other people are bewitching them. The women are not to blame. Merab will have children when the right time comes."

Merab, who felt bad hearing her aunts quarrelling because of her, went inside the house.

"Abigail, because you are married to a reverend you think you know everything but believe me, witchcraft works," Namagembe continued.

"Do you use it? Are you a witch yourself?" Abigail asked.

"Are you trying to call me a witch?" Namagembe asked, annoyed.

"If you don't use it you can't tell me that it works," Abigail said. "You have no proof."

And so the two sisters continued arguing, only stopping when Merab returned to where they were seated.

❊   ❊   ❊

While Merab was away, Mukuza spanked Kulumba and Nakiyingi for what she called their mischievous behaviour. Nabukalu reacted by telling Mukuza that she was too harsh towards the children. Mukuza retorted by asking Nabukalu why she was not married and living in her own home. The comment annoyed Nabukalu so much that she needed someone to speak to about it. And since her friend Merab was not home, she went to the home of her other friend, Nakatudde, where she met another woman who was there. Samanya told Nabukalu that she and Mukuza had grown up in the same village, and that she knew Mukuza well.

"Her family is large—she has many brothers and sisters but none of her sisters is married," Samanya said. "People say that their father is a 'night dancer.'"

Nabukalu knew what that meant. People said that a person who was a night dancer was sometimes possessed by evil spirits, going into other people's plantations in the wee hours of the night, performing weird dances around each plant and causing the crops to fail. People even said that some night dancers were cannibals. "No wonder that woman's behaviour is weird," Nabukalu said. "Sometimes she stares blankly at you as if she were half asleep in broad daylight."

When Merab returned home two days later, Nabukalu eagerly whispered to her everything she'd heard from Samanya. "And none of Mukuza's sisters is married," she concluded. "I think men stay away from them because they are night dancers, too."

"What about her brothers?" Merab asked sceptically. "Why is it always the women that are singled out?"

Nabukalu did not answer.

"Nabukalu, you are not married either. Are you a night dancer?"

"No, I am not."

"Then why do you believe such things about others? Those are myths. Have you ever seen a night dancer? Or do you know anybody who has ever seen one?"

"No, but people say—"

"You can't believe everything that people say."

"But while you were away, Mukuza made some rude comments about me," Nabukalu answered.

"I don't want to sound like I am defending Mukuza—I know she is not friendly to you or to anyone else—but let's not spread rumours about her."

❋   ❋   ❋

Seven-year-old Kulumba started attending Kalasa Primary School, and his behaviour made Merab a frequent visitor to the school. If she was not summoned because he had hit another student, it was because he had insulted a teacher.

"I try my best to teach him to be polite but I guess the message falls on deaf ears," Merab said apologetically one day when she was called to the school after Kulumba had yelled at a teacher.

"We wanted to tell you that the next time he misbehaves, we will send him home," the headmaster said. Kulumba was cowering in a corner.

"Kulumba, why did you yell at the teacher?" Merab asked the little boy.

"I did not yell at the teacher. I only answered her question very loudly."

The headmaster laughed.

"You've got to behave better. Otherwise you'll be in trouble if your father finds out about it," Merab said.

"I'll not do it again, Mother."

When Kulumba returned home after school, Merab reminded him again that if he behaved badly in school, she'd have to tell his father.

"He is only a child," Mukuza said. Merab hadn't noticed her standing nearby. "You can't get him to behave better by talking to him like that—you've got to spank him."

Kulumba stood there silently, and before Merab could respond to her statement, Mukuza slapped the boy on the shoulder, making him cry.

"Really? Did you have to beat my son? What did he do to you?" Merab asked.

"He looked at me defiantly and I don't like that. You'll have more problems with him if you don't spank him," Mukuza said, walking away.

Merab shook her head as she calmed the boy down. *Mukuza's beatings have worsened my children's behaviour. I don't think she will stop hitting them unless I tell Mwami about it.*

It was Mukuza's *kisanja* that week and while Lutalo was waiting for dinner in the living room that evening, Merab brought a mat like she usually did, placing it on the floor and sitting down. After she had greeted Lutalo and asked about his day, she said, "*Mwami*, today I was called to the school because Kulumba yelled at a teacher—"

"Sorry about that, but you didn't have to go there," Lutalo answered. "He's only a little boy. Schools these days can't handle such children without involving the parents?"

"That's not what I wanted to talk to you about. What I wanted to say was that while I was talking to him about his behaviour at school after he returned home, Mukuza slapped him. Please intervene because we can't correct his behaviour by hitting him. It would be like teaching him to do what we want him to stop doing," Merab said.

"Mufuzi," Lutalo said, "you worry too much about these children. You won't be able to change them—their stupidity is inborn. They take after their mother."

"But I don't like it when—" Merab stopped in the middle of the sentence when she saw Mukuza entering the dining room with a pile of plates.

Lutalo was relieved when the conversation was interrupted. *It is okay to spank the children*, he thought. *It does no harm.*

❋   ❋   ❋

The following morning, Mukuza went away for a very rare visit to her parents' home.

"The children will have some relief at home now," Nabukalu told Nalunkuma while they were preparing lunch. "I think Mukuza is too harsh on them."

"Yes, I've noticed that she is not home. Where did she go?" Nalunkuma asked.

"She went to pay a visit to her parents. And she was very excited about it. I guess she was looking forward to enjoying some delicacies."

"What kind of delicacies?" Nalunkuma asked.

"She is a night dancer. You know what I mean?" Nabukalu said, laughing.

Nalunkuma also laughed. "Actually, Samanya told me a while ago that Mukuza is a night dancer. Do you think it is true?"

"I don't know, but it might be true. Sometimes she behaves in a weird way."

They did not know that Mukuza's son Jonah was sitting in the empty space between the outdoor kitchen and Musirise's house, and that he had heard everything they said.

A few days after Mukuza returned, Jonah asked her, "Mother, is it true that you are a night dancer?"

"What? Who told you that?" Mukuza asked.

"I heard Nabukalu telling Nalunkuma that you are a night dancer."

"Really? When and where did they say that?"

"They were preparing lunch in the kitchen."

Mukuza wept. She wanted to confront the two women about it but she did not. *It must be Mufuzi spreading rumours about me.* In the evening, while she and Lutalo were in her bedroom, she wept again, told him what Jonah had said to her and accused Merab of having started the rumour. Lutalo did not respond, which annoyed Mukuza. *He is so fond of her that he can't even reprimand her about her bad behaviour.*

The following day, when his friend Kabali went to see him at the shop, Lutalo asked him, "Do your wives also cry and whine about every small thing?"

"It depends," Kabali answered. "Are your wives giving you a headache?"

"Last night Mukuza accused Mufuzi of slander. I didn't respond because I didn't know what to say."

"Yes, you did the right thing. Simply ignore them."

"For how long will I be able to ignore them?" Lutalo said. "It seems they have something to complain about every day."

"Don't think their complaining will stop when you intervene in every small problem they bring to your attention. So long as they are not physically fighting each other, simply ignore them."

❋   ❋   ❋

Mukuza was so annoyed by the "night dancer" accusation that for about three days she did not talk to any of the members of the family except her own children. When they were going to the farm to dig and Merab noticed that Mukuza was sulking, she asked her what was wrong, but Mukuza did not respond. Merab did not insist on an answer, chatting instead with Musirise.

"Mufuzi, is your brother Absalom single?" Musirise asked her. "I have a younger sister that he might like. If you want, I could make arrangements for her to come visit so he can meet her."

"Thank you very much," Merab said. "That would be good for my brother but isn't he too old for your young sister to marry?"

"No, and he seems to be a kind, caring man. It would be nice if my sister married him."

"Thanks for saying that," Merab said. "Let your sister come to visit. We'll take it from there."

Musirise wrote a note to her sister Dahlia and gave it to Lutalo who handed it to a bus driver who came from the same village as Musirise. The bus driver promised to deliver the note to Dahlia the following day.

Dahlia came to visit a week later. Merab sent Yafesi to ask Absalom to come see her, and Absalom dressed nicely and came to see the visitor. His heart skipped a beat the moment he laid his eyes on her. Absalom only greeted Dahlia that evening but didn't talk with her. But when Merab took her to see him at the coffee store the following day, they enjoyed their conversation so much that by the end of the following week, Dahlia had moved into Absalom's home. They were married a few months later.

❋   ❋   ❋

Once Merab's cousin Scovia completed her course in midwifery, she started working in Kampala's Mulago Hospital. A year later Scovia married Boaz Lumbuye, a doctor with whom she'd often worked the night shift. Merab visited Kampala for the first time for their wedding reception, where Philemon spoke on behalf of the bride's family. While Philemon was speaking, Mulinda, who had disowned his daughter Scovia and then reconciled with her when she joined nursing school, remorsefully wiped away his tears.

❋   ❋   ❋

One night the following week, Merab woke up in the middle of the night feeling sick. She had a headache and felt a little light-headed. When she told Lutalo about her condition the following morning, he gave her two aspirins for the headache but she vomited soon after. She got worried. *Could it be symptoms of malaria?*

The following day, her frequent visitor, Aunt Namagembe, came to see her. Merab told her aunt about her sickness and that she had vomited two more times during the day. Namagembe asked her a few more questions, took a close look at her and said, "Merab, this will sound strange to you but I'm glad to say that this is likely to be a good sickness."

12

JANUARY 1963

ONE EVENING, RUTH was cooking dinner when Jude brought a letter home addressed to her. Ruth opened the letter anxiously as she tried to guess where it had come from. Maybe it was from Miss Cook? The former headmistress had written to her once before, when Herbert was born. She looked at the signature to see who it was from—she'd been right. The letter was from Miss Cook.

London, 27ᵗʰ January 1963

Dear Ruth,

How are you? I hope you and your family are well.

I wanted to inform you that the Commonwealth Scholarship Fund will, in the next few months, be accepting applications for scholarships for various courses. I have no doubt in my mind that you are an excellent candidate for further studies. And while I was perusing the prospectus, I saw a number of courses being offered at the London School of Economics that would be suitable for you, such as courses in Economics or in Public Administration. I know such a move would be intimidating for a young mother and wife but the truth is that you are a born leader. The women in your country need your leadership. Most likely it will be difficult for you to decide, so, let me anticipate your questions:

"Will I, as a woman, qualify for a scholarship?"—I don't know but it does no harm to try.

"How about my family?"—I know it is extremely hard to leave one's family behind to go to live overseas, but the rewards will be great, not just for you and your family but for your newly independent country as well.

Therefore, my dear Ruth, please think about it and then go ahead and apply for a scholarship. You never know. Remember that if you came to study here in London, you would always be welcome to my home. I am here to support you and to offer you company and guidance. I hope that by the time I receive your response to this letter you will have submitted your application. Let me keep my fingers crossed.

I wish you success.

Miss Cook

Ruth was thrilled by the possibility of studying in England but she did not think that Jude would let her go. Since Jude did not ask about the letter, she did not talk to him about it, deciding instead to discuss it with her father.

"Daddy, my former headmistress wrote to inform me that there are scholarships for studies overseas," she told her father in his office the following day. "I'm thinking of applying for a course at the London School of Economics."

"Great. Why don't you apply for one?" Collin asked.

"It would be great if I got a chance to study in London but how would I do it now that I am a wife and a mother? I'm worried about leaving my husband and children behind, especially my children."

"Your mother and I can take care of your children. I mean, we are still strong. Submit an application—you never know."

The following day when Jude returned home from work, Ruth decided to talk to him about the scholarships. "Jude, do you remember the letter you brought home yesterday?"

"Yes. What about it?"

"It was from my former headmistress, Miss Cook—"

"So?"

"She wrote that there are Commonwealth scholarships available for foreign students in Britain. She advised me to apply for a course at the London School of Economics."

"Of what use would that be to you? You are already a teacher."

"Yes, I'm a teacher. But haven't I told you many times before that I don't want to be a teacher all my life?"

"You can apply for a scholarship—it's up to you," Jude said as he went to read the copy of *The Uganda Argus* he'd brought home. "I don't care."

Ruth learned three months later that not only had her application to study Public Administration at the London School of Economics been accepted, she had also been awarded a full scholarship.

"Jude, this letter has good news!" Ruth told her husband after she'd read just the first paragraph of the acceptance letter. She handed it to him.

"Good," he said, perusing it. "I'm happy for you."

Good. He is happy about it. Now his next question is going to be, "Who will take care of us?"

"Who will take care of the children and me while you are gone? How long will the course be?"

"Four years."

"Four years? Are you serious? I will have found another wife by the time you return."

Ruth, ignoring the comment, called in her children to celebrate with her. However, it was hard for her to tell them that she would be away for four years.

❋   ❋   ❋

A week before Ruth's departure both her family and Jude's met for dinner at her parents' home to bid her farewell.

"Do you feel ready for the adventure?" Belinda asked Ruth.

"I am ready. I am excited about studying in London but I miss my children already."

"They will be all right," Belinda answered. "We will take good care of them."

"Would you want to keep them?" Ruth asked. She knew that her mother also wanted to keep the children.

"Oh yes. I will take them home sometimes. You and I know that their father cannot take care of them."

"Then you will have to share time with them with my mother."

"No problem. They will spend one week here, one week there. They will be spoiled..."

Of course you are good at spoiling children.

"That's what grandparents are for."

They both laughed.

❋   ❋   ❋

When Ruth arrived at London's Gatwick Airport, she took a taxi to the offices of the Commonwealth Education Office as her orientation letter had instructed. A young woman, Jenny, received her and gave her a folder containing all the information about her four-year course. Ruth was to take general courses during the first year and units in Public Administration for the final three years. Jenny gave her an envelope containing a month's living allowance and the address of her students' residence. "Lucky you; you have a full scholarship and you won't need to worry about anything. You've got two days to rest. Classes will begin promptly on Monday," she told Ruth. "There is a taxi waiting outside to take you to your residence of the next four years. Welcome to London."

"Thank you," Ruth said as she lifted her suitcase, ready to embark on the next leg of her life.

"I'll be your contact person in case you have any questions or concerns," Jenny said. "Here's my business card."

Ruth started feeling homesick the moment she sat in the taxi.

❊   ❊   ❊

At the end of her first week in London, Ruth went to pay a visit to Miss Cook.

"Hello Ruth, I'm glad to see you. George, meet Ruth. She is one of my favourite former students in Uganda," Miss Cook said while Ruth was still at the front door. "And Ruth, meet my husband, George."

They entered.

"You look surprised!" Miss Cook added as she led Ruth to the living room. "It took me a while to fit in here," she explained, telling Ruth that her life had been quite hard when she'd returned to England. "This country had just gone through a devastating war and it was very different from when I left it. I missed Africa so much that I wanted to go back there. I missed the people. I missed the simplicity. I was used to living life at a slower pace. When I returned here, I felt that people were distant and I felt lonely. That explains in part why I remarried George. Isn't that so, George?"

"Sweetheart, you didn't tell me that you remarried me because you were lonely," George said as he placed a cup of tea on the small table where Ruth was seated. "You said it was because you couldn't live without me."

"What matters now is that I love you," Miss Cook said.

George kissed her on the forehead and left the two women together.

"So, I will ask you questions like a proper Ugandan would," Miss Cook said, laughing. "How is your life, your family, marriage, everything?"

"Uh, where should I start? I think that now I am away from home I'm relieved," Ruth said. "But I find that my life has been harder compared to that of my brothers, for example, because I am a woman."

"Tell me about it," Miss Cook said.

"I love my parents, and I have no doubt that they love me, too, and did a lot to make me the person I am today. However, I find that right from my childhood, my parents, especially my mother, were more demanding of my sister and me than she was of our brothers. She was critical of how we girls dressed and told us many things we should do and shouldn't do."

"But what is the problem now?" Miss Cook asked. "You don't live with your parents anymore."

"I thought that once I grew up, I would be free from that situation but I am not."

"So what's going on?"

"My mother-in-law is very critical of me. We live so near my parents-in-law's home that she can drop into my home any time she wants to criticize me, and—"

"Have you done anything to stop her?"

"No. What would I do?"

"You can't solve problems by sitting there and wishing they didn't exist. Honey, when you return home, I'm afraid you will have to confront the troublemaker."

"How can I confront her? She is my mother-in-law."

"Talk to her directly. Well, I know you can talk to her because I know you as someone who stands up for herself."

"I don't know why she thinks it is okay to mistreat her daughter-in-law," Ruth said.

"All she is doing, sweetheart, is to impose her biases and values on you. Don't blame her, though. She is not aware of them being biases and values— and that's a common problem, probably in all cultures."

❋   ❋   ❋

One Saturday morning, after studying in the library, Ruth went to the cafeteria for lunch. Looking around for a place to sit, she saw a table with an empty seat, with just one young woman seated there, having her lunch alone. "Would you mind if I joined you?" Ruth asked.

"No, I wouldn't mind. Sit down."

Ruth introduced herself as she placed her tray on the table and sat down.

"I am Manisha. How are you, Ruth?"

"I am very well, thank you."

"Are you a student?"

"Yes, I am a student. How about you?"

"Me too."

"Where do you come from?" Manisha asked.

"I come from Kampala, in Uganda," Ruth answered.

Ruth and Manisha chatted until they had finished eating. They went out of the cafeteria and continued talking for about half an hour. Manisha told Ruth that she was from India and that she was studying business and finance so that she could run the family home furnishings business when her father retired.

"I'm also interested in things to do with homes—cooking, baking, decorating, you name it," Ruth told Manisha.

"Then you can start a similar business in your city," Manisha said, smiling. "I can give you all the necessary information. Actually, my father has a friend in Kenya, in Mombasa, who buys from the same factories as my father. His name is Hussein Mohammed, and I think he'd be willing to help you."

Manisha and Ruth found each other easy to talk to and their friendship began that afternoon. Ruth thought that Manisha was a bit too enthusiastic about business and for a moment regretted why she had said that she was interested in home furnishings, but when they met the following weekend and Manisha showed her a catalogue filled with beautiful photos, an idea formed in Ruth's mind. *I could do this. I could start a home furnishings shop.*

Manisha was a funny and talkative young woman, spending a lot of time with Ruth and helping her to overcome her homesickness. When she completed her course before Ruth had completed hers, she even enrolled in a sports program in order to hang around until Ruth had completed hers.

The two friends spent their free time cooking and tried numerous recipes, from desserts to dishes that Ruth had never heard of, while still watching what they ate, balancing their meals and exercising twice a day. Ruth decided to change her children's diet when she returned home.

Manisha took Ruth on adventures, too.

When Ruth told her that she did not know how to ride a bicycle, Manisha laughed until she cried. "What? Why not?" she asked, laughing even more.

"Actually, I've never seen a woman riding a bicycle in my village," Ruth said. "Never—that's the truth. I think it would look funny if anyone of the women in my village was seen trying it."

"Really? Would you like me to teach you how to ride?"

"Yes of course. Let's do it."

Manisha helped Ruth get on the bicycle. She fell several times over the following weeks but she did not give up, and by the end of the third week she was riding on her own. She added "bicycle" to her list of things to ship back to Kampala.

Next, Manisha took Ruth to register for driving lessons, and after several months of practice, she learned how to drive, too.

Whenever she wrote home, Ruth mentioned her new skills.

She also frequently visited Miss Cook. They would chat and sometimes pick fruit together from her backyard garden.

13

IN THE NINTH year of her marriage, Merab was very pleased when she realized that she had conceived, just like her aunt Namagembe had guessed. She was so happy to learn that she was pregnant that she sent Yafesi to her aunt Abigail's home to tell her the news. Yafesi also went to see Namagembe, who gave him a bag full of dried herbs for Merab.

Yafesi sat down to relay the instructions to Merab and showed her which herbal mixture she would drink, which ones she would bathe in and which herbs she would use to smoke herself with. Merab accepted the bag of herbs politely and carefully tucked them away under her bed, never using them.

Lutalo seemed to be happier than he had ever been when his other wives were pregnant. He started returning home earlier than usual in the evenings to spend time with Merab in the living room, talking and asking about her pregnancy. He did not hesitate to buy the foods she craved, even if it meant going to buy them from markets in the neighbouring villages. But Lutalo's reaction to Merab's pregnancy also caused trouble for her.

"We knew all along that you are the favourite wife but *Mwami's* behaviour these days only confirms that," Mukuza said.

"I don't think it is fair for you to say such a thing to me. After all, I am the legally wedded wife," Merab answered.

"You are the legally wedded wife and us, what are we? Rubbish?"

"Don't put words in my mouth," Merab said. "If you have a complaint about *Mwami's* behaviour, talk to him about it, not me."

Mukuza fumed. *Don't think because you are the so-called legally wedded wife you are very special. I'll make life very hard for you in this home.*

When it was time for her to deliver her baby, Merab's labour pains were intense and seemed to last what felt like an eternity to her. She spent hours at the health centre and the midwife checked her periodically to see if the baby was due. Merab felt that the pain was unbearable and vowed not to have another child. When in the evening she finally gave birth to a girl, she named her Leah. Merab spent the night at the health centre and was very pleased when Lutalo came there to see her and the baby—he had never visited any of his other wives there when they gave birth. So, although he seemed a little disappointed when he learned it was a girl, his visit was proof to Merab that Leah was going to be a special baby to her father.

When Merab returned home with Leah, the first person to greet her was her aunt Namagembe, who had come to help her take care of the baby. Namagembe took the child to the back of the house. Merab followed her aunt and she realized that a metallic basin with herbs mixed in water had already been prepared. "We will wash her before she enters into the house for the first time," Namagembe said.

"Isn't it a bit cold for a bath outside?" Merab asked.

"No, it will not take long." Her aunt began to wash the child while saying some inaudible blessings upon her.

Merab tried to figure out what Namagembe was saying to the baby but didn't understand what it was.

Soon after they had taken the baby inside the house, Lutalo's sisters Nalwanga and Nakirijja also arrived, with more herbs, also wanting to wash the baby. Namagembe told them that she had already washed her, so they just took turns holding her.

Nalwanga put two coins in Leah's palm and closed it firmly. "I'm declaring all sorts of blessings on you, my niece," she said. "May you grow up to be a responsible woman and be as prosperous as your father."

❋   ❋   ❋

When Leah was two months old, Yafesi took Merab and the child to pay a visit to her parents.

As soon as Yafesi had stopped the bicycle in the front yard, Dolosi came out, shouting for joy. "I am glad to see you, Merab," she said as she took the baby in her arms and looking closely at the child. "Is it a girl?"

"Yes," Merab answered. "Her name is Leah."

"I am very glad to see you, Leah," Dolosi said. The child tried to open her eyes but it was too bright outside. "Let's go inside."

Levi was already seated in the living room, waiting. "I am glad to see you, Merab," he said.

"I am glad to see you Father," Merab said as she knelt to greet her father.

"Congratulations on the birth of your child. How is your husband?"

"My husband is well. He asked me to convey greetings to you."

"Do you have the letter?" Levi asked with his hand outstretched. "Please sit down, Yafesi."

Merab opened her bag and took out the letter. Levi read it in silence then put it in his shirt's pocket.

❋   ❋   ❋

The birth of Leah was a source of joy for Merab. She felt that because of the baby, Lutalo loved her even more and she remained his favourite wife. Because of that, and thanks to Namagembe's tips as well, Merab made Lutalo feel even more special. When she prepared his favourite dish of chicken and sweet potatoes, she cooked the chicken in a small saucepan, apart from that of the rest of the family. And when the meal was ready to be served, she would place the whole saucepan on the table for him to serve himself. It seemed that Lutalo enjoyed his meals more when Merab cooked than when the other wives cooked—she seemed to put more love and attention into hers. And, he was a little more talkative during Merab's *kisanjas*.

When Leah turned one year old, Merab's cousin Philemon organised a party at his home in Kampala to celebrate the child's birthday and to get her christened.

"I can't stand this favouritism!" Mukuza said just as Lutalo and Merab were about to set out for Leah's baptism in the city, unable to hold her tongue for one more moment. "You would think that Leah is the first child to be born in this home! No other child here has ever been taken to the city. Even I, a grown woman, I've never been to the city. *Mwami* will have to explain himself when he returns."

Merab, Lutalo and their daughter arrived at Philemon's home on Saturday but they did not know what kind of arrangements Philemon had made for Leah's baptism. They were surprised at the big party he had organized. Several people they did not expect, including Levi and Dolosi were there, and so were Merab's sisters Eseza and Nawume, who were very happy to see their niece for the first time. Lutalo was a little uneasy when he saw his parents-in-law—he had never met them since he'd gotten the two new wives but they welcomed him like nothing had happened. Levi shook hands with him and they chatted at length. Dolosi greeted her son-in-law from a distance, sitting on a mat in a room next to the living room and walking away as soon as she had greeted him, since culture did not allow her to sit near him.

In the morning, the entire family went to the church for the baptism ceremony and returned to Philemon's house for lunch afterward. After lunch, it was time for speeches.

After Philemon spoke briefly to welcome the family to his home, Levi spoke. "My wife Dorothy and I are very glad to be here to celebrate our granddaughter's first birthday and her baptism." Dolosi's husband was the only person who called her by the English version of her name. She beamed—to her, the name sounded so much better that way.

Lutalo sat quietly and uneasily throughout the party. He thought they were not happy with him and that they were judging him although no one mentioned his other wives.

Lutalo returned home two days later without Merab and Leah, telling the others nothing about the journey or about Leah's baptism. After his chair was brought out into the front yard and everyone had greeted him, he went to Musirise's bedroom, changed his clothes and hopped on to his bicycle to go open his shop.

"He doesn't even have the courtesy of telling us about his travels. This man is very conceited," Mukuza said to Musirise who was seated on the veranda, weaving a mat.

Musirise did not respond.

"Did you hear what I said?" Mukuza asked.

"I don't care. He is a grown man and he owns this home. He can do whatever he wants to do."

"What? You don't care that he is treating us like rubbish?"

"No, I don't care."

"Now that Mufuzi is your sister-in-law, you don't care. I think you are stupid."

Musirise still did not respond.

✻   ✻   ✻

During her visit to Philemon's home, Merab enjoyed herself. She wished she lived in the city or at least nearby and didn't want to return to Kalasa.

"Philly, is there a way you can help me to move?" she asked her cousin.

"Do you want to divorce your husband?" Philemon asked, laughing.

"No, but if I could, I would move to the city."

Philemon took Merab to Nateete, near Kampala, to see a large house that he was building. Philemon was becoming more and more prosperous—his boss Mitego's wealth seemed to be rubbing off on him—and it was obvious, which made Merab wish even more that she could live in the city. She thought she could also prosper there.

✻   ✻   ✻

Merab loved Leah, her only child, so much that she watched over her all the time. By the time Leah turned four and despite Namagembe's relentless efforts in supplying herbs, including Nsigo-Emeluka's clay bars, it was clear to Merab that she might not have any more children. Mukuza, out of Merab's hearing, referred to her and Leah a lioness and her cub, and because of Leah, Merab's relationship with Mukuza worsened.

One day, Leah returned home with some of the other children after they'd been playing at the stream and they were covered in mud. Mukuza got a stick and beat them—the first beating ever for Leah. She did not stop crying until her mother returned from the garden.

"Listen to me, you woman!" Merab screamed at Mukuza. "If you want someone to beat, I am here for you to beat but for goodness sake, never ever again touch my daughter!"

"I am sorry," Mukuza said, but plainly she was not. "I didn't know that some children in this home were untouchable."

Merab did not respond, she just walked away, fuming, to go wash her daughter.

That incident aggravated Mukuza's hatred for both Merab and Leah. "Who do they think they are?" Mukuza said. "They should go live elsewhere if they think they are so special."

"What did you say?" Musirise asked.

Mukuza did not respond. *I will make Mufuzi's life in this home miserable until she leaves.*

"Mukuza, you should try to understand what Mufuzi feels about her daughter," Musirise said. "Unlike you and I, Mufuzi has just one child. Let her mother discipline the child herself."

"No, I'll beat her whenever she misbehaves," Mukuza said, furious, striding into the kitchen. "If Mufuzi wants special treatment for her daughter, she should go live elsewhere."

14

WHILE RUTH IS busy studying in London for her degree, I will do whatever it takes to get her husband, Clotilda thought when she learned that Ruth was away studying in Britain.

When she found out where Jude worked from one of his former classmates, she followed him secretly for a week to learn his evening routine. After Ruth had left for London, Jude had gotten into the habit of not going straight home from work. Now Clotilda knew that he and his friend Darlington met every evening in Suzana Night Club to drink and to eat fried chicken. She also noticed that he often went to Kamulu's Bar to drink.

One Friday evening, she dressed and made herself up very nicely. Looking at herself in the mirror, she was so pleased with her look she knew that Jude would not be able to resist her.

She arrived at Kamulu's Bar and ordered a drink and when three men asked if they could join her, she told them she was waiting for her boyfriend.

When Jude arrived at the bar, he was very surprised to see Clotilda. "You look beautiful," Jude said. "Can I join you?" he asked, indicating the chair opposite Clotilda.

"Oh yes, join me. It's you I've been waiting for."

"How did you know that I would be coming here?"

"Why wouldn't I know?" she said. "You know I care so much about you."

But although Clotilda and Jude shared a plate of fried chicken and drank several bottles of beer that evening, when she asked him to drive her home, he refused.

"I can't—I've got to go see my children before they go to bed," Jude said. "But I'll see you next Friday," he added as he walked out of the bar.

❋   ❋   ❋

When she returned home that evening, Clotilda felt both aroused and lonely. She waited until dark, then checked to see that nobody was watching her and walked to the caretaker's room two doors from her own. Kyotera was surprised to see the uninvited visitor but was pleased, too—he'd had a crush on her since he had first laid eyes on her.

The young man was dressed quite well and it seemed he was going out but he changed his plans when Clotilda entered his room.

"Here, go buy some beer, Kyotera," Clotilda said, handing the young man some coins. "I would like some."

When Kyotera returned with the bottles of beer, he and Clotilda drank and talked in low voices. It was in the middle of the night before Clotilda opened the door to return to her room.

❋   ❋   ❋

After several such night-time visits, Clotilda felt sick and hatched a plot and asked a woman who lived in the next room to help her. "I don't think Kyotera is fit to work here any longer," Clotilda began.

"Why not?" The woman asked, smiling. "I thought you two were friends."

Clotilda was shocked—she hadn't realized that she had been spotted going in and out of the caretaker's room. "It is a long story but I need your help in getting him fired from his job. If the landlord asks you to corroborate my story, please help me."

"Do you want me to lie? I don't know what your problem is with Kyotera."

"Never mind—just corroborate my story," Clotilda said. "If you do, I will get you a job at my school. I know you are looking for a job. Help me and I will help you."

So Clotilda accused Kyotera of entering her room without her permission and the woman confirmed that she had seen him. Kyotera was fired immediately.

❇   ❇   ❇

Despite her insistence, Jude resisted visiting Clotilda's home. When he finally gave in, he realized that it made him feel less lonely—and since there was no one at home to ask where he had been, he went to see her some nights. It was during the third month of their affair, while he was resting on Clotilda's bed, that she told him that she was pregnant with his child.

"That's very unfortunate," Jude said, sitting up in the bed.

"What do you mean unfortunate? It's a child like any other," Clotilda replied.

"It's a child like any other, but remember, I am a married man."

"So what?"

"Listen, I will admit to being the baby's father only on condition that Ruth does not know about it."

"And I am willing to keep it a secret on one condition," Clotilda said.

"And what condition is that, if I may ask?"

"That you provide for the child like a responsible father would do," she said. "And if you avoid me, I will tell the world that you are a cheater."

"I don't usually deal with stupid people...I am so sorry that I got involved with you."

"I may be stupid but you, wise man, will take care of your child. Otherwise, I will expose you."

"Tell me what you want and I'll give it to you. But you must leave me alone after that."

"Your parents have a lot of land," Clotilda said. "Everybody knows that your father is very rich. I want you to give me a piece of land that's large enough to build a school. If you do, I'll leave you alone."

"Give me one week," Jude said as he put his clothes back on. "But, in the meantime, keep your big stinky mouth shut," he said, walking out of Clotilda's room without another word.

When Jude informed his parents about Clotilda's pregnancy, all his mother said was that he had done a bad thing that he should never do it again, but Dawson promised to give him ten acres of land after the child was born. He reported back to Clotilda.

Jude had said that Clotilda was stupid and she was angry with him, but he resisted visiting her again for only two weeks. After that, he went to see her several times and a few times, he spent the night. At his own home, Nampa soon noticed that her boss wasn't coming home some nights and after a while decided to tell Eunia.

"Listen, Jude is a grown man," Eunia told her. "I trust him to do what is good for his family. We don't know where he is or what he does on the nights he doesn't return home. I don't want you to tell Ruth about it when she returns. Is that clear?"

"Yes."

"Good."

15

December 1960

MERAB'S MAT WEAVING was getting even more skilful and more women and girls came to her home to learn the craft from her. Her friend Nakatudde used the meetings to teach the younger women about their culture and their roles as women in their homes. The meetings became so popular that Lutalo's home became a centre of social activity for the village women. However, some of the husbands, thinking the women were gathering just to gossip, tried to stop their wives from joining the group. One such woman was Samanya, but she didn't want to miss the meetings and continued to briefly go there under the guise of going to fetch water from the stream.

"Mufuzi, I want to join you and the other women in weaving mats," Samanya told Merab. "But my husband won't let me."

"Ask him to pay us a visit so he gets to know what we do here," Merab answered.

"I don't think he would come here unless your husband invited him or you talked to him yourself," Samanya replied.

"I can't go talk to your husband but I can write a letter to him."

"It would be useless to write to him—neither of us can read," Samanya answered, laughing. "And he is too proud to let one of our children read to him."

"I don't see why he stops you from joining us," Merab said, and told Samanya that she would ask Lutalo to talk to him.

Merab thought that it was a good idea for the women to gather in her home because people had always been welcome there. But not everyone in the home now thought so, including Mukuza.

"But the women meet under the tree, not inside the house—I don't see why that bothers you," Merab told Mukuza. "And the head of our household hasn't complained about anything we do."

"Take your meetings elsewhere! I don't want to see those many women—"

"Who do you think you are? We will continue to meet here until *Mwami* asks us to stop! If you don't want to see the women, lock yourself up in your bedroom until they've left," Merab said, walking away. She was surprised by her own reaction. *My mother would be shocked to know that I talk to people like that.*

While they were in bed the following night, Lutalo asked Merab about her mat-weaving gatherings. "Mufuzi, other than weaving lots of mats, what else do you do?"

Is Mukuza giving him false information about our gatherings? She wondered. "We talk about our families, how to take care of our children, what nutritious foods we should feed them, how to organize our homes—things like that."

"A few men came to me at the shop to complain about your meetings, including Deogratias, Samanya's husband. I promised them that I would talk to you," Lutalo said.

"Did they say what the problem was? Is their wives' behaviour deteriorating?"

"No, they didn't give details. Now that you've told me the things you talk about, I will tell them exactly what you have told me," Lutalo said. "But if a man feels that his wife is not benefitting from your activities, he should simply not let his wife come back. Isn't that so?"

"I guess so," Merab answered. "But it would be unfortunate for some of the women to miss our meetings, considering the benefits that we get out of them."

"I don't see any problem with your mat weaving," Lutalo said.

"Thanks for saying that, *Mwami*. I know some people in this home are bothered by our meetings," Merab said, hoping that Lutalo would say whatever he knew about Mukuza's complaining but he did not respond to her prompting. He simply rolled over and covered his head.

※　※　※

When a team of medical officers came to Kalasa to immunize the children, Merab was one of the many mothers who came with hers. The young nurse doing the immunizations who looked so beautiful in her pink uniform especially impressed her, and Merab paid a lot of attention to her later, too, when the nurse gave the women tips for caring for their children and how to prevent diseases. In fact the young nurse impressed Merab so much that she decided that her daughter Leah must become a nurse.

Two days later, she went to see her brother Absalom. "I have given a lot to Lutalo's family and now it's time for me to get something in return," Merab said to her brother. "It might sound selfish but I am not going to let Leah grow up in the midst of the confusion in her father's home. I would like to send my daughter to a good boarding school in Kampala. But I don't have the money to do so."

"But you do," Absalom told his sister firmly, smiling. "Listen," he continued. "For two years now, whenever Yafesi has delivered coffee to the store, I measured it and paid him the money to take to his master. But I know that Yafesi doesn't know how to count, so, each time, I deducted a little money that I kept for you." Absalom moved close to his sister and whispered, "At night, I wrapped the money in several pieces of cloth and buried it in my coffee plantation, in places that I carefully marked."

"What? Have you really done that or are you just joking?"

"No. I'm not joking."

"That's very kind of you," Merab said, "but it is shocking, too—isn't that theft? I can't accept that money."

"It is all up to you," Absalom answered. "It is your money; you work hard for it."

On the way home, Merab struggled with what Absalom had just told her. *Sneaking chicken when I'm not supposed to be eating it means I'm already stealing... and would I really be stealing from Lutalo if I used the money to pay for his own daughter's education?*

Merab went back to see Absalom the following day and told him she would take the money to pay for her daughter's education. "But what will I tell Lutalo if he asks me where the money for Leah's education comes from?" she asked him.

"Tell him that Philly pays," Absalom said without any hesitation.

❋   ❋   ❋

That weekend, Kulumba met his mother Gemma for the first time. It was Merab who sent him to his mother's home in Kampala, without Lutalo's knowledge. When the boy was there, Gemma told Kulumba to be careful with Merab and with the food that she fed him. "Remember, you've got to be careful in your father's home. Here, take this," she said, as she slipped a potion into his bag. "Before you go to bed, put this under your head. It will protect you. You've got to protect your sisters, too, because you are the only man they have to rely on. Your father is useless."

That weekend, while Nakatudde and Merab were weaving mats and talking, she asked about Kulumba. "I don't see Kulumba here today. Is he home?"

"He went to visit his mother. He is a teenager now, and I thought that it wasn't good that he hadn't seen his mother all these years. I organized the visit," Merab said, immediately regretting opening a topic she had avoided for years—she knew that Nakatudde would start talking about Lutalo's ex-wife.

Nakatudde did just that. "Was Lutalo happy about it?" she asked. "About you sending Kulumba to visit his mother?"

"No, he wasn't. He said that I shouldn't have let his son go to see—I will quote his exact words—'that woman'—but he did not say why," Merab said, feeling bad that she was encouraging Nakatudde to gossip.

"I know why," Nakatudde said. "You see, Kulumba's mother is older than Lutalo. It is said that she is a distant relative of Lutalo's stepmother. She lived in this home shortly before Lutalo's father passed away and it seems Lutalo got into a relationship with her later without really falling in love with her. Let me tell you, there were constant fights in this home while she was living here…" Nakatudde had just noticed that Nabukalu was coming to join them and quickly changed the topic.

※　　※　　※

When it was time to return to Kalasa, Kulumba did not want to leave the city. He refused to go back because, he said, Merab mistreated him. "You have to go back to Kalasa—my room is too small to share with a teenage son. Go back before it is too late," Gemma said, giving some money to Kulumba and leaving the house for her choir practice.

So Kulumba returned to Kalasa but refused to go back to school, and when Merab asked him why, he said he wanted to live and work in the city. She told Lutalo as soon as he returned that evening.

"Kulumba, you either go back to school or go live with your mother. I won't tolerate big-headed people in my home," Lutalo told his son.

When Kulumba woke very early two days later and boarded the bus for the city, Merab wept most of the day for him.

✳︎ ✳︎ ✳︎

When Philemon came on his monthly visit, Absalom told him about Merab's plan for Leah's schooling. "I have already collected the money she needs to begin but she will also need your help. If Lutalo asks, she would like you to tell him that you are the one paying the school fees."

"Educating a child is a good thing. Why does she have to be secretive about it?"

"Lutalo would not let her send the child to a boarding school when there is a school here."

When Philemon talked to Merab, she confirmed her plan. "And I will need your help in finding a good school for my daughter," she told her cousin. "I will do everything I can to educate her so she doesn't end up living in a miserable rural area like me."

"I know a few good schools that she can attend. Actually, I think she can be enrolled in the same school as my son, Sam," Philemon said.

"That's very kind of you. Please let me know as soon as possible," Merab said. "There's also something else that I wanted to talk to you about. We have a lot of beautiful mats here that our women's group has woven. Can you help us find a market for them?"

"I can't, but I know somebody who possibly can—my boss, Mitego. He is one man who never runs out of ideas and contacts. He even knows people in foreign countries."

"Foreign countries—isn't that wonderful!" Merab said, mesmerized.

"Yes, and I will talk to him about your mats. Who knows? Perhaps he can get you buyers abroad," Philemon said.

Philemon's statement raised Merab's hopes for Leah, and she couldn't wait to pass on the news about the mats to the rest of the women.

16

CLOTILDA GAVE BIRTH to a baby boy whom she named Clement. As agreed, the Kiyagas gave her ten acres of land to build a new school. She used that land to secure a bank loan and built two very large classroom blocks on it as well as several houses for the teachers and a very large house for herself with the money. Within two years she had relocated Lungujja Primary School. The school's performance continued to improve every year and was soon one of the best schools in the district.

※　　※　　※

Collin and Eunia organized a party to welcome Ruth home three weeks after her return from England. "Ruth, I knew that you could do well in your studies because I know how hard you work," Eunia said in her speech at the party. "My friends, let us educate our girls," she added, now addressing the guests. "My daughter is proof that it is worthwhile for us to invest in our girls' education. I'm glad to report that Ruth is the new Assistant District Education Officer— she got the job just one week after she returned from England!"

Jude spoke, too, saying how very proud he was of Ruth for completing her course. When he said, his hand on Ruth's shoulder, "My wife Ruth and I are alumni of the London School of Economics and Cardiff University, respectively," the audience gave a loud cheer.

When Ruth made her speech switching back and forth from Luganda to English, people were amazed by her transformation and many admired her new English accent. She thanked her husband, her parents and her parents-in-law for taking care of the children while she was away. She said that she had acquired a lot of knowledge in England that she was ready to pass on to her compatriots.

When Dawson Kiyaga rose to speak, his speech was short. However, in a gesture that annoyed Belinda, he handed over the keys of a new Fiat to Ruth to congratulate her for having successfully completed her course in London.

Eunia was very happy that evening and even after the party sat in her bedroom and thought how lucky she was. All her children were doing well in life. Ruth was back and had just completed her course in London. Hannah was an accountant. Thomas was a teacher and Mark, a civil engineer, had started working in his father's company.

❋   ❋   ❋

Ruth was very eager to start her new job but she was not prepared for the resistance she encountered at work right from the first day from male colleagues like Sebbowa. Sebbowa had been an office clerk for fifteen years and didn't want to report to a female boss, deliver her mail or prepare her tea, feeling insulted when he had to take orders from a woman. Worse still, Ruth was younger than he was. He asked to be transferred to another office but the DEO told him that he had two options—either to stay and work under Ruth or quit his job.

Sebbowa was the most critical of the way Ruth dressed. Because Ruth occasionally wore trousers to her office, the men had nicknamed her *Mwambala mpale*—the one who wears trousers. "Her husband must be a weak man," Sebbowa said. "Why would he let his wife leave home dressed like that?"

"It is obvious that she is the man in the home. I wouldn't allow my wife to wear the same clothes as I," another man, a technician, agreed.

"The office is not a nightclub. Ruth should not be allowed to dress like that here. She distracts us," Sebbowa added.

Except for the typist, the rest of the employees were all men, and Ruth felt isolated since they did not seem to want to talk to her. She had many new ideas that she wanted to share with them but most did not even stop at her office to say hello. An early riser and always the first person to arrive in the office, she'd see the men pass by her wide-open door not saying hello, their faces buried in newspapers, busy reading, she thought, so they could avoid talking to her.

Ruth remembered Miss Cook's advice: "Don't think that you can solve a problem by wishing it went away. You've got to do what it takes to solve it." So she soon started to think of ways to change the office atmosphere. One Friday morning, she brought in a breakfast of bread, omelette, bananas, fruit juice and tea in a thermos as well as beautiful cups and plates to serve it with, inviting three of her co-workers to eat, including Sebbowa. The men were very surprised to see her cheerfully serving breakfast to them, and from that time onwards, Ruth served breakfast once every month and the men looked forward to it. They became friendly with her, gradually opening up to her and telling her about their problems, including about money and their families.

❋   ❋   ❋

One year after she returned to Kampala, Ruth received a letter from her friend Manisha. Manisha had contacted Hussein Mohammed in Mombasa and wrote that Hussein would be sending ten rugs free of charge to help Ruth start her home furnishings business. "This is my gift to you, Ruth," Manisha wrote. "I hope it will be enough inspiration for you to start your business."

Ruth was thrilled and grateful to have such a caring and generous friend and wrote Manisha back immediately to thank her. When the rugs arrived in Kampala three months later, Ruth left them in their packaging and placed them in an unoccupied room in her house. Until Manisha wrote again to ask about the progress she was making with the business, she'd almost forgotten about them.

Why hadn't she told Manisha right away that she wasn't ready to start the business? *I'm an Assistant District Education Officer. What would people say if I quit my job to start a home furnishings shop? I might have to start the business and hire somebody to run it for me.* And what could she tell Manisha now? *"Thanks for the rugs, but I'm sorry I failed to sell them?"*

❋   ❋   ❋

But Ruth did know how to handle her extended family. She knew that her paternal aunties Miriam and Eva did not approve of some of her ways but were a bit tolerant. After all, they had learned to tolerate her mother over the years and she was her mother's daughter. Whenever Miriam or Eva complained that Ruth did not go to visit them, she'd turn up with bags of groceries and that appeased them every time.

However, Jude's family did not see things in the same way. One hot Saturday morning, Ruth went to the hair salon dressed casually in trousers. Jude came by later and when Ruth saw him waiting outside, she wondered why he was there and came out as soon as her hair was done. Jude said, "You look stunning, darling."

"Thank you," Ruth answered. "But why are you here?"

"I just remembered that we were invited to a baptism party for my sister Catherine's son."

"When is it?"

"Actually, it has already started. We should be heading there now," Jude said. "Sorry I forgot to tell you earlier."

"But I can't go to a party dressed like this!"

"Why not? You look fine to me. It's just a baptism party, not a wedding."

"It would be okay if it were my family organising the party but it's your family. Your mother is so critical of me."

"Don't worry about her. Besides, she will not be at the party. Let's go," Jude said as he pulled Ruth by the hand.

As soon as they walked into the party, all eyes turned to Ruth. Jude's uncle Kasolo, a Second World War veteran, was there, his war medals pinned to his jacket. The old man looked at Ruth with disgust when he saw her dressed in trousers. He immediately rose from his seat and walked out of the room without saying a word to his nephew or to Ruth. Ruth put on a bold face and tried to enjoy the party but the entire evening she felt scrutinized and saw the disapproving glances.

The following day, Jude, Ruth and their children went to pay a visit to his parents. Immediately after the greetings, Belinda called Ruth to her bedroom. "Ruth, I would like to talk to you, not as your mother-in-law, but as a grown woman who respects our culture."

"Yes, please go ahead," Ruth said as she fixed her mother-in-law with a bewildered gaze.

"I am sorry to say but ever since you returned from England, I noticed that you are a changed woman."

"How?" Ruth asked.

"To say the least, the way you dress is inappropriate and you are disgracing our family. I heard that you wear trousers wherever you feel like."

"For your information, Belinda, I am free to wear what I want so long as my husband is okay with it."

"Your husband is okay with the way you dress?" Belinda asked, shocked also that Ruth had addressed her by name.

"Yes he is. He has never told me that he finds my dressing inappropriate."

"He might not say it—" Belinda began but Ruth was already walking away, fuming.

When Ruth walked into the living room, Jude noticed that she was upset. "I don't want to talk to your mother again," Ruth said. "I don't know why she is making life hard for me."

Jude got up and went to his mother's bedroom. "Mummy, what did you say to Ruth? She's angry with you."

"I talked to her about her dressing. It is inappropriate. Your uncle Kasolo told me that yesterday at the baptism party she was wearing trousers."

"Yes, she wore trousers because we were late for the party. But I'll talk to her about it," Jude said, leaving his mother's room.

Ruth was in the front yard, playing with the children. When Jude went out to join them, he did not tell her about his conversation with his mother.

That evening Ruth wrote in her diary:

> When I returned from England I felt a lot of scrutiny, of what I wore, of what I said, of how I conducted myself. This evening my mother-in-law attacked me because of the way I dress. For goodness' sake, girls, women, and especially young women, are free to wear what they like. I want things like the weather or my mood to determine what I wear. Neither my mother-in-law nor my culture should impose restrictions on the way I dress.

17

December 1960

"LADIES, MY COUSIN Philly told me that his boss can find people abroad to buy our mats!" Merab said that afternoon as soon as the women sat down to start weaving.

"That's wonderful news," the women answered in unison.

"How soon will that happen?" Samanya asked.

"He didn't confirm anything but I know my cousin well. Once he commits himself to doing something, he does it," Merab answered. "Actually, I have another idea. One day I would like to establish the largest crafts shop in Kampala, where we would sell our mats."

"What?" Nakatudde asked. "Where would you get the money to start a shop? You never run out of crazy ideas, Mufuzi!"

The rest of the women laughed at Merab.

"I would start small. All those big companies that you've heard of did not start out big," Merab said.

"Of course they did not start out big," Nakatudde answered, "but I have never heard of any company that was started by a rural woman like you."

The women laughed at Merab again.

"It can be done," Merab said. "Our mats are the best. I bet you can't find any better than ours."

❋   ❋   ❋

"Philly, you know that I can sell anything," Philemon's boss Mitego said to him when he talked to him about Merab's mats. "But handicrafts are the one thing I've never tried to sell. These days the people who can afford to buy things want to buy imported, manufactured goods for their homes. I think for now you have to let your cousin and her friends use the mats themselves and for their children to sleep on."

Philemon laughed.

"But in the future if people no longer want manufactured goods, they might buy handicrafts."

❋   ❋   ❋

When Philemon visited Kalasa the following month, the first question Merab asked him was, "Did you talk to your boss about our mats?"

"Yes, I did. Unfortunately, he told me that he can't sell handicrafts."

"But you said that he knows some people in other countries who—"

"Yes, he does, but he made it clear to me that he can't help you. However, I have good news about Leah's schooling—she has been admitted to City Primary School, which is a boarding school. If you get her ready—including the school fees, of course—I will take her with me tomorrow."

Later that day Merab told Lutalo the news. She had also prepared some answers for him about where the money to pay for the school was coming from but

GEOFFREY KIGGUNDU

Lutalo never asked, only saying, "That's good. Please thank Philly for his help."

The following day, Merab accompanied Philemon and Leah to the bus. "Listen, Leah, what we are doing is for your good—you are going to a good school which will give you a better future," Merab said to her crying six-year-old daughter, who did not want to live far away from her mother. "You will be seeing me during the school holidays."

When the bus started moving away, Merab cried, too, and walked back home in tears. She missed her daughter already.

"I'm tired of the favouritism in this home," Mukuza said as soon as Merab returned home. "How come Leah is the only child who has got the opportunity to study in a good school in the city?"

Merab did not answer. She went to the kitchen, picked up her hand hoe and a basket and went to harvest some cassava for dinner.

A few weeks later, one mid-morning, after Lutalo had bathed and was getting ready to go to the shop, there were no clean clothes for him to wear in Mukuza's bedroom, where he had slept. *That's going to be a good lesson for him*, Mukuza thought. *He is so passive that he expects everything to be done for him.* But Lutalo knew where to find clean clothes. He went to Merab's bedroom, got some clean ironed clothes and dressed there.

Mukuza watched as he walked out of Merab's bedroom, hopped onto his bicycle and headed to the shop before she went to the front yard where Merab and Nabukalu were spreading out coffee beans in the sun to dry. "Mufuzi, tell me, why you are undermining me? You went behind my back and washed and ironed clothes for *Mwami* yet it's not your *kisanja* this week," she said.

"I'm sorry I don't understand. Please say that again," Merab said.

"You know what I'm talking about! *Mwami* has just taken the clothes that he is wearing from your bedroom. I don't know what that is if you think it is not undermining."

"Why are you blaming me? I have been out here working for the past half

151

hour. Did I ask him to go to my bedroom to find clothes to wear?"

"Perhaps you did. How come he knew that there were clean clothes in your bedroom even though he did not sleep there?"

"*Mwami* owns this home and I think he is free to pick up his clothes from wherever they are. He knew that there were clean clothes in my bedroom, so he went there and got them. I don't see why that would be an issue."

"I don't see why that would be an issue either," Nabukalu added.

"Don't meddle into our affairs!" Mukuza yelled at Nabukalu. "These are matters between us wives. You are not a wife in this home."

"I know I am not a wife in this home but I can't just keep quiet and let you insult Mufuzi. I've got to defend her."

"Don't talk to me ever again. What I'm talking about is none of your business."

Mukuza and Nabukalu went on quarrelling for a few more minutes while Merab remained silent. *I don't think the aunts of these so-called wives talked to them about the importance of caring for a husband,* she thought, fuming. *It's not my concern that they cannot clean their husband's clothes.*

※　　※　　※

Merab decided that if she was going to be able to keep Leah in a boarding school, she couldn't go on relying on Absalom setting aside money for her. From that time onwards, whenever she sold firewood or sugarcane, she handed most of the money to Lutalo but kept some for herself. Then, like Absalom had done, she would sneak out at night and hide the money in carefully marked places in the garden.

※　　※　　※

When Lutalo's servants had moved out of his home and built their own houses, Yafesi's nephew Enos had come to live with him. All the servants except Yafesi had gotten wives and now had children. Guste, the most prosperous servant, worked with Merab on her income-generating activities including sugarcane and firewood. Later he asked Lutalo to lend him land to grow his own crops, hiring temporary workers to grow cotton, beans and groundnuts. He was able to build a larger house and eventually some of his relatives came to live in his home.

18

SEPTEMBER 1971

A LETTER FROM the Minister of Education informed all employees in the Ministry that after a long career in the civil service, the District Education Officer was about to retire and that interviews would soon be conducted to find his replacement.

Ruth received the news with mixed emotions. *I think I've carried out my duties well as Assistant DEO, but they are probably not satisfied with my performance. If they were they would simply promote me to DEO.* However, she was the first to submit her application for the DEO position.

A week before interviews began, she met one of her father's friends, Bethuel Bulega, who was visiting her father at home. Mr. Bulega told Ruth that he had heard that she was the only woman who had applied for the DEO job and that there were four other candidates.

"That's a crowded field with lots of competition," Collin said.

"True, but I think Ruth has an advantage. She is the most academically qualified," Bulega told them.

During her interview, Ruth highlighted her earlier experience as a teacher. She also said that she knew the demands of the job well and as the current Assistant DEO, she knew what was expected of the DEO. Her international education and having lived in London and graduated with honours in Public Administration would also be an asset to the office, she told them.

When she met one of the interviewers a week later at church, he told her that her candidature was strong. "You did very well in the interview. I think if everything were equal, the job would be yours."

"What do you mean by that?" Ruth asked.

"The fact that you are a woman doesn't help you," the man answered.

Was it possible she wouldn't get the job simply because she was a woman? Ruth decided that if she was not appointed DEO, she would quit her job as Assistant DEO and start her home furnishings business. She still had the ten rugs that she had received from Manisha safely kept in her house.

When she saw the letter on the office notice board the next week announcing the appointment of Mr. Shem Malungu as the new DEO, Ruth was not happy, and walked around the office to talk to somebody, anybody. But the doors to most offices were closed and the offices whose doors were open were empty, unusual for that time of the day.

Ruth returned to her office and dictated a letter to the copy typist, resigning immediately.

When she told Sebbowa that she had resigned he said, "Ruth, it's just a small setback in your career. Are you sure you want to quit your job because of a minor disappointment?"

"It's not a minor disappointment—it's a major blow to women in this country. The men have discriminated against me and it's not funny," she said, picking up her handbag and walking out of the office without saying another word.

＊   ＊   ＊

"Ruth, I didn't expect to see you here at this time of the day," Collin said when

Ruth appeared in his office later that day. "Are you all right?"

"The job has been given to somebody else. The DEO job."

"That's unfair—you have all the necessary qualifications and the international exposure that this country needs. I expected you to be hired."

"It's too late, Daddy. I have resigned from the civil service."

"What? What are you going to do instead? Become a housewife?"

"That's why I have come to see you first—Jude doesn't know about my idea yet. I would like to start my own business. I've had enough and I can't take the mistreatment at work anymore."

"I have an appointment now, but why don't you come home this evening and we can talk further?" Collin said.

❄   ❄   ❄

When Ruth arrived at her parents' home that evening, Eunia started yelling at her as soon as she walked into the living room. "You have to go back to your job now! You can't quit!"

"I can't go back Mummy," Ruth replied. "I have already resigned from the job."

"You are so bigheaded, Ruth! All your education is going to be wasted? Are you going to sit at home now and wait for your husband to provide for all your needs, like an uneducated woman, in this day and age?"

"Let's give her some time to figure out what she would like to do," Collin said as Ruth sat beside him on the sofa.

"I have already planned what I am going to do. I am opening a business, a shop."

"What? You are going to waste your education just like that? You are going to become a trader? Who is it that bewitched you?" Eunia said. "That's witchcraft, pure and simple!"

But despite Eunia's annoyance, Ruth was not ready to change her mind. *She has always told me that I can do things that men do but she is now getting in my way.* "It is not witchcraft, Mummy. I am making a conscious decision to pursue my dream."

"That's a bad dream and let me tell you, you will regret it," Eunia said, rising from the mat on which she had been seated.

"It's a good dream and I am determined to pursue it. I am going to start my own home-furnishings business."

"What? You? A woman? You want to become a trader? It's men with no ambition who become traders," Eunia said. Ruth knew that it was a veiled reference to her mother's stepbrother Simon, who repaired bicycles and sold spare bicycle parts in Katwe, near the city.

"Mummy, this is the first time in my life that you are telling me that I can't do a job that men do."

Eunia was caught off-guard by that remark and she remained silent for a while, not knowing how to respond. "Ruth, you always rush your decisions," she finally said, "but this time I think you are making a grave mistake."

Why? Ruth wondered, but she said nothing.

"*Kabiite*, please calm down. Go to the bedroom and find something else to do, something else to think about. I will continue this conversation with Ruth," Collin said.

As Eunia walked away, muttering, Ruth only heard "…waste of the time and money we paid in school fees!"

"Ruth, you are going through a difficult time and I see that we are not making it any easier for you," Collin told his daughter.

"My mind is made up, Daddy—and I don't have any self-doubt about what I want to do."

"But can you put yourself in your mother's shoes for a minute?" Collin asked. "You know your mother's history and how hard she worked, against all sorts of odds, to get to where she is today."

"Yes, of course I do—she achieved her success through her education and a stable career," Ruth said. "I wanted to follow the same path but circumstances have forced me to abandon that path and to pursue other dreams."

"But as an entrepreneur myself, I will tell you right away that the path you are choosing is a very difficult one."

"I know it will be difficult," Ruth said. "But that doesn't mean that I should abandon it, Daddy."

Jude returned home that evening too drunk for Ruth to tell him that she had resigned from her job. When she did the next morning, he told her she should take a break and look for another job the following month. When Ruth said, "No, I have other plans," Jude did not respond. He just picked up his car keys and went to work.

Two days later, Ruth went back to see her father. "On one hand, I think you are entering a risky kind of business. Who do you expect to sell home furnishings to?" Collin said. "On the other hand, I am very optimistic about your success. You have the determination and the education you need."

Ruth listened attentively.

"I am a successful builder, yet my level of formal education is low—unlike your mother, I learned what little English I know by befriending members of the colonial administration I met through my father," Collin said. "My father was successful but illiterate, and it was they who taught me English and eventually gave me business opportunities. But how are *you* planning to start your business?"

"I know what I want and I have a plan to get me what I want," Ruth said. "I intend to start small. I already have ten rugs in stock and I will eventually grow my business into the biggest home furnishings shop in the city."

"You have my full support."

"Don't pledge support to her because if you do, she will not think of looking for another job," Eunia said as she emerged from the corridor. She spread a mat on the floor and sat down.

"*Kabiite*, please go back to the bedroom. I will handle this. Ruth needs our support."

Eunia never argued with her husband, especially while their children were present. She walked back to the bedroom, muttering something else inaudible.

"Ruth, look for a place to rent for your shop. I will pay your rent until when you don't need my support," Collin said when Ruth was leaving.

"Thank you, Daddy," Ruth said as she entered her car.

❋   ❋   ❋

Ruth's Boutique opened its doors one month later, but although many people stopped by to admire the rugs, six months went by and she had not sold a single item. She soon realized that many of the shoppers were only curious about the former Assistant DEO who, according to an article in *The Voice of Uganda*, was "a brilliant London-educated woman who quit her career in the civil service to open a shop."

But even without sales, Ruth was surprised by the amount of energy she put into the shop. She opened at 10:00 every morning and happily talked and gave home décor tips to those who wanted them.

When Daisy dropped into the shop one evening, Ruth confided in her friend. "It is harder than I thought, Daisy, but I've not lost hope," she said. "I've already figured out everything on paper. I've studied home décor magazines, and I've got big plans for the shop. Every day I do something small to get me where I want the business to go."

"That's very clever," Daisy said, laughing.

"Yes, I've got everything planned out. It may sound crazy to you but whenever I see my detailed plan on paper, I picture this shop all large and beautiful, with customers lining up to pay for merchandise and me, the busy managing director, working in my office. I know it sounds silly, but that's what gives me the energy to come here every day."

"Really?" her friend said, impressed. "Then that determination and the burning desire mean that you'll achieve your dreams. I believe in you."

On her way home that evening, as Ruth replayed the conversation with Daisy in her mind, she felt even more encouraged to keep working at the shop. She arrived home a little later than usual and saw Jude's car parked in the front yard. She realized as soon as she entered the house that he had been waiting for her.

"You are late today. Have you had a busy day at the shop?" Jude asked, lighting a cigarette, his fifteenth of the day.

"Hey, how are you, Jude? Why don't you first greet me before you tell me how late I am?"

"Answer my question, woman. Have you had a busy day at the shop? If yes, how much money have you made in sales?"

"Jude!"

"Show me the money you are making," Jude said. "You go to the city every morning, now I want to see the money you are making."

"We've got to give the business time to grow, darling. Rome was not built in a day," Ruth said, trying to keep her voice low so the children wouldn't hear the quarrelling.

"For how long are you going to wait? You don't want to admit it but I see that you are discouraged. Why don't you swallow your pride and go find another job? It won't take you even a week to find one."

"I am going to do everything I can to grow the business."

"Ruth, you can actually stay at home," Jude said. "You don't need to work. I make enough money."

"Is that the best thing you thought of telling an educated woman?"

"Actually, my mother also thinks that you are wasting your education by becoming a trader."

"Hey, I don't care what your mother thinks," Ruth said as she went to the bedroom.

The following morning, Ruth felt less motivated than usual to get out of bed. Jude's comments the previous evening had caused a little doubt in her mind for the first time about her struggling business. After a while, when she did get out of bed to prepare breakfast, she was surprised to hear him ask her to forgive him for his behaviour the previous evening. "I am very sorry darling," Jude said, and kissed her on the cheek.

"I know it's frustrating for you to see me making no progress but we have to give the business time to grow," Ruth said. "And Jude, you have to take better care of yourself. Your eyes are red and you are drinking and smoking too much—be careful, you might end up messing up your life."

"I am very sorry, darling," Jude answered.

❋   ❋   ❋

That weekend, Ruth and her friends met for lunch at her sister Hannah's home. When she got a moment alone with Daisy in the sitting room, Ruth asked, "Daisy, how are you my dear?"

"I am doing well, thank you."

"Good to hear. How is your marriage going?"

"It's good but I have too much to do both at work and at home. I feel overwhelmed."

"Don't we all? How is your husband behaving?"

"He is okay but he is totally passive at home."

"You are probably wondering why I am asking but I have a problem in my home. Jude behaves badly. He insults me and he is not respectful."

"I am sorry to hear that you are going through such a hard time, Ruth. You are a good person. You don't deserve that," Daisy said. *And there were red flags right from the beginning*, she thought.

Their friend Sanyu came in as they were speaking. "You both look so serious—what are you talking about?"

"My husband insults me and he is not respectful," Ruth told her.

"Leave him," Sanyu said.

"What?" Ruth asked.

"My brother Cornelius loves you so much that if you and he were single again, he would be happy to marry you," Sanyu said.

"What?" Ruth asked, looking shocked.

"Ruth, didn't you know that Cornelius is deeply in love with you?" Daisy asked.

"Are you serious? Of course I didn't know that—he never told me anything!"

"I can talk to him for you," Sanyu said, laughing, "and then we can kick Jude out."

"Are you crazy?" Ruth said. "Jude mistreats me but I love him very much and I will always be loyal to him."

＊　＊　＊

Cornelius Bulega was now the headmaster of the prestigious Musasa High School. Ruth had just opened the shop a few days later when he walked in. "Hey, hello, Cornelius, it's been a long time. I'm glad to see you," she said. "What brings you here today? Are you furnishing your home?"

"No, I happened to be walking by and decided to drop in to say hello. I am attending a meeting of head teachers this morning."

"Are you sure you just happened to be walking by?" Ruth said, smiling. "Sanyu told me that you love me. How come you've never said anything about it?"

Cornelius smiled, too, but he could not hide his nervousness. He glanced at Ruth then looked away. "I didn't have the courage to tell you."

"Oh, you find me scary? Anyway, it's too late now. Cornelius, whenever you want something, ask for it. I hope this is a lesson you've learned for the future."

Cornelius laughed but he did not respond.

"Have a look around the shop if you have time and please help me pass the word around among your acquaintances," Ruth said.

Cornelius was speechless. A woman walked into the shop and he made for the open door. "I'll see you soon. Bye, Ruth," he said as he walked out.

＊　＊　＊

A week later, Jude returned home late and Ruth realized he was drunk when he started snoring on the sofa soon after he had sat down. She woke him up to go bathe before she served him his dinner.

Jude held onto the wall so he wouldn't fall. "Ruth," he said as he slowly made his way to the bathroom, "you've been running that lousy so-called boutique of yours for several months but I'm yet to see a single shilling you've earned from it. What's going on?"

"Hey, you call my business lousy? Don't insult me."

"Just show me the money you are making from it if it's not a lousy business."

Could he be faking it? I don't think he is so drunk. Ruth went to the dining table where she sat down to face him. "Do you know how businesses work? You thought that I would open the business one day and the next day the money would start coming in? It's going to take some time, my dear, for the business to become profitable."

"I didn't want you to open the damn boutique in the first place! Now you are eating my food for free," Jude said, still leaning on the wall.

"I'm eating your food for free? Do you cook it?"

"Oh, anybody can cook. I'll be forced to kick you out of my house if you go to the city to work but earn no money."

"Hey, this is not your house; it is our house."

"It is *my* house. It's my parents who gave it to us."

"Oh, dear. Well, my bedroom is still vacant in my father's house. And for your information, Daddy has a few other houses as well. He can give me one of them."

"Shut down the damn boutique!"

"Sometimes I wonder if you want to support me or simply to sabotage my efforts."

"Silly. Why would I sabotage your efforts? I do want to support you. It is you who is sabotaging yourself."

"Do you know what I'm thinking? I am going to work hard and one day build my own house."

Jude laughed. "You go to the city every day, supposedly to work but you don't earn any money."

"Hey, let me repeat. You've got to be patient if you want the business to grow at all."

"Nonsense! How much longer should I be patient?"

"For as long as it takes for the business to take off. I'm in it for the long haul. You'd better get used to that fact."

"Go get a real job. Go back to teaching."

"No, I won't," Ruth said as she went to the bedroom. She was so annoyed that she decided not to serve his dinner. *If he really wants to eat, he will serve himself.*

* * *

The following day, while Ruth was wiping down the counter, her father's friend Mitego entered the shop. "Good afternoon daughter of Wamala," Mitego said as soon as he entered.

"Good afternoon Mr. Mitego," Ruth answered. "Why don't you call me Ruth?"

"Oh yes, Ruth. I'd forgotten your Christian name. How is your father?"

"My father is well."

"I'm glad to see that you have started your own business. How is it going?"

"The business is not yet doing well but I'm hopeful about its future."

"That's right, you should be hopeful but there are ways to accelerate business. How much marketing do you do?"

"Marketing? None."

"Let's meet sometime this week and I can show you the ropes. You can benefit from my long experience in business." A man came into the shop and Ruth went to greet him. "I will be in touch later this week," Mitego said, smiling to himself as he left the shop. For a long time, he had wanted a date with Ruth.

*　　*　　*

When Clotilda's son Clement's class was graduating from kindergarten, all the parents were invited to attend a Speech Day.

"Mummy, all the children's fathers were at the school today," the six-year-old said to his mother at home that evening, while they were having dinner. "Where is my father?"

"Your father is in Nairobi," Clotilda answered. "That's in Kenya."

"Is that where he lives? Nairobi?"

"Yes."

The following morning, Clement asked again, "Mummy, does my father love me?"

"Yes, he does."

"Then why doesn't he come to see me?"

"Clement, I'm busy right now."

Two days later while Clotilda was preparing dinner, Clement asked again about his father. Clotilda didn't answer this time, she just slapped the boy twice on the shoulder. "Don't ask me about your father ever again," she said to the crying boy. "Don't I provide everything you need? Do you lack anything?"

19

HOW DID I let myself settle for a life that I never wanted in the first place? Why am I still here in Lutalo's home, toiling for him? What benefits are there for me? I've got to go away. Thirty-two-year-old Merab spent a month thinking these thoughts but she did not know how or where to go. She did not want to divorce her husband—she had eventually fallen in love with him—and she did not want to live alone. She feared that if she went away, she would end up as a *nakyeyombekedde*—a single woman who owns and runs her own home, but she knew the kind of ridicule that "Small," the woman who sold alcohol in the village endured as a *nakyeyombekedde* and did not want to go through that. *Maybe I can ask Philly for help. He seems to be so successful and rich now.*

When Philemon visited Merab as usual, they sat under the tree and talked in low voices. She told him that she no longer wanted to live in Kalasa. "Now that my daughter is away at school, I think there is nothing more for me to do here. I am wasting the most productive years of my life in this home. I don't think there is anything new that Lutalo is going to do for me and I don't think I will have more children. Help me to go away."

"Where do you want to go? Were you thinking of coming to live in my home?" Philemon asked his cousin. "Wouldn't that be a source of trouble?"

"No, I wasn't thinking of coming to live in your home. I was hoping that you could find me a place to live. I would do everything possible to sustain myself and my daughter."

"I have land in Kawempe, about six miles from Kampala. It would be large enough for you to build a house and to grow some food," Philemon said. "But you would need money to build the house. How much do you have?"

"I have about three thousand shillings," Merab said.

"You would need a little more—but where do you keep all that money? In your house? Three thousand shillings is a lot of money to keep in the house."

"No, I don't keep it in the house," Merab said as she lowered her voice and looked around to see whether someone was within earshot. "I keep it in various places in my garden."

Philemon laughed. "Like I said, you would need a little more, but I have some bricks left over from when my house was built. I can give you those, and they'd be enough to build three rooms, which I think would be enough for you to start—two for you to live in and one for storage. As you earn more money, you can pay for my land, and I would buy elsewhere. Does that sound like a good plan?"

"Yes, please—thank you very much! I knew that I could always count on your help. I'm so excited about that idea."

"Are you divorcing your husband, then?"

"No, I'm not divorcing him. But I know that if I left him here, he would follow me wherever I went."

"You still love him, then. Why do you want to go away?"

"There is no way I can fulfill my plan here. I want my daughter to lead a better life, to succeed in school, to get a good job and to marry in the city. In other words, all the things that I wanted for myself," Merab said, her voice full of determination. "My dreams were cut short when I was married off to Lutalo. I'll see to it that my daughter leads a better life. In the city."

"Merab, you've really changed."

"Let me tell you, Philly," she said, sighing. "Having sister wives *has* changed me. I am both irritable and quarrelsome. Mukuza is so critical of me these days that I think she wants me to leave this home. And many times I ask myself what I am still doing here. Honestly, there is nothing for me to do here anymore."

"Prepare your money and give it to me tomorrow. I'll spend the night at Absalom's and when I return to Kampala, arrange for construction of your house to begin in a few weeks' time."

When Philemon told Absalom about Merab's plan, her brother was very happy. "My sister now has the chance to be the woman she was meant to be— she will manage her life, raise her daughter and she will get rich," Absalom said.

When Philemon returned to the city, he hired a man to clear an acre of his five-acre land and construction of Merab's three rooms began. Four months later, the house was ready and food crops, including beans and maize were thriving in the garden. When Philemon reported this to Merab, she made up her mind that it was time to leave Lutalo's home.

❋　❋　❋

Lutalo had gone to visit his servant Guste's home one evening and had seen Guste's pretty young niece Adah there. From that evening, Lutalo went to Guste's home more often and finally asked Adah to visit his shop. She started frequenting Lutalo's shop, and he gave her several small gifts, like handkerchiefs and a pair of bath sandals. Lutalo was so engrossed in his new relationship with Adah that he became less attentive to his wives. But when Nakatudde told Merab about Lutalo and Adah's relationship Merab said she did not care. "It's none of my business," she'd said.

❋　❋　❋

Three weeks after Lutalo had befriended Adah, Merab was seated under the tree weaving a mat when she saw Mukuza walking towards her looking angry. "Mufuzi, who do you think you are?" she yelled, standing right in front of her.

"What do you mean?" Merab asked, perplexed. "Please calm down, sit down and tell me what I've done wrong."

"No, I won't sit down."

"Then I won't talk to you. If you want to talk to me, you've got to sit down."

"You are a witch!" Mukuza yelled. "*Mwami* does not want to talk to me anymore or show me any affection even when it is my *kisanja*..."

"If you have a problem with *Mwami*, talk to him, not me."

"You are a witch," Mukuza said again, walking away.

Merab abandoned the mat that she was weaving and went to see Absalom at the coffee store. By the time she arrived, she was crying. "Absalom, I think it's time for me to leave Lutalo's home."

"What happened?"

"Mukuza attacked me with a lot of anger just minutes ago," she said, still sobbing. "I don't know what for—if I don't leave, I think that woman will harm me one of these days."

"I, too, think that you should walk away," her brother said. "What are you waiting for?"

Merab returned home and started thinking of a way to escape.

❋   ❋   ❋

Guste heard about Adah's visits to his boss's shop but he did not know how to stop her without Lutalo finding out. However, on the day he'd gathered just enough courage to confront her about it, Lutalo went to his home and asked his permission to have Adah as his fourth wife. Guste was speechless—he thought it was wrong for Lutalo to take his young niece as a wife but felt powerless before his boss.

A week later, when Lutalo arrived home with Adah, who balanced a small suitcase on her head, Merab did not wait for any explanations. She remembered how he had acted on the two previous occasions when he had brought home her sister wives. While some of the members of the family gathered in the living room to find out what was going on, she went to her bedroom, packed her suitcase and walked out the back door.

Absalom was alone in the coffee store seated at his desk working on his accounts when Merab arrived, crying. "I've made up my mind. I'm leaving Lutalo," Merab said as she placed her suitcase on the floor.

"Good! The timing is perfect," Absalom said without asking why she had decided to leave. "Philly will be coming this weekend and he will take you to your new home. You'll spend a couple of days at my home until he comes."

"Good. But I am scared. I don't want to live on my own," Merab said. "Is there anything in my new house?"

"There should be—we will find out from Philly. But you have three hundred shillings here," Absalom said, pointing to his books. "You can start off with that money."

✳   ✳   ✳

Merab spent two days at Absalom's home with him, Dahlia and their two boys. Her sister-in-law tried to convince Merab to stay but she said she was ready to go away, saying that if she failed in the city, she would return. Absalom noticed with surprise that Lutalo did not come looking for Merab but he did not comment about it.

When Philemon and Merab arrived at her new home in Kawempe, she was so happy to see it, even though there was nothing other than two mats, two small saucepans, an old mattress and a lantern inside the three-room house, and just a heap of firewood on the veranda. Men had just completed work on the latrine and the smooth cement layer on its floor was still wet.

"Your new home, your new life," Philemon said as he placed a mat on the floor to sit. "Are you ready for this?"

"No. I'm not ready. I miss my husband and my children," Merab said. "I miss my home."

"So, do you want me to take you back to Kalasa?"

"No."

"Then stay—everything will be all right eventually," he said, smiling at his cousin. "Now, take a tour of the garden, see how much food is growing. There is actually more food than you need. I'll go to Kampala and will be back in the evening. I will spend the weekend here with you, to keep you company."

"Thank you so much for your kindness to me, Philly. I am very grateful," Merab said. But when Philemon left for the city, she stayed inside the room, crying, and scared by the new life she had just begun.

Philemon returned in the evening with some groceries, including a kilogram of beef, some tomatoes, onions, potatoes and *matooke* plantain. After Merab had peeled the *matooke*, she put them in a saucepan and prepared to cook the beef.

She had already gotten three bricks to make a fireplace. "But how do I make a fire?" she now said, almost to herself.

"Here," Philemon said, pulling a matchbox out of his pocket. Merab knew that Philemon wasn't a smoker, so she was surprised at how prepared he was.

"I've been wondering about how everything seemed to fall into place for my move." Merab said after their dinner. "Absalom was sure that you'd be visiting

Kalasa this weekend and that you'd take me with you. And everything here was ready for me—"

"We had actually prepared for you to move this weekend."

"What?"

"Yes, two weeks ago, Absalom told me that you had gone to see him crying, after a bizarre encounter with Mukuza—"

"Oh, he did? Where did he meet you to tell you that?"

"I came to visit."

"You came to Kalasa and I didn't see you?"

"You didn't see me because I returned here right away to do the final touches," he said. "We knew that you were fed up with your life in Kalasa and we knew that you wouldn't hesitate to walk away."

"I can't believe that you had actually planned all this!"

"Do believe it—and it turns out that our timing was perfect."

❊   ❊   ❊

In the days that followed, neighbours dropped by to talk to Merab and to welcome her to the village. Philemon came to pay her a visit every other evening after work and to bring her groceries.

"Philly, I've got to find something to do, some kind of job," Merab said one evening. "I can't continue relying on you; you have a family of your own to look after."

"I have no problem taking care of you, Merab. You'll need some time to settle down."

"You're right, but I'm very bored here."

"Let me think about what you can do," Philemon said. He knew that his cousin was not the kind of person to sit around doing nothing. "I have to caution you, though. Be careful about people here and in the city. They behave differently from people in rural areas. You've got to have your guard up while you deal with people here."

Merab listened attentively.

"I'm not saying that everybody in the city is bad," he continued, "but you'll find some who will want to take advantage of you and some who will want to steal from you. Be assertive and don't hesitate to stand up for yourself. And of course, I'm available to advise you whenever you feel you need it."

❊ ❊ ❊

When one of Merab's neighbours, Kamaadi, realized that Philemon did not live there, he started visiting her home frequently, which made Merab uneasy for two reasons: one, even though she was separated from Lutalo, she was still married to him. Two, Kamaadi was also married and she knew that his wife would not like his visits to Merab's home. Another man, Katiiti, also started visiting Merab's home and competed with Kamaadi to do Merab favours—when one fetched water from the stream, the other split her firewood. Merab found both men overbearing but she did not have the courage to tell them to leave her alone.

And when the women in the area noticed that a young good-looking woman lived alone there, they started harassing her. After dark, Merab would sometimes hear women calling out to her, "*Nakyeyombekedde*, we know your plans. You want to steal our men but we warn you—you will get in trouble if you try to steal any of our men." Another time she heard, "*Nakyeyombekedde*, go back to wherever you came from. We will torch your shack if you don't." Kamaadi assured Merab that she would not be harmed but she was still very worried by the women's tormenting.

Six weeks passed. After working in her garden in the mornings, Merab would sit in her room to weave mats or read copies of *Uganda Eyogera* that Philemon brought. One morning, she prepared two mats to show to shop owners and for the first time took a bus to Kampala alone. Each of the shop owners she showed them to declined to purchase her mats, and they all seemed surprised when Merab then politely asked how much rent they were paying for their shops, some telling her and two only asking why she wanted to know. When Merab answered that she was thinking of soon starting her own mat-selling business, one of the men just laughed at her, but another encouraged her to pursue her dream.

"I can't stop worrying about my husband. I don't trust my sister wives to feed him properly," Merab said to Philemon when he visited that evening. "I know they can cook for him but when I was still in the home, I would keep an eye on what they fed him and what time they served his meals ..."

"Hey, come on! He is an adult and he decided to treat you like rubbish," Philemon said. "That's why you left him. Can't you get over it?"

"The poor women must be overwhelmed by all the responsibility in my absence, and—"

"Merab, listen to me," Philemon said. "I know you are a very kind person and your compassion seems to have no limits but I think now is the time for you to work for your own wellbeing and that of your only child. Forget about your husband and his wives."

"You are right," Merab answered, rising from the mat to go prepare a cup of tea for him. *But I still wonder what Mwami is doing right now.* When she was pouring the tea, Merab said, "But I spend a lot of time awake at night, struggling with my thoughts and wondering how I ended up here, alone and not knowing what to do next with my life."

"Just like other people, you have to make choices in life, whether you like to or not," Philemon answered, sipping his tea. "Things are hard for you now but I think the future will show that you made a good decision. I'd advise you to persevere and to stay here. After all, when you left, you had strong reasons to leave."

That night, Merab had trouble sleeping. *I don't know what I'm doing here. I have no job and no money. I can't rely on Philly—he has his own family to look after. By coming here, I intended to ensure a better future for Leah but now I don't know where I'll get money from to pay for her next school term. I think I'm failing in this adventure.* By the following morning, Merab had made up her mind to return to Kalasa without first consulting or informing Philemon. She decided to wait an extra month so that she could harvest her beans and maize before moving back, but the fact that she would be returning to Kalasa soon gave her some peace of mind.

❉　❉　❉

Lutalo missed Merab. His other wives did not serve his meals on time and they did not organize the home as well as she had. There were so many disputes between Mukuza and the newest wife, Adah, that Lutalo delayed going home whenever he could. He stayed at the shop later than before and even when he closed, he would go to join his friends to drink, something he rarely did before Merab left Kalasa. He wanted to go to ask Merab to return but was too proud to do it. But one day, he missed Merab so much that he went to Absalom to ask where she was and Absalom told him that Philemon had settled her in Kawempe.

One Sunday evening, Lutalo was seated in the living room listening to the radio while waiting for dinner when a fight broke out between Adah and Mukuza in the front yard, with Mukuza yelling at Adah for calling her a "night dancer." Lutalo broke up the fight by threatening to beat both of the women, so they stopped quarrelling and he returned to the living room. But as soon as he had walked back into the house, Mukuza said that she would beat Adah up. Adah left briefly and returned with a bunch of girls, ready to attack Mukuza. Mukuza ran and locked herself in her bedroom.

The next day after that stressful evening, Lutalo woke up early but decided not to work on his farm, instead going straight to the shop. A few minutes after he had opened it, the bus to Kampala arrived. Deciding he was going there to look for Merab, he took money for the trip from a drawer, and took a seat on the bus. He was soon lost in thought.

His friend Kabali got on the bus and sat next to him. "You didn't tell me Friday night that you would be traveling to Kampala this morning," he said, but soon realized that Lutalo seemed preoccupied and did not want to disclose the reason for his trip. "This morning there are fewer people in the bus than usual. The wait is likely to be long," Kabali said, to change the topic. "So, are you going to buy merchandise for the shop?"

"No."

"What are you going to do?"

"What do you think I am going to do?"

"If I had known the reason I wouldn't have asked."

"It's nothing serious," Lutalo answered.

"I can't believe that," Kabali said. "I know you very well, and know that you never go anywhere without a strong reason."

"I am going to see Mufuzi," Lutalo said.

"So you know where to find her?"

"I have a rough idea."

"What are you planning to do? Bring her back home?"

"We'll see," Lutalo said, changing the topic. "Have you started harvesting your beans? You planted plenty this season."

Kabali answered him but was aware that the previous topic was closed. He leaned forward to speak to the man in the seat in front of them.

Lutalo kept quiet for most of the journey, lost in thought. *I will ask her to return home. Will she want to return? Probably not—I might have to force her to return. If she says no, I will go talk to her Aunt Abigail.* He gazed out the bus window, admiring a large well-cared-for banana plantation. *I did not treat her well. I should apologize. No, I shouldn't, I am her husband—she is supposed to obey me. Why did I let her go away in the first place? No, I shouldn't have let her go away.* By now he felt a little annoyed with himself.

Lutalo got off the bus in Kawempe not knowing where to start his search. Kawempe was a big village but he was determined to look for Merab, even if it took most of the day to find her. He approached a few people and described his wife but they did not know her.

"Sir, I am looking for a tall woman," he said to a young man he'd met after about half an hour of searching. "She smiles almost all the time and she has a small gap in her teeth."

"Did she move to this village recently?" the young man asked.

"Yes."

"I think I know her—she lives that way," the young man said as he pointed to a path that led up a small hill. "Follow me, I will take you there."

"Thank you very much," Lutalo said, following the young man.

Merab saw her husband even before he walked into her front yard. It turned out that it was Mudasi, Kamaadi's son, who brought Lutalo to her home. "I am glad to see you *Mwami*," Merab said.

"I am glad to see you too, Mufuzi," Lutalo replied, surprised that his anger had immediately turned into joy when he saw his first wife. He and Merab both thanked Mudasi and then Lutalo followed Merab into her house.

Lutalo enjoyed a very calming day at Merab's house and wanted to spend the night there as well, but he decided not to because the people at home did not know where he was—he knew they assumed he was still in Kalasa, working at the shop. "I will be back soon," he told her after lunch.

When Philemon came to visit that evening, Merab told him about

Lutalo's visit.

"Oh, great. What did he say when he arrived? Wasn't he surprised to see you living here?"

"He must have been surprised but he didn't show it," she said. "He said that he was happy to see me again. Then he asked, 'Is this your house?' When I told him that it was, he hugged me and sat down. He did not ask any more questions."

"He did not even ask who built the house or where you got the money from to build it? What a character!"

"All along I knew that if he came, he wouldn't ask questions," Merab said.

"Really? Obviously, you know him better than I do," her cousin replied.

20

RUTH'S BROTHER THOMAS went to pay a visit to her at home on the day that Mitego visited her shop and while they were chatting, Thomas asked about her business.

"I am still having trouble getting the business off the ground," Ruth admitted to Thomas. "However, Mr. Mitego came by the shop and promised to give me some tips. Perhaps that will help."

"Mitego?" Thomas asked, laughing. "Don't take Mitego seriously. What did he say to you?"

"He said that we can meet sometime this week."

Thomas laughed again. "Mitego is only looking for a date. Don't expect anything useful from him."

"Come on, Tom! Surely Mitego knows that I am married. He is Daddy's friend and he attended my wedding!"

"Of course he knows, but that wouldn't stop him from developing ideas about you," Thomas said. "I know Mitego well, Ruth—but you don't seem to know him that well."

When Mitego returned to Ruth's Boutique the following morning, she was talking to a customer. Ruth went to talk to Mitego as soon as the customer left.

"Good morning Mr. Mitego," Ruth said, offering her hand to shake his.

"Good morning, Ruth," Mitego answered. "If you are not busy this evening, let's meet at the Silver Springs Hotel to discuss your business."

"Thanks Mr. Mitego, but why don't we talk here?" Ruth asked.

"No, this wouldn't be a good place for serious discussions. We should meet at a quiet place. If the hotel is not convenient, I know a couple of bars, or a restaurant where we can—"

"What? I am a married woman. I can't meet you in a bar."

"Your husband meets a woman in a bar every week, and you can do so, too" Mitego said, "After all—"

"What are you talking about?"

"You know what I am talking about. I often see Mr. Kiyaga drinking with Clotilda. You know Clotilda Kayiza, don't you?"

"That's just a malicious rumour," Ruth said, her voice rising. It was obvious to her now that Mitego had had no intention of advising her about business. "Get out of my shop—now."

"Bye, Ruth," Mitego said coolly as he left. "And don't tell your husband that I told you these things."

Ruth sat on a stool, fuming. *Tom is right. Mitego is evil. But what about Clotilda? Could it be true that Jude is seeing her?* The encounter with Mitego was going to ruin Ruth's day.

But while Ruth was cleaning the counter, her landlord, Mr. Visram, entered the shop.

"Good morning Mr. Visram," Ruth said. "How may I help you?"

"Good morning Ruth. How is the business doing?"

"Not well—in fact, I haven't sold anything yet."

"I know it is none of my business, but I have been in business for more than twenty years and maybe can give you some useful advice," Visram said. "What are you selling? Can I have a look at your stock, if you don't mind?"

"I don't mind. Over there," Ruth said, pointing to the rugs in the corner.

"These are beautiful," Visram said. "I would love to have one of these rugs in my sitting room. But are these all you have, or you have more in storage?"

"They're all I have for now."

"That's a mistake," Visram said firmly. "These are too few. You wouldn't want to run out of stock when customers start buying, would you? How long does it take for you to receive a new order?"

"At least three months. The goods are shipped from Iran to Mombasa and it takes more time to get them here."

"If I were you, I would order more stock now, and sell other things too, not just rugs. That way you'll make money quickly. You are here to make money, aren't you?"

Ruth thanked her landlord for his advice. "I'm glad you came by," she told him.

After Visram had left, Ruth sat at her desk trying to get Mitego off her mind as she began to draft an order for new stock. But what to order? She hadn't sold anything yet, so how could she know which items customers would buy?

With Hussein Mohammed's catalogue on the counter in front of her, she made a list: 25 rugs, 150 curtains (all available sizes), 4 dozen floor brushes, 60 plastic carpets, 20 flower pots. *Wait a minute—who is going to buy those?* She removed the flower pots from the list. 20 chandeliers, 100 wall decorations. She typed out the list and a note, folded the two sheets of paper and slid them into an envelope, then locked the shop and went to post the letter.

Only then did she go to the bank to check the balance on her bank account. *Good!* She had enough money to pay for the goods she had just ordered.

Walking back to the shop Ruth got an idea, and rushed to her father's office to tell him about it. Since he built houses, maybe he had clients that would be interested in the home furnishings his daughter sold—it would be one way to spread the word about her business. "Can you do that Daddy?" she asked.

"That's a brilliant idea," Collin said. "Of course I can recommend your business to my clients, and surely they can buy some items from you. Why didn't I think about that earlier?"

And so Ruth returned home that afternoon, happy that she had ordered new stock and deciding to ignore what Mitego had said about Jude and Clotilda.

✳   ✳   ✳

"Do you think it would be a good idea for me to hire a shop attendant now?" Ruth asked Jude one evening. "Actually, I ordered a variety of stock, and do you know what I'm thinking? When the stock arrives, customers are going to start flocking in."

"Yes, it would be a good idea," Jude said. "And then you won't have to be at the shop all the time. You can put a small advertisement in a newspaper and also pin a handwritten poster on the shop's door. People are always walking around the city looking for work."

I am glad that he seems to have changed his mind, Ruth thought. *He now likes my business.*

Ruth made a poster and pinned it on the door when she closed the shop the following evening. Three candidates were waiting outside the shop for her by the time she arrived the following morning. All three were men.

"Hello, good morning," Ruth said as she shook hands with each of them. "How can I help you?"

"I saw the note on the door and would like to be your shop attendant," one man said, but the others stared at her, awed by her beauty.

"Sorry, I should have been more specific. I'm looking for a female attendant," Ruth said. "But do check once in a while in the future. I'm likely to have jobs for you, too."

Ruth rewrote the poster, pinned the new one on the door, and six women responded that week, but none of them was suitable. She told Jude about it.

The next evening, when Jude met Clotilda at Suzana Night Club, he mentioned that Ruth was looking for a shop attendant.

By Wednesday of the following week, Ruth still hadn't found a candidate to fill the job, when a cheerful young woman came into the shop. "I read the note on the door," she told Ruth. "I would like to apply for the position of shop attendant. My name is Petua Nakakawa."

Ruth pointed to a stool for the young woman to sit. "Do you have retail shop experience?" she asked. Unlike the previous candidates, Petua impressed Ruth with her eye contact.

"Yes I do," Petua said. "I worked in my brother's shop here in Kampala for two years and sold a variety of products, including cosmetics."

"Good," Ruth said, impressed by the young woman's direct manner. "What do you think is the most important thing for a business like mine?"

"Service to the customers and attention to their needs would be the two most important things—without happy customers who buy and come back to buy some more, a business won't do well, however good the items it sells may be."

"Yes, great," Ruth said. "But what makes you a perfect candidate for my boutique?"

"I love home furnishings, and I am meticulous and organised."

"Do you know what I'm thinking? I like you. However, my business is new and I don't have enough money to pay you a big salary—"

"I wouldn't mind. I'm ready to help your business grow. I can earn a good salary later," Petua said.

Ruth asked her to begin the next morning and Petua accepted. They chatted a little longer and both were very happy by the time they parted. When the new stock arrived a few days later, they spent a busy two weeks sorting and displaying the various items.

※　　※　　※

Petua was standing behind the counter of the shop one morning when she saw a beautiful Mercedes-Benz park on the street in front of the boutique, and watched as a soldier hopped out to open the back car door for a very tall smartly uniformed officer.

The officer and two bodyguards strode into the shop. "Good morning," he said to Petua.

"Hello," Petua replied.

The officer walked around the shop, the bodyguards close behind him, touching and examining the rugs. "These are very good," he said.

"Yes, they are very beautiful," Petua said.

The men remained in the shop for about five minutes, examining several of the items, before nodding to Petua and walking out.

When Ruth arrived, Petua told her about the visit and described the officer. "He was very tall with a few grey hairs at the front, and he had a slight limp."

"That must have been Zoki, the army officer in charge of training,"

Ruth said. "I don't know him well but I met him two times while I was still Assistant DEO."

The following morning, Ruth was the first to arrive at the boutique and shortly after she had opened, Zoki came again, this time in a Land Rover and with three soldiers. One soldier stood at the door while the other two entered the boutique with their commander. As soon as they walked into the shop, Ruth rose from her seat and walked straight to Zoki with her hand stretched out to shake his. Zoki looked surprised.

"Good morning, Colonel Zoki," Ruth said as she gave the officer a firm handshake. Zoki was not only impressed by Ruth's looks and confidence but was also happy that she had addressed him as "Colonel"—one rank higher than his actual rank of Lieutenant-Colonel.

"Good morning my, lady," Zoki answered. "What is your name?"

"My name is Ruth Kiyaga, the owner of Ruth's Boutique. Are you looking for an item in particular or do you need a moment to look around?"

"Have we met before?" Zoki asked, smiling.

"Yes. Twice, when I was an Assistant DEO."

"Yes...Ruth. Sorry, I think I'm getting old," he said. "How else would I explain why I forgot who the beautiful lady is?"

Ruth asked again, ignoring his comment, "Are you looking for an item in particular or do you need a moment to look around?"

"I came here yesterday—I love those rugs," Zoki said, walking towards the stack of rugs in the corner. "Pick two, one in each pattern," Zoki said to two of his men in Swahili as he stood, staring at Ruth.

They picked a rug each and carried them out of the shop while the third soldier stood beside his commander. Ruth looked at Zoki inquisitively. *He hasn't asked how much the rugs cost.*

"How much do I owe?" Zoki asked, pulling a wad of cash out of his pocket.

"Two thousand shillings," Ruth answered.

"That's too cheap for such beautiful rugs. But it's your business, beautiful lady, not mine. You'll not make profit if you sell each rug at one thousand shillings," Zoki said, as if he knew what they had cost her.

Her first sale! Ruth's hand shook as she took the money.

"I'll send more customers your way," Zoki said as he and the soldier walked out the door. "I know many men who will want one of these rugs and your other merchandise."

Petua had just been walking into the store and had heard what the lieutenant-colonel told Ruth. That evening she went to present a report to Clotilda, as she'd agreed to do when there were "noteworthy events."

"If Zoki and others like him are going to spend money like that, they are going to enrich Ruth," Clotilda said. "That's not good." She began to think of how she could sabotage Ruth's business.

When Zoki returned to the boutique two days later with two men and a woman who bought between them six rugs, a dozen curtains and three chandeliers, Petua again reported to Clotilda.

Zoki returned twice the following month, bringing people with him who'd always buy something, and each time it happened, Petua reported to Clotilda.

When Clotilda and Jude met at the Speke Hotel one weekend, she asked him, "Do you know that Ruth has dealings with Colonel Zoki?"

"Colonel Zoki? The soldier? What kind of dealings would Ruth have with Zoki?" Jude's heart was racing. "I know of no connection between Ruth and Zoki!"

"Zoki is a regular at the shop—why would he frequent the shop if he had no deals there?" Clotilda asked, her voice insinuating. "That shop doesn't sell day-to-day essentials."

Jude lost his temper. *What could Ruth be doing with a soldier? But can I trust Clotilda? She probably wants to tarnish Ruth's name.* He decided to ask Ruth about Zoki.

21

APRIL 1962 – MAY 1963

"PHILLY, I HAVE noticed that you leave work early these days to go to Kawempe. Are you seeing a woman there?" Philemon's boss Mitego asked, laughing.

"No, I'm not seeing a woman—I do go to Kawempe frequently but it's because my cousin has just moved into her home there. She is the one I go to see."

"Tell me more about her," Mitego said. Philemon knew Mitego must be thinking about meeting for a date with her.

"Her name is Merab. She has just left her marital home to settle in Kawempe, to start a new life. She would like to start—"

"That means she is divorced from her husband," Mitego said, a smirk on his face.

"No, she is not divorced. She is establishing a new home here in the city."

"A woman? On her own?"

"Yes, she is very determined to start a new home. She is very hardworking."

"But why do you care so much about her?"

"Levi, her father, helped me when my own father kicked me out for refusing to go to church. Levi actually paid for my final two years in school."

"Can I meet Merab? I think I can find a way of helping her," Mitego said.

"That's very kind of you. I will make arrangements for you to meet," Philemon said, although he did not want Merab to meet Mitego.

❋   ❋   ❋

In Kalasa, Nabukalu noticed that the home no longer functioned properly. It was no longer as clean as when Merab still lived there. Meals were late, and many chores were not done. When Nabukalu returned home one afternoon and found that coffee beans that Mukuza had put out in the front yard to dry in the sun had been washed away by rain, she confronted her about it. "Mukuza, this is unacceptable. How could it happen? Everybody was here at home when the rain started!"

"Don't talk to me like that! You are getting too familiar with me," Mukuza replied.

"Sorry, but I have to speak up," Nabukalu said. "We shouldn't expect Lutalo to manage his shop, plan for the family and at the same time be here at home to take care of things which the rest of us can do."

"If you knew that there were chores that needed to be done, why didn't you do them? You chose to go away to gossip all afternoon," Mukuza answered.

Nabukalu ignored the comment. "I have noticed that since Mufuzi left this home, everything is not right. It seems some of you—"

"So what's your point? If you expected us to stop living our lives because Mufuzi is no longer here, you are mistaken. Besides, if you think that she was so great, why don't you go live with her, wherever she is?"

"You forced Mufuzi to abandon the family that she worked hard to build.

You wanted to take her place as the favourite wife, but let me tell you—you can't compete with Mufuzi," Nabukalu said. "She is in a class of her own."

"Stop praising her! She is a witch," Mukuza answered.

"You are the witch. You used your magic medicine to send Mufuzi away from her home," Nabukalu answered before walking away fuming, and now determined to go to live with her friend, Merab.

❉　❉　❉

Lutalo returned to Merab's home two weeks later with a few of his belongings, including his newest bicycle. When he arrived, Merab was digging in her garden near the front yard.

"I'm very glad to see you, *Mwami*," Merab said.

"I'm very glad to see you too, Mufuzi."

Merab stopped digging and they went into the house. She brought a mat and placed it on the floor for Lutalo to sit on. "I'm sorry I don't have a chair," she said.

"There's no problem with that. I'll sit on the mat," Lutalo said. After the greetings, he went back outside, and while he was getting the things that were tied to the bicycle, Merab went to the back of the house for a quick bath.

When Merab sat down twenty minutes later, Lutalo had untied the load of things he had wrapped in a tablecloth and took out some new cloth, which he gave to Merab. "Take this," he said. "It's for you to make a *gomesi* for yourself. I would like to say how truly sorry I am for mistreating you and for breaching my vows. Today, I have left the other women and I'm returning to you."

"Thank you very much," Merab said, taking the cloth into her arms and starting to cry.

Lutalo watched his wife in silence as she struggled to compose herself.

"I'm very glad to hear that you're recommitting to me. Are you abandoning your wives for good?" Merab finally asked.

"I'm not abandoning them; they'll still live at home. However, I'm officially done with them. Each of them will do as she wishes from now on."

"Did you tell them that?"

"No, I did not. I have come to live here with you for now. After we've settled down, I'll inform them. There's no hurry. They are not going anywhere."

Poor women, what are they going to do next? Merab thought. *They trusted a selfish man who has now decided to abandon them. That's very sad.* "You're welcome to our new smaller home. The land belongs to Philly," Merab explained. "He gave me an acre to build this house on but we are free to till his entire plot of land, which is five acres large. He said that if I get money in the future, I can buy the rest of the land from him."

"That's very kind of him. He is a very organized man, unlike some of us."

Merab was surprised to hear Lutalo criticizing himself for the first time.

"I think it would be a good idea for us to buy the entire land. My plan would then be to construct another building here to open a shop," Lutalo said.

"Would you like to operate the same kind of shop here as in Kalasa? Have you thought of looking for a job in the city instead?" Merab asked.

"What kind of job would I do at my age? No, I'll continue as I'm doing now. We need to talk to Philly so I begin construction right away."

"Philly often comes to pay me a visit. You'll talk to him," Merab answered.

Lutalo kept quiet for a few minutes and Merab realized that he seemed to be worrying about something. "Are you all right?" she asked.

"There is something I haven't told you. I was never in a relationship with the young woman, Adah."

"What do you mean?"

"When I brought her home, I thought that she was going to be my wife but I found out that very evening that she did not love me. She has never let me enter her bedroom or even touch her. I realized later that she only wanted a place to live."

"What?"

"Yes. So, throughout the time she has been living at home, whenever I spent the night in her house—I had put her in that small house that faces west—I slept on a heap of dried coffee beans while she slept in the bedroom."

"Oh, oh, that's very strange!"

"I continued doing that because I wanted to save face. But two weeks ago I heard rumours that she is pregnant with Enos's child, so—"

Merab looked puzzled. "Enos?"

"Yes. Enos, Yafesi's nephew. So, the day before yesterday, I asked her about it and she admitted that she was indeed pregnant with Enos's child. I sent her away immediately."

"I'm sorry you had to go through all that, *Mwami*."

"So I told myself I'd better sober up, leave the mess that I created and go to my beloved wife. That's why I am here, Mufuzi. I can't say how sorry I am. Please forgive me."

Merab wept again. "I am sad to know that you've gone through all that, *Mwami*. I forgive you. Let's start our relationship afresh. Leah will be very happy to see you living here with us. She loves you very much."

"Even after everything I have put you through?"

"She loves you very much," Merab repeated firmly. "I am sure about that."

A few days later, Lutalo and Merab were having lunch when he said, "I wish you had told me that you planned to move to the city. I have land in a village called Bukoto which is even nearer to the city than Kawempe."

"Oh, so wouldn't it have been better to live there instead of in Kalasa?" she asked.

"I could not move out of the large chief's home in Kalasa to a place where there was no home. The land I'm talking about is vacant. A friend of my father's who was a county chief in this area gave it to him and I inherited it—it's still all bush. But now that I am here I'll see what to do about it."

Two months after Lutalo moved into Merab's home, he started constructing a small building for his shop. And Kamaadi and Katiiti had already stopped coming to Merab's home as soon as her husband had appeared.

※　※　※

Kamaadi had told Merab that he'd heard that Philemon's boss was very rich. Merab had remembered what he'd said and now, a few months later, she asked Philemon where Mitego's money came from.

"Mitego's main source of income is from trading in coffee beans," Philemon told her. "He and his friend Patel own a building in the city—that's actually where I work—and he has several retail shops, too. He is really a jack-of-all-trades. Oh, he also owns rental properties, from shacks to bungalows."

"That's interesting. Is he very educated?"

"No. He has no formal education whatsoever. He's simply smart. He has never seen the inside of a classroom."

"What?"

Philemon nodded. "And by the way, people claim that Mitego has between seventy to ninety children. He has concubines in every trading centre around Kampala."

"What?"

"Yes, listen to this strange incident I witnessed. One day, I went with him to a school where many of his children studied. While he was talking to the headmaster in the school compound, a girl of about eight years came and knelt down and greeted him, addressing him as 'Father.' When Mitego asked her who her mother was, I saw the headmaster discreetly shake his head in disbelief."

"What?"

"Yes. That's Mitego for you."

"Thanks for all that information about your rich boss," Merab said. "I would like to meet him."

"What? Do you really? You would have to do one of two things for Mitego in order to get anything from him. Either you join his army of concubines or you make money for him."

"I can make money for him."

"How do you think you can do that?"

"I'll find a way—trust me, Philly."

"Don't get yourself into a mess that you'll regret, Merab. Now that you have Lutalo back, you don't want to cross paths with Mitego. By the way, do you have food?"

"Thank you," she said. "I do need some groceries."

"You are welcome," Philemon said. "I'll buy you some groceries and send one of our drivers to deliver them."

❉   ❉   ❉

Two hours later, while Merab was napping, the sound of a truck in her front yard woke her, and she went out to see what was going on. She watched as the driver switched off the engine, fetched a bunch of *matooke* plantain and other groceries from the back of the truck and offered them to her.

"Hello, my name is Karoli," the driver said to Merab. "Philly sent me to deliver these to you."

"Thank you, Karoli. Please come in," Merab said.

After greeting him, she opened a thermos and poured him a cup of tea. "Karoli, tell me about Mr. Mitego. I would like to ask him for some business opportunities. What are my chances—"

"You are a beautiful woman. Of course Mitego will want you to be his girlfriend. I don't see any other way you can deal with him. Let me warn you, he has an insatiable desire for women."

"Aren't there any business opportunities? Philly tells me that Mr. Mitego has many businesses."

"True, there are some business opportunities," Karoli said, thinking for a moment. "Mitego buys a lot of dry produce like maize, beans, soya beans and sesame for resale. If you can find those at a very cheap price, you are in business."

"Thank you very much for that information, Karoli. When and where can I meet him?"

"The easiest place to meet him is at his maize mill—it's only about a half hour's walk from here," he said. "Go straight to the main road, turn left and then continue for about two kilometres. The maize mill is on the right side of the road. You can't miss it, and I'm sure he'll be there tomorrow morning."

"Then I'll go there to meet him."

✳   ✳   ✳

When Merab arrived at the mill the following day, she asked a man sitting at the reception desk and typing, whether she could speak to Mr. Mitego.

"Do you have an appointment?" the employee asked, surprised. "What's your name? Who should I say wants to speak to him?"

"My name is Merab. I'm Philemon Mukuye's cousin."

The employee asked her to wait but didn't stop typing so she sat on a bench and waited. Half an hour later, three men came in and joined her on the bench. It was clear that the receptionist knew them because he told them right away that Mitego would be late. Only then did Merab realize that Mitego was not yet in the office.

When a large man speaking at the top of his voice walked in shortly after, Merab did not need to ask who he was. He shook hands first with the men and then with Merab, giving her an inquisitive look before the employee explained who she was. Mitego said he would see her first, before his appointment with the men. The men exchanged glances with each other and the employee and smiled as Mitego pointed Merab in the direction of his office and walked behind, ogling her.

"How are you, dear?" he asked, embracing Merab in a bear hug as soon as they reached his narrow office at the back of the noisy maize mill.

"I am very well, thank you," Merab answered, trying to keep her voice steady after the awkwardness of the hug. "Philly has told me a lot of great things about you."

"Philly exaggerates sometimes," he said, obviously pleased. "How do you find life in the city?"

That was the kind of question that Merab was waiting for. She did not want to give Mitego an opportunity to ask about her social life—straight to business was much better. "Life is challenging without a job. But Philly tells me that you can help me. I can supply dried maize for your mill if you gave me the opportunity."

"Do you grow it yourself?"

"No, but I can buy it from farmers at a good price, a lower price than what you are buying at now. I am good at bargaining."

"You're sure?" he smiled. "Okay, come back here tomorrow morning before 8 o'clock and ask to speak with Karoli. He will give you further instructions. Everything should go well because you're a brilliant woman," Mitego said. He hugged Merab again, this time tightly.

❋　❋　❋

Philemon could not believe his ears when Merab told him that she had met Mitego. "Where did you meet him?" he asked.

"When you sent Karoli here, I asked him about Mitego and his schedule. He told me that the best place to meet him was at the maize mill," Merab answered. "So I walked there and talked to him."

"Wasn't he surprised to see you?"

"Not so much. You could even think that he was expecting me."

"Did he ask questions about you?"

"No, we discussed only business."

"That's good. However, you should be careful when you talk to Mitego. He is like a big child. He says whatever crosses his mind. He can't keep secrets."

❋　❋　❋

"Good morning, Mufuzi," Karoli said when he and Merab met at the maize mill the next day. "Mr. Mitego instructed me to help you to start buying produce. I guess you have some money to start? And what crops do you intend to buy?"

"I don't have any money but I know people in the village where I was born who can supply dried beans and maize on credit. We can pay them later," Merab said.

That very morning they drove to Senge and to Karoli's surprise, returned with the truck a quarter-full of produce without having paid a single coin for it. From that time on, Merab would go twice a week with Karoli and three of Mitego's other workers to buy beans and maize. She soon decided that instead of sitting at home the rest of the week, she would go into the city to look for other people who could buy more produce from her. She went to Nakasero Market and established some contacts. Soon after, she regularly delivered sacks of fresh produce in the evenings which she left out in the open for the buyers to find in the morning, going back during the day to collect her payments.

One morning, Merab had gone to collect her payment from Mitego's office in Kampala when she saw a large group of workers at a multi-storey office building that was under construction. She watched the men for some time. *There are many men working here. I don't think they can go without food the whole day—I could cook food to sell to them. Nabukalu can join me in the business.*

When she returned home, she told Lutalo about the possible business opportunity. Two weeks later, Nabukalu came to Kawempe with her few belongings. "Mufuzi, I really missed you! Thanks for inviting me to join you," she said. "It had become increasingly difficult for me to live in the same home as Mukuza—"

"Mukuza is a very difficult person," Merab said. "You'll be all right here. We'll find some work for you to do."

Merab had Nabukalu move her belongings into the second room, leaving the third for storage.

Lutalo also opened his shop and the villagers responded well, immediately coming in large numbers to buy from him. Three days after Lutalo had opened the shop, Musirise's firstborn son, Roger, also came to stay in Kawempe so he could go to study in Kololo Secondary School. The home became lively and Merab was happy to have the company.

When Merab talked to Mitego about her idea of cooking food and selling it to the men at the construction site, Mitego was positive about it. "That's a brilliant idea, Mufuzi. You really are a money-maker. You can set up at the back of my building—for now, free of charge," and he asked one of his employees to show her the back alley where she could start her business. Merab bought four big saucepans, some plates and cups and two charcoal stoves, and borrowed two benches from Mitego's office. The following week, Nabukalu started cooking and selling breakfast to the workers at the construction site, with Merab joining her in the day to serve lunch. Merab was the business owner and Nabukalu was the worker.

Merab's makeshift eatery became popular so quickly that she and Nabukalu started getting customers other than the men who worked at the construction site, and she had to buy four more benches for customers to sit on while they ate. At that stage, Mitego started collecting monthly rent from her. Soon, there were even more customers and Merab gave up the business of buying produce in order to work full time at the eatery.

"I'm glad your business is growing so fast," Philemon told Merab one afternoon.

"I'm very glad too, but my poor husband has to endure the loneliness at home while I am here working every day," she said. "It's too bad that I can't be home to serve him his lunch. He is used to being served."

"Don't worry about Lutalo—change is catching up with him and men like him who have chosen to leave the rural areas, and he will get used to the loneliness, if he is lonely. He is a grown man and knows the necessity of what you are doing. That's what it means to settle in the city."

❋   ❋   ❋

Early one morning six months after Merab's eatery had opened, two men came to talk to her. From the formal way they were dressed, Merab guessed that they were not her typical customers. "Madam, can we have a look at your trading licence?" one of the men asked. "You need a licence to operate a business in the city."

"I didn't know that, sir."

"Ignorance of the law is no defence," the second man said. "How did you start operating here?"

"The owner of this building, Mr. Mitego, gave me permission to operate my business here," Merab said. "I pay him to use this place."

"You pay him?" the men asked simultaneously, laughing.

"I know Mr. Mitego but this alley has nothing to do with him. It's not part of his building. It is the property of the city," one man said.

Merab looked shocked.

"You've got seven days to vacate this place. Your business here is illegal," the first man told her, as he signed and handed an eviction slip to Merab. "If you continue operating here, your property may be confiscated and you could pay a hefty fine."

Nabukalu had been busy boiling milk in a large saucepan during this conversation, and soon after the men left, several customers turned up for breakfast and business went on as usual. But Merab was furious. *I have been paying Mitego to use a place that does not belong to him?*

"What?" Nabukalu said, almost in tears when Merab told her about the eviction notice. "Does it mean that we have to close the business down and stay at home?"

"No. That's not what we're going to do," Merab said. "We'll move the business elsewhere in the city. Our regular customers will follow us so long as we don't move far away. I'll ask Philly to help us find a new place. But I'm really angry with that man Mitego."

When Philemon came for lunch as usual, Merab told him what had happened. "And we have just seven days to vacate this place," she said, handing the eviction slip to Philemon.

"That's bad news, but I knew that it would happen because you didn't have any experience," Philemon said to his cousin. "But now you know this business works, and you can relocate it."

"But did you know all along that this place didn't belong to Mitego?"

"Yes, I knew that."

"Then why didn't you tell me? I've been paying Mitego rent for it every month!"

"Merab, before you met Mitego, I told you that you could do only one of two things for him, either to become his mistress or to make money for him. You did the latter."

"That's so sad," Merab said. "He needs to fleece me, a poor woman?"

"Don't regret it," Philemon said. "After all, now you have a business. I think the best place for you to relocate will be to Nakasero Market, in the heart of the city. I know you will succeed there."

* * *

"*Mwami*, you seem to be settling comfortably here but I am concerned about what's happening in Kalasa. Why don't you entrust the responsibility to someone who can report to you? We can't rely on Yafesi alone to run the farm," Merab said to Lutalo that evening.

"You've read my mind—I am planning to ask Absalom. He is a trustworthy man and I think he will accept the responsibility," Lutalo said. "What I lack is the courage to face Mukuza and to break up with her. I fear her." He paused, thoughtful. "It will be easier to break up with Musirise."

Merab did not respond.

A few days later, Lutalo went to Kalasa and asked Absalom to help take care of his farm. Absalom accepted gladly, but only after Lutalo told him he was ending his relationships with Mukuza and Musirise.

Absalom accompanied Lutalo to his home, and after the greetings, Lutalo asked the two women to sit down to talk in his presence. "Mukuza and Musirise," Lutalo began, "I love and respect both of you because not only are you the mothers of my children, you are wonderful people. However, I am sorry to say that I will no longer be your husband."

"What do you mean?" Mukuza asked.

"Bringing you to this home was a mistake, which I have regretted numerous—"

"Do you mean that our relationship with you was a mistake?" Mukuza asked sharply. "Our children are a mistake?"

Musirise started crying. Absalom buried his face in his hands.

"No, our relationship was not a mistake. What I meant..." he hesitated. "...What I wanted to say was that from now onwards, I have entrusted the responsibility of caring for the farm with my brother-in-law Absalom."

"Are you abandoning us and your children?" Mukuza asked.

"Absalom will take care of everything on my behalf. If you have any complaints, address them to him," Lutalo said as he rose.

Mukuza continued to quarrel and Musirise to cry.

22

"PETUA, SINCE WE are not busy this afternoon, let's close the shop early. I don't think any more customers will be coming in," Ruth said.

"I don't think so either," Petua said, opening the drawer to count the day's cash.

When Petua went to Ruth's office to hand her the money, she looked nervous. "Are you all right?" Ruth asked.

"No. There's something I have wanted to tell you for the past month," Petua said and then paused. "I wanted to tell you that Clotilda Kayiza asked me to spy on you and the business and to report to her ever since I started working for you."

"Really?"

"Yes, but I didn't pass on any information to her that would be detrimental to you and the business," Petua said.

"I'm glad to know that you did the right thing," Ruth said, seemingly unshocked by what Petua had just told her.

"However, because reporting to her was a condition for her to help me get the job, I've been reporting trivial occurrences to her." When Ruth didn't say anything, Petua continued. "It was Clotilda who tipped me about the vacancy and coached me for the interview. Before I started working for you I was a teacher in her school."

"Thank you for being honest and for letting me know," Ruth said, and then the two women were silent.

"Have a good evening," Petua said as she closed the door on her way out.

❋   ❋   ❋

The following day, Mrs. Kawuka, the deputy headmistress at Clotilda's Lungujja Primary School, happened to be visiting Ruth at her home.

"Yesterday Petua finally spilled the beans," Ruth told her. "She told me that Clotilda hired her to spy on me and my business. And what was most surprising was that I hadn't asked her anything. She just volunteered the information."

"Actually, I don't think she is getting anything from Clotilda in return for the information," Mrs. Kawuka said.

"I don't think so, either. Poor girl, I won't fire her. She does a very good job at the shop. And now that she has come clean, I don't think I'll need *you* to spy on Clotilda anymore."

"Mrs. Kiyaga, you still need someone to keep an eye on Clotilda at all times. She will do everything she can to try to bring you down. And I must confess that the money you pay me here and there really helps me and my family. Clotilda rarely pays our salaries on time."

❋   ❋   ❋

Jude was walking out of Kamulu's Bar shortly after 7 o'clock one evening when Clotilda accosted him. "Hey, what do you want now?" he asked. "I'm going home."

"Listen, Jude, I'm tired of your son asking me who his father is. He is with me in the car. I'll introduce him to you."

"Right now? Are you stupid? It's already dark!"

"It doesn't matter. Talk to him and if you want, I can arrange for you to meet him during the day."

Jude saw Clement for the first time, and the boy seemed very happy to see him. But Jude himself felt somewhat distant.

❋   ❋   ❋

"Ruth, do you know Colonel Zoki?" Jude finally got the courage to ask Ruth one evening, a month after Petua's confession.

"Yes, I do," Ruth answered.

"Why does he frequent your shop?"

"How do you know that he frequents the shop?"

"You didn't answer my question," Jude said, his voice rising.

"Zoki comes to the shop sometimes to buy, sometimes to see what's in stock."

"I see."

"And you didn't answer mine—how do you know that Zoki frequents the shop?"

Jude got up and went to the bedroom without answering. Ruth followed him there a few minutes later. "So instead of going to work you hang around to find out what's going on at the shop?"

"Don't be silly. I just wanted to know why Zoki frequents the shop, that's all."

"Have you been meeting with Clotilda?"

"Clotilda who?"

"You know who I am talking about. Clotilda Kayiza. She is the only person who could have informed you about Zoki's visits to the shop."

"How do you know?" Jude asked, his heart racing.

"Have you been meeting with Clotilda?"

Jude did not answer. He stalked out of the house and drove to Kamulu's Bar. He'd join his friend Darlington for the evening.

Ruth put some clothes and toiletries in a bag and went to the backyard, where the children were chatting. "I'm going out now. I'll be back tomorrow," she told them.

"Mummy, where are you going to? You look upset," Herbert said.

"I'm going home to see Daddy and Mummy. I'll be back tomorrow."

"All right, we'll see you tomorrow," Kate said.

❄   ❄   ❄

Jude returned late at night, drunk. It was unusual that Ruth was not in the bedroom but he did not look for her. How had she found out that it was Clotilda who informed him about Zoki's visits to the shop? He laid awake for an hour, puzzling over that question before he finally fell asleep.

When he woke up in the morning, there was still no sign of Ruth. After he had dressed, he went to Kate's bedroom and woke her. "Where is your mother?"

"She went to our grandparents' home last evening."

"Oh, I see. You prepare my breakfast, then—otherwise I'll be late for work."

That afternoon, Jude left his workplace earlier than usual to go talk to Ruth. But when he got to the Boutique, Petua told him that Ruth had not come to work at all.

Jude wondered what he should do. He knew his children would ask about her when he got home, so he decided he'd drive to his parents-in-law's home to talk to her.

When he got there, Collin opened the door. "Jude, I am glad to see you. Please come in," his father-in-law said.

"I'm glad to see you too, Daddy," Jude said as he entered the living room. But after the greetings, as they chatted about the weather, Jude could not hide his nervousness.

Eunia came into the living room and left immediately after formally welcoming Jude to their home, which made him even more uneasy. Eunia had always been cheerful towards him.

"Ruth and I had a disagreement last evening," Jude said to Collin. "She then left home without my knowledge. Is she here?"

"Yes," Collin said. "I'll let her know that you are here to see her."

Eunia and Ruth were in Ruth's old bedroom and Ruth was crying. "Ruth, will you go talk to your husband?" Collin asked.

"No, I don't want to talk to him," Ruth answered.

"It's a very complicated matter. I don't think this is the right place to discuss it," Eunia said to Collin. "Your sister Miriam might have to mediate."

"What's the matter?" Collin asked as he closed the door and sat on the bed.

"I have reasons to believe that Jude is having an affair with Clotilda Kayiza,"

Ruth answered.

"Who?" Collin asked.

"Clotilda is Walter Kayiza's niece," Eunia told him. "She was one of my students."

"What makes you believe your husband is having an affair?" Collin asked.

"I don't think we should investigate that now," Eunia said. "Ruth, go talk to your husband—he is waiting."

"No. I don't want to talk to him."

Collin went back to the living room. "It seems Ruth doesn't want to talk now. I suggest you give her some time."

"I'm happy that she is safe and sound here," Jude said as he rose to go.

"I'll ask her to go home this evening," Collin said, walking Jude to his car.

Back in the bedroom, Eunia was continuing to plead with Ruth to go back to her home. "I know it is hard, but you are also a mother. You have to go back home to see your children."

❋ ❋ ❋

Ruth returned home later that evening. She greeted Jude, who was in the living room reading a newspaper and Herbert, who was watching the news on TV, before going to the kitchen where Victoria, Kate, and Nampa the maid were preparing dinner.

During dinner, Ruth talked to everybody except Jude, who left most of his food on the plate and went back to his newspaper. She went straight to the bedroom after dinner.

Jude followed her there soon after. He was very nervous. "Darling, I'm sorry," he said. "I'm sorry that I upset you."

"Have you been meeting with Clotilda?"

"Yes, I have," he said. "I'm sorry about it. But Clotilda is my friend, that's all."

"Are you having an affair with Clotilda?"

"Come on!" Jude said. "Don't be silly."

"Jude, you'll have to tell the truth if you don't want me to leave you."

"I don't care. You can leave if you want."

"I don't want to leave but I want to know the truth," Ruth said, emptying her bag.

As Ruth began picking out dresses to place in the suitcase, Jude watched her in silence until he seemed to explode, shouting, "Where do you think you are going?"

"You've just said that you don't care if I leave. I *will* leave unless you tell me the truth now." She paused. "My room is still available for me in my parents' house."

"Yes," Jude said. "I did have an affair with Clotilda in the past but not anymore."

Ruth started crying. She was seated on the bed facing him but Jude did not move or say anything "Why did you do it?" Ruth asked when she had regained a bit of composure.

"I don't know. I am very sorry."

Ruth jumped up and tried to open the bedroom door but Jude blocked the way.

"Sit down. Don't go out," he said. "The children shouldn't see you in this state. We can't involve the children in these—"

"You are going to tell us everything," Ruth said. "And you will apologize to the children, too."

"I'm sorry, Ruth. When you left for England, Clotilda tempted me—"

"Your relationship started while I was in England?"

"Yes, but I left her when she became pregnant."

"So it is you who are the father of Clotilda's son? Does the boy know that you are his father?"

"Yes."

"But why, Jude? Why did you cheat on me?"

"I am so sorry, darling. I don't know how I can describe how sorry I am. Clotilda is a terrible woman. She used me."

"Do your parents know that you have an illegitimate child?"

"Yes, they do."

"You told them about it but you didn't tell me?"

"I am so sorry, darling."

"We have to tell the children," Ruth said. "And let the boy come meet them if he really is their half-brother."

23

July 1963

"HOW DO I go about starting a business in Nakasero Market?" Merab asked Philemon. "This time, I want to go through the proper channels."

"I think the first thing you need to do is go visit the market to get acquainted with it," Philemon said.

"Where do I begin?"

"Simply walk around to see what goes on there. If you want, I can take you on a tour of the market tonight after work."

"Yes, thanks. That will help."

Philemon took Merab to the market for a tour, and went back a second time so that Merab could arrange to rent a stall. Before she wound up her business in the back alley, she let her customers know where she'd be relocating.

Two weeks later, Merab opened her food-vending stall in Nakasero Market. The two women already selling food there seemed to be welcoming. One of them, Balinja, helped sweep the area while Merab and Nabukalu placed two benches and a large table on the bare ground, started their two charcoal stoves and began cooking. Towards the lunch hour, Merab was very happy to note that several of her regular customers from the back alley had followed her to the market to enjoy more of her delicious meals. Balinja and the other woman were very surprised by the number of customers that the newcomers already had. "You are not new in the food business, are you?" Balinja asked Nabukalu.

"No, we are not," Nabukalu said, and told her about the eviction.

By the end of the month, the two benches and one table were no longer enough to seat all the customers they were getting. Merab got permission from the market's managers to add an extra table and another two benches and hired a girl to serve the meals.

As Merab's business grew, Balinja became less and less friendly. At the end of business one day about three months after she'd opened her market stall she asked Balinja if, as usual, she wanted some leftover tilapia and *matooke* plantain, Balinja's favourite dish.

"No, I don't want any food," Balinja said, curtly, and soon she even stopped responding to Merab's greetings in the morning and stopped chatting with her.

Twice a week, after work, Philemon went to see Merab in the market and he was happy to note her progress. "Do you still miss the back alley? Business is certainly a lot better here than there."

"That's true, but a problem is cropping up here. Our competitors are not happy with us," Merab said, gesturing in Balinja's direction.

"Well, there's nothing you can do about that. Carry on with your business. If they find that they can't cope with your pace, they will relocate or go out of business altogether," Philemon whispered.

A month later, Philemon noticed two men eating in silence at one of Merab's tables when he came by, and saw that when the men finished their dinner, they washed the saucepans and the dishes, dried the plates and cups and placed them in the saucepans and then picked up the rubbish that littered the ground. They then placed some food in banana leaves and secured the packages with banana fibre. They thanked Nabukalu and Merab for the meal and left with the packed food.

"You hired two more employees?" Philemon asked.

"No, those men can't afford to pay for their dinner, so they help us by washing the dishes and cleaning up in exchange for the food. You noticed that they also take some food—that is for their families," Merab said, smiling. "It's a good arrangement. They get their dinner and we get our work done."

A few days later, Mitego asked about Merab's business. Philemon told him that it seemed to be doing well. "Merab surprises me," he added. "When I think about her, I get a feeling that she has a split personality."

"What do you mean?" Mitego asked.

"There is Merab the very kind, caring, motherly woman, then there is Mufuzi the shrewd businesswoman," Philemon answered.

Mitego laughed. "Is that so?"

"Oh yes. For example, when I went to see her at the market the other day, I noticed that she feeds two men every evening free of charge. Well, but not really free of charge. They don't pay for their dinner but they clean her dishes and the stall in exchange for food."

"Really?" Mitego said. "That woman is going to make a lot of money. I'd want to have her as *my* wife."

Philemon laughed very loudly.

* * *

"*Mwami*, my business is doing better than I expected," Merab said to Lutalo one evening.

"Good. Since you are now sure about its viability, we can invest more money in it," Lutalo answered.

"That's exactly what I wanted to talk to you about. I was thinking of moving the business away from the market—it is now too crowded and my competitors are becoming more and more hostile. I would like to open a real restaurant."

"If all goes well," Lutalo said, "that will be possible. Today I went to see my vacant land in Bukoto—and there is a group of doctors who want to buy half of it on which to build a medical clinic."

"Oh, that would be a huge boost to my idea!"

"Do you think you know enough to run a restaurant?"

"I can hire people who have the knowledge," Merab told her husband. "I'll ask Philly for advice."

❋   ❋   ❋

"Philly, I've got an idea and as usual I trust you to tell me if it is good or bad," Merab said to Philemon a few days later. "My business has performed better than I expected. Now I'm thinking of opening a restaurant. Would it be a good idea?"

"What kind of restaurant were you thinking of opening?"

"A well-furnished restaurant in a permanent building. *Mwami* is willing to help with the initial capital, and I think I am ready to do it."

"It is a good idea but you would need, among other things, to hire qualified staff. You should visit other restaurants to get an idea how they operate, ask about rents," he advised her. "Look around, and I will help you, too, by asking around how much it would cost per month to rent a space for a restaurant."

Merab thanked Philemon but for the next three months, although finding a place to open a restaurant was at the back of her mind, she did not do it. *How can I? I have no time!* She thought. *I'm too busy running* this *food stall!*

One morning, when Merab arrived at the stall, Nabukalu and Balinja were quarrelling, and when Merab tried to intervene, Balinja silenced her abruptly.

"Shut up, Mufuzi! You are a witch! You've taken away all our customers and you are running us out of business."

"Pardon me?" Merab said.

"I'll repeat it—you are a witch."

"What?" Merab said, trying to keep calm as she placed her handbag on the bench. "I don't intercept customers—people *choose* to eat at our stall. What do you want me to do?"

"And people choose to eat at our stall because yours is filthy!" Nabukalu yelled at Balinja.

At that, Balinja started crying, and the quarrelling only stopped when customers started coming in for breakfast.

After the busy lunch hour, Merab walked along a few city streets, looking for vacant business premises that would serve well as restaurant locations. She saw two, but the rents were too high.

Over the next two weeks she walked around the city after lunch with a notebook, writing down the location, amount of rent, a brief description and what the neighbouring businesses were for each of the premises she visited.

Merab's search for a place to rent led her back to Mitego's building, the same one in whose back alley she had started her business venture in the city. The first thing she noticed was that Wamala & Sons Construction, which originally occupied most of the ground floor, was no longer there.

She entered the vacant premises and saw that two men were repainting the spacious main room—it would be ideal for a restaurant!

"Good morning sir," Merab greeted one of the painters. "Sorry to interrupt your work, but do you know if this place is available to rent?"

"We don't know. You have to go upstairs to ask someone in the office," the man said, pointing. "The stairs are on the north side of the building, over there."

"Thank you sir," Merab said and walked out to take the stairs.

Upstairs, Mitego's secretary opened the door for her, and took her to look around the vacant premises.

The space was perfect for a restaurant. "I'll take it," Merab said.

❉   ❉   ❉

"Merab, our secretary tells me you are going to rent a space in our building. Congratulations!" Philemon told Merab when he saw her the following week at the market. "I didn't tell you it was available because I thought it would be too expensive," he explained. "But by the way, I can take two weeks off work to help you prepare for your restaurant."

"Oh, what a surprise! Thanks Philly. I appreciate your help."

"Is your husband also available to help? There is a lot that needs to be done before you can open."

"Yes, *Mwami* will help with the furnishings while I concentrate on things like the menu and staffing."

"You will also need to open a bank account now. This business of keeping money in the ground or under your mattress will not work for this business."

Merab laughed.

❉   ❉   ❉

During the following weeks, Philemon helped Merab to plan the menu and to recruit staff, hiring a woman named Kulabako to be the manager and two cooks to join Nabukalu in the kitchen. He also hired two of Merab's nieces, her sister Nawume's daughters, as servers. Lutalo brought a carpenter and two electricians and by the end of the second week, the restaurant was ready. The carpenter put a sign above the front door: "KYATELEKERA RESTAURANT—GET VALUE FOR YOUR MONEY."

※　　※　　※

The restaurant was even more successful than Merab had thought it would be. But its success presented a new challenge—she had to supervise work in the restaurant, and sometimes even stay until 11 o'clock at night. *How can I stay out late when my husband is at home alone?* Sometimes she would leave work unfinished so that she could go home to cook for her husband.

After a while, she found it harder to return home before 10 o'clock, and told Philemon about her predicament. When he saw her trying to run her restaurant as efficiently as possible and also ensure that her husband was happy at home, it confirmed his notion that his cousin had a split personality—she was Merab the wife and mother and Mufuzi, the hardworking businesswoman; Mufuzi wanted to work hard at the restaurant while Merab preferred to return home early to be a wife. She struggled to reconcile the two.

It was the end of the work day three months after the restaurant opened when Mitego saw Merab walking out of the building and sent a security guard to ask her to meet him in his office.

"How is the restaurant doing?" Mitego asked.

"It is doing well but I don't think it's the kind of business I wanted to do," she said. "It's robbing all my time."

"What did you expect? That's the normal life of an entrepreneur."

"True, but it leaves me no time to take care of my husband."

"Come on now! The husband whom you want so much to take care of also benefits from the money you make, doesn't he?"

"Yes, he does," Merab admitted.

"Then he has to choose, either to have you at home cooking for him or to let you work to earn the money that the family needs."

"I wish it was as easy as that."

"I know it is not easy and I don't think your husband is going to change overnight, either. You are going to persuade him to change by your actions. I know your abilities and I have seen you succeed where many other people have failed. You are Merab, the very kind woman, but you are also Mufuzi, the very hardworking one. Think like Merab but act like Mufuzi."

"That's a good idea," Merab answered, laughing.

When she was leaving, Mitego rose from his chair and hugged her, which still felt awkward but by now she was used to his hugs.

After their brief conversation she decided to stay a little longer at the restaurant, but she still felt uneasy as Lutalo's dinnertime approached. So after half an hour back at the restaurant, she decided to go home.

There was an unexpected visitor there when she arrived—Yafesi. She was very glad to see him.

"How are you? How are the folks at home? I miss my home," Merab said.

"I am well, Mother, and everybody else is well but we miss you, too. The home is not the same without you." And he told her that Kulumba hadn't been back even once since he left.

Yafesi talked at length with Lutalo who asked him about everything, from the children to the chickens, to the crops. They drank a lot of beer and by the time dinner was served, Yafesi was drunk. Roger was walking the drunken man to a room where he could sleep when they heard him yell, "Mama Merab, you will be my friend forever! You cared for me, a labourer, like I was your son. Yes,

I am your son. My colleagues are your sons, too. But that woman, your sister wife Mukuza, she treats us like rubbish."

24

"I CONFESSED EVERYTHING to Ruth," Jude said while he and Clotilda were waiting for the waitress to bring their drinks. However, he did not tell her that he had asked Ruth about Zoki and things had turned out badly for him.

"What do you mean?" Clotilda asked.

"I told her that I had an affair with you and we have a child."

"Good! What did she say? Did she cause a scene?"

"She was angry, of course. But she wants Clement to meet the family—my family."

"No, I will not let my son meet—"

"He will meet them," Jude said and paused. "…if really he is my son."

"No."

"Yes. Ruth insists."

"Ruth is very stupid. Don't even talk to me about her! You are the man in the home; it's up to you—"

"Let me repeat," Jude said. "Clement will meet the family if he really is my son. Have him ready for me to pick up at 10 o'clock on Saturday."

❋　❋　❋

Jude told Ruth what he had arranged, the following day. "Okay. Now, tell the children about it," Ruth answered.

"You can tell them. Do I have to be the one to tell them?"

"Yes, you fathered the child. Tell them yourself," Ruth said then called out loud to her children from the living room. "Herbert, we have a family meeting. Call your sisters."

"Mummy, can't we talk later?" Herbert said from the dining room. "I've got a lot of school work to complete."

"It's going to be a brief discussion," Ruth said.

Herbert and his sisters sat on the sofa facing their parents, and the awkward silence lasted close to a minute. Ruth looked at Jude in a way that indicated that he was the one to start the conversation. Jude cleared his voice. "My children, I wanted to tell you that I have a young son by another woman. His name is Clement. He'll be visiting us on Saturday."

Ruth and her daughters dropped their eyes simultaneously as if they had choreographed it. Herbert smiled.

Another silence followed.

"Do you have any questions for your father?" Ruth asked finally.

There was no response for a short while, then Herbert asked, "When is he coming?"

"Saturday morning," Jude answered.

The girls rose and walked out, looking unhappy—Victoria was about to cry. But as sixteen-year-old Herbert walked out of the living room he continued smiling.

❊ ❊ ❊

Jude returned home with eight-year-old Clement on Saturday morning and Ruth opened the front door for them, shaking hands with the boy and scrutinizing him in a way that seemed to make him a little nervous. She saw that Clement resembled his mother.

Clement sat on the sofa while Jude went to the back to get Herbert. Herbert came into the living room and shook hands with Clement. "I am glad to see you, Clement," Herbert said as he vigorously shook Clement's hand. "I am *very* happy—I have a brother at last!" It was obvious that they were both happy to meet each other.

Now Ruth walked out of the room and went to the backyard. "Please go in to meet your brother," she said to her daughters.

"He is not my brother!" Victoria said.

"Do we have to?" Kate asked.

"You don't have to but it is good manners to greet people when they visit your home, isn't it?" Ruth said.

Jude was watching his daughters from the corridor and saw that the girls didn't respond. When Ruth re-entered the house and he whispered, "I am very sorry," Ruth didn't respond either.

Herbert and Clement chatted for an hour, until Jude asked them to both accompany him on a visit to Jude's parents. They too were going to meet Clement for the first time.

❋   ❋   ❋

Like she had predicted, with the arrival of new stock customers had eventually flocked into Ruth's Boutique, even though many didn't buy but simply wanted to admire the merchandise. Collin had referred his clients to the shop, too, and by the end of the second year, Ruth had had to rent even more space and hire more workers, two men to provide general labour and a woman to clean the shop and arrange the merchandise. The shop was now also carrying large items like sofas, dressing mirrors and sideboards. When Collin brought Eunia to the shop for what was her first visit, Ruth gave them both presents—a rocking chair for Collin and a dresser for Eunia. "Ruth, I'm sorry. I will never stand in your way again," Eunia said, patting her hair as she gazed into the mirror.

That evening, Ruth wrote in her diary:

> *I have established my shop and it is doing very well. I feel very good. I realize that this is what I have always wanted to be—an independent woman. From now onwards, neither my mother nor my husband will control me.*

When Mitego returned to Ruth's Boutique, she thought he was there to chat and thought of telling him to go away. The last time he had visited they had parted on a bitter note. However, she was surprised when he asked to talk to her alone in her office, and wondered what his intentions were this time.

After he had sat down, Mitego said, "Ruth, I know that you are a good administrator, a successful businesswoman, a former teacher, and that you love netball."

"Thanks for the compliments," Ruth said, still wary.

"I'd like to appoint you as the new coach for the City Netball Club, my team," Mitego said.

"I would be honoured to coach the team," Ruth answered, surprised.

"However, I imagine it's quite a demanding role and I don't know where I'll get the time to fulfill it. And Mr. Mitego, if I may ask, how do you know that I enjoy netball?"

"Don't even ask! I've never met a man more proud of his daughter than your father," he said. "Even when you were just a student in Buweela he used to tell me about your successes on the netball field! Coaching my team will be easy for you!"

"Great, but do you know what I'm thinking? I will coach your team but for only two years— that's all I can fit into my five-year plan," she said. "And please draw up a contract too, for two years—I don't rely on verbal agreements," she added. "When do I start?"

"I'll arrange for you to meet with Constance, the outgoing coach."

❄   ❄   ❄

One week later, after introductions at Mitego's office, Ruth asked Constance for the team's records.

"What are you talking about?" Constance asked.

"I need any records that you have, like players' files and any other information that you have pertaining to the team," Ruth answered.

"Do you need to have records for a bunch of girls who meet once a week to practise—" Constance began.

"Oh yes, of course you need records—how else do you monitor and track progress?"

"That's the problem with you overly educated people," Constance said. "You theorize everything and in the process create unnecessary work for yourselves. Just get the girls together and help them to score goals—that's what matters."

"Give me a list of the players' names, then."

"You can get the list from the manager."

Ruth took the next day off work and spent most of it at her dining table planning for the netball team. She wrote a list of things to do, including a one-on-one meeting with each of the players, ideas for routines for the team on and off the pitch, and social activities.

For the first practice session, she arrived at the field with fifteen minutes to spare before the session began at 5:00 PM. She put her bag and the ball on the ground and walked a few times around the field to familiarize herself with it, glancing at her watch every few minutes. By 5:15 still no player had reported for practice. At 5:20 the first two players arrived together. Ruth saw them chatting as they walked. *They are 20 minutes late and they are simply dilly-dallying? There is, without a doubt, a serious problem of late-coming.*

"Hello, I am Ruth, your new coach," Ruth said, offering her hand to greet the young women.

"Hello Mrs. Kiyaga. I am Nabaggala," one woman said.

"And I am Akullo," the other said.

"Please call me Ruth. And, can we use our first names from now on? It will be easier that way."

"Okay," Akullo replied. "My name is Dinah."

"And my name is Sandra," Nabaggala said.

Ruth shook their hands again. "I'm glad to meet you, Dinah and Sandra." *Their eye contact is not great. Either they have self-confidence issues or they are nervous. That's something to work on.*

The entire team had arrived for practice by 5:40 PM. After she had introduced herself, Ruth asked each of the players to introduce herself as well and to say a little bit about herself.

"Hello, I am Akiiki," the team captain said. "That's all I can say. There's nothing interesting about me."

The rest of the team laughed.

"Akiiki, there must be something interesting about you, but you have to look for it. Everyone is special, you too are special, Akiiki."

"I know that but can we leave it at that?" Akiiki said. She seemed to be on the verge of crying.

"Every practice session will begin on time with a brief chat—some sort of talk about where we are at in other areas of our lives," Ruth said to steer the conversation away from Akiiki. "Then we will stretch and warm up before we play."

After the practice session, all the players remained behind to talk to Ruth except Akiiki, who hurried away as soon as the session ended although she had been the last to arrive.

The following week, each of the players went to meet Ruth at her boutique for a chat. At the beginning of her one-on-one meeting with Ruth, Akiiki said, "I am sorry for my attitude when we first met, Mrs. Kiyaga, but—"

"Call me Ruth," Ruth interrupted.

"I can't call you Ruth—you are my coach!"

"I am your coach but that does not stop you from calling me by my Christian name. Everybody calls me Ruth. I may appear to be highly-placed or whatever other ideas you may have about me but I am not any different from you."

Akiiki kept quiet for a while. "Ruth, I am sorry for my attitude—"

"There is no need to apologize; we were meeting for the first time."

"Thanks for your understanding. I love netball and I cherish the time I spend with the team but I have serious personal problems."

"I'm very sorry to hear that. Is there any way I can help?"

"I love my boyfriend and we have a son together. But he has made my life very miserable," Akiiki said, and started crying.

Three customers walked into the shop and Petua welcomed them.

"Please follow me," Ruth said and led Akiiki into her office. She closed the door.

"Would you like to tell me more about your situation?" Ruth asked as Akiiki wiped her tears.

"Other than when I come to netball practice once a week, I don't leave home. When I go anywhere else, my boyfriend beats me. He is very jealous. I have tolerated his behaviour because if I left him, I wouldn't have the means to take care of our son."

Ruth had been listening attentively. "How old is your son?" she asked.

"He is two years old. My boyfriend's sister looks after him when I come to netball practice. She lives in the same neighbourhood as us."

Akiiki and Ruth talked for close to two hours, not realizing for how long until Petua knocked on the door. It was getting dark and it was time to close the shop.

"I'm very glad for having had the opportunity to talk to you, Ruth," Akiiki said.

"I'm available for you to talk any time, Akiiki."

"Oh, it's very late," Akiiki said as she and Ruth walked out of Ruth's office. "Atwoki is going to beat me. That's my boyfriend—he doesn't know where I am."

"I'll drive you home," Ruth said. "And if you want, I can talk to Atwoki."

When Ruth parked the car in the front yard of Akiiki's home, the young woman said, "Thank you, Ruth. You are very kind."

"You are welcome. Would you like me to talk to your boyfriend?"

"No, I'm fine," Akiiki said as she opened the door and exited the car.

"Good night, Akiiki."

"Good night Ruth," Akiiki said, looking very anxious as she hurriedly walked into the dark and to the back of the house.

"Where have you been?" Atwoki yelled at Akiiki. He had been waiting in the poorly-lit backyard, holding his son in one arm and a stick in the free hand.

"I've been talking with my new netball coach," Akiiki answered.

"Until this late? Don't lie to me," Atwoki said, as he walked toward Akiiki, the stick already raised.

"No, she is not lying," Ruth said as she stepped forward into the dim light. Akiiki turned, surprised, when she realized Ruth had followed her. "My name is Ruth Kiyaga. I am Akiiki's new coach. It's true that she has been talking to me."

"Oh, hello, Ruth," Atwoki said, changing his tone immediately and quickly throwing the stick away. "Please come in."

After the greetings, there was silence. Ruth just wanted to say goodbye but she felt she had to talk to Atwoki. "Atwoki, I saw you had a stick in your hand, but that's not right. Decent men don't beat women."

Atwoki kept quiet.

"When you are angry, instead of beating your girlfriend, go out. Take in some fresh air. Take a walk. That will help cool you down."

It was plain that Ruth's beauty and demeanour had captivated Atwoki. When he and Akiiki went to see her off, he admired her car. "That's a classy woman," he said.

"She is very kind, too," Akiiki said.

Two weeks later, Akiiki told Ruth that her intervention had helped. "Atwoki still yells at me but he has never hit me again since you talked to him."

"Good. Let me know whenever you need my help."

"Are you sure? I don't want to be too much of a burden to you."

"You can count on me to help."

"Okay, thanks," Akiiki said. "Actually, Atwoki lost his job just a few days after you visited us. Can you—"

"Oh yes, I can help with that too," Ruth answered.

And a week later, because of Ruth's recommendation, Atwoki started a new job as a bus conductor at the Uganda Transport Company.

＊　　＊　　＊

The morale of the netball players improved under Ruth's tenure and they told her that they were very eager to come to practice. "We appreciate your motherly love, care and coaching skills," Dinah told her. "There is no team we can't beat!"

Ruth was glad to hear that.

At the end of the month, when they met with the East Mengo Netball Club, the City Netball Club beat them for the first time in the club's history. That evening Ruth's fame went beyond the city.

After the match, Mitego met with the victorious team to hand them their salaries. The thankful players hugged each other and shook hands with the fans as they made their way out of the stadium. Ruth stayed behind to talk to Mitego.

She told him that she was not happy with what she called "meagre" pay for the "hardworking players." "Mr. Mitego, it is high time you paid our players the kind of salaries that they deserve. I think you are paying them peanuts."

"Listen Ruth, aren't those girls happy to be earning money while at the same time doing what they love?"

"Sure, I know they are doing what they love. However, presently, doing what they love can't put food on their tables."

"Do any of them own a home? They are young girls who most probably still live with their parents."

"No sir, some of them have homes. There haven't been any complaints about pay but as a resident in this city, I know what it costs to—"

"Those are ideas that you educated folks have developed to turn our young people against us."

"Oh, dear," Ruth said, sighing. "With all due respect, Mr. Mitego, I think you must not be serious when you talk like that."

The conversation ended there when Mitego's assistant, Philemon, walked into the stadium and tapped him on the shoulder. "Let's talk some more another time, Ruth," Mitego said.

"Talking will not help, Mr. Mitego. You've got to do something," Ruth said and walked away.

✳   ✳   ✳

Ruth, her sister Hannah, and her friend Sanyu loved to chat outside their church every Sunday after the service. "I really like our Sunday morning conversations," Ruth said one Sunday. "Why don't we ask other women to join us? After all, the topics of our discussions might interest them."

"You are too funny, Ruth," Sanyu said. "How many women do you think would be interested in chatting at church instead of returning home to serve lunch to their families?"

"No, no, let's tell them. Those who think it's useful will join us," Ruth said.

Three other women joined Ruth, Hannah and Sanyu in the church hall the following Sunday after the service. They talked about their children's education and Ruth discussed the importance of a balanced diet and physical exercise.

In a year's time, over fifty women were attending the weekly meetings. Ruth suggested they form an association, and the women voted to support her idea. The Women's Development Association was born in the hall of St. Mark's Church. Women from various walks of life now joined the WDA and when its membership grew to about one hundred, the members changed their meeting time to Thursday evening. Ruth was elected the first president of the association. Sanyu became the secretary and administrator.

※　※　※

Two years after Ruth took over as coach, the City Netball Club beat the Maroons to win the national championship. Hundreds of fans shook hands and hugged Ruth and her team in the stadium. Ruth became an even bigger celebrity.

A week later, during the dinner that Mitego organized to congratulate the victorious team, Ruth tapped him on the shoulder and said, "Mr. Mitego, I have something important to tell you before you drink more beers."

"Do I drink that much?" Mitego asked, laughing.

"That's not what I meant to say. Let me talk to you now because I'll be leaving soon."

"I am listening."

"As agreed, this was my last season as coach—"

"Don't tell me that you are resigning! You are doing so well!"

"No, Mr. Mitego. I am not resigning; my contract has ended and I don't intend to renew it."

"What can I do to make you continue for at least one more year?"

"Nothing," Ruth said. "But I can help you to find a new coach."

"You are a stubborn girl, hm?"

"No, I'm not stubborn. I plan my life."

Mitego was sorry to see Ruth's tenure as coach end but he could not convince her to stay. Two days later, she received a call from Dr. Dickson Okecho, the chairman of the board of the Uganda Development Corporation, asking her to join the board. He said that her business knowledge would be very useful to the corporation. Ruth said she was honoured and hesitantly accepted the role.

✳   ✳   ✳

With time, rumours started going around that the WDA was just an excuse for women to get together to gossip and to learn new ways to rebel against their husbands. An article in *The Voice of Uganda* reported that on one hand, it was good to see women coming together to develop themselves through the WDA. On the other hand, the article then added, the association was already two years old and it had no tangible benefits to show for its members. The article infuriated Ruth. She wrote a letter to Timothy Mbogo, the article's writer, to protest.

Dear Mr. Mbogo,

I would like to thank you for the article that you wrote about the Women's Development Association in The Voice of Uganda of 18th October 1976. I am sorry to inform you, though, that the article contains a number of regrettable errors. You point out that the Association, to quote your actual words, "has no tangible benefit to show for its members." I wonder how you arrived at that conclusion. Did you interview any of our leaders or members? That should certainly have been the intelligent thing to do. I am not a journalist and would not want to pretend to teach you how to do your job but I think the best thing for you to do would have been to check the material for your article with a reliable source before sitting down to write.

I would like to invite you to one of our meetings to give you a chance to experience first-hand what we do and to give you an opportunity to talk to some of our members. Hopefully, after doing so, you will have a more positive article to write about our Association.

Yours truly,

Ruth Kiyaga

Timothy Mbogo arrived a few minutes before the next WDA meeting started. He introduced himself to the secretary of the Association and sat at the back of the hall to listen and to observe. At the end of the meeting, when he asked Ruth whether he could interview her for another article about the Association, she agreed.

"What are the objectives of the Women's Development Association?" Mbogo asked Ruth, ready to take notes.

"There are several, but the three major ones are to unite women in this city irrespective of their religious or ethnic background, to educate women in the areas of diet and physical exercise, and to create a forum through which to discuss and create income-generating projects."

"That last objective sounds vague."

"Mr. Mbogo, are you here to learn or to judge?"

"You have been accused of having established the WDA for your own personal agenda."

"Accused by whom?"

Mbogo ignored the question. "What are your personal goals in all this?"

"I would be lying if I said that I don't have personal ambitions. However, I don't think that my personal ambitions and the objectives that I am pursuing for women through the WDA clash."

"For example?"

"I am a businesswoman. I am one of the female pioneers in Ugandan business, if you will. When women, especially young women, learn about my achievements—mind you, like you've seen this evening, in the weekly meetings of the WDA the first half hour is dedicated to showcasing professional and business success stories—so, back to my point, when I share my achievements, young women gain the inspiration they need to start their own businesses and the drive they need to advance their careers."

"I think that is a source of problems for women leaders like you. Our men are not yet used to living with independent women, yet the things that you discuss and promote through the WDA create exactly that—independent women."

"No, no, no! Make no mistake—our aim is not to compete with our men! Our aim is to contribute to our families and to society as equal partners, as full human beings. Remember, we are the mothers of the nation. When you educate a mother—when you give power to a mother—you educate a nation, you give power to a nation."

"Your Association has been accused of being out of touch with our country's reality. It is allegedly an association of elite women, and it is out of reach for the majority of women in this city who are uneducated and marginalized."

"That's news to me. That's hearsay. Can you please name the source of your information?" Ruth asked.

"What do you say about those accusations?" Mbogo asked, again ignoring Ruth's question.

"Membership in our association is open to all women from all walks of life. It is only a coincidence that the majority of our members are educated urban women. However, it is still a young association and with time, we will devise ways through which to reach more women. We will strive to reach all those mothers who have to work very hard to care for their families—"

"Those who work very hard while their husbands are out having fun?" Mbogo interjected.

"I didn't say that. Please don't put words in my mouth. I'm not here to accuse men. What I am trying to do is advocate for women. And to quell your baseless rumours."

"And, it seems there is no connection between your advocacy work and your business. You have a clientele of well-to-do people. Can an ordinary woman afford to buy anything in your boutique?"

"Hey, listen! My business and my work in the area of social justice are two separate domains of my life."

"You are a very busy woman, a board member of the UDC, the president of the WDA. You are a mother. You are a model of a progressive modern woman, an advocate for women's rights. If you were to evaluate your efforts at the end of your career, what would need to be in place for you to know that you have achieved your goals?"

"Equality between men and women!" Ruth said emphatically. "Women in this country should be free, like their fathers, their husbands, their boyfriends, you name it. Women should be free to dress in any way they want, to go wherever they want, to own property. Basically, to live the life they want."

A few days after his interview with Ruth, Timothy Mbogo wrote another article in the newspaper in which he praised Ruth and the WDA. He wrote some excerpts from the interview and that Ruth was an excellent leader.

Ruth was very happy about the second article and wrote another letter to Mbogo thanking him for "having set the record straight."

After he had received Ruth's letter, Mbogo went to Ruth's Boutique and asked if she had time to chat with her at length. They arranged a meeting for the next day. The following day, when he entered the shop, Ruth said, "We can chat in my office if you don't mind, Mr. Mbogo."

"You can call me Tim," Mbogo said.

"Good morning, Tim. What can I do for you?" Ruth asked as soon as they had sat down in her office.

"I don't know whether you are aware of this, but I am a son of the late Tito Mbogo, the man who founded the school that now belongs to Clotilda Kayiza."

Clotilda! Oh, that makes sense now. It was Clotilda who was the source of the rumours about the WDA! "Oh, I didn't know that," Ruth said.

"Clotilda has a long history with my family. She was actually the one who paid my school fees and those of my three younger siblings right from when I was in secondary school."

"Really?" Ruth said. "That was very kind of her."

"It was because of an agreement that she had with my late father. Unfortunately, being illiterate, my mother and my uncle—my father's younger brother—did not know how she had managed to secure that agreement. And they never knew how she later got ownership of the school."

"That's strange."

"Yes, 'strange' is the right word to describe that situation. I was too young when my father passed away to know or even to care about what the agreement between him and Clotilda entailed. What I remember was the suffering that we went through after my father's death. True, Clotilda did pay our school fees," Mbogo said. "But only very late every term, and whenever I went to her office to get the fees, she'd first give me a long lecture each time, telling me that my siblings and I needed to work hard and that we should not expect to get anything for free. Although she did not say so, to me it sounded like she wanted us to work for her to earn the school fees. My mother was so hurt whenever I recounted my encounters with Clotilda to her that when I grew a little older and realized that telling my mother such things was not helpful, I stopped doing so."

Ruth listened attentively.

"Unfortunately, the school is not the only property that Clotilda stole from my family. She also bought land, very cunningly and cheaply, from my uncle to establish a school farm."

"I went to school with Clotilda," Ruth said, "and all I can tell you is that I know that she is a very difficult woman, and one has to be careful when dealing with her."

"Oh yes, she is very difficult," Tim agreed. "I still have to deal with her on many occasions and always wonder why she is so nasty."

Tim talked with Ruth for over an hour and each of them appreciated the other's candour. Their friendship started that morning, and Tim would now sometimes go to Ruth's Boutique to chat with her. Ruth eventually introduced him to her family and he introduced her to his.

*   *   *

One evening, when Ruth returned home late after a board meeting of the

Uganda Development Corporation, Jude was furious. "Now that you are rich, you feel so powerful and important that you often forget that you are still a wife!"

"I know you are intimidated by my success in business but isn't my success good for both of us and our children? Don't you appreciate the fact that I go out to work and contribute to our family's financial wellbeing? Would you prefer to have me stay at home and wait for you to provide everything?" Jude didn't respond.

For the next two days Ruth saw that Jude stayed in bed when she left for work in the morning and found him still in bed when she returned in the evening. Then his friend Darlington came to take him out to drink. When they left, Ruth took out her diary and noted her feelings for the day:

> *I don't like it when my husband spends the day in bed.*
> *The level of energy here is low when he is lying in bed*
> *instead of working. I would rather have him out there*
> *drinking in a bar than in bed idle.*

Ruth stayed up late thinking about her children. She had hoped that all three would go to university and find good jobs. However, while Herbert and Kate studied hard, Victoria seemed to be more interested in doing housework, and when Ruth asked her what she wanted to do later in life, the teenaged Victoria said that she wanted to get married and stay at home to raise her family.

And like she had said, when she completed high school, Victoria did not apply for admission to university. She had met a doctor called Dan Bugembe while she was visiting her paternal aunt Catherine and had fallen in love with him. Ruth insisted that Victoria go to the university but she refused. *I now understand the heartache I caused to my mother when I did not pursue the career she dreamed of for me*, Ruth thought. Victoria married Dan five months later and joined him in Boston, Massachusetts, where he lived.

❋　❋　❋

Three days after Victoria's wedding, Ruth went to Nairobi to attend a women's conference. After the conference, a magazine interviewed her about her work with the WDA. Three weeks later, she received a letter from Ms. Cook. Ruth was always happy to hear from her former headmistress.

> *My dear Ruth,*
>
> *Judging from what I have been reading in magazines about women leaders in East Africa, you are having the time of your life. I was very glad to read the text of the interview that you gave to* Modern Woman *during the recent women's conference in Nairobi. Your ideas are wonderful and I hope that they will trickle down to ordinary women.*
>
> *I was glad to learn from your last letter that your business is thriving. I couldn't be prouder of you. That's a wonderful job, honey! However, I know how hard you work and I would like to remind you to take time off for yourself. We women want to work all the time and in the process we forget that we need to slow down once in a while and to create time for ourselves. Remember, sweetheart, the best way for you to care for your loved ones is to take care of yourself first.*
>
> *Please also remember to give the same benefits to your employees—they need time off to recharge, too. Excuse me for the lecture, but I will always be your teacher. Convey my greetings to your wonderful family.*
>
> *Warm regards from George.*
>
> *Miss Cook*

PS: I harvested a lot of fruit from my backyard garden. Do you remember it all? Grapes, blueberries, strawberries, you name it. I wish you were here—you would enjoy some.

Ruth was writing back to Miss Cook when Jude called home to inform her that his father had been admitted to hospital.

Jude, Herbert and Clement arrived there as soon as they could and realized right away that Dawson was very ill. Dawson gazed at Clement for a long time, so long that it made the young man nervous. After a while, Dawson asked his grandsons to leave so he could talk to their father.

"Jude, I am glad that I have got this chance to speak to you alone—I'm sorry to say it but I am not convinced that Clement is your son."

"I doubt it, too," Jude told his father.

Jude and his sons had just left when Ruth arrived to see her father-in-law. "Ruth, please have a seat," Dawson said. "As you can see, I am nearing the end of my days. However, before I depart, I would like to speak to you sincerely and to tell you how sorry I am."

Ruth took her handkerchief from her handbag and started to wipe her eyes, trying to hide her dismay and sorrow at the resignation in his voice.

"You are very misunderstood in my family. I am very sorry for the bad treatment that you have endured all these years."

It was against her culture for a daughter-in-law to hug her father-in-law or to touch him, but Ruth wanted so much to hug Dawson. Instead, she knelt by the bed and wept.

A nurse came and asked how she could help and Dawson changed the topic. "Ruth, I am very proud of the work that you have accomplished in building a first-class business in the city. I have heard fantastic comments about you and your business acumen, even from Kampala's most chauvinistic men."

"But it has not been easy to deal with some of those chauvinistic types," she admitted, her eyes still glistening with tears. "I guess you know Mitego. When he came to the shop the first time, it was clear that he was there not to buy anything. He wanted a relationship that had nothing to do with business."

Ruth had always found it easy to talk to Dawson but, even still, it was a bit awkward to have such a conversation with her father-in-law. "But when he realized that I was not the type to fall for his tricks and fake charm, when I became his netball club's coach, he attempted to develop some kind of father-daughter relationship, expecting me to kneel to greet him and such nonsense."

"Mitego is an interesting man, a self-made businessman who started from nowhere and succeeded in building an empire," Dawson said, and smiled faintly. "And he has always been a ladies' man."

❋　❋　❋

Dawson died a few weeks later, and a month after his death, his children sat in the offices of Kasiita & Company Advocates to learn the contents of the late tycoon's will. Jude, his only son, inherited most of the property.

> My son and heir Jude shall receive dividends from his shares but he shall not be involved in the running of the company. The following persons shall oversee the management of the entire business and property of Kiyaga Holdings: My daughter Catherine Kiyaga Kalule shall become the Managing Director and Chief Executive of the company. She shall be assisted by a board with the following members: my daughter-in-law Ruth Wamala Kiyaga, my grandson Herbert Kiyaga and my nephew Hezekiah Mubiru.

> My grandson Herbert Kiyaga shall inherit my home in Kololo and the land on which it is built after the death of my wife Belinda. The keys to the home shall be handed to him the day after she is buried.

25

OCTOBER 1967 – DECEMBER 1977

LEAH STUDIED DILIGENTLY to complete her primary education, and even during the school holidays would spend several hours every day and night studying. She wanted to be admitted to Buweela High School and she knew that to do so she'd need high grades. Merab thought that if her daughter studied at Buweela High School, it would be a great achievement not just for Leah but for her, too, a woman from a little-known rural area of the country.

When the examination results were released, Leah and Merab celebrated— Leah had passed very well and would go to Buweela High School. Merab was very pleased to accompany her daughter to the school for her first day of the term, and thankful that she had been able to pay the school fees in full and to buy everything her daughter needed without borrowing any money.

❋   ❋   ❋

During her third year at the high school, Leah and five friends formed a group that bullied younger students and one evening a matron caught them. They were suspended and given warning letters to take to their parents to sign but Leah did not give the letter to her mother. Instead, she gave it to her aunt Nabukalu, asking her to sign it and to not to tell her mother. Nabukalu scribbled something on the letter—she could not write—and promised not to tell Merab.

Before the next term ended, Leah and her friends bullied another girl, and this time their victim reported the matter to the deputy headmistress. Leah denied having participated in the bullying not knowing that a matron had witnessed the entire incident, and she was the first of the group to be expelled from the school that morning.

Leah regretted her actions but she knew that it was too late to seek a pardon. When she arrived at her home in Kawempe, crying, her father was not there; he had gone to Kalasa. She sat on the front veranda of the house to wait for her mother to return. After about an hour of waiting, she went to the neighbours' home to ask for some food. After she had eaten, Mrs. Kamaadi invited her to wait there until Merab returned.

"Are you all right?" Mrs. Kamaadi asked, noticing that Leah was crying. "What's the matter?"

"I'm scared. I don't know how to tell my mother. I have been expelled from school. I stupidly got myself involved with a group of girls to bully a young student. Now I regret my actions."

"I like your honesty. You are a good girl. Don't you think they could let you go back to the school if your mother—"

"Not a chance. Expulsion from Buweela High School is final. There's no chance for appeal."

"Would you like me to speak to your mother on your behalf?"

"No, thanks—I will find the courage to tell her, but I know she will be devastated. She has devoted her life to seeing me succeed. I've let her down," Leah said as she cried even more.

❋ ❋ ❋

It was already dark when Merab and Nabukalu returned home. Merab opened the door and went into the house. Nabukalu went to the back of the house to the latrine. A few minutes later, there was a knock on the door.

"Who is it?" Merab asked. She wondered who would be knocking at that time.

"It's Leah."

Leah? She was supposed to be in school. "Are you sick?" Merab asked.

Leah came in, dragging her belongings behind her. Nabukalu followed the girl into the house, helping her with the suitcase. "No, I'm not sick. I've been expelled from school," she said quietly. "I'm very sorry, Mother."

"Sit down and tell me why you were expelled from school," Merab said as she picked a mat from a corner to sit down. There were already tears in her eyes.

Leah sat on the mat facing her mother. "I'm very sorry, Mother," she said again. "I got involved with a group of bad girls who led me into bad behaviour. We bullied a young student and we were caught. I tried to deny my involvement, but a matron—"

"What? You bullied a student?"

"I'm very sorry, Mother. I regret my actions."

"You know how hard I work for you, Leah. I am an uneducated woman trying my best to give you opportunities in life that I never got. Is this the best way for you to pay me back?"

Leah did not answer.

Merab, very disappointed by Leah's behaviour, spent a sleepless night trying to think what to do next for her daughter. *Who throws away an opportunity to study in Buweela High School?*

When Lutalo returned the following week, Merab let Leah tell him what had happened herself. Leah couldn't look her father in the eye as she did so. "That's not good, Leah," was all Lutalo said when she had finished, walking away to his shop. "You'll just have to find another school."

Leah spent a week at home, helping her father in the shop sometimes and worrying about the possibility of dropping out of school. But she did not know what to do next.

Merab spent several more sleepless nights worrying about Leah until she decided to talk to Philemon. She went to see him at his new hardware shop. He had recently quit his job as Mitego's personal assistant.

"Philly, I have a problem," Merab said to Philemon after he had greeted her. She explained what had happened.

"Talk to Mitego," Philemon said. "There's no door he can't open in this country. Or if you want, I'll talk to him tomorrow."

"Okay, tell him if you think he can help."

Philemon went to Mitego's office the following day and when he told him that Merab's daughter had been expelled from Buweela High School, Mitego took a pen out of his pocket to take notes. "What's her name?" he asked. "In what class? When was she expelled?"

Mitego immediately called Mrs. Kakeeto, the school's headmistress, and by the time he got off the phone ten minutes later, Leah had been readmitted to the school.

Mrs. Kakeeto wanted Mitego himself to take Leah back to the school that day, before she left her office. Mitego told her that he would bring her.

Philemon wanted to tell Merab the good news first. "No, you will tell her later," Mitego said as he rose from his seat. "There's no time to waste—let's go!" Mitego drove Philemon to Merab's home and while he was exchanging some pleasantries with Lutalo, Philemon told Leah the news—that thanks to Mr. Mitego's intervention, she had been readmitted to the school and they were taking her back immediately. Leah was overjoyed but said that she was not ready to return to school right away since all her clothes were dirty.

Mitego always carried a whip in his car to discipline his many children and "mischievous" employees. When he heard what Leah was saying, he took it out and whipped her twice. Lutalo was shocked—neither he nor Merab had ever spanked the girl.

Leah returned to school that day with dirty laundry and in tears.

*   *   *

The following month, Merab started building a large house on the vacant plot of land that had been her garden when she'd first moved to Kawempe. When the large house was completed, a row of rooms were built to form an enclosure for the whole backyard. At around the same time Merab's nephew Yosiya, her sister Eseza's son, came looking for work. Merab sent him to a driving school. A few months later she bought Mitego's used car, a Peugeot 504, and Yosiya became her driver.

*   *   *

Since she had a few vacant rooms, Merab wondered if Kulumba could come to live in her home. One day she said to Musirise's son, Roger, "Can you please find a way of contacting Kulumba? I miss him."

"That's easy—I know where he lives," Roger said. "I'll ask him to come see you."

Merab looked forward to seeing Kulumba, and wondered why the boy she had loved and cared for so much since he was two years old had never come to visit his father and her.

"He is stupid, so it is not surprising to me that he is behaving that way," Lutalo said. "His mother and her family are all good for nothing. And, by the way," he added, "if he ever came here, don't let him into the house—he might steal from us."

Merab decided not to tell Lutalo that she had already asked Roger to look for Kulumba, and just three days later, he came to visit in the company of another young man.

"Mother, I am sorry for not visiting sooner," Kulumba said. "Life is hard, and I don't have a job."

"I forgive you my son," Merab said. "You are welcome home but make sure your father does not see you here. He doesn't want to see you."

"Please tell him that I have reformed my ways."

When Nabukalu told Lutalo that Kulumba had come to visit he was fuming. "Mufuzi!" Lutalo called out to Merab, "Why did you let Kulumba come here? I don't want him in this home."

"He came in the company of another young man, and he apologized—"

"Who is the young man he came with?"

"He was a very tall man, about the same age as Kulumba, but he did not introduce him."

"A very tall man? That must be one of his cousins, probably a son of one of Kulumba's maternal uncles. The people in that family are all very tall," Lutalo said, "—And they are all thieves! Don't let them come here again."

But Kulumba and the young man, whom he later introduced as his cousin Ndugga, did come back. Merab gave them a room in the back where they lived in hiding. She knocked on their room's door whenever she returned from the restaurant, and she noticed that sometimes they were not in.

One morning, Merab said to Kulumba, "Sometimes I knock on your door to check on you as late as 1 o'clock in the morning and realize that you are not in. Where do you spend the nights?"

"Mother, we are still young. We go out to dance some evenings."

"Oh, I see. So you have become night dancers?"

The young men laughed.

"Please stay out of trouble because if you cause trouble, I will have no choice but to send you away. Remember your father is still not aware that you live here."

❋   ❋   ❋

When she graduated from Buweela High School three years later, Leah was admitted to a secretarial course in the National College of Business Studies. In the same year, her half-brother Roger graduated with a B.A. Honours in History and Philosophy from Makerere University. Many people attended the graduation party in Kalasa, and Musirise made Mukuza's day when she thanked her in her speech for her ruthless and indiscriminate spanking which, she said, had made Roger more serious with his studies in primary school.

❋   ❋   ❋

Clotilda was all smiles as she waved to Clement as he boarded the plane to go to India for a four-year course in Pharmacology in the University of Calcutta. *Go study and do well, my son. When they expelled me from school, they thought that I was good for nothing. But the sky is the limit for me.*

26

RUTH WAS ONE of the many Old Girls of Buweela High School, most of them Londoners, who attended the funeral of their former headmistress, eighty-nine-year-old Ann Kaitlin Cook. On a Uganda Airlines flight home, Ruth was thumbing a copy of *The Voice of Uganda* when she glanced at a headline: "Woman Found Murdered in Bed." She almost skipped the story before she noticed a familiar name. Akiiki, one of her former netball players, had been stabbed in her bed; according to the article her husband, Atwoki, was the suspect and was still on the run. Ruth wept quietly for the young woman. For a few years she'd been planning to organize a get-together party at her home with her former players but had somehow never been able to do so.

When she arrived home, there was a letter on her dressing table. That weekend, the executive committee of the WDA wanted to recognize and honour her and the other founders of the Association. When she told Jude that the WDA was going to honour her, he said that he would accompany her to the ceremony, to stand by her side as she received the recognition. *He wants to be in the limelight but he doesn't deserve it.* Ruth almost said that his presence would not be necessary until she remembered Akiiki, and then agreed that it was important for Jude to accompany her.

At the event after Ruth, Hannah, Sanyu and a few other women had been awarded their meritorious certificates, Ruth rose to speak.

"Ladies, it is indeed a great honour for me to see that you have found it fitting to recognize my contribution to the WDA. Thank you very much. However, before we continue, let me ask us to observe a moment of silence for my friend and a former player in the City Netball Club, Akiiki, who was murdered this week."

After the moment of silence, Ruth continued. "The newspaper reported that Akiiki's husband abused her for a long time. There were signs that the abuse was going on but nothing was done to help her. Remember, my sisters—protect yourselves. Talk to somebody, don't suffer in silence." She paused as she held back tears. "I mean, we set a good example for women everywhere when we, the so-called powerful women, speak up against abuse. I know what I am talking about because, powerful as I may seem to be, I have endured verbal abuse for years. I have endured verbal abuse throughout my marriage." She paused again, wiping her eyes with a handkerchief. "My loving husband Jude has been abusing me verbally since the beginning of our marriage and it is only now that I have gathered the courage to speak publicly about it. I am sorry I am telling you this, and I know what some of you must be thinking because what I am doing is contrary to our culture. What takes place in the home stays in the home—*eby'omunju tebittotolwa*—but it would be hypocritical if I, as a role model to many young women, did not speak up."

The audience gasped in disbelief as Jude rose to his feet, walked up to the platform where his wife was standing as he, too, wiped his eyes with a handkerchief. "It is true, I have abused my wife for many years, but I am ready to change. I promise you, darling," he said as he turned to face Ruth, "I will never again abuse you. I will honour and respect you. I promise this to you before this gathering." He then pulled her close to him and kissed her on the mouth. Several photographers snapped photos.

On Monday, Ruth was unhappy to note that it was the photograph of Jude kissing her that made the headlines of several newspapers. Only *Ngabo* mentioned what the event was really about.

❋ ❋ ❋

Jude's mother Belinda died two weeks later after a short illness. "After my father died, my mother wasn't the same again," Jude told the mourners at St. Mark's Church, the church his parents had helped to build. "I have never seen a greater love than the love that my parents had for each other."

A week later, Ruth and Jude's daughter Kate married her long-time boyfriend Ham, who she had known since he and Herbert were students together in Musasa High School, and who was now a lawyer.

A few weeks after his grandmother had been buried and shortly after he had completed his university studies, Herbert moved into his late grandparents' large and beautiful home, in accordance with Dawson's will.

❋   ❋   ❋

During a visit to Kalasa, Merab took many presents for the family, including cloth for making *gomesi*, one each for Mukuza and Musirise. Mukuza thanked Merab profusely and did a happy little dance in the living room. "Thank you, Mufuzi—may you earn much more than you spent on us!"

"You are welcome," Merab said. *A present once in a while will cheer her up. She is a different person when she gets something she loves.*

Merab had expected her friend Nakatudde to be one of the first to come meet her, and when she did not come and Merab asked about her, Musirise told her that Ezra, Nakatudde's husband, was ill. Merab went to see Ezra and realized that he was very sick. She asked Nakatudde to dress him and took them to Mulago Hospital in Kampala.

For a month Nakatudde helped to nurse her husband in the hospital, sleeping on the floor by his bed and going daily to Merab's home to bathe and to get home-cooked meals to take to him until he died. A few months after Ezra's death, Nakatudde returned to Kampala to thank Merab for her kindness.

"Mufuzi, I'm very impressed by your work. I didn't believe you when you said you wanted to start a business in the city one day. How were you able to establish this business?" Nakatudde asked, looking around on her first visit to Kyatelekera Restaurant.

"The business is successful now," Merab said, "but it didn't start that way. We built it gradually."

Nakatudde spent the night in Merab's home in Kawempe. When she went to bed, she took a while to sleep. *Mufuzi often spoke about her ideas for business and I said they were crazy. It's quite impressive how much she has accomplished. By working with Mufuzi, I, too, could succeed in the city.* By the morning she had made up her mind. "Mufuzi, if it's okay with you—and this might sound strange to you because I am so old—I would like to stay here to work with you. I don't want to return to Kalasa."

"That's fine," Merab said without hesitation. "There's a free room in the servants' quarters. You can live there. I'll be glad to have you helping us at the restaurant."

Nakatudde started working in the kitchen of Kyatelekera Restaurant the following week. She was the fastest peeler of *matooke* plantain that Merab had ever seen.

A few weeks after Nakatudde had started working at the restaurant, she heard Merab arguing with the young servers about "the way young women dress these days." Nakatudde found the conversation interesting and she joined in. "I have noticed that our young women, and even some older ones, are copying foreign cultures. I don't like the way women in the city dress," she said.

"You are right, Mama Nakatudde," Merab said, smiling. She was enjoying the conversation and the exchange of ideas. "Why don't we resume the kind of talks that we used to have while we were weaving mats in Kalasa?"

From that day, whenever she had finished her work in the kitchen and there was a lull, Nakatudde sat on a bench with the servers at the back of the building to talk about culture. Soon a few other women, some of whom just happened to be passing by, joined the talks. "My fellow women, even though you live in the city, you should not forget what our culture expects of you—good behaviour!" Nakatudde said.

A few months later, several other women who worked in the neighbouring businesses joined the talks, and they became known as *Omukyala Omugunjufu*—the civilized woman—or OO. The OO gatherings grew in number and continued to take place at the back of the building until the landlord, Mitego, heard about them.

When Philemon came to the restaurant for lunch soon after, Merab told him that Mitego wanted to stop the meetings. "He said that they are illegal," Merab told her cousin.

"I think he just wants you to pay him for holding your meetings on his premises," Philemon said.

"Why would I pay him? I don't collect any money during the meetings."

"Remember that it is Mitego we are talking about. He reaps even where he doesn't sow."

But Merab convinced Mitego, for a small fee, to let the OO meetings continue once a week in a vacant room upstairs.

The OO meetings became popular, especially among older women in the city, and some of the participants were inspired to start similar meetings in their own towns. An article about OO in *Munno* commended the organization for being a good vehicle to promote Ugandan culture among women.

After Ruth had read that article, she went uninvited to one weekly OO meeting and listened to the discussions. At the end, when Nakatudde called for questions, Ruth was the first to raise her hand. She said that even though OO itself was not bad, a lot of its messages were negative because they promoted the subjugation of women. Several women responded in unison, telling Ruth to shut up, and then Merab rose to speak. She and Ruth argued for about five minutes. When their argument turned into yelling at each other, Ruth walked out.

*   *   *

Kyatelekera Restaurant became very popular in the city, known for its excellent food. Every month when they received their wages, the two men who worked at Ruth's Boutique treated themselves to lunch at the restaurant. While they dined, they often talked excitedly about their boss, *Mwambala mpale*, and what they called her "European ways"—she required them to take breaks even when they were very busy, and if she did not take a 20-minute nap in her office, she walked for half an hour along the streets. Whenever the men sat near the restaurant counter, Merab would overhear bits of their conversations and formed a rough image what kind of woman *Mwambala mpale* was.

So she did not need to ask who it was when one afternoon a woman dressed in a black pair of trousers and a white blouse came into the restaurant. As soon as the woman entered, the activity in the restaurant seemed to come to a standstill as all the men present turned to look at her. Ruth walked to a few tables where she shook hands and greeted them before she went to join the table where the two employees from Ruth's Boutique were seated.

Ruth's self-confidence surprised Merab, who gazed intently at her. *This must be the famous Mwambala mpale—oh, but isn't this the same woman who was arguing with me at the OO meeting?* After Ruth and her employees had been served, Merab glanced several times at their table, trying to overhear the classy woman's conversation, noticing that Ruth switched between Luganda and English and seemed to say "oh dear" in every other sentence. Merab was happy that the woman seemed to be enjoying her meal; she was one of the few people who left a tip for the waitresses. "Please thank the chef for me," she said as she walked out of the restaurant.

*   *   *

When Merab asked Leah to work as a cashier at the restaurant whenever she did not have classes, Leah agreed, but only reluctantly. Leah was a slender young woman now, with an easy smile, a calm, composed look and beautiful, kind eyes. Her work at the till was meticulous, organized and unrushed. But she did not enjoy dealing with the customers—most seemed to complain about anything and everything. And she did not like the attention of the male customers, some of whom seemed to enjoy talking to her for no particular reason.

Soon, however, one customer in particular caught her attention, a handsome, well-dressed young man who always came for lunch at exactly 1:00 o'clock, and in the following days as she watched him, Leah found herself starting to like working at the restaurant and looked forward to seeing him. But one day he did not show up for lunch, and then not the next day either. It was only when she was getting ready to return to her college at 6 o'clock that he entered the restaurant. She put her handbag down and waited until he had finished his dinner. She wanted to be the one to collect his payment from him.

When he went to pay, he greeted her for the first time, speaking in English.

"Hello, how are you?"

"I am fine, thank you," Leah answered, smiling.

"So how was your day?"

"We've not been busy today."

"Oh, that's good sometimes. By the way, my name is Herbert."

"Hello, Herbert. I am Leah." She smiled again.

"Keep the change," he said as he turned to leave. "Have a good evening."

❋   ❋   ❋

From that evening onwards, Herbert came to the restaurant in the evenings instead of for lunch and he would sometimes chat with Leah at a table near the restaurant's entrance. One day he asked her to go to the cinema with him.

Leah accepted.

After the movie they walked for several kilometres in the city, talking. Leah laughed a lot when Herbert told her that people had nicknamed his mother *Mwambala mpale* because she frequently wore trousers. "She knows but she doesn't care," he told her, laughing. "My mother is very stubborn."

They said goodbye, and Leah had just stepped onto the bus to return to her college when Herbert told her that he loved her. Leah stepped back off the bus. "I'm so happy to hear that, Herbert! I love you too. Let's talk a little longer." She took the next bus—and five months after they first spoke, Herbert proposed marriage to Leah at the Norman Godinho Cinema. She said yes.

❉   ❉   ❉

"Leah, who is the young man you have long conversations with these days?" Merab asked the following day.

"His name is Herbert," Leah answered.

"Herbert? That's all you can tell me about him? Who is he? Where is he from? He certainly enjoys your company."

"Yes he does," Leah said. "And I enjoy his company too."

During the following two weeks, Merab noticed that Leah was more enthusiastic about work at the restaurant than usual, and when the young woman mysteriously disappeared for one or two hours every evening, Merab thought she knew why.

"Leah, it is a good thing that you go out and I am not saying this to stop you, but can you tell me what's going on? Who is the young man you're spending so much time with these days?"

"His name is Herbert Kiyaga. He is in love with me."

"Good. He seems to be well brought up; he is polite and well-mannered," Merab said. "But do you know where he is from and what he does for a living?"

"He lives in Kololo and has just completed his studies in Makerere University. His mother, *Mwambala mpale*, has dined at the restaurant a few times before."

"What? I don't like that woman."

"Why don't you like her?"

"She is rude and she said nasty things about us in one OO meeting. I am afraid you will have to end your relationship."

"No, I am not in a relationship with his mother. His mother has nothing to do with me."

"But will he marry you? I wouldn't want him to waste your time."

"Yes, he has already proposed to me."

"And?"

"And I said yes."

"Should I tell your father about it?"

"Yes."

❊　❊　❊

"Mummy, I proposed to my girlfriend and she's agreed to marry me."

"Hey, that's great news my dear but I didn't know you had a girlfriend."

"We've been together for about half a year."

"What's her name and where is she from?"

"Her name is Leah and if I remember correctly, she said she lives somewhere in Kawempe."

"Kawempe? Um, Herbert, what kind of people are those?"

"What do you mean?"

"What is her father's name?"

"His name is Lutalo. Her mother owns Kyatelekera Restaurant. You know that restaurant, don't you?"

"Yes. I know the restaurant and the woman who owns it," Ruth said and paused for a few moments. "No, that's not the kind of girl I would like you to marry."

"Mummy, you were not planning to find a wife for me, were you?"

"No, but we know a few girls from decent families. Why don't you—"

"I have chosen Leah and I don't care that she doesn't come from a prominent family."

"That's not what I wanted to say," Ruth told her son, "but I didn't think you would choose a girl like that woman's daughter."

"Do you know Leah?"

"No, but I've seen her mother a few times."

"A few times are not enough to judge a person," Herbert said, his voice rising.

"Oh dear, I know that but—"

"Mummy, you always pretend to promote women's rights and to empower women. Actually, it's the rights of women like Mufuzi that you claim to promote—women with low levels of education!"

"Okay, you win, Herbert. Oh dear, what should I say?" Ruth said, shaking her head. "And I *would* like to meet that girlfriend of yours that you seem to be so much in love with."

"Mummy, let me make it clear to you. I don't just seem to be 'so much in love' with Leah. I am madly in love with her, and of course you can meet her. Shall I invite her home?"

Is the boy crazy? "Not at home, dear, not yet. She will meet me at the shop."

"But I guess Daddy would like to meet her, too."

"Not now, he will meet her after I have approved of her."

"What? We don't need your approval. What matters is that Leah and I are in love."

"That's all right," Ruth said as she placed a cup of tea on the table for her son. "Please let her come meet me."

"Promise me one thing, Mummy. Don't embarrass my girlfriend by asking her irrelevant questions," Herbert said.

"What kind of questions are those or do you mean that I should not ask her any questions? Do you know what I'm thinking?" Ruth said, irritated. "Shall I give you a list of questions that I want to ask her, for your preapproval?"

"No, that's not what I meant. What I am saying is that you should let her feel comfortable, because I love her."

✳   ✳   ✳

The following week, Leah went to Ruth's Boutique. Petua was cool as she showed her to Ruth's office. *What an unpleasant woman,* Leah thought, but she quickly focused on her first encounter with *Mwambala mpale.* She was very nervous. As soon as Leah entered Ruth's office, she knelt to greet her future mother-in-law.

"No, no, don't kneel. Please sit on that chair," Ruth said as she showed Leah a chair to sit on.

Leah hesitated. According to her upbringing it would not be good manners to sit on a chair while talking to her future husband's parents. She wondered whether Ruth was testing her manners, and felt a bit uneasy because Ruth seemed to scrutinize her as she talked.

But Ruth soon got a good impression of Leah and their first meeting went well. Ruth's sister Hannah walked into the office just before Leah was leaving and it was obvious that she had been invited to see her.

"Hannah, I can't believe that what I said to my son is contrary to what I preach on a daily basis," Ruth told her sister once Leah left. "I tried to deny him the freedom to choose a wife!"

"You behaved just like other human beings—we are all like that," Hannah said. "But let me give you a piece of advice. You'd be wasting your time standing in his way. Let him marry the woman he loves."

"I think you are right. I wanted him to marry a girl from a prominent family," Ruth paused and tears started rolling down her cheeks. Hannah held her hands. "But I know that marrying into a prominent family is not all that matters. Jude continues to abuse me. He is a great father but a bad husband. Hannah, you know that I have no self-esteem issues but honestly, living with Jude, I have to remind myself that I'm worthy."

Hannah was crying now, too, as she and her sister held hands.

* * *

"Your mother tells me that you've found a man to marry," Lutalo said to Leah in the living room.

"Yes, Father. His name is Herbert Kiyaga."

"That makes me very glad. But before you go any further with your plans, I would like to meet his parents, to chat with them and to get to know them better."

"Do we need to write them a letter?"

"No. A verbal invitation will suffice. If they are free, let them join us for lunch on the last Sunday of this month."

❋　❋　❋

Merab prepared a big meal and invited several friends and members of Lutalo's family. Mukuza and Musirise also attended. But Merab and her family, who expected at least five visitors, were shocked when just Ruth and Jude showed up. The visitors arrived on time and inconvenienced the hosts who were not yet ready to receive them. *The problem with educated people*, Merab thought, *especially these ones that were educated in Europe, is that they take things literally. When you invite them, they arrive fifteen minutes early. We are not even ready yet to receive them*! "It's just the two of them visiting? They've underrated us," Mukuza said to Absalom while they were in the backyard.

At first glance, Merab and Ruth could be mistaken for sisters. Both of them were tall and beautiful with big eyes and deep voices. But aside from their outward appearance they were different in every other aspect. While Ruth was an outspoken well-educated woman who said right away what she thought, Merab was reserved and took time to think about what was said to her. When Merab came into the living room to greet the visitors, Ruth, who was seated on the sofa next to Jude, surprised her by informing her that she should not sit on a mat but on the sofa, next to Lutalo, her husband. Merab was also uncomfortable when Ruth then engaged her in a lengthy conversation, asking questions about Leah. As the hostess, Merab thought it was inappropriate for her to be sitting there in the living room while the rest of the family prepared the meal in the backyard.

"By the way, Jude, this lady is the owner of Kyatelekera Restaurant,"

Ruth said.

Merab could not believe her ears. *What a badly behaved woman! She calls her husband by his name?* And when Ruth crossed her legs, Merab found her very disrespectful. *What? She crosses her legs in the home of her son's future in-laws? At least she is wearing a* gomesi. *But then, who crosses her legs in a* gomesi?

Philemon came late for lunch and after he had apologized to Lutalo and Merab, he greeted the visitors. "Hello, Ruth, I am glad to see you again. How are you?"

"Oh, do you two know each other?" Jude asked.

"Yes," Ruth answered. "Philemon used to work with Mitego."

"I used to work *for* Mitego, not *with* Mitego," Philemon said.

They all laughed.

"It's a small world," Jude said. "How did you come to work for Mitego?"

"At first he hired me to teach him English but a few months later, I was doing more than just teaching him English," Philemon said. "For example, I delivered groceries to his mistresses' homes and I ran errands for one of his companies. I actually had many duties and soon accompanied him everywhere. In the meantime, I did not have a proper job description or title."

Jude laughed but Ruth did not. *I worked for years without a proper job description. And it's not funny.*

"I must say he was a very diligent and quick learner in his language classes. At some point he did introduce me to his friends as his Chief Executive Officer, obviously something he had read in a magazine...but apparently, when he found out that the title would technically place me above him, he dropped it."

Jude laughed again and this time Ruth joined in, too.

At the end of the visit, Leah's uncle Lumu formally addressed the visitors.

"Thank you for coming," he said. "We are glad to have met you and we will be happy when your son marries our daughter."

❄ ❄ ❄

The following week, Herbert wrote a letter to Lutalo requesting his permission to marry his daughter Leah and also to allow him and a few of his friends and family to meet Leah's family in a formal ceremony. When Lutalo's sister Nakirijja delivered the letter to him, he convened a meeting in their home in Kawempe to discuss the matter.

"We are very honoured to marry our daughter off," Lumu said. "However, before we discuss anything concerning the ceremony, I want us to agree on one thing. The ceremony must take place in our ancestral home in Kalasa."

"Of course, that goes without saying," Nakirijja said.

"I don't know whether Leah will be happy with that," Lutalo said.

"What's wrong with you?" Lumu said. "Leah can't decide for us. She's only a child."

The following day, Roger who had attended the meeting, told Leah that the family had decided to hold the ceremony in Kalasa.

Leah was not pleased. "Why would we hold the ceremony in a distant rural area when we have this beautiful home in the city?"

"Don't worry," Roger said. "I can find you a rainmaker to make it rain for a whole week before the ceremony. They would have no choice but to hold the ceremony here; the road in Kalasa is impassable during the rainy season!"

Leah laughed. "That's funny, but it would save me a headache if it were actually possible. I don't want my visitors to drive all the way to Kalasa."

Roger did not need to look for a rainmaker. The rainy season began the following week. The ceremony was held in Kawempe.

＊　　＊　　＊

"Herbert, before you get married there are some important things that I would like to tell you," Ruth said to her son. His parents were hosting his bachelor's party in their home later that day.

"Mummy, is it some sort of premarital counselling?" Herbert asked.

"Yes, why not? After all, girls have been getting premarital counselling for generations but the men they marry haven't—*they* are free to do whatever they want in their marriages!" Ruth said, laughing.

"Get on with it, Mummy. I have some loud-mouthed friends coming anytime now," Herbert said.

"I wanted to talk to you about your father and the way he has treated me over the years. He's been very mean to me, and has treated me like rubbish. I don't want you to emulate him."

Herbert didn't say anything, he just listened attentively.

"When people see us they imagine a perfect harmonious couple, but all that is a lie. Our real life is far from harmonious. I've spent many years of my life advocating for women in this country and in my speeches I've been asking women to speak up against abuse. Yet, I've not spoken up for myself, except one time when unfortunately it was your father's kiss on my mouth that made the headlines. Actually, sometimes I feel like I'm a hypocrite."

"Why, Mummy?"

"Simply because I've been telling women to speak up yet I don't speak up— well, I do speak up—I've been asking your father to respect me and to treat me like the equal partner I am—but he continues to abuse me."

"I know that," Herbert said, "and it has always made me angry."

"I'm telling you these very confidential things because you are not only my son, you are my close friend," Ruth said softly. "Please remember that I'm not telling you this to criticize your father—I'm telling you this so you don't follow his bad example." She started to cry.

Herbert smiled at his mother and touched her hand.

"Your father is a very brilliant man who lacks ambition and he has wasted his life," Ruth said sadly. "He has helped build things through his job, but other than that, what has he built? What kind of man fails to build a house for himself, not even a small one? A man of his calibre?"

Herbert knew that his grandfather had given his parents the house they lived in. "I promise, Mummy. I'll not follow Daddy's example."

"Good. Remember, I'll be watching you."

❋   ❋   ❋

While Lutalo was walking his daughter to the altar, he looked straight ahead, his eyes glued to the altar, avoiding the looks of his relatives. He knew they were judging him—the man who abandoned his own home and land to go to live in a wife's house.

During the reception, many in the audience were surprised when for the first time in their lives they saw a mother speaking at a wedding instead of a father, but they clapped and laughed when they heard what Ruth had to say.

"Leah, I tried to judge you before I met you," she said, addressing the beautiful young bride. "But I was wrong—as soon as I met you I saw what a brilliant young woman you are. My son is lucky to have you as his wife."

A month after the wedding, Herbert started working as an economist in the Bank of Uganda. Soon after, Leah began her career as a secretary in the

Ministry of Commerce.

*   *   *

After Clement had completed his course in pharmacology, Clotilda organized a party to welcome her son back home from India. After the party, she asked Jude to co-sign for a bank loan to enable Clement to open a pharmacy in Kampala with his friend Jairus, who had been his classmate at the University of Calcutta. Jude reluctantly agreed and the pharmacy opened soon after.

27

"MOTHER, I THINK you are overworking yourself. You need some time to rest. You should take some days off work," Leah said to Merab one Saturday evening.

"I have to work, my child. I don't want to be lazy," Merab answered. "Besides, if I hadn't worked hard, we wouldn't be where we are now."

"That's right, but you need to take time off to rest, and to take care of yourself."

"I guess those are your mother-in-law's ideas that she got from Europe. Do they work here?" Merab asked, laughing.

"Yes, they are my mother-in-law's ideas but they are good ones. You need time to take care of yourself. You are aging fast."

"I am aging fast?" Merab said, amused. "I *am* old—were you expecting me to grow younger?"

"You are just one year older than my mother-in-law but you look almost ten years older."

"But I heard that she runs every morning and she eats very little food—what for? I find it strange that such an old woman is not ashamed of running down the street like she does," Merab continued. "What do her neighbours think about that strange behaviour?"

"Actually, some of the women in her neighbourhood go out and run with her," Leah told her. "She has taught them the value of physical exercise. They no longer find it strange at all to run for their wellbeing."

"What? Where is this country heading to?" Merab shook her head in disbelief. "Women lack self-respect to that extent? I can't imagine a bunch of old women running down the street like schoolgirls!"

"She rides a bicycle, too. In fact, at times she rides to work."

"That lady has no manners. Don't tell me anymore about her bad behaviour."

"She will be paying us a visit this weekend and I know she'll ask me about you."

"Why would she ask about me?"

"She's just a friendly person who cares about your wellbeing."

"If she asks, tell her to mind her own business. It's rich educated people who can afford to be idle." *I have changed very much and don't like the person I've become—I taught my daughter all her life never to speak ill of people but now I'm doing it? If my father were still alive, he would not recognize me now.*

❊　　❊　　❊

"Leah, how is your mother? I haven't seen her lately," Ruth said while she was helping Leah to arrange her pantry the following weekend.

I knew she would ask. "She is very busy with her work but I told her that she doesn't rest enough," Leah said.

"Does she know that working constantly and never taking time to take care of herself is not good for her health?"

"My mother worked hard against many odds to get to where she is. She therefore thinks that slowing down is a sign of laziness. She says that she doesn't want to be lazy."

"Oh dear, I too worked hard to be where I am but I know the importance of taking time to rest and to take care of oneself."

Those are what my mother called your European ideas. Leah almost laughed.

A few minutes later, Ruth went to the living room to talk to Jude. "I've been talking to Leah about her mother and her health. The poor woman doesn't know the importance of taking care of herself."

"Come on now!" Jude said. "How many women in this city and in this country in general have the kind of exposure you've had?"

"That's not the point. Since I first met Merab, I have talked to her about the importance of her wellbeing but she doesn't want to listen. Her lack of education doesn't help."

"Live your own life—it is not your job to teach others how to live theirs."

"But I don't like it when someone doesn't heed good advice. And the way she dresses is atrocious. I wonder where she puts all her money. She is a rich woman."

"Stop that, will you?" Jude said.

28

October 1978 – December 1979

WHEN THE UGANDA-Tanzania war broke out towards the end of 1978, many people were forced to flee their homes. Schools in areas where the fighting was intense closed and the students were sent home. The Tanzanians were advancing very fast into Ugandan territory and it was apparent that the Ugandan Army was going to lose the war.

Mitego was worried—his eighteen-year-old son Adrian's boarding school had been closed and the students sent home but his son had not returned. Mitego, who'd never seemed to care about his many children, now became restless and focused less on his businesses. Adrian was one of his favourites.

There was no news about Adrian for over a month until one of his friends who had also disappeared turned up. He told Mitego that he, Adrian and several other schoolmates had joined the Ugandan Army when it had been recruiting in the village where the school was located, to help with the war effort. "Adrian is alive," the boy reassured Mitego. "We didn't go to the front line—we helped the more experienced soldiers in the war zone. But I will not be going back."

"Didn't Adrian think of deserting and returning home with you?"

"No, I didn't discuss anything with him. I don't think he knows that I ran away. He actually seemed to be enjoying himself in the army," the young man said. "He performed the drills faster and better than most of us."

Mitego's friends got concerned about his safety when he said that he would try to go to the area where his son's school was located to look for him.

When the fighting got closer to the city of Kampala, Ruth locked up her shop and decided to flee the city. She, Herbert and Leah, now pregnant, left the country for Nairobi in the middle of the night, and they monitored the situation back home day and night from there.

A few days after the Tanzanians had captured Kampala, some people started returning to the city. Collin called Ruth in Nairobi to inform her that her boutique had been looted, like many other businesses. He had gone to check on the shop and seen two men walking away with the last rug. Ruth wept. It was well-known that some of the looters had even been Kampalans who'd been left in the city.

When Ruth returned from Nairobi and toured her shop a month and a half after it had been looted, she saw that nothing of value was left inside. It appeared that the boutique had at some point served as a resting place, and the two sofas the looters hadn't taken were stained by bits of food and drink. Ruth estimated that she had lost hundreds of thousands of shillings in stolen and damaged merchandise. *I don't think I can rebuild this business now. I've got to reassess my options. Perhaps I should go look for a job.*

She visited the filthy, empty premises twice during the week she returned from Nairobi. The second time, while she was still pondering her situation, her father came to the shop. "Do you think you can rebuild the business?" Collin asked her.

"Probably I can, but I don't want to, Daddy."

"Then I have a suggestion for you," Collin said. "The war did not affect my company. Now that I'm very old—"

"You are not very old, Daddy."

"Okay," he said, smiling and continuing, "—now that I'm old, why don't I let you manage the company? Your brother Mark helps out mostly in the field and he can keep doing that. You can concentrate on administration and take over from me as Managing Director. Given your business skills, the company will grow even further—more so because the city will have to be rebuilt. You'll get many contracts."

"Thanks for the offer, Daddy. I can take the job—"

"You can take the job or you will take the job?"

"I will take the job but we need to discuss my remuneration. I wouldn't want to work for free simply because I am an unemployed daughter of the company owner."

"I don't work for free," Collin said, laughing. "And neither will you."

❋   ❋   ❋

Leah had such severe morning sickness at the beginning of her pregnancy that she was admitted to hospital for close monitoring. Herbert told Merab when she got there that the doctor had told him Leah was dangerously dehydrated and that she was pregnant with twins. The doctor planned to carry out further tests that morning.

When she left the hospital, Merab was so worried about her daughter's health she decided to go see Reverend Kasi.

"Let's have a cup of tea after which we will pray for Leah," Reverend Kasi said when Merab told him about Leah's condition. "She will get well and deliver her children safely." They prayed together, and when Merab left, she felt reassured.

When she arrived at the restaurant, Nabukalu asked her how Leah was, and Merab told her.

"Mufuzi, I know you don't believe in our traditional medicine but wouldn't it help if we consulted a healer?"

"No," Merab answered. "Don't talk to me about those things."

"Think about it," Nabukalu said. "This is a serious matter—and since she is carrying twins, it makes it even harder. Twins are not ordinary children. You'll need a healer to advise you on how to prepare before they are born and what cultural ceremonies you will need to perform after they are born."

Merab sat quietly thinking about her daughter's condition. After about a half-hour, she told Nabukalu she was going out and would be back soon—she'd decided to visit a healer although she did not want Nabukalu to know that she had taken her advice seriously. Merab knew that Philemon also believed in traditional religions and regularly consulted healers. She went now to her cousin, and he volunteered to take her to see a healer that night.

While Merab went in to consult the healer, Philemon waited in the car. The room was so dark that Merab could not see the man even when she looked straight in the direction of his voice, which was deep and very authoritative. At one moment she thought she recognized it. Was he one of the regulars at her restaurant?

"You are dating a married man, aren't you?" the healer said.

"No, I am not," Merab answered. "My husband was a polygamist but he left the other women. I am his only wife now."

"I see another woman here," the healer said as he shook what sounded like empty gourds with small pebbles in them. "This woman has three grown children with your husband."

Merab thought about Kulumba's mother.

"This woman does not want your daughter to have children."

"Oh!" Merab exclaimed.

"But I have a solution for you. We can stop all her evil powers. But I will ask a few things of you before we proceed."

The man then recited a long list of herbs and other things, including a molar tooth of a leopard, which he required before he began. Merab had never heard of most of the things. "Of course you can pay for one of my assistants to collect all these things for you," the healer said.

Merab said that she would return to pay the following day.

Merab tried to replay in her mind what had transpired at the healer's as Philemon drove her home. She thought the visit had been useless, and felt guilty, too, that she, a Christian, had consulted a "witch doctor."

"So, what did he say?" Philemon asked.

"He recited a long list of things to take back," Merab said, but did not tell him what the man had said about Kulumba's mother.

"So, will he help?"

"He said he would—but I will not go back. I wasted my time, and yours."

"It's up to you," Philemon said. They drove in silence the rest of the journey.

When Leah got better, she was discharged from the hospital. However, she developed complications in her final month and was hospitalized again, and two days later her labour pains started. Merab did not leave her daughter's bedside while she went through her twelve-hour labour. Leah delivered two tiny girls early in the morning.

"I have always been told that twins are not ordinary children," Merab said to Herbert while Leah was asleep, "but we will treat them like ordinary children, like any others."

"I agree with you," Herbert said.

"Here's my plan," Merab continued. "I'm going to ask Reverend Kasi to baptize the babies here in the hospital. If anyone asks us, we will tell them that the children are already Christians and can't be subjected to any traditional cultural ceremonies."

Herbert agreed. Reverend Kasi baptized the children in the hospital. The firstborn twin was named "Eunia" and the second one "Dorothy." But people were already calling them by the traditional names given to twins—Babirye, "the first of twin girls," and Nakato, "the second of twin girls," and those were the names that stuck.

Leah was very happy with her children but a bit disappointed that they were both girls. She had hoped that at least one of them would be a boy, a future heir for Herbert.

29

MARCH 1981 – JUNE 1987

LEAH WAS VERY happy with her daughters but still she prayed hard for a son. Her prayers were answered when the twins turned three and she gave birth to a boy whom Herbert named Brandon. Another girl, Hellen, was born three years later.

The twins started school and Leah and Herbert were pleased to note that the girls were very clever in class. Merab frequently visited Leah's home to see her grandchildren and to ask about their progress in school. Schooling was very important in Leah and Herbert's home.

When Eunia and Collin Wamala fell sick at around the same time, their children took very good care of them. Collin was the first to die, and Eunia died two months later.

A month after Eunia's funeral, the Wamala siblings met in the office of a lawyer. He read them their parents' will. "I can't tell you how impressed I am with the four of you," he said after he'd read the last sentence. "There has been total silence in the room. This is not what I encounter on similar occasions with other clients, believe me, and I read wills at least twice a month." The sons Mark and Thomas inherited the bulk of their parents' property but Ruth and Hannah also inherited some property. In addition to two houses in Kampala, Ruth inherited ten acres of land near Kawempe, and within two days had figured out what she wanted to do with it.

Just two months after she got title to the land Ruth officially donated it to Merab's church, St. Peter's Church, in the company of Merab, her son Herbert, his wife Leah and her daughter Kate, and following a brief speech. "I'm happy to donate this land to the church," she said. "The only condition is that a school must be built on it and that at least twenty-five percent of the student population must be girls from needy families." Reverend Kasi cheerfully accepted.

Merab was very happy with Ruth's donation and decided to donate something to the school as well. When it opened its doors two years later, Merab was there, serving porridge to the needy boarding students. She did not know it then, but that she would have the energy and the commitment to serve similar breakfasts at the school every day, rain or shine, for years to come.

❋   ❋   ❋

One Friday evening, wanting to rekindle her on-off relationship with Jude, Clotilda went to the White Nile Club to wait for him to arrive. She had secretly watched him for over a week to know his new evening routine and she had visited the bar several times to get acquainted with the place and its staff. She ordered a beer and perched on a high stool by the counter. A few minutes later, Jude came into the bar, and saw her.

He had decided to avoid her for good but there she was. He would not have wanted to greet her but she had sat in a place where he could not ignore her. He had mixed feelings about her. "Hey, how are you?" Jude said.

"I'm doing well, sweetheart. How are you?" Clotilda smiled.

"Don't call me "sweetheart.""

"I'm doing well, Jude. Can I order a drink for you? Wilber, can you please serve a cold Bell to this gentleman?" Clotilda said to the barman.

Jude was surprised to note that Clotilda knew the barman's name. "I don't drink beer anymore—"

279

"But you do," Clotilda said as the barman placed a bottle of Bell Lager and a glass in front of him, Jude's usual. "Pick up your drink and follow me," Clotilda said as she rose to go to an empty room. Jude followed her hesitantly. She looked at him with a smile. "You've never visited my school, have you?"

"Do I have to?" Jude asked.

"You don't have to but it would be nice if you did."

"I can't visit your school because like I told you years ago, you are very stupid."

"I know what you said," Clotilda answered, "but my stupidity shouldn't stop you from coming to see the progress I've made at the school."

"I don't care, stupid woman! It's your progress, not my progress. You got what you wanted—free land—and I don't owe you anything."

"Mind you, whatever I'm doing I'm doing it for your son. I don't know whether—"

"Hey Jude, how are you?" Jude's friend Darlington said as soon as he entered the bar, interrupting their conversation. "Oh, I didn't realize you had company. I'll let you two enjoy your evening."

"No, no problem. Join us," Jude said as he motioned Darlington to sit down.

As soon as Darlington sat down, Clotilda rose. She did not greet or acknowledge him. "You should visit the school, Mr. Kiyaga," she said as she walked out of the room.

❋　❋　❋

Two weeks later, although Jude had repeatedly told himself that he did not want to, he did go to see Clotilda's school, and she took him for a tour around.

"This is very impressive," he said. The school was bigger than he'd thought it would be, with beautiful buildings and well-kept grounds. "Great job," Jude said as they passed a group of young students who were playing soccer in a small playground.

"Thank you. I'll show you around my house too," Clotilda said, and Jude did not decline that invitation, either.

"You have a beautiful home," Jude said, stepping into the living room.

"Thank you."

Clement emerged from his bedroom. "Good afternoon, Father."

"Hey, good afternoon, Clement. How are you?"

"I'm well. Sorry I can't sit to chat. I have an appointment with Herbert."

"Good to see you. Tell Herbert I'm here," Jude said. "They shouldn't look for me."

"Okay. See you," Clement said as he walked out, wondering what Jude meant by that.

Clotilda smiled as she went to the refrigerator and took out two cold beers.

Later that evening Jude called home. "Hey, listen," he told Ruth. "I will not be returning home for a while."

"Why not? Where are you?" Ruth asked.

"Where I am is none of your business. I only called so you don't start looking for me. I'm safe here," Jude said as he replaced the receiver.

Ruth shook her head. *He has resumed his relationship with Clotilda. I'm not going to let him back into my life.*

"Clement told me that Daddy went to see their home for the first time last week," Herbert told his mother three days later.

"Yes, and that's where he is. I have not seen him since Friday evening."

❋   ❋   ❋

A month passed. Jude still lived in Clotilda's home. When one of his colleagues told Herbert that his father did not go to work some days, Herbert went to Clotilda's home to talk to him. When he knocked, it was Jude who opened the door. He had a glass of beer in his hand and he was already drunk.

"Come in," Jude said. "How are you? What brings you here? Come in and have a seat."

Herbert looked around and it appeared that his father was alone in the house. "Daddy, what's going on? Why aren't you home?"

"I live here now."

"Is there a problem between Mummy and you?"

"It's none of your business."

"Daddy, you've become a nuisance. I met your boss Mr. Fadamula yesterday and he told me that sometimes you don't show up for work."

"Herbert, you are not trying to police me, are you?"

"Go back home, Daddy. You are disgracing our family."

"I'll go back when I want," Jude said, slurring his words a little. "Say, do you want a beer?"

"No, thanks," Herbert said and walked out without another word.

❋   ❋   ❋

Herbert went right away to see his mother at Wamala & Sons Construction and told her what had been said, as soon as he closed the door behind him.

"And he was drinking there in the middle of the afternoon."

"Really? Oh dear."

"Mummy, Daddy is a nuisance and I told him that. Why don't you divorce him?"

"Listen, Herbert. You are not just my son—as I have said, you are my close friend. The thing is, I love your father and I will remain loyal to him. If there is a problem between him and me, it is in his mind, not mine. He'll return home when he feels like."

❊   ❊   ❊

Jude lived in Clotilda's home for over a year. He only returned home to pick up a suit or other dress clothes when he needed them for special occasions. When his daughter Kate once asked him what the problem was, she got the same answer as Herbert had: "It's none of your business."

❊   ❊   ❊

One evening after dinner, Ruth was watching TV and thumbing through a home improvement magazine when she heard a familiar voice. The TV program was about developments in education and Clotilda was being interviewed. The interviewer was asking her how she had developed her school from one that was little-known to one of the best schools in the district. "If you are to succeed at anything, you need to work hard at it and focus," Ruth heard Clotilda say. "It's only those of us who focussed on what we wanted to achieve that succeeded in the long run. People have started all sorts of businesses—retail shops, so-called 'boutiques' and other things," she said disdainfully. "They failed simply because they didn't focus."

People started boutiques and failed? Who does Clotilda think she is? As soon as Clotilda's interview had ended, Ruth picked up the phone.

Mark Wamala was at home watching TV when the telephone rang. It was his sister Ruth. He glanced at his wife Enid on the sofa next to him and smiled. He and Enid had watched Clotilda and had both heard her mention "so-called boutiques" among the businesses that failed.

"Good evening, Mark," Ruth said. "I'll be coming to the office late tomorrow. I am planning to reopen my boutique…" Mark glanced at Enid again and smiled. "…so I will need to tour a few premises for rent in the morning."

"You are planning to reopen the boutique?" Mark asked, glancing again at Enid. "Ruth, how long have you been planning—that? Just now? All right then. I'll see you tomorrow," he said and replaced the receiver.

"You seem to be amused," Enid said. "What's going on?"

"That was Ruth," Mark answered. "She's planning to reopen her boutique."

"Could it be because of Clotilda's comments?" Enid asked.

"Most probably, but once Ruth has made up her mind, there's nothing you can say that will make her change it. We'll only have to help her with her plans."

The following morning, Ruth visited several buildings along the upscale Kampala Road business area. By noon, she had seen one vacant shop that she thought would be the ideal location for her new boutique.

She arrived at her office at Wamala & Sons Construction in the afternoon. "So, you want to reopen the boutique?" Mark asked her, laughing. "You seem to be rushing the idea. Are you reacting to Clotilda's comments on TV last night?"

"Hey, you watched that interview, too, didn't you? Who does Clotilda think she is? She doesn't even know why I abandoned it—"

"You need to plan before you reopen and I know someone who can help guide you," her brother said. "Do you remember my friend Tucker Kabanda?" Ruth shook her head. "Tucker used to work in the Ministry of Commerce but now he is married to the bottle—"

"What do you mean?"

"He drinks so much that he lost his job two years ago. But he is still sharp, and you can make good use of his knowledge of business. I can drive you to his home tomorrow morning if you want."

❊   ❊   ❊

"Mark, are you sure you know where Mr. Kabanda lives? This is a slum," Ruth said as Mark stopped the car in Kamwokya-Kifumbira, about five kilometres from Kampala's downtown.

"Yes, Tucker lives here. He has no job—it's his sister who pays his rent. I guess this is the area she can afford."

Mark knocked hard on the door before opening it and going into the room. A curtain divided the room into two, one space for the bed and another for two chairs. Both sides were full of books and dirty clothes littered almost every inch of the floor.

"Tucker, wake up. Good morning. It's Mark. My sister Ruth is right here with me. She would like to consult you for her business. Please help her," Mark said, and went back outside.

"How are you, Mark?" Tucker mumbled from his bed.

"Go in," Mark said to Ruth. "It's not the most beautiful room you've ever entered but Tucker is knowledgeable. I'll be back in an hour."

Ruth entered and stood by the door. The room stunk. "Good morning, Mr.

Kabanda. My name is Ruth Kiyaga—" Ruth began.

"I know who you are, Ruth. I went to school with Mark," Tucker answered as he pulled the curtain away and rose from his bed. "Call me Tucker," he said as he rose from his bed. It was plain that he was drunk.

"Tucker, my shop, Ruth's Boutique, was destroyed in the 1979 war," she began. "I need your advice about how to reopen it. You've been highly recommended—" *But could it be true?* she thought.

"Yes, I'm available to answer any questions that you might have. I'm always here; you don't need an appointment," Tucker said, grinning.

"I'm very glad to hear that," Ruth said.

"Sorry about the mess. You know I live alone and I'm quite busy. There's no time to clean this place," Tucker said as he removed a pile of books from a chair for Ruth to sit. "Feel at home, Ruth."

"Thanks, dear," Ruth said, sitting gingerly on the dusty chair.

"So, Ruth, can you tell me a little about your new boutique idea?"

"I want to re-establish it and make it even better than before."

"Good. Then the first thing we will need to do is to modify the name," Tucker said. "Not an entirely new name—just modify the old name to give the boutique a new vibe. Change it to something catchy. Remember, times have changed since '79 and you are not only going to have a new clientele, you are going to face tougher competition. The earlier you distinguish your business from others before you relaunch, the better it will work for you."

"That's a great idea Mr. Kabanda. I—"

"Well, you came to me because you heard I had great ideas, didn't you Ruth?" Tucker said, chuckling. "The other important factor to consider is the location. You've got to reopen the boutique in a new location where the nouveaux riches hang out."

"That would be a good idea but such places cost a lot in rent, and I don't have that kind of money."

"Come on, now! The Managing Director of Wamala Construction doesn't have money? You expect me to believe that?"

"Looks can be deceiving sometimes."

"Just do as I recommend and believe me, you'll make your money back and get so much more," Tucker said. "Make your reopening a big event by inviting an influential figure, like the mayor. TV and radio advertising prior to the event also works but I'd invest mostly in radio advertising several weeks before the reopening. In addition, you've got to make sure that you get positive messages out to potential customers using any means you can find."

"Just a moment, please. Let me take some notes," Ruth said as she took her notebook from her bag.

"Don't worry about it. I can write up something for you. My fees are not high."

"Please do write everything down for me. I'll pay you," she said. "Now, can we discuss the location a little more? I looked at some spacious premises on the Crested Crane Building on Kampala Road."

"Wonderful, that's what I was talking about! In a location like that, you can be sure that potential customers with money will easily find you."

"Good," Ruth said. "And you know what I'm thinking? I am going to hire you full time to relaunch the business."

"You want to hire me?" Tucker asked, laughing. "That'd be great but do you think I can work? I am a gone case, Ruth—I miscalculated life and now I live like a pauper."

"I'll help you to get your life back. We can't let such a smart man as you waste your life," Ruth said. *But I failed to stop my own husband from wasting his.*

"So, when are you planning to reopen the boutique?" Tucker asked, "…and saying 'as soon as possible' is not specific enough—you need a timeline, and that will depend on the resources at your disposal. It could be three, four or six months."

"I think six months would be the most realistic timeline."

"Do you know where you are going to source the goods from? Where did you get them before?"

"I used to buy from a supplier in Kenya."

"Times have changed. Traders nowadays buy their goods from such far-off places as Dubai and London."

"I'll contact my friend Manisha. She is very knowledgeable in that area."

Six months later, in addition to arranging the radio advertising for the reopening, Tucker also sent several young people to restaurants, hotels and bars to deliberately start conversations about the new "Ruth's Classic Boutique" and to subtly promote it.

✳   ✳   ✳

When Ruth returned home one evening just a week before the reopening of Ruth's Classic Boutique, Nampa told her that Jude was back and that he was in the bedroom, sleeping.

Ruth went in and woke him up. "I have no problem with you returning to live here," she told her husband. "But for goodness's sake, stay away from my bedroom."

"Okay, I will, but I promise you that I am a changed man. I am very sorry for what I have done to you and I will never do it again," Jude said then he went to Herbert's old bedroom to resume his sleep.

There is no way I can trust him again, Ruth thought. And when in the following days, Ruth returned home around midnight, Jude knew that she was busy with the reopening and he did not complain.

The mayor graced the reopening, and was led on a private tour of the boutique before it was opened to the eager shoppers. Seven sales assistants together with their new boss, Petua, walked about, welcoming and greeting the multitudes of customers to the large, sweet-smelling, inviting shop, and Ruth smiled, remembering Tucker's words: "Just do as I recommend and believe me, you'll make your money back and get so much more." She was delighted to see so many affluent Old Girls of Buweela High School who had come and had just greeted a couple of them personally when all of a sudden she found herself face to face with Clotilda. They stared at each other speechlessly.

Tucker appeared from inside the shop. "Isn't the foot traffic impressive?" he said. Ruth turned to speak to him and Clotilda walked quietly away.

30

July 1987

THE FOLLOWING WEEK Herbert took Clement to Kyatelekera Restaurant for lunch, the first time his half-brother had ever eaten there. Clement enjoyed his lunch and complimented Merab for having established such a popular restaurant.

Two weeks later, he returned with his mother. "The restaurant serves the best food in the city," Clement said as they sat down. "I know you will like it."

"Don't exaggerate things, Clement. How do you know they serve the best food? Have you been to all the restaurants in the city?" Clotilda asked, annoyed. But while they were eating, an idea formed in her mind. She could befriend and get close to Merab to annoy Ruth.

From that time on, Clotilda frequented Kyatelekera Restaurant until she became quite close to Merab, who soon invited her for a meal at her home in Kawempe.

When Ruth heard Leah mention that her mother and Clotilda had become friends, she became alarmed. *What mischief could that woman be up to now?* "Tell your mother not to associate with Clotilda if she doesn't want trouble," Ruth said.

But when Leah relayed Ruth's comment to Merab, Merab fumed, "Who does Ruth think she is? She wants to choose friends for me?"

❋　　❋　　❋

"Mufuzi, I have a business idea for you. If you'd like to, I can invest in your restaurant so we can expand it. We can improve it by purchasing modern appliances to help speed up cooking or we can open another even better restaurant," Clotilda told Merab one evening at the restaurant.

"Thanks for the offer," Merab answered. "But I wasn't planning on growing it beyond what it is now."

"What would prevent you from doing so? The business seems to be doing well—so now is the time to expand it! I'm speaking to you from my experience with my school." Merab had already heard Clotilda say that she had taken a small little-known school and turned it into one of the best schools in the country. "I have all the money that we'd need to modernize the restaurant. We wouldn't need a bank loan."

"Okay. I'll talk to my daughter about it. I'll let you know what she thinks."

Merab left the restaurant early to go pay a visit to Leah at her home and when she saw Ruth's car parked in the front yard, she almost went home. *Ruth is the last person I would like to talk to now. She is too judgmental*, she thought. *I can see Leah another day.* But she went in anyway.

"Hello, Merab," Ruth said as soon as Merab had entered the house. "I'm glad to see you."

"Hello, Ruth, I'm glad to see you too," Merab said.

After they had chatted for a few minutes, Leah went to prepare a cup of tea for her mother.

"Merab, I know that Clotilda has befriended you these days. I told Leah but now I'd like to warn you in person. Clotilda is not a nice person—be very careful as you deal with her," Ruth said.

"I appreciate your concern. Thank you," Merab answered politely but inside she was fuming. *How dare you tell me how to conduct myself? Your problems with Clotilda don't concern me.*

"I've known Clotilda for so long that I can even imagine what she is planning next for you," Ruth continued. "I am guessing that she is interested in your business. She is likely to come up with an enticing proposal that may sound too good for you to turn down. And then she'll ruin you."

Does she already know that Clotilda is interested in investing in the restaurant? Probably she does. "What kind of proposal?"

"I don't know. I'm just thinking aloud—but what I *do* know is that the family of the man who used to own her school still don't know how she came to own it. It's still a mystery to them up to this day," Ruth said. "I know it's none of my business, but I thought I'd warn you about her. As they say, 'forewarned is forearmed.'"

"Thanks for your concern. I'll be careful while dealing with her," Merab said, but Ruth's "meddling into her affairs" annoyed her so much that she left earlier than she had planned, and she did not tell Leah about Clotilda's proposal.

And by the time she arrived home, she had decided to say yes to it. She told Clotilda two days later, and in less than a week Merab had signed a formal agreement with Clotilda, who then deposited 500,000 shillings into Merab's bank account.

❋   ❋   ❋

Clotilda's visits to the restaurant, sometimes as many as three a day, became too frequent for Merab's liking. Merab had originally given Clotilda a free meal once in a while but when she started eating an entire day's worth of free meals, Merab got concerned. However, she did not want to confront Clotilda herself—since her son-in-law Herbert was Clement's half-brother. Clotilda was a member of the family. Merab finally asked the manager to demand payment from Clotilda before she was served any food.

When Clotilda ordered a lunch of tilapia stew with *matooke* plantain, Kulabako walked to her table and said, "Please pay for your meal before we serve you."

"What? What kind of restaurant is this? You want me to pay before I eat your food? What if I don't like it?"

"What do you mean? You wouldn't pay for the food after eating it simply because you didn't like it?" Kulabako asked her.

"Call Mufuzi. I want to talk to her right now," Clotilda said.

"Mufuzi is busy. I handle all the restaurant's financial matters."

"What? Who puts somebody like you in charge of a business's finances?"

The rest of the customers looked at Clotilda but she did not seem to be bothered by that. From her office in the back Merab could hear the commotion, too.

"Don't insult me," Kulabako said. "Get out now."

Clotilda picked up her handbag and walked out of the restaurant. "I will never step foot in your smelly restaurant again. And don't think you'll still have that job you seem to be so proud of by the end of the week," Clotilda said to Kulabako as she strode to her car parked just outside the restaurant's front entrance and its waiting driver.

Merab came into the dining room. "Gentlemen, I'm very sorry for the disturbance," she said to the other diners.

"That woman is crazy!" one man said. "And she is a freeloader—my sister is a cleaner in her school, and she says that the teachers are in constant fights with her over their pay."

Merab shook her head. *Ruth was right. I shouldn't have befriended that woman.*

❋   ❋   ❋

Merab was just leaving her house the following morning when Clotilda's car pulled up, her driver parking it beside Merab's.

"Good morning, Mufuzi," Clotilda said. "I want my money back."

"Come for it this afternoon at the restaurant. I haven't touched any of it."

"Good. And you will pay it back according to the terms of the agreement."

"Okay. See you this afternoon."

But why did she say that I should pay back the money according to the terms of the agreement? What does the agreement say? Merab decided she had to go to the bank first thing to withdraw Clotilda's money. She was in a panic when she arrived at the restaurant and took the agreement out of a drawer in her office. She read it through and although she did not entirely understand the English it was written in, she did not see anything alarming in it, either. She decided to take it to Leah.

"Mother, why did you sign this? What did you need the money for?"

"I didn't need the money. Clotilda almost forced me to—"

"She tricked you—here, look, you agreed to pay her back her money in full with fifteen per cent interest."

"No, I didn't agree to any such thing!"

"Yes, you did—that is the agreement you signed. You are going to have to pay her back 575,000 shillings!"

That afternoon, Merab paid Clotilda the full amount in the offices of Buwule, Sekitto & Company Advocates. Clotilda smiled as she walked away with the money in her bag.

"I wish a pickpocket snatches it all from her," Merab said, wiping away angry tears as she and Leah walked out of the law firm's office.

❋   ❋   ❋

"Merab, I'm sorry to hear that you lost money to Clotilda," Ruth said to Merab when she went for lunch at the restaurant three days later.

Oh, she knows about the money? I should have warned Leah not to talk about it! "It was my fault," Merab said. "I should have listened to you."

"Anyway, as they say, experience is the best teacher," Ruth said. "But please, don't relax my dear. Now Clotilda will not leave you alone."

31

OCTOBER 1987

"MERAB, I DON'T think you have ever taken a vacation," Ruth said. "You need to take time off work to rest."

"Even though I have built a successful business I am still an ordinary woman," Merab answered. "Where would I go?"

"If you want, you can come with me to Nairobi and Mombasa next month. I'll be going away for two weeks."

"Oh, I wouldn't want to travel that far at this age—I'm old!"

"I'm not asking you to walk there, my dear! We would travel by air," Ruth said, smiling. "Think about it and tell me your decision next week."

Merab had never travelled anywhere and didn't want to go away, so she decided to ignore Ruth's invitation.

But two days later Leah asked her about it. "Mother, are you travelling to Nairobi? My mother-in-law told me that she wanted you to go with her." Leah told her mother that it would be good for her to see another part of the world and urged her to go.

So the following month, Merab and Ruth flew to Nairobi and checked into a small hotel. As they strolled through the city, Ruth talked to Merab at length about the importance of taking care of herself.

"Thank you for bringing me out here," Merab said to Ruth on the third day of their vacation. "I didn't know that I could be happy anywhere away from home."

"Hey, thank you for accepting to come with me," Ruth said. "This is a good opportunity for us to get to know each other better."

Merab paused before confiding something that had been worrying her. "You know what's funny?" she began. "I don't know whether I'm just making wrong assumptions but ever since Clotilda stole my money and we parted on such bad terms, city health inspectors have been coming to the restaurant, much too frequently."

"See? Didn't I tell you? She must be sending malicious messages to the City Council. Fortunately your restaurant is always sparkling clean."

✳   ✳   ✳

Kulumba's mother Gemma was very ill in hospital. When Kulumba's cousin Ndugga went to tell him about his mother's illness, he found him sleeping in the doorway to his room, drunk. Ndugga, thinking that he had to cure his cousin's hangover before he took him to the hospital to see his mother, dragged Kulumba into his room, closed the door, and went to the market to buy some food for him. When he returned Kulumba was awake.

"Your mother is very sick," Ndugga said.

"Which mother?" Kulumba asked.

"Your mother Gemma. Eat some food before we go to see her. She is in a very bad condition, in hospital."

When Kulumba and Ndugga arrived at the hospital, Reverend Father Semuyaba was sitting on a stool near the bed looking distraught. Gemma, one of the best singers in the parish choir, was on the verge of death. When Kulumba and Ndugga entered the room, he asked them to help her to sit up in the bed and then asked them to leave the room.

"Gemma, I'm sorry to see you in this state," Father Semuyaba told her. "I will pray for you because you are very sick but before I do so, I would like to know if there is something you would like to say."

"No, I have nothing to say Father," Gemma replied.

"Are you sure?" he said gently to the dying woman. "Aren't there things you would like to put right?" Gemma began to cry. "Don't be upset," Father Semuyaba said. "I am not here to judge you. I would like you to say whatever you have on your mind. Anything you want to put right."

"Yes, I have a confession to make," Gemma said, sobbing. "I regret the way I have treated a certain woman I've never met."

"Who is that woman?"

"Mufuzi—the woman who raised my children," she said. "I said bad things about her over the years, yet deep down I knew that she was innocent. She did a job that I failed to do—she raised my children. I would like to apologize to her if she can come to see me here."

Father Semuyaba called Kulumba and his sister Nabbosa, who had been helping to look after her mother, into the room again.

"My children," Gemma told them, "it is clear that I don't have a lot of time left in this world. There is something I want to ask of you. I would like you to ask your mother Mufuzi to come see me."

Kulumba gasped and Nabbosa looked incredulous.

"Please ask Mufuzi to come see me," Gemma repeated, her voice pleading. "I have to tell her that I am sorry for having been so unkind to her. I would also like to thank her from the bottom of my heart for raising you."

"Mufuzi is away," Kulumba said. "She is visiting Kenya."

So Gemma died without ever meeting Merab.

When Merab returned, Kulumba told her about Gemma's last wish. Merab cried and said that she would have liked to meet Gemma, but she was not totally sure that what Kulumba had told her was true. Had he just invented the story to make his late mother look good?

32

LUTALO FELL SICK and his condition deteriorated quickly. Merab stayed in the hospital to help nurse him for a week, then asked Kulumba to go to Kalasa to ask Musirise to come take over from her.

"Oh, it's now that he is sick that they remember us?" Mukuza asked. "Why does he need us after having abandoned us here for years?"

Musirise did not respond.

"Was it your father or Mufuzi who asked for Musirise to go to the hospital?" Mukuza asked.

"It was Mufuzi who requested—"

"Don't go there, Musirise! Let Mufuzi take care of him," Mukuza said.

Musirise said nothing as she got up to go prepare for the journey to Mulago Hospital.

When she and Kulumba arrived at the hospital, Merab was just preparing to leave for the day. "Thanks for taking care of him," Musirise said.

"Don't thank me," Merab said. "I am just fulfilling my pledge to him—in sickness and in health."

Had Merab said that to remind her that she was Lutalo's only wedded wife? Musirise shook her head to banish that thought. She knew that Merab was not a malicious person.

Left alone with Musirise Lutalo was uneasy, feeling guilty that a woman he had abandoned now had to take care of him. He felt it was lucky that Musirise didn't talk much—it would have been harder for him if it had been Mukuza sitting at his bedside there in the hospital.

When Lutalo was discharged a week later Musirise stayed in the home in Kawempe to take care of him for a few days and then return to Kalasa. But Lutalo fell sick again and again was hospitalized.

Merab and Leah were in the hospital by Lutalo's side the night he died, at seventy-five. They wept loudly and people who had come to visit other patients in the ward gathered to console them. Afterward, when Leah informed the rest of the family they too began wailing. Leah sent announcements through Radio Uganda to inform relatives, in-laws and friends far and near about her father's passing.

Lutalo's funeral was attended by hundreds of people. During the burial, Merab almost fainted as she wailed for Lutalo: "Lutalo, you were my best friend. I was a young girl when you took me from my father's home. Now you are gone, forever!"

※　※　※

A month after the burial, all of Lutalo's children met in Kampala in the offices of Buwule, Sekitto & Company Advocates to learn the contents of their father's will. Lutalo had listed all his children by name and date of birth and then all the assets he owned. After he had read all of these, Mr. Buwule began reading how this property was to be allocated.

As soon as it was clear that Mr. Buwule was finished, there were murmurs among Lutalo's children. "Is there a problem?" Mr. Buwule asked. Nobody answered so he resumed reading.

"Sorry—yes, there *is* a problem," Jonah said. "I did not hear the home in Kawempe being mentioned in the will."

"I am aware of the existence of the home you are talking about but your father did not include it in his will. So, what that means is that it did not belong to him," Mr. Buwule said.

"That's not possible!" Jonah answered. "It is my father's home."

"Sir, I will ask you to keep quiet and pay close attention to what I am reading to you. These are very important matters and I will not allow any interruptions. If you have any complaints, I'll tell you later the right procedures to follow," Mr. Buwule said. "*My son Roger Bbosa, the firstborn son of my former wife Musirise, shall be my heir,*" Mr. Buwule read.

Jonah had kept quiet but he was fuming, and now he rose and stormed out of the room. Kulumba lost his temper, too—as the late Lutalo's firstborn son he had thought that he'd automatically be the heir. He too rose from his seat and went out of the room.

Mr. Buwule resumed reading. "*'...Roger Bbosa shall be my heir. However, he shall not inherit the family home in Kalasa. The home shall remain the property of the entire family to enjoy.'*"

Jonah returned a few minutes later still disappointed and sat down just in time to hear *'My daughter Leah Nalutalo Kiyaga has the overall responsibility of overseeing the family home in Kalasa and all the property that I have not allocated to anybody. She must be consulted first before any major decision is made.'*

When they heard this, Jonah and Dunstan both jumped to their feet. "I don't accept that!" Jonah said. "Leah is a woman—she can't be entrusted with that responsibility!" Jonah himself had been looking forward to inheriting the large house in Kalasa.

"Besides, she is married and no longer belongs to our clan. She belongs to her husband's clan," Dunstan said.

"Gentlemen," Mr. Buwule said coolly, "you should not air your objections through verbal statements. That will not help anybody. I advise you to convene a clan meeting to raise all the matters that you don't agree with. If that doesn't work, then you can submit a formal complaint to the law courts."

The two brothers stormed out of the meeting and did not return.

❋   ❋   ❋

"Hello. Thanks for calling *Munno* Publications. Can I help you?"

"Hello, can I please speak to Mr. Timothy Mbogo?"

"Hold on."

"Hey Tim, it's Ruth. How are you?"

"Hello, Ruth, I'm well. How are you?"

"Very well, thank you. Listen, my sister will be celebrating her restaurant's twenty-fifth anniversary in two weeks' time. Can you please interview her for an article in your newspaper?"

"Yes, I can. I didn't know Hannah owns a restaurant."

"No, it's not Hannah," Ruth said, laughing. "It's Mufuzi. Kyatelekera Restaurant."

"I know that lady. She is not your sister."

"She is not my sister but she is my son's mother-in-law. We've become like sisters."

"Mufuzi is Herbert's mother-in-law? Yes, I can interview her. I'll contact her to set up an appointment."

*　　*　　*

When Mbogo called her, at first Merab declined the invitation to do the interview. "I'm an uneducated woman. Will I be able to say anything sensible for a newspaper article?"

"Don't worry, I will guide you. You managed to establish and manage a successful business; you are an intelligent woman," Tim said.

Merab reluctantly agreed to do the interview. She and Tim met at the restaurant one Sunday afternoon.

After fifty-eight-year-old Merab had introduced herself and given a brief history, Mbogo said, "Tell me a little about how you grew this restaurant. Some of your competitors alleged that you used magic medicine to grow it and to drive them out of business. What do you say about that?"

"Who told you that?" Merab asked, laughing. "Mr. Mbogo, I'm a Christian and I've never been involved in magic medicine. I run my business as honestly and honourably as possible."

"Is it true that you didn't go far with formal education?"

"Unfortunately, my parents did not know the value of education. They married me off very young and so I missed out on fulfilling my dream of becoming a teacher."

"To what factors do you attribute your success?"

"Honesty, hard work, and giving my customers what they really pay for," Merab said, "and that's value for their money. From day one, Kyatelekera Restaurant has delivered its promise to its customers—feeding them to their fill with real food that's fresh from the farm. As far as hard work is concerned, I am involved in the day-to-day running of the restaurant. You will find me here toiling January to December."

"Let's go back to what you said about value for money—as someone who started out as a food vendor in the market, don't you think you snub the majority of people in this city with your high prices? Yours is the most expensive local restaurant in the city."

"Mr. Mbogo, this is a business. When I established it I wanted to sell good food in a decent place. Obviously prices in a restaurant such as this will be higher than in the market—it is true that our prices are high but so is the quality of our food. I think this restaurant has acted as a good ambassador for local Ugandan cuisine. Thousands of people, including tourists, dine here every year."

"The meetings that you started in your restaurant for young women years ago grew into a movement—*Omukyala Omugunjufu*—popularly known as OO. What led to the demise of OO?"

"Unfortunately, many people misunderstood the teachings of OO, claiming that OO's teachings promoted the subjugation of women. Yet our major objective was to promote our own culture, which, unfortunately, has been eroded by foreign cultures."

"You encouraged women to obey their husbands, among other things. Your critics said that was one of the things that would promote the subjugation of women."

"It's the Bible that teaches women to obey their husbands. I didn't invent that myself."

"What message do you have for the young women who, like you, did not get a chance to go far with their formal education?"

"I would like to tell all young women that they have talents. You've got to know yourself in order to discover those talents. When you do, use them every day. The rewards will be big."

"Your name is Merab but you are popularly called Mufuzi. What is the origin of that name?"

"Oh. That actually relates to the previous point—talent. My husband nicknamed me Mufuzi—the Administrator—when he noticed my qualities as a manager. I was a very young woman when I married him and I increased the home's income in a short time."

Merab answered many other questions. She was thrilled to see the article and her picture in *Munno* two weeks later.

33

WHEN LEAH'S YOUNGEST daughter Hellen completed primary school, her aunt Victoria took her to live and study in Boston. Both Babirye and Nakato studied in Makerere University, became doctors and married later.

When it was time for Brandon to start university he decided to do a Diploma course in Music, Dance and Drama. Herbert did not like Brandon's choice. He had wanted him to become an economist like him.

"So your ambition is to go to the university to study dance? You want to become a dancer?"

"The course includes Music, Dance and Drama. I want to be an all-round artist," Brandon said.

"Is that the best course of study you could find?"

"That's what I want to study."

"Brandon, I want you to be serious with your life. I want you to study something that will help you make a living."

"I can make a living with music."

"No, find another sensible course."

"Daddy, music and dance are what I want to study."

"You know what you should do? Go live down the street in your grandmother's home. She is the only person who can tolerate your nonsense."

Brandon packed his suitcase and walked to Ruth's house. "Study what you want and become whatever you want to become," Ruth told Brandon when he recounted his conversation with his father. "I went through a similar situation and I know that it is not easy to do something different than what your parents have planned for you. But it is your life, isn't it? You've got to pursue your dreams."

❋   ❋   ❋

When Brandon completed his course two years later, Ruth invited Herbert and the other members of the family for lunch to celebrate his achievement. Merab couldn't attend because Kyatelekera Restaurant was short-staffed—its long-serving manager, Kulabako, had just left to go take care of her elderly parents.

While they were preparing lunch, Ruth overheard Babirye say to Leah, "Mummy, I often think about my two grandmothers. They are totally different."

"Oh yes, but they are both interesting women—and they both beat the odds against them to build their businesses," Leah said.

"How did they manage to do that at a time when women didn't have many opportunities?"

"Your grandmother Ruth is an educated woman and she had made a concrete plan to set up and to run her business, while my own mother says she just followed her gut and that her success in business was accidental," Leah said. "But I don't believe her."

"Why don't you believe her?" Brandon asked.

"My mother had one goal in mind. Everything she did was aimed at securing a good future for me."

"And I guess that worked?" Brandon said. They all laughed.

"Of course it worked," Leah said, laughing. "I turned out fine and raised a good family that I'm very proud of."

While they were having lunch, Nakato asked Ruth, "Grandma, we've been asking Mummy about your history. Can you please tell us about your past and how you managed to set up the Boutique?"

"Hey, you know what's funny? I had the ambition to start my business but I didn't find it easy to decide when to start. However, I was treated unfairly at my workplace and that forced me to take action. I resigned. You know I'm impulsive. Who of you is impulsive? There must be somebody in the family that inherited the gene."

The siblings laughed. "It's Babirye," Brandon said.

"No, I'm not impulsive," Babirye answered.

"Yes, you are!" Brandon said.

"Anyway, I resigned from my job and started Ruth's Boutique but it wasn't easy. I got a lot of resistance from my family, especially from my mother and my husband."

"Why did they resist? They didn't think the idea of starting a business was good?" Babirye asked.

"She had a good job and she'd just walked away from it," Jude said as he bit a chunk of meat off a bone.

"My mother said that I was wasting my education by becoming what she called a "trader," yet my goal was not merely to be a trader. I planned to do more than just buying and reselling goods. And actually soon after I started, I taught people things like how to furnish and decorate their homes, and even how to keep their homes clean and tidy!"

"Really? You taught people how to clean their homes?" Brandon asked.

"Yes I did," Ruth answered. "It was some kind of after sales service through which I would demonstrate how to furnish a room. I would say something like 'this rug must be cleaned regularly' or 'take these curtains down to wash them every six months because they collect dust'."

"Would you demonstrate such things to groups of customers or to individual customers?" Babirye asked.

"I would demonstrate not to customers only but to whoever dropped into the shop. You see, many people knew that I had studied in England and that fascinated them. In the past it was a big deal. Is that what you say, 'big deal?' It was a big deal to travel to Europe, let alone to study there. So, some of the people came just to ask about my experiences in England. Actually, at one point, we people who had spent time overseas became the subject of ridicule when a theatrical group staged a play in which the main character returns from England and ends up messing up his life—"

"Oh, that's interesting. Please tell us more about that play," Brandon said.

"Yes, it was a very interesting play by the Kayayu Film Players. Darling, do you remember that play?"

"Yes I do. Who can forget Bulime's story?" Jude answered.

"So, the main character Bulime returns to Uganda from England after a couple of years' stay," Ruth continued. "He pretends to have forgotten his mother tongue Luganda and pronounces things in a very funny way, mimicking the English accent. People get amused and some follow him everywhere because they think he is great. However, with time, the jobless Bulime becomes broke and ends up stealing chickens in the neighbourhood in order to sell them to get money to buy alcohol and cigarettes. When he is caught one day, he pleads for mercy in perfect Luganda."

"Actually, most people who returned from England spoke with a fake English accent," Herbert said.

Ruth continued. "The play ended with a moral. People should never steal chickens because if anybody did, it would bring bad luck to them."

The three siblings laughed.

"You live in the city where there are no chickens scratching around in search of food so these things probably don't make much sense to you," Ruth said. "Anyway, let me go back to what we were talking about. I think women these days are having an easier life than when I was younger."

"Why do you think so, grandmother?" Nakato asked.

"There is no doubt that you still have challenges especially in our male-dominated society but at least now you can dress the way you like, you can freely own property, and you have more or less the same opportunities as men."

"We still have to fight to get some of these things," Nakato said.

"Sure, but probably not as hard as I had to fight," Ruth answered. "In whatever you do now, you have the support of your parents and your husbands. But I had to fight to convince my parents, especially my mother, to let me do what I wanted to do. Women faced a lot of criticism everywhere. Whatever went wrong in society was blamed on women. When children failed in school, the blame was put on their "dumb" mothers. Oh, dear!"

The siblings laughed.

"Ruth, you exaggerate sometimes," Jude said.

"What she is saying is true, Daddy," Herbert said.

❋   ❋   ❋

The following day, Herbert took Petua's daughter Veronica to Kyatelekera Restaurant. He said that she had just completed her university studies and recommended her for the position of manager. Merab hired her right away.

❊   ❊   ❊

Four months later, Brandon's singing career rose to new heights when he released his song *Tobbanga nkoko*—"Never Steal Chickens." The lyrics of the song came from the Kayayu Film Players' play that Ruth had told her family about and followed the plot and the moral of that play. The chorus of the song became so popular on FM radio stations that even toddlers began to imitate it.

Munnange ebintu bikalubye

Era tukitegeera tolina wadde ekuba ennyonyi

Naye genkuwa tobbanga nkoko

Kubanga ojja kuba ng'ono gaayi Bulime

Kale yasoma naye kati abba nkoko.

Things are tough, dear friend / We know you are broke, but listen, don't steal chickens / Because if you do, you will be like Bulime / An educated man who ends up stealing chickens.

❊   ❊   ❊

Family and friends met in Herbert and Leah's home to celebrate Merab's eightieth birthday. After lunch, Merab blew out the candles on the cake. After she had cut the cake, Herbert suggested she say a few words but Merab refused.

"I'll speak on her behalf," Leah said. "Everyone, thanks for coming. I'm very glad for having had this opportunity to organise this party for my wonderful mother. As some of you know, my mother was married when she was just fifteen—she told me once that she sometimes felt like just a child herself in her husband's big house—and she waited for almost ten agonizing years before she got me. I am the only child she bore and all my life I have been the centre of my mother's life. She sacrificed everything for me, working hard to build a business, to make sure I was educated and to pay for my education. And throughout all those struggles, there was never a day that she showed that I was a burden to her." Leah and Merab were both crying now. "I am very proud of you, Mother, and so happy to have you around," Leah said, hugging Merab.

After the guests had left, Leah and her daughters sat in the living room to chat.

"Mummy, that was a great speech. I'd never heard you speak so emotionally," Nakato said.

"Neither had I," Babirye said. "While you were speaking, I visualized the things you were talking about and thought how lucky we have always been to have such a hard-working grandmother."

Merab, who had been outside seeing off her cousin Scovia and her family, came into the living room.

"Grandma," Nakato said, "You were so young when you married!"

"Oh yes, I was very young," Merab said, smiling at the girls. "I didn't want to get married at fifteen. I dreamed of becoming a teacher." She picked up a glass from the tray and poured some water for herself. "One day, I returned home from school and my aunt—God rest her soul—told me that I was getting married in two weeks' time."

"What? Two weeks? So your dreams of becoming a teacher were cut short?" Nakato asked.

"But that was not the worst part," Merab continued. "The worst part was that I didn't know who I was going to get married to. I was getting married to a complete stranger."

"So you see why I always say that most things have become easier for your generation, girls?" Leah said. "And for my generation too, to a large extent—at least my husband was not a stranger when I married him."

"That's right, things are easier for our generation," Nakato said, laughing.

"Actually, Babirye even chose a husband for herself."

"Babirye chose her husband?" Merab asked.

"Yes she did," Nakato said, laughing some more.

"No I didn't! You exaggerate things, Nakato," Babirye said, embarassed.

"I'm not exaggerating," Nakato said. "Babirye almost forced Brian to propose to her."

"Is that so? What happened?" Leah asked.

"Mummy," Babirye said, "the thing is, Brian and I had been classmates for five years, so we knew each other quite well. One day, he invited me for a drink and roasted chicken at a restaurant near the university. Two weeks later, when he came to our residence room and I was lying on the bed, very tired after a long day, and Nakato was reading at a table in the room—"

"Brian asked to talk to her alone in the corridor but she refused to go out of the room," Nakato said.

"Nakato, let Babirye tell her story," Leah said.

"Brian knew Nakato well—there was no reason why he couldn't say what he wanted to say right there in the room," Babirye continued.

"Obviously he wanted some privacy," Merab said.

"Anyway, he sat down on the only other chair in the room and started talking about our studies. So I asked him, 'Brian, is that what you wanted to talk about in the corridor?'"

"At that point I said I could go out of the room and let them talk but—" Nakato began.

"Nakato, don't interrupt the story," Leah said.

"So, Brian invited me," Babirye said, "to a fancy restaurant this time."

"That was when Babirye forced him to say—" Nakato began.

"Nakato!" Leah said.

"I did nothing wrong," Babirye said. "I just asked him why he was inviting me to such a fancy place."

"Brian said then and there that he loved Babirye! Fortunately for him, she accepted the invitation right away," Nakato said. "But she did so too enthusiastically, in my opinion."

"You girls of today are very courageous," Merab said. "Babirye, how could you do that?"

"I've noticed that Babirye is often like her grandmother Ruth. They are both blunt and sometimes that bluntness borders on rudeness," Leah said, smiling.

"Oh dear. Brian was a friend—I didn't see why he was beating about the bush," Babirye said.

34

CLOTILDA LEFT HER office one afternoon and had her driver take her to the school farm. When she asked to see the farm's manager, the workers told her that he was not around and that they didn't know where he could be found.

"He should be at his desk during working hours," she said. "Who is in charge when he is away?"

"No one is. He did not delegate any duties."

"I think he is getting too familiar with the job, but he should know that there are thousands of other people who would be happy to replace him," Clotilda said, furious, heading toward the banana plantation on foot as her driver waited in the car. The workers watched as she disappeared from sight.

When the manager returned about an hour later and saw her car parked next to the farm's office building, he panicked and braced himself for a confrontation, since Clotilda was habitually rude to him. The workers told him that she had gone to tour the farm and that it was taking her longer than usual. The manager and Clotilda's driver set off to find her.

A few minutes later, the workers heard the two men shouting for help. They had found Clotilda lying face down in the afternoon heat, unconscious. They suspected that she had been bitten by a snake—but then they saw her puffer lying on the ground beside her handbag. They rushed her to a nearby clinic but by the time they got there it was too late. She was pronounced dead on arrival.

*　　*　　*

Ruth asked Jude to go with her to Clotilda's funeral service but he refused. "I left Clotilda for good when I walked out of her house the last time," Jude told his wife, so Kate went with her instead. When Kate asked her mother why she wanted to attend the funeral service of a woman who had caused misery in her life for many years, Ruth told her daughter that it was for Clement, but also for her own son Herbert, who was Clement's close friend.

Hundreds of people turned up for the funeral service. During the service, speaker after speaker praised Clotilda. One speaker called Clotilda "a great educator, a selfless woman who had done a lot to educate the children of the nation." Another said that "her untimely death has robbed the nation of one of her great daughters." Were the speakers talking about the girl and woman Ruth had known? *People don't publicly speak ill of the dead, but did Clotilda have a good side that I never got to see?*

Clement said that his mother was not only a great mother, she was a very hardworking woman. "Not only did she educate thousands of children, she invested in herself, too. She worked hard and took correspondence courses, graduating with a degree in education from Landsborough College in Nairobi."

Ruth shifted on the pew. *Oh, I never heard about that. Is it true?*

During Clotilda's burial at the school farm Ruth stood next to Herbert and his half-brother Clement, Clotilda's son. When Tim Mbogo saw Ruth standing so close to the grave he almost laughed, unable to dismiss the thought that she was standing there to be sure that Clotilda was being buried.

Afterward, while Kate was talking to Clement, Ruth waited under a small tree near Kate's car, thinking about Clotilda and how hard she had worked in her life. *What kind of life did Clotilda live? Did she set aside some time for herself or did she concentrate on acquiring wealth, as it seems? But am I any better off? It looks like* many *of us don't have our priorities right.*

As her thoughts flowed, Ruth began to cry. She took a handkerchief out of her bag and wiped her eyes. Many people passed by on their way to their cars, but when Tim Mbogo saw her he stopped to speak to her.

"Ruth, are you really crying for Clotilda?" Tim asked. "I can't believe it."

"Of course I have been thinking about her," Ruth said. "She was a woman who lived her life for work—she died working. Timothy, please go find my daughter Kate," she asked him, trying to compose herself. "I want to go home."

✳   ✳   ✳

A few weeks later, Jude fell sick. Ruth thought it was his usual smoker's cough when she heard him coughing through the night, but when he lost a lot of weight Kate took him to hospital. He was diagnosed with lung cancer, and stayed in the hospital for the two months before he died.

Ruth wept a lot, and said in her speech during the funeral service, that she had enjoyed a "good almost three decades with the new Jude." After the burial, she told her children that she would return to work two weeks later.

But when the time came, she called Herbert to come see her at home because she had something important to tell him—something she couldn't tell him over the phone.

Herbert arrived at his mother's home at 6 o'clock the following day.

"Would you like a cup of tea?" Ruth asked.

"No thanks. I'll have a beer if you've got some." Herbert got a bottle of beer and sat down on the sofa facing his mother. "So, what's going on with you?"

"I am done working at the boutique and you are taking over from me," Ruth said. "I've decided to retire, and I'm entrusting the responsibility of managing the shop to you."

"What's going on, Mummy? Are you all right?"

"Herbert, I had a full hour of exercise this morning and I enjoyed every minute of it, something I have not done in months! I am retiring—or should I say I have retired? I will stay at home from now on."

"But you are still energetic and vibrant! Retirement will wear you out too quickly—why don't you simply reduce your working hours gradually?" Herbert said. "Besides, I have no idea how to manage a shop."

You'll learn. I didn't know either when I started out."

"Mummy, I can't accept the responsibility! Why don't you close down the shop if you don't—"

"Herbert, what I mean is that the boutique is now yours. Do with it what you feel like."

"What's wrong with you?"

"There's nothing wrong with me. I'm eighty years old and I need to enjoy the rest of my life."

Herbert was still talking to Ruth when Leah called him. She was at the restaurant chatting with Merab.

❄   ❄   ❄

"Leah, I'm now old and it seems I'm getting weaker every month. It's high time you got involved in the running of the restaurant," Merab said.

"Mother, the restaurant has a manager," Leah objected.

"I don't have a manager, actually—Veronica just quit and she gave me just two days' notice!"

"But what kind of work would there be for *me* to do?"

"I think you should leave your job and take over the running of the restaurant from me—you would take over gradually. Unless, of course, you think I have no work to do here," Merab said, laughing.

"Um, Mother, that's not it—I don't think I would be capable of doing it. But I will tell Herbert about it to see what he thinks."

"That's all right. Please do talk to your husband," Merab said. "But time might be running out. There are mornings I feel that if I had a choice, I would stay in bed."

35

WHEN LEAH ARRIVED home that evening, Sam Mukuye, Philemon's oldest son, was there waiting for her. He was sitting in the living room, deep in thought and had not touched the glass of fruit juice that Brandon had served him.

"Hello, Sam. I'm glad to see you. How are you?" Leah said.

"Good evening, Leah. I'm not well. I've just been laid off from work."

"Oh, I'm sorry to hear that," Leah said, trying to hide her shock. "It's certainly terrible to lose a job at your age, but don't beat yourself up or lose your faith—you should start looking for another job right away."

"Certainly, and I'm not losing my faith. But what's worrying me the most are my two youngest children. They are still in school—how will I be able to pay their fees without a job?"

"We can help you with that," Leah said to her cousin. "Don't worry." She paused. "Actually, can you in the meantime, help my mother manage the restaurant?"

"Yes, I can," Sam answered, smiling. "Alleluia! And thank you, thank you." He rose to hug Leah.

When Ruth called Herbert two weeks later, he said that he was still on the plane, on the way back from a work-related trip in Germany. It was clear to his mother that he had not taken their conversation about the boutique seriously.

"Mummy, were you serious about retiring?" Herbert asked his mother when he called soon after he landed at the airport.

"Yes and I am at home enjoying myself."

"Okay, I'll check to see what's going on at the Boutique."

"You'd better go check. Because you know what I'm thinking? Somebody has got to keep an eye on the cash at the Boutique."

"Haven't you gone there since we last talked?"

"No. The business is now entirely your responsibility."

"Mummy!"

"Yes. I told you in clear terms that you've got to take over. I'm now old and I need to enjoy my retirement."

"Okay Mummy. Bye. Talk to you soon."

※　※　※

However, Herbert decided not to go to the boutique. He instead called Clement, "Hey, hi Clement. Listen. Mummy is no longer working at the Boutique."

"Yeah?"

"Uh, can you go there and see what's going on there? I am actually just returning from Germany and I have other urgent matters to handle."

"No problem. What exactly do you want me to do at the Boutique?"

"Just look around. See how everything is running and let me know."

"Okay. I will do that. Talk to you soon."

❄   ❄   ❄

"One of your clients has arrived," Lawyer Sekitto's secretary told him when, through the office's window, she saw Clement exiting his car in the parking lot the following week.

Sekitto glanced out the window. "Clement? Who invited him to this meeting?"

The secretary perused a copy of the letter the office messenger had delivered to the Kiyaga family. "No, there is no Clement on the list. He is not invited."

Sekitto was already at the door when Clement came in. "Hello Clement," Sekitto said, shaking hands with Clement. "How are you?"

"Very well thank you," Clement answered.

"Can I have a word with you in my office?"

Clement followed Sekitto into his office. He closed the door. "Have a seat please. Clement, I was not expecting you this morning. Are you here for the reading…"

"…of the will. Father's will."

"We didn't invite you—"

"No. It was Herbert who told me about the meeting—that's why I am here."

"We didn't invite you because you are not named in the will. It's a delicate matter, I'm sorry to say," Sekitto said, capping and uncapping his pen. His nervousness was making Clement nervous. "My late client, Mr. Jude Kiyaga, did not leave you anything in his will because he was not your father."

"What are you saying, he was not my father?" Clement asked, shocked.

Clement stared at the ceiling, speechless, and Sekitto watched him in silence before he gently said he understood how difficult the news must be for him and suggested that they meet back in his office that weekend. "It is a long story and I witnessed part of it," the lawyer said. "Come here on Saturday morning and I'll tell you everything I know."

When Herbert and his sisters drove into the parking lot and saw Clement drive away, they wondered why he was leaving before the meeting and why he did not stop to talk to them.

Sekitto soon informed them that Clement hadn't been included in their father's will. "And I will tell you why," he added. "Clement was not your father's son."

Victoria smiled.

Kate sighed.

Herbert said, "Really?"

"Yes, it is true," Sekitto said. "Let's proceed with the morning's agenda."

※   ※   ※

Clement arrived at Sekitto's office ten minutes before ten on Saturday. Sekitto hadn't been sure how to begin such a difficult conversation but decided to plunge right in with the truth. "Jude Kiyaga is not your father." Clement, calmer than he had been, listened attentively. "Your father was a young man called Kyotera—well, he is not young anymore—he was a young man when your mother conceived you."

"Kyotera? What kind of name is that?"

"It was a nickname. Your father was a caretaker for the houses where your mother lived at the time. The houses belonged to my father and that's why I know everything that I'm about to tell you. Actually, it was my father who nicknamed your father 'Kyotera,' after the town where he came from near the Uganda-Tanzania border."

"Do you know where he is?"

"I don't know where he is or whether he is still living or not."

"Did he know that my mother had his child? Did he just decide to walk away?"

"He was too young—he must have been just a teenager. Your mother was ashamed about the whole matter because she took advantage of him. Like I said, he was the caretaker of the houses where your mother lived. I think she was already in a relationship with Jude Kiyaga when she conceived, and she wanted Jude to be your father. She told my father—her landlord, Kyotera's boss— that the young man was disrespectful and that he had walked into her room uninvited on two occasions. My father checked the story with another long-time tenant, and when she confirmed that she had seen Kyotera walking into your mother's room at night without knocking, he was sent away immediately. He was not given a chance to plead. I never saw him again."

"Are you sure about these things?"

"Yes, I am. One night I was outside one of the rooms in the dark, just hanging around, and I overheard your mother and the woman who later testified against Kyotera plotting against him. I heard everything, but I did not want to risk being beaten by my father for saying that what the two women were telling him was not true. In any case, children were seen and not heard in those days. I wouldn't have even gotten a chance to talk to my father about it."

"I am not surprised," Clement said. "I know that my mother was capable of doing such a thing."

"We can try to look for your father."

"No, that won't be necessary. Thanks for the information, Mr. Sekitto,"

Clement said, as he shook the lawyer's hand. "But Herbert will still always be my brother."

36

LEAH'S YOUNGEST DAUGHTER Hellen had just graduated from Harvard Business School when she decided to return to Kampala to find a husband. She spent a few days in her grandmother Merab's home, where her sisters went to see her.

"How much time do you have? I don't think you'll find a suitable man in a few weeks," Babirye said to Hellen.

"It's an important matter. You know what I'm saying? I can stay for a month or two until I find a man. I'm lucky that I can do all my work online," Hellen answered.

"We can recommend a few guys to you," Nakato said. "Even if you don't find one this time, you can return next year. You are young and beautiful."

The first man with whom Hellen met, who introduced himself as "Joe" although Nakato had told her his name was Kenneth, had placed both his cellphones on the table in front of him during their date and he answered them each time they rang, which was several times. Hellen was relieved when he did not call her for a second date.

The second man that Hellen met seemed to be shy and self-conscious, not even asking her name or anything else about her. When she asked whether he wanted to have a drink or dinner, he said that he had already eaten and that he had somewhere to go urgently. "I will call you tomorrow," he said. He did not call.

Hellen met with two other men but she found them as rude as "Joe."

The fifth man, Derek, had been recommended by one of Leah's workmates. On the day that they were supposed to meet, he sent a text message saying that he was held up in a meeting. They rescheduled the date to the following evening.

* * *

Hellen, late for her appointment with Derek, parked at the side of the road to send him a text message to let him know she'd be about five minutes late. "No prob. Will B late 2," Derek texted back. Hellen drove to the hotel through a traffic jam and worried that she might be even later—she hated being late for any appointment. *What kind of impression will it be on a first date?* She saw a gap in the traffic and tried to squeeze in so she could change lanes to enter the hotel's property through the south gate but two *boda bodas*—motorcycle taxis—squeezed in. Once they'd moved away, she tried again, but now another driver had the same idea. He closed the gap, lowered his window and yelled at her. "Hey, watch your driving! When will women learn how to drive?" and then drove on, cutting her off.

Hellen was upset—an inconsiderate driver had spoiled her mood and now she was really late. Once she had parked her car, rushed up the stairs into the hotel's dining room and sat down at a table, she tried to compose herself. *Thank goodness Derek hasn't arrived yet!* She did not want him to see her in the mood she was in.

Three minutes later, the door to the dining room opened and in walked the man who had yelled at her in the road a few minutes earlier—it was Derek, and he could not hide his embarrassment. "Hi, Hellen?" he said, stretching out his hand out to her. "I'm so sorry—I mean, I don't normally behave—"

"That's okay. You don't need to apologize," Hellen answered as she picked up her handbag and rose from her seat. "Anyway I am happy I got to know so much about you so quickly."

❋   ❋   ❋

Hellen had lost hope in finding a man to marry in Kampala when her aunt Kate gave her the telephone number of a young man, Conrad Bulega, whose parents she knew well.

Hellen and Conrad agreed to meet at the Grand Imperial Hotel. When Hellen arrived at the hotel before Conrad, she just had time to text her friend in Boston—"Hi, Gwen. I'm at the hotel. He's not yet here but for some reason I'm freaking out. LOL!!! Keep you posted"—when she saw a man smiling and walking shyly towards her. He seemed to be nervous. *This must be Conrad.*

"Hello, you must be Hellen. I am Conrad," Conrad said as he stretched his hand to shake hers.

"Hi, yes, I am Hellen. I'm glad to see you, Conrad. Please have a seat." He smiled as he pulled up a chair and she smiled back.

I wonder who of the two of us is more nervous. "So Conrad, how are you doing?"

"I'm doing well, thanks. How are you?"

"Good, thanks."

"I am sorry for being late."

"No problem," Hellen said, laughing. "You are late by just a couple minutes, which gave me a chance to send a text to my girlfriend. You've been at work?"

"Yes. Actually, I work not far from here, so I just walked. That explains the slight tardiness," Conrad said, hoping that his words were impressive.

It was the gentleness of Conrad's voice that was impressing Hellen. *And he's hot! Good eye contact. A little bit shy, though*. "Can I order a drink for you, Conrad? A beer, a coke, water or something?"

"No, thanks. The drinks will be on me. That's the Ugandan way," Conrad answered, signalling the waiter.

There we go. He's already figured out that I'm not from here.

After they had ordered their drinks, Hellen asked, "So, Conrad, what do you do?"

"I am a Chartered Accountant. I work in the Ministry of Finance."

"Ministry of Finance? You must know my dad, then. He's been working there for years."

"Oh yes, I know your father. He is our Chief Economist. And what do you do, Hellen?"

"I am an entrepreneur. I hold an MBA from Harvard and my girlfriend Gwen and I have a business as consultants. We've already advised several startups."

"That sounds like an interesting career," Conrad said. "Do you work here in Kampala?"

"No, I don't work in Kampala," Hellen said hesitantly, not wanting to disclose as yet that she lived in the United States. "What do you do in your free time?"

"Free time? Uh, let me see…do I have free time?" Conrad answered, gazing into the air in a mock-pensive manner.

"Holy smokes! That means you work, like, 24/7?" Hellen asked, laughing.

"When I am free I go to the village to help my parents on their farm."

"That's good," Hellen said. "That means you are a good, helpful son. You are not like me. You don't suck at helping out your folks."

"Kind of. And you, what do you do in your free time?"

"I go to the gym most evenings though sometimes I don't go when I work till late—you know what I mean, demanding projects and stuff."

They talked for two hours. Hellen enjoyed Conrad's company and felt that the evening was going well. *Should I ask him for a second date?* She wondered. *He is a Ugandan man. Will it be appropriate or will it scare him away instead?*

But Conrad saved her from the embarrassment. "I really enjoyed talking to you, Hellen. I wonder whether we can meet again sometime this weekend."

"Of course we can. Same place? What day and time?" Hellen asked, wondering whether she sounded desperate.

"Let's meet here on Saturday at three," Conrad said.

"Let's make it five. I'm kind of busy until three. We can have dinner together around six."

"That sounds good. See you on Saturday," Conrad said as they rose.

"Yeah cool. See you on Saturday," Hellen said.

Conrad turned to cross the street while Hellen proceeded to the parking lot. As he walked through the hotel's gate, he glanced back a little to check Hellen out. His heart raced. *I hope she likes me.* He was smitten.

I hope he likes me, Hellen thought. Her heart was racing, too.

❋   ❋   ❋

Hellen looked forward to the second date with Conrad. She spent half an hour on Saturday going through her suitcase to choose the best outfit. She arrived at the hotel a few minutes to five and she was happy to find him already seated.

"So, Conrad, how are you?"

"I am okay, thanks," Conrad said, glancing at her expensive outfit. *I hope she is not high maintenance*, he thought.

"Just okay?" Hellen asked, laughing. "I'm very happy to see you."

"I'm very happy to see you, too," Conrad admitted, smiling. "I couldn't stop thinking about you since we met last time."

"Same here," Hellen said. *I'm happy about where this is going. This is insane! I can't believe we are falling for each other this fast.*

While they were having dinner, Hellen said, "Conrad, I have a confession to make. I didn't tell you that I live in Boston. Wouldn't that be a problem if everything else worked out fine between us?"

"No, no problem. I actually already knew that you live in Boston," Conrad said. "I don't want you to think that I was gossiping but when I told one of my coworkers that I had met Mr. Kiyaga's daughter he asked, 'Which one? The youngest one, the one who lives in Boston?'"

"What?" Hellen said.

"But that's not so surprising," Conrad said. "Your father is very popular at the Ministry. People know about his family."

"I'm glad to hear that. I actually left Uganda after I completed primary school. But don't tell me you knew that already, too," Hellen said, smiling.

"No, I didn't know that but I could tell from your accent that you have lived outside for a long time."

"Pardon me!"

"Sorry, I meant "overseas." I could tell from your accent that you have lived overseas for a long time."

"Yeah, I know. It's crazy. It's like a totally different culture over there, but I love Uganda. Do you know what I mean?"

"I know."

"What kind of woman would you like to have for a wife?" Hellen asked, getting right to the point—and Conrad didn't seem surprised by her question.

"I don't know. I guess I am open to—"

"I am kind of a go-getter and I love some independence. You know what I'm saying? I hope that would be okay with you."

"I guess so."

When Hellen returned to Boston, she happily talked about Conrad to her friend Gwen. Conrad surprised her three months later when he sent her a ticket back to Uganda. They were having dinner with his brother at Kampala's Serena Hotel when he proposed. Hellen accepted to marry him.

37

"MOM, I'M VERY happy," Hellen said. "I'm so looking forward to the big day, and I want to invite Conrad home so you guys can meet him. I can't wait!"

"No, not so fast—that's not how it's done," Leah said. "He'll meet your aunt Kate first and she'll tell you the necessary procedures to follow."

"Come on now, Mom, are we gonna do things the old-fashioned way?"

"No, I'm not suggesting that you do things the old-fashioned way but there are aspects of our culture that should still be followed."

"How do we go about it since there are time constraints? I'll be returning to Boston before the Introduction ceremony."

"Talk to your fiancé so he arranges a visit to your aunt's home. His family will arrange the rest for him. They'll know what to do."

When Hellen met with Conrad that evening, she told him that he would need to meet her aunt Kate first of all. "My mom insists," she said.

"Yes of course. We won't do everything the old-fashioned way," Conrad said, "but there are certain cultural procedures to be followed."

"That's interesting. My mom said exactly the same thing."

"You'll need to call your aunt to find out when we can pay her a visit."

"No problem," Hellen said as she looked up her aunt's telephone number on her cell phone.

"Are you calling her now?" Conrad asked.

"Yeah, that's how I am. I do my stuff right away," Hellen said, dialing her aunt as Conrad looked at her. "What?" Hellen asked him, seeing that he was a little uncomfortable with them discussing the matter in his presence. "Do you find it weird that I am calling—oh hey, Aunt Kate. I'm here with Conrad. He proposed—yes, I said yes—and, Auntie, we were wondering whether Conrad can come pay you a visit. We are kind of in a hurry to do everything this week as I—" There was a pause and then Hellen smiled. "Sunday, for lunch? Okay, great! See you on Sunday."

❄   ❄   ❄

When Conrad and Hellen arrived at the gate of Kate's home, they rang the bell and a gatekeeper promptly let them in. After they had parked the car, Conrad opened the trunk and took out a big basket full of groceries.

"Hey, what do we have in there?" Hellen asked. "Did you have to bring stuff?"

"Of course I had to!" Conrad said. "I wouldn't visit your aunt for the first time empty-handed."

"Have you, like, started paying for me?"

"No, I'm not buying you. I'm just being courteous, as our culture dictates."

"Just kidding," Hellen said, laughing. "But I didn't think you'd bring anything."

Kate was already standing at the veranda. She took the basket from Conrad, led the couple into the house and placed the basket on the dining table before she showed the young couple to a sofa in the living room. As soon as they sat down, Hellen took Conrad's hand in an affectionate way but he immediately let go, embarrassed to hold hands in front of Hellen's aunt.

Kate noticed and was pleased. "Feel at home," she said, placing a mat on the floor to sit on and greet Conrad. Hellen was amused by the formal greeting and that her aunt had even chosen to sit on a mat to greet Conrad. At that moment, Kate's husband Ham came into the living room and shook hands with both Hellen and Conrad in a less formal greeting.

After lunch Conrad presented a letter to Kate, his request to be introduced to Hellen's family and to marry her. Kate accepted the letter and she said that she would deliver it to Herbert. "I'm very glad for both of you," she said.

Conrad then presented the groceries that were in the basket, four kilograms of beef, a big pack of tea, two kilograms of sugar, a tin of margarine and two bars of soap. Kate and Ham thanked him for the presents.

※　　※　　※

Several meetings now took place in Merab's home in Kawempe, led by Sam Mukuye, to arrange Conrad's introduction ceremony to Hellen's family. Merab watched in amusement as family members argued over the details of the big ceremony—how many people to invite, who would cater the event, the seating arrangements, where to park the cars and so many other details that she thought were minor and unnecessary. She could not help but remember the similar ceremony organized decades earlier for Lutalo before they were married and how small and simple it had been.

Two weeks before the introduction ceremony, when Herbert went to see his village's Local Council chairman to arrange for where his many guests would park, he also used the opportunity to invite the LC chairman and all the members of his council to the ceremony. The chairman gladly accepted the invitation.

Hellen returned to Kampala at the beginning of the week and asked to go through the details of the event. It was obvious that she was stressed. "They've done a great job of arranging everything," Merab told her. "Watching them, you could think they were preparing for the actual wedding. Just sit back and enjoy the party."

On the eve of the ceremony, two large tents were placed in the large front yard of the house, each facing the other—one for the host family and the other for Conrad and his entourage. The tents were decorated with helium balloons and fresh flowers.

On the day of the ceremony, there were over two hundred friends and family in Hellen's family's tent. The decorations, the music, the food, and the people's clothes all showed wealth and class. Conrad came accompanied by one hundred and sixty guests, ten more than he had said would accompany him—and ten more than the hundred and fifty plastic chairs furnished for them. When it was time to sit, Sengo, the spokesman that Herbert had hired for the ceremony, made the extra ten people stand in the hot afternoon sun and did not arrange for ten more chairs to be brought out until Conrad's own hired spokesman, Katantazi, had paid a fine.

The introduction ceremony itself was very colourful, with music, a lot of food and drinks. After lunch had been served, Katantazi gave out so many gifts on Conrad's behalf, to Hellen's family, including a new sofa set, an electric stove, a solar electricity system and a beautiful rug, that Katantazi said that Herbert and Leah's home was going to have a completely new look. "You'll excuse us for transforming your décor," Katantazi said in a teasing tone.

"Not so fast, my friend," Sengo replied. "Before you boast, remember that the home you are visiting belongs to Herbert Kiyaga, a grandson of Dawson Kiyaga, the late, great industrialist. His house is already expensively furnished."

As part of the ceremony Conrad placed an engagement ring on Hellen's finger, and then they danced to show their joy as they walked around in front of the guests. Merab was shocked. *How did we come to this?* she thought, rising from her mat to go back inside the house. *Where are our people heading to? Since when did a man dance in his in-laws' home?*

✻   ✻   ✻

"Grandma, did yesterday's ceremony bring back memories of the day when Grandpa was introduced to your family?" Hellen asked Merab the next day as they sorted through Conrad's gifts.

"Of course it did, but things have changed a lot from back then."

"Certainly. Can you tell me more of your annoying stories?"

"If really you find them annoying, why do you want to listen to them?"

"You know what? They are annoying but interesting too. I know you were married young and it was not your choice—"

"Of course not. It was not my choice," Merab answered. "My father and my aunt decided for me."

"They chose a man for you to marry and you let them get away with it?" Hellen asked.

"Yes, what could I have done?"

"You could have said no and walked away."

"Walked away? To where? Women back then didn't have the kind of power and freedom that women of your generation have. You could never say no to your parents' wishes. Actually, there was only one girl that I know of who said no. That was my cousin Scovia and even then, she couldn't stay in her father's home after she had said no to the man they had chosen for her. She had to go live with a family, strangers—people were very kind back then. They cared for her and helped her through her education, like she was their own child. She reconciled with my uncle only after he found out that she was likely to become successful in her career."

"That's interesting," Hellen said, "but I think I am like Scovia. I would run away."

*   *   *

Hellen returned to Boston to prepare for her wedding and was overjoyed when at one of her bridal showers her friend and business partner Gwen told her she'd be attending.

Conrad called Hellen two weeks before the wedding, asking her to go to Kampala a little earlier than she'd planned so she could be at the last wedding meeting. "Friends and family have contributed money and ideas for the wedding," he explained.

"What? Are you crowdfunding the wedding?" Hellen asked.

"That's how we do it. Anyway, come to the last meeting and that evening there'll be a dinner in our honour."

"Okay, see you then, honey. I can't wait."

*   *   *

"Hellen, as your paternal aunt, I play an important role in your married life," Kate told Hellen when they met a few days before the wedding. "Traditionally, I am supposed to prepare you for your marriage and guide you."

"I kind of know a little bit about that, Aunt Kate," Hellen said.

"So let's sit down to talk. I know you may not find some of the things I tell you useful, but—"

"No problem, Aunt," Hellen said, smiling. "I'll listen to whatever you have to say then I'll take to heart what works and ignore what doesn't."

"You were born here in Kampala but you've lived most of your life in America. Your fiancé has lived here all his life. That means you'll have different world views."

"That's for sure."

"You should therefore have that in mind whenever you have a disagreement or very divergent points of view on a given matter. You'll be a couple that looks the same on the outside but different on the inside, due to your differing world views."

"I understand that and I think Conrad understands it as well."

"Yes. That also means that you'll need to be tolerant of each other. Many times, if your husband says or does something that you don't agree with, let it pass for the sake of your marriage. Don't dwell on it unless you think that it is so major that it will affect your relationship in a negative way. Ignore all minor disagreements."

"Sorry for interrupting, but—is Conrad getting a similar kind of talk from his folks?" Hellen asked.

"He should, but most probably he is not. What I know is that the two of you will get premarital counselling from his church. And remember, when you have an argument with your husband—yes, you'll have arguments once in a while—try to understand his feelings and try to find a solution. In such situations, you should always ask yourself, 'What can I do to make things better?'"

"All those things sound good, Aunt Kate, but I hope Conrad is getting the same tips as well."

"Of course it goes without saying that you should love your husband unconditionally, trust him always and forgive him for his mistakes," Kate said. "Do you have any questions for me?"

"Yes, I do. I know you've been married for a long time and when I look at you and your husband, you guys seem to be, like, the happiest couple I've ever seen. What's the one thing that has helped your marriage to last?"

"It's the last point I mentioned to you. I love my husband unconditionally, I trust him one hundred percent and I forgive him whenever he wrongs me. I think he strives to reciprocate that."

✳   ✳   ✳

After the last wedding meeting, Nakato drove Hellen back to their parents' home to change. The two sisters and their aunt Kate were walking back to the car when their aunt Victoria arrived from Boston. "Hellen, you can't go to the dinner dressed like that!" was the first thing Victoria said. "Your skirt is too short!"

"It's too hot here, though."

"I said, 'Your skirt is too short.'"

"Why do we need the freaking fundraising dinner anyway? We have all the necessary resources," Hellen said.

"Hellen," Kate answered, "here, marriage ceremonies are a friends and family affair; you cannot exclude family just because you have all the resources you need."

"Hellen, you can't go to the dinner dressed in such a short skirt," Victoria said. "All the young men there, instead of focusing on the party, will be staring at your body. You don't want—"

"Whatever. Should I wear a snowsuit simply because somebody is going to stare at my body?"

✳   ✳   ✳

As Hellen and Conrad exchanged their vows in English, Ruth listened and smiled while Merab just watched her granddaughter in awe. She did not understand any of the things that Hellen said but Merab was impressed by her confidence and was happy for her. She knew that her granddaughter was saying 'I do' with both her heart and lips, not just her lips as she herself had done when she exchanged vows with Lutalo.

When the congregation went out of the cathedral, they took many photos with the bridal party on the steps and as it left half an hour later, Merab smiled when she saw the decorated limousine and the expensive cars following it.

"You seem to be amused by all the day's events, Mother," Leah said.

"Yes, I am," Merab told her daughter. "And why wouldn't I be amused? On my wedding we were transported on bicycles! This is a very good change."

Cornelius Bulega smiled as he walked towards Ruth. "Ruth, I am glad that what didn't happen for us has happened for our grandchildren."

"I'm glad too," Ruth answered as she shook Cornelius's hand.

"Shall we sit together and talk at the reception?" Cornelius asked. Ruth noticed that he held her hand a little too long. The poor man was there alone— his wife had died just in the past year.

"Yes. I am lonely. I'd love to chat with you," Ruth answered.

38

"YOU KNOW WHAT, Nakato? We are enjoying this good life partly because of the sacrifices that our grandmothers made," Hellen said as she and her sister chatted in her hotel room after the wedding. "We need to celebrate them while they are still alive."

"You are right—Babirye and I had a similar discussion the other day. What kind of celebration did you have in mind?" Nakato answered.

"I was thinking, like, we organize a dinner in their honour in some cool hotel and make speeches. You know what I mean? And talk about them and that kind of thing. We are fortunate…"

"… to still have them around—I hear you. Let's organise something pretty soon. I know you can lead us in that regard because you make stuff happen."

"Thanks for the compliment, sister! I'm flattered."

❊ ❊ ❊

Hellen and Conrad returned from their week-long honeymoon in Mauritius and the Kiyaga siblings hosted a dinner to celebrate their grandmothers' lives at the Sheraton Kampala Hotel soon after. Many friends and relatives of the family attended, including some of Brandon's fans. Because the attendees were of various nationalities, the event would be conducted entirely in English.

"Grandma, I'll sit next to you so I can interpret everything for you," Babirye said to Merab.

"You don't need to interpret everything; just the things that concern me directly. Enjoy the party," Merab answered.

Hellen wore a stylish tightly fitting suit, with a skirt that was an inch above the knee. During the dinner, when she walked up the short flight of stairs to the platform to give her speech, a slit at the back of her skirt exposed the lower part of her thighs. Ruth smiled, seeing a free woman, but Merab, cringed—she saw a skimpily dressed woman. In her written speech, Hellen outlined each woman's history, challenges, strengths and the qualities that helped her to succeed. "My grandmother Merab discreetly ate chicken without her husband's knowledge. As a woman, she was not supposed to eat chicken." She paused and looked at the audience. She abandoned her written speech for a while. "Really? A woman was not supposed to eat chicken? Weren't our grandfathers just greedy?" She returned to her written speech. "My grandmother's brother hid money in the coffee plantation in order to pay for my mom's education." She abandoned her speech again. "I know more about the history of my grandmothers than they think I know."

The audience laughed.

Hellen returned to her written speech. "Although their relationship is now cordial, it has not always been that way. For a time, each one of them seemed to be opposing everything that the other was doing; everything that the other stood for. Later, they became friendly to one another. They are our Frenemy Matriarchs. That's who they are. My grandmothers have funny stories but they also have sad stories. I wish they would write their own 'tell all' books!"

Hellen concluded by saying that she was very grateful to be enjoying a success that was born from the sacrifices that her grandmothers made. "And I am very thankful that they are both alive to hear me say this."

Leah walked to her mother and told her that she should give a speech. Merab refused. "I am an uneducated old woman," she whispered to Leah. "What can I say to this crowd of educated people? Please leave me alone."

There was a lot of cheering and a standing ovation when Ruth rose to speak. She placed her eyeglasses on the podium and looked around the room with a smile as she waited for the clapping to stop.

"Ladies and gentlemen," Ruth said, "thank you for coming to this happy occasion that our family has organised to celebrate us. Our culture teaches us not to blow our horns but I must say that my sister Merab and I deserve the honour of such a colourful and well-attended occasion."

While Ruth was delivering her speech, Merab was half-dreaming, thinking about the people who had helped her to achieve her success. They were all dead. *This is the painful thing about a long life like mine; all the people who were close to me and were helpful to me are gone.*

"…Although there is still a long way to go on the road to equality between men and women in this country," Ruth continued, "I think women like Merab and me have been successful—we had to fight hard, but we won freedoms for our female descendants."

Merab thought sadly of her brother Absalom, who had died so suddenly and unexpectedly at much too young an age.

"Our granddaughters are better off now than we were, in several respects," Ruth said. "I am glad to note that all my granddaughters are accomplished career women."

Merab remembered Nabukalu, her long-time friend and workmate, who had also died. Merab was consoled only by the fact that she had been there for her friend, caring for her during her long illness.

"All of you young women present here today, I have a message for you. Don't give up your dreams simply because you face obstacles. For anything worth pursuing, there will always be obstacles."

Merab remembered Mitego, who had died at ninety a heartbroken old man. His beloved son Adrian had joined the army during the Uganda-Tanzania war of 1978 and 1979 at eighteen and had never been seen again. It was only at his funeral that Merab had learned that "Mitego" wasn't even his real name. Yobu Mugula had been nicknamed "Mitego"—"traps"—because of the traps he seemed to set for everyone he dealt with, whether there were apparent benefits for him or not. Merab was not surprised that many of his descendants had proudly adopted "Mitego" as their last name, and that there were Mitegos everywhere—in the media, in banking, in the police, in hospitals, and in the diaspora.

"…You should always stay focused on your goals and not on the obstacles you are facing," Ruth continued.

Her cousin Philemon's death had been the most shocking to Merab. Three days before his youngest daughter Priscilla's wedding, Philemon had insisted on driving to Nairobi for a "very urgent business trip" with some business to do in a town on the way. On the very day of the wedding on their way back in the wee hours of the night, his driver had fallen asleep at the wheel and driven off the road into a steep cliff, and both Philemon and the driver had died at the scene. Later in the day, after Sam Mukuye had received the police phone call with the news of his father's death, he had kept quiet about the terrible news and put on a brave face, not wanting it to ruin his little sister's big day, and he walked her down the aisle—she fuming because her father wasn't there. Merab had confronted Sam while the bridal party were still out taking photos. "Sam, something must have gone terribly wrong, and something is telling me that you know what it is—please tell me! Philly is the most reliable man I know and he would give anything to be by his daughter's side on her wedding." Sam had broken down and announced the sad news. Merab had wailed for minutes before she fainted.

"I would like to thank my son Herbert, his wife Leah and my grandchildren for having organised this party," Ruth concluded, and the assembled guests raised their glasses to celebrate Ruth and Merab.

* * *

"That was an amazing tribute to our grandmothers, Hellen," Nakato said as they walked out of the ballroom after the dinner. "There is a big problem, though. Both our grandmothers' businesses are dying. Since your job is to help turn businesses around, I suggest you visit the restaurant and the boutique to see what can be done to salvage them."

"Nakato, I don't have time. I am going back to Boston on Thursday."

"Please go there, even for a few hours. I can take you there on Monday morning."

"Okay, if you insist," Hellen said. "We'll drop in briefly on both."

* * *

That evening, Ruth stayed up late at night, reflecting on her long life. She sat up in bed and brought out her diary, reading it for a few minutes before adding one more entry.

> *I have had a good life. Although there have been some haters—there will always be haters—generally, I have had healthy relationships. I have realized, though, that on one hand, as I am now older, I feel less visible than when I was younger. Like millions of other women, I was very attractive. When I was younger and at the peak of my powers, I know that I had a captivating smile, lots of charm and wit. On the other hand, now I feel more in control of my life than back then. Is the invisibility I am feeling now good or bad?*

39

LEAH AND HERBERT felt greatly honoured the following week when the veteran journalist Tim Mbogo wrote an article about their mothers in the *Daily Monitor*:

Family Celebrates its Matriarchs

Ruth Wamala Kiyaga. Merab Nantamu Lutalo (Mufuzi). I know those names don't ring a bell for many of our readers. However, these two women, in the prime years of their lives, were among the movers and shakers in business in the city and were, in a way, pioneers in their respective businesses. Ruth owned Ruth's Boutique and Merab owned Kyatelekera Restaurant—the first women to own major businesses in these fields—and these two businesses, unlike many others in Kampala that opened in the 60s and 70s, are still standing.

Last Saturday, the two women's family celebrated them with a grand dinner at the Sheraton Kampala Hotel. In her speech, their granddaughter Hellen Kiyaga-Bulega called her grandmothers "Frenemy Matriarchs," because the two women, despite the marriage of their children and their friendship in later years, did not always agree with each other.

The traditionalist and the moderniser

Omukyala Omugunjufu (OO) was begun in Merab's Kyatelekera Restaurant as a conversation between an older woman and her younger female employees, a forum that encouraged women to safeguard their culture. It later became a popular movement in the city. It was around the same time that Ruth founded the Women's Development Association. The two businesswomen once clashed when Ruth said that OO promoted the subjugation of women.

However, even though Merab and Ruth both succeeded in business, they started out in life very differently.

Reserved and shy—to me, anyway, she seemed shy— Merab was born to poor rural parents and she did not complete primary school. "Unfortunately, my parents did not know the value of education. They married me off very young and so I missed out on fulfilling my dream of becoming a teacher," Merab told me when I interviewed her for my 1989 article on the twenty-fifth anniversary of Kyatelekera Restaurant.

Ruth, in contrast, was born to rich urban parents. Her mother was a teacher and her father owned Wamala & Sons Construction, a company that built many homes in and around Kampala. She studied in Buweela High School, the National Teachers' College and the London School of Economics. Ruth made headlines when she resigned from her job as Assistant DEO to start her boutique. Such a move was rare at the time, even unheard of.

When they grew older, it seems the two women must have talked through their differences because we know they cooperated on a generous project. Ruth donated the land on which St. Peter's Primary School was built in Kawempe, then led the fundraising campaign to build the school, stipulating that at least twenty-five percent of the students must be girls from poor families. And for many years Merab prepared breakfast for the boarding students of the school at her own expense.

So all I can say is, "Thank you for your generosity, Ruth and Merab. The women of this country thank you, Frenemy Matriarchs."

40

"MOM, DAD, I visited both the boutique and the restaurant on Monday," Hellen said to her parents when she visited them at their home a few days later. "Aren't you guys supposed to be running those businesses?"

"Yes we are," Leah answered, laughing.

"Mom, it's not a laughing matter. I visited for just a few hours but I noticed a number of problems, especially at the restaurant. Do you really know what's going on there?"

"Yes we do," Leah answered.

"I don't think so. I actually doubt whether you are making any profit from that restaurant. My professional recommendation would be to close it down."

"We can't close the restaurant. What about my mother's legacy?" Leah said, and added, almost to herself, "I prefer we leave things the way they are for now, as long as Mother is still alive."

"Hellen, there is nothing you can do about that restaurant. Leave it as it is for now," Herbert said.

"No, Mom, Dad. I can't leave the restaurant as it is. I am flying out later this evening but I will do a thorough analysis of the two businesses when I return to Kampala in two months' time," Hellen said, hugging both her parents goodbye. And, speaking over her shoulder as she headed to the door, she said, "Something's gotta change."

If you enjoyed Frenemy Matriarchs, you will love the next novel.

Sign up here for pre-launch specials and notification about the book.

www.geoffreykiggundu.com

www.facebook.com/geoffreykiggunduauthor

GEOFFREY KIGGUNDU was educated at Makerere University and Université de Rouen. He taught French in Makerere University before emigrating to Canada.

He currently lives in Milton, Ontario with his wife and three children. His first novel, *The Son of Kasaka* was published in 2013.

www.ingramcontent.com/pod-product-compliance
Lightning Source LLC
Chambersburg PA
CBHW050916250626

47155CB00001B/259